"How

"Three."

She lifted his hand. "I bet it was this one." She kissed his index finger. "This one." She kissed his ring finger. "And this one." She kissed his thumb.

"I also broke my wrist."

She placed her lips on his inner wrist.

"And I once shattered my shoulder."

She raised an eyebrow, then placed a kiss on his shoulder.

"And my nose."

She shook her head. "You never broke your nose. Your face is too symmetrical."

"I have a scar on my thigh."

Claudia raised both eyebrows in feigned innocence. "Inner or outer?"

"Inner. On my right leg."

She lowered herself to the ground, stifled a grin then kissed him there. "Is it this?"

"It's a little higher."

She kissed him again.

"Higher."

She looked up at him with amusement. "If I go any higher, I won't be kissing your thigh."

"And you won't hear me complaining."

Books by Dara Girard

Kimani Romance	Kimani Arabesque
Sparks	*Table for Two*
The Glass Slipper Project	*Gaining Interest*
Taming Mariella	*Carefree*
Power Play	*Illusive Flame*
A Gentleman's Offer	
Body Chemisty	
Round the Clock	
Words of Seduction	
Pages of Passion	
Beneath the Covers	

DARA GIRARD

fell in love with storytelling at an early age. Her romance writing career happened by chance when she discovered the power of a happy ending. She is an award-winning author whose novels are known for their sense of humor, interesting plot twists and witty dialogue.

When she's not writing, she enjoys spring mornings and autumn afternoons, French pastries, dancing to the latest hits and long drives.

Dara loves to hear from her readers. You can reach her at contactdara@daragirard.com or P.O. Box 10345, Silver Spring, MD 20914.

Beneath the COVERS

DARA GIRARD

KIMANI
ROMANCE

To adventurous women!

KIMANI PRESS™

Recycling programs
for this product may
not exist in your area.

ISBN-13: 978-0-373-86207-8

BENEATH THE COVERS

www.kimanipress.com

Printed in U.S.A.

Dear Reader,

Welcome to the third and final book in my Ladies of the Pen trilogy about three friends and their rocky roads to romance. You've already met Suzanne in *Words of Seduction* and Noreen in *Pages of Passion*. Now in *Beneath the Covers*, you'll get Claudia's tale.

Claudia Madison loves being single. So does Peter Warren. Getting these two together was a challenge. However, the research wasn't—they were putting together a travel program and I love to travel.

I gained inspiration from travel shows for the sights, sounds and feels of travel. I also used holiday pictures and let's not forget the food. I watched The Food Network and indulged in French pastries, Italian cuisine, Hawaiian fruits and Bahamian snacks.

So I hope that you'll enjoy not only a sizzling romance, but lush locales and sumptuous foods. How's that for armchair travel?

Best regards,

Dara Girard

Chapter 1

A blackout. Claudia Madison flipped the light switch again just to make sure. Nothing. She sighed. Just what she needed to end a hellish day. She'd started off the day excited about her trip to Hawaii, but things had gone downhill from there. She'd missed her first flight. Then when she was put on another flight two hours later, she found herself in a seat between a man with a hacking cough and a woman who, because she was afraid of flying, had drunk herself into a stupor. And, in her rush, she had forgotten to say a proper goodbye to her cat, Madame Curie.

At the baggage claim, the latch on her suitcase had broken, scattering her clothes on the ground. On the way to the hotel, her taxi driver, a talkative man with a rotund figure that hinted at his love of a good meal, had gotten lost. And to top it off a storm opened up, darkening the sky and obscuring the view of the island.

Fortunately, once they reached their destination, the rain had lightened a little and Claudia could see the massive wrought-iron gates which opened to a private sanctuary of luxurious villa residences. Unfortunately, because it was evening, she didn't get to see all eleven acres of manicured gardens and colorful exotic flowers. However, she had noticed the tiki torches as they blazed throughout the facility, creating an oasis of tropical splendor. Claudia felt as if she were on the movie set of *South Pacific.* After she registered at the "main house," the taxi driver drove Claudia to her villa, which was located on the far side of the property, overlooking the beach.

Once she was safely in the entryway, Claudia paid the driver handsomely, since he'd helped her with her many bags while she fumbled with her umbrella, and assured him she would be okay. She then struggled through the hand-etched, frosted-glass front door and entered into darkness.

Claudia stood in the foyer soaking wet, tired, hungry and convinced that she'd made a mistake. This trip was supposed to be the beginning of something new. A promise of more fame and influence. A top producer, Frank Brady, was turning her bestselling book *No Commitment Required: Fun, Freedom and Romance for the Single Woman* into a television show. She'd pinched herself when her agent had given her the news. She'd come far from her middle-class upbringing in a small town in Virginia, her former medical practice in Charlotte and a failed first book.

"You know why it bombed, don't you?" her friend and colleague Tamara Bell had said about that first book several years earlier. She was visiting Claudia's office for lunch, but looked as though she was heading for a gala event dressed in a lime green silk minidress with matching high heels. "It's dry and soulless. Unremarkable and technical. No wonder it sunk like a stone. I know you've been through a lot, but you're wasting away behind your desk." She motioned to the oak table where Claudia sat absently spinning a paper clip. "Okay, so our college days are over," she added when Claudia didn't reply. "But I'm positive you have something to say. Something besides this." She poked the book with her perfectly manicured finger as if it were a dead animal. "Your dissertation had more sex appeal."

"I don't care about writing success. I achieved my goal. I wrote a book that—"

"Five people read!" Tamara said, making a dismissive gesture with her hand, which made her large diamond engagement ring sparkle. "So you want to stay in this boring little town, listening all day to your neurotic patients?" Claudia frowned, but Tamara continued. "Fine, I can't stop you, but at least say something interesting. Your college papers used to set the class on fire. Write something deep with meaning. Don't let him win."

Claudia looked up.

"You know who I'm taking about."

She did. And she was glad that her friend didn't say his name. At the time it had been only a few years since their breakup, and her feelings were still raw.

"He was a jerk. Don't let him do this to you. Success and living well are the best revenge. If you can't find his replacement, at least write something fabulous to show the bastard."

Claudia took her friend's advice to heart that night when she entered her dreary little apartment. She hadn't settled down, still hoping that her ex would somehow return and she'd move in with him. But that night that hope died. She needed a change and to reclaim her life. Over the next few months she wrote her second book, *Living Alone and Loving It,* a book about how she'd gotten over the Cinderella myth and claimed her own happy ending *without* a prince. She didn't expect it to do anything and wasn't surprised when it was turned down by twenty agents who thought her ideas were interesting but unmarketable.

"Look, most women want to get married," one agent told her over the phone. "Write about finding a man, keeping a man or having a baby, then we can talk."

Undeterred, Claudia decided to skip agents and send directly to editors. Initially, this route was equally frustrating. Some told her to get an agent, others didn't reply. She was about to give up when she received an email from Hannah Rabin, a woman who'd idolized *Ms. Magazine* and as a result had started her own small press. During their first of many conversations, she told Claudia that she loved the manuscript and thought it was radically feminist and pro-female, without male bashing. That autumn she published the book, and it took off.

The day *Living Alone and Loving It* hit the bookstores, Claudia threw out her wardrobe of sensible shoes and monochromatic outfits and replaced them with flowing dresses and bright colors, becoming the woman she'd been before her heartbreak. Soon guest spots on local talk shows followed, then a weekly column in a glitzy magazine. Her third book quickly followed, also becoming a blockbuster. Money afforded Claudia the life she'd dreamed of. A life away from her patients, schedules and obligations. Although the academic world found fault with her work, she didn't mind the criticism.

She was making millions of women happy. And that was better than any prescription she'd handed out.

Not only had her writing expanded her world, it had brought into her life her two best friends Suzanne Gordon and Noreen Vaughn. Neither women had read Claudia's books or believed in her free-living—and free-loving—lifestyle, but all three had developed a close friendship since meeting at a writing conference in North Carolina, and they were extremely proud of her success. They had, at one point, all been single and enjoyed girls' nights out, spa trips, extended lunches and vacations together. But now her two closest friends were happily married. At times, Claudia keenly felt their loss and the fun times they'd had in the past.

The proposed TV series was a great reprieve, and Claudia hoped it would help take her mind off things. She wasn't going to head down the aisle just because her friends had. She'd once gotten perilously close, but fate had other plans and she'd learned a hard lesson she didn't need to be taught again. No, she'd remain a happy bachelorette the rest of her life. She had no interest in being tied down. There were too many benefits to singlehood to give up those privileges. Plus this show would do a lot for her career. It was everything she'd ever hoped for, except for one thing—her cohost.

But she wouldn't think about him. She hadn't thought about him for years, and she didn't need to start now. She had more pressing problems to handle. She needed to find her room and change out of her wet clothes. She dropped her suitcases and handbag in the hallway and tried to adjust her eyes to the blackness.

"Hello, Claudia."

She froze. The voice came through the darkness with the chilling gossamer feel of a ghost. In a way, it was—a specter of something from the past long gone. It called to her. The sound of the low, resonant voice was beautiful and smooth, like hot caramel over ice cream. Claudia held her breath, hoping she'd imagined it. *Please don't let it be him.* She didn't need this right now.

"Who—" Her voice cracked. She cleared her throat and tried again. She wouldn't let him frighten her. "Who are you?"

"You know who."

Her heart sank. "What are you doing here?"

"We're sharing this villa. Not that you can see it now, but to your left the hallway leads to the living area and from there the kitchen is to your right. Straight ahead are two separate bedrooms. I've claimed the one on the left."

Her hellish day was turning into a nightmare. She was alone with her cohost, Peter Warren—the man she'd almost married.

Claudia looked around, desperate to see something. "Where are you?"

"I'm right here," he said in a bored tone, as if they were at a cocktail party instead of alone in a darkened room.

He was close, but she still couldn't place him. "That's not helpful," she mumbled. "Aren't there any flashlights or candles?"

"The lights haven't been out that long."

"So? Why are you standing in the dark?"

"You know why."

Claudia cringed. He wasn't going to allow her to pretend that they were strangers. He was ripping through her wall of politeness and revealing a former closeness she wanted to ignore. He was trying to destroy her defenses and leave her vulnerable to the memories of their past. But Claudia was strong and wouldn't surrender. She fought not to remember that he used to love watching a rainstorm. That he could sit and watch one for hours. Sometimes she'd watch it with him. They'd had an old sofa at that time and liked to crawl on it and snuggle while eating a large bowl of potato chips, drinking cold beer and listening to the rain pounding the roof. He'd hold her close while she fed him. Once he'd said that watching the rain helped him think, but she sensed there was more to it than that. Something deeper.

Claudia knew he had secrets, and, although she never felt as if she truly knew him, back then she'd loved him and didn't care. Claudia brushed the thought aside. It didn't matter now. The past was dead.

Her eyes adjusted to the darkness and she could now make out shadows, but she still couldn't see him.

"Where are you?" she asked again, sensing that he knew where she was. "And don't say 'right here.'"

"You'll find me. Just follow my voice."

His voice. He knew its power. She did, too. She remembered how he used to whisper her name, the huskiness of it early in the morning or after making love. It was one of his best attributes. On the radio his voice could make a woman forget her name. Right now it caused goose bumps to form on Claudia's skin. In the darkness, it caressed her, embraced her, thrilled her.

"Never mind." She ran her hand along the wall until it hit a solid form. A life-size statue. Her fingers skimmed over the smooth, muscular chest and arms, and she imagined it looked as impressive as a bronze sculpture by Rodin. She splayed her hand against it. It was surprisingly warm to the touch. When her finger brushed against a hard nipple, it felt remarkably real.

Claudia jerked her hand away as a realization struck her. Embarrassment heated her face. "Oh, that's you."

"In the flesh."

"I hope not."

"You can always find out."

Claudia quickly folded her arms, ashamed by how intimately she'd been touching him and annoyed that he wouldn't drop the subject. "I didn't know you were *that* close."

When he spoke, she heard the smile in his voice. "Now you do."

Chapter 2

Yes. Now she knew where he was, but that didn't calm her frayed nerves. She knew he wasn't naked. He probably had on a pair of jeans or shorts; he wasn't the type to go around bare, although the image was always pleasing. She silently swore. What was wrong with her? Had jet lag obliterated her common sense? She knew how dangerous it was to be susceptible to him. Yes, he was still good-looking with a great voice, but cyanide was said to smell like almonds. Both could destroy you. Annoyed by her wayward thoughts, Claudia moved past Peter down the hall and crashed into a stand-alone glass wall cabinet.

"What are you doing?" he asked, amused.

"Trying to find my way around. I need to find a flashlight."

"Still afraid of the dark?"

"I was never afraid, just uneasy."

"Right."

Claudia didn't care if he didn't believe her; she would focus on her task not on him. But she could feel herself starting to panic. She'd never admit that she was still afraid of the dark. It was ridiculous to have such a childish fear. She was a trained health-care professional. She'd studied the roots of phobias and helped others conquer theirs. She opened the doors and frantically searched the cabinet for a flashlight or candle while quietly counting to calm herself. *One Mississippi*. She wouldn't think about the elevator. *Two Mississippi*. And how she'd gone in although something said she shouldn't. *Three Mississippi*. And she'd almost been…

She nearly screamed when a warm, solid hand wrapped around her forearm and pulled her close. "Breathe, Claudia."

"I'm all right," she said, although her shrill voice said otherwise.

"You're shivering."

"I'm cold."

"I'll get the candles."

"But—"

"I know where things are. It will be faster if I do it."

He was right. Claudia let him lead her to the sofa then stopped. "Wait. I can't sit down."

"Why not?"

"I'm wet."

Peter seemed to stumble over his words for a second then said, "So what?" He gently pushed her onto the couch. "You'll dry."

She sat and folded her arms. She was going to be fine. She was in a safe environment. No one was going to hurt her. Not like last time. She had to focus. She turned her gaze to the rain-soaked moonlight, but it cast a weak glow as it filtered through the window, so she focused on the sound of the rain.

"How long have the lights been out?" she asked, again anxious to know where he was.

"About twenty minutes. They're working on them now. Fortunately, the lightning has stopped."

"Where is everyone?"

"The crew is in the villa next door."

"So it's just us?"

"Yep."

Claudia wrung her hands together, feeling on edge. Just hearing his voice was enough to cast a spell. And in the dark it was dangerously intimate, and that was something she didn't want. Not with him. She tried to imagine him as he was now. She knew he hadn't changed much in eight years. She'd seen his latest photo in a national men's magazine. He had looked attractive and cocky, wearing a crisp light blue shirt and gray tweed jacket that complemented his toffee-colored skin and imposing dark eyes. He'd looked handsome, boyish *and* charming. The type of guy men could trust and women thought they could tame.

But in real life he was a lot more dangerous. A photo couldn't capture his virile, rugged strength and magnetism. He looked uncomplicated but she knew that behind his seductive smile was a dark, complicated man few people really knew. But he was off-limits to her. She didn't want to remember when he hadn't been.

"You're still shivering."

"I'm fine," she said through clenched teeth.

Claudia jumped when a large, soft vellum blanket wrapped around her. She hadn't heard him move.

"Thanks," she said, feeling awkward. Why was he being nice to her?

As if he'd read her thoughts, he said, "I don't want you to get sick."

"Hmm."

"We couldn't have the show without you."

Claudia's wariness subsided. At least she knew it wasn't personal. She was a commodity. That made sense. This was the way it needed to be. It had to be.

She heard Peter set something on the coffee table. Then he lit a candle and she breathed a sigh of relief as light pushed away the darkness. She felt the cushion shift as he sat down beside her. The faint scent of his cologne drifted toward her, reminding her of jasmine. She glanced at him, not wanting to appear overeager to see his face. He was still mostly in shadow, but the flickering candle flame highlighted his strong jaw and sensuous mouth. He hadn't put on a shirt, but just as she'd guessed, he was wearing a pair of dark blue jeans.

"Here," he said.

Claudia felt a soft package placed in her hands.

"It's a sandwich."

"Thank you."

Claudia unwrapped the sandwich from its plastic encasing then bit in with gusto, too famished to be dainty. "Mmm, a BLT with extra mayo. My favorite."

"I know."

He would. It was his, too. She swallowed hard. Why couldn't he let the past stay buried? What was he up to? She glanced down at the sandwich. Was she eating his dinner?

"I bought two at the airport. Don't worry, I've already eaten."

Unnerved by how easily he could read her, Claudia squeezed the sandwich until mayonnaise oozed out the sides. Even back then he'd been able to pierce her thoughts like no other man.

"You might as well finish it since you're still hungry."

"Stop doing that."

"Doing what?"

"Reading my thoughts."

He turned to her and grinned. "You used to think it was romantic."

"That was a long time ago."

Peter shrugged. "I'm hardly a mind reader. Otherwise—" He stopped and his grin dimmed. He turned away.

Claudia took another bite, determined not to force him to finish what he was about to say, although part of her wanted him to. *Otherwise what?* They would have been married? Las Vegas wouldn't have happened?

"We've always had a strange connection, that's all. You can read me as easily as I read you."

He was only partially right. They did have a connection, but she hadn't been able to read him as well. Otherwise, she wouldn't have let him break her heart.

She looked at him again, sensing he was lost in thought as he stared at something in the distance. In the past she would have asked him what he was thinking. Back then every thought, feeling or mood he had was important to her, but now she didn't care.

She dabbed her mouth with a napkin he'd given her. "You don't have to stay here with me."

Peter sent her a look but didn't reply. He stretched out his legs.

To someone else he might have looked relaxed, but

Claudia knew he wasn't. She sensed he was waiting for something. What, she couldn't guess. It had nothing to do with the power outage; it was more instinctual, predatory and patient.

Peter was his most formidable when he was patient, because he was a man of movement. Always in motion, he could cook, watch TV and hold a conversation all at the same time. But when he concentrated on a goal, he expected a specific outcome that always landed in his favor.

"Are you expecting someone?" she asked him, trying to gauge his mood.

His gaze slid to her face. "Not anymore."

Claudia finished her sandwich then rubbed her hands together. Somehow the darkness didn't seem as frightening as the man beside her. But she was a professional. She'd dealt with drug-addicted surgeons and crisis-driven top executives. She would handle him by being cool and detached from the situation. Emotions altered objectivity. Perhaps he was *also* uncomfortable with the situation. She would put him at ease and then take control.

"Congratulations on your last book and your radio show," she said, making sure her voice was suitably impressed. "I'm so happy you've done so well for yourself."

A bitter smile touched Peter's mouth. "Don't even try that with me, Claudia. You know better than that."

She stiffened, feeling caught and exposed, but quickly hid her emotions behind defensiveness. "I was only trying to have a conversation."

"By treating me as one of your patients? Do I look that stupid?"

"I don't have patients anymore." She sighed fiercely.

"This isn't going to work. In less than an hour we're already getting on each other's nerves." She looked at him. "Why did you say yes to this show, anyway?"

He continued to stare at something else. "Why did you?"

"Opportunity, money, exposure."

He nodded. "Sounds about right."

"At least no one knows about us." Few people knew about their relationship, and even fewer knew about their rash decision to meet in Las Vegas and get married. "That's a relief, don't you think?"

He ignored the question and stood. "I have another reason why I'm here."

"What is it?"

He took her hand and lifted her to her feet. "I wanted to see you again."

Claudia's heart began to race. "Why?"

He showed her. His mouth covered hers, stirring feelings of longing she hadn't realized were still there. Years floated away, and in an instant she was a med student again, in love with a man she'd known only a few weeks. A man who made her laugh and feel beautiful. Who believed in her. Claudia closed her eyes, sinking deeper into the special allure of the past.

His warm, wet lips called to the core emptiness in her, uncovering a hollowness she'd been desperate to keep hidden. It scared her how he made her feel vulnerable, but fear was quickly banished by ecstasy. Then, just as quickly as he'd started his sensual assault, he abruptly stopped and drew away. Claudia opened her eyes, startled by his sudden change, then noticed the electricity had returned. The lights blazed bright, causing her to squint against the glare. Her eyes surveyed her surroundings.

And what she saw was thirty-three hundred square

feet of absolute elegance. The villa had floor-to-ceiling solid glass, and screen doors which faced the ocean and retracted into hidden pockets, creating a complete open-air living experience.

The interior design consisted of inlaid mosaic tile floors in the entryway, polished dark mahogany and rosewood floors and cabinets, ceilings outlined with mahogany trim, bamboo handrails, and in the kitchen sea-foam green marble counters. The walls were a mix of soothing natural colors with Hawaiian Print wallpaper, and in the living area were silky handwoven Tibetan area rugs and imported leather and Italian furnishings.

Then her eyes moved to the tall man in front of her. Yes, he was still gorgeous, with silky dark brows and lashes and eyes smoldering with desire so evident her throat went dry.

Peter shook his head, reading her face. "Don't think of running away from me. We have unfinished business."

"That business ended years ago."

He moved in closer and brushed his thumb against her lower lip. "You really think so?"

Claudia turned her face away from his touch. "Yes. What just happened was a release of tension after a highly stressful situation. Nothing more." She folded her arms, trying to create some distance. "I was anxious about the lights being off, and it was an adequate diversion."

"But the lights are now on."

"I know that."

Peter glanced at her arms, then her face. "And you're still scared." He winked. "Night, Claudia." He turned on his heel and left.

Claudia watched him disappear into his bedroom, amazed by how easily he'd gotten past her guard. She

knew she'd need all her strength to fight him, but that
wouldn't be tonight. She sank back into the couch and
buried her head in her hands.

Chapter 3

"The camera loves her, but she's going to cost us money."

They were on location shooting a scene in the villa. The weather was perfect as the camera crew moved about.

Peter looked over at the producer, Frank Brady, a compact man with a bald head, an eye for detail and an uncanny ability for stating the obvious. He'd been working with Frank for the past five years. Frank had known him before his fame when Peter used to create documentaries for public and cable television, traveling the world to give voice to the voiceless. They'd gotten malaria together; he'd been at Frank's wedding and commiserated with him through Frank's divorce. Peter credited Frank as the man behind his fame.

Peter's bestselling book *Your Bed or Mine?: Tips from the Ultimate Bachelor* had started out as a dare when Frank was tallying up his legal fees after the breakup of his three-year marriage.

"I didn't know a divorce would cost this much," Frank had said, spreading papers out on the dining table. He was staying at Peter's expansive bachelor pad while he tried to get his life back in order. Peter came from money, although he never talked about it. He let Frank stay with him rent free and wouldn't discuss payment of any kind. Frank was glad, because he needed all the money he could get. His ex-wife had ended up with the house (Frank hated the rambler, anyway), the dog (a purebred Pomeranian named Zou Zou) and all the china (what the hell did he need expensive china for, anyway?). They had split the rest.

"That's the price you pay for dreaming," Peter said as he lay on the couch and flipped through the TV channels.

Frank looked up from his bills. "What?"

"Weddings, marriage. They're all a big fantasy meant to prevent us from seeing the truth."

Frank rested his arms on the table, curious. "Which is?"

"If you want to stay happy, you don't get married."

"I had to get married."

Peter shook his head. "No, you didn't."

"But she wanted to get married. I would have lost her otherwise."

"You believed that you would." He held up his forefinger. "That was your first mistake. Never let a woman know your fear, or she has the upper hand. She sold you a myth that you paid for. Ultimatums are manipulations. I never fall for them."

"But I loved her."

"And you told her, right?"

"Yes."

Peter shook his head. "That was your second mistake. There are only three times to tell a woman you love her. In the heat of passion (few women take that declaration seriously, so you can retract later), when you don't mean it (just to see what she thinks of the relationship) or three, when you want something."

"Like what?"

Peter sat up. "Say you've been seeing a woman for three months and she's still skittish. You tell her that you love her, and in an instant—" he snapped his fingers "—you're in. She feels special and safe with you."

"Isn't that cruel?"

"No. You can love a lot of things without being stuck with it forever, and don't be fooled—women play the same game. Tamika said she loved you, too, right?"

"Yes."

"But you're sleeping in my guest bedroom. Most women care about the ring more than the man. Again, it's about not falling for the myth. The moment a woman knows your weakness, you're a lost man."

"But if you really love a woman…"

"You remind yourself that there's always someone better. And if that doesn't work, remember the definition of love by Ambrose Bierce: *'Love: a temporary insanity, curable by marriage.'*"

Frank sat back and shook his head. "You don't really believe that. You were the best man at my wedding! You were the one who gave a speech that left half the women in tears."

"I know how to be sentimental."

"Why didn't you tell me any of this before?"

"Because you wouldn't have believed me. Back then

you were blinded by love. Now your eyesight has been restored."

Frank folded his arms. "Haven't you ever been in love?"

Peter paused. "Once."

Frank waited, but when Peter didn't expand on his answer, he shook his head again and gave a low whistle. "She must have been some woman to turn you off love completely."

"I believe in love. I just don't believe in forever."

Frank rubbed his chin. "Everything you've said sounds nice in theory, but if you want a good woman…"

"You don't have to get married to have a good woman. I have had my fair share."

"But you're different."

"No. I know the traps, and I avoid them. I plan to stay a bachelor for life."

"Impossible."

"I could show you how."

"I don't believe you."

"It's easy. There are key modes of operation that a man must follow in order to stay free. Here are a few pointers. The best women for great sex are divorced women. They have something to prove and aren't ready to 'settle down.' Avoid women with small children. They deserve someone stable and committed—that's not going to be you. And…what are you doing?" Peter asked when he noticed Frank writing something down.

"I'm taking notes. This stuff is good."

So he talked and Frank wrote. For weeks they worked on the book. Then when they were through, they stared at the computer screen where Frank had cleaned up his notes.

"What should we call it?" Frank asked.

They brainstormed different titles then decided on *Your Bed or Mine?: Tips from the Ultimate Bachelor.*

Frank hit Print and watched the pages pile up. "This is going to make you a fortune."

"It was just for fun."

But Frank disagreed. Without Peter knowing, he acted as his agent, typed up a marketing plan and sent out Peter's photo, along with the manuscript. Publishers scrambled to buy it. Frank sold it to the one he thought would do the best job of promotion and distribution. Once the book hit the market, it was an instant bestseller and shot to the top of *The New York Times* list. It led to guest appearances on TV talk shows, covers of magazines, a radio talk show and a weekly online column. Peter wanted to share the credit, but Frank refused, preferring to stay in the background. "I just typed the book," he said. "You wrote it." When the book's second edition came out, it reached number two in *Publishers Weekly.* The number one spot was held by Claudia's book. That's when his plan was born.

During this period, Peter used his connection with industry insiders to negotiate a way to turn the two books into a television series. He wanted to see Claudia again, because she was more than unfinished business: she was his ultimate challenge. The woman who'd gotten away and almost destroyed him. He still couldn't remember what he'd done the two weeks after she'd jilted him. The last thing he remembered after returning to the apartment they'd shared and finding all her things gone was going to the local liquor store to buy a bottle of scotch.

The next thing he remembered was waking up in a Sudanese hospital, getting a bullet removed from his arm. He discovered he'd accepted an assignment

to film the warring factions in the western region of
the Sudan. Peter didn't remember accepting the job or
anything prior to that moment, so he decided then to
stop drinking. But he didn't stop taking risks. Instead
of embarking on the radio career he and Claudia had
talked about, he decided to stay behind the camera and
not use the voice she admired.

Once released from the hospital, he finished his
assignment, then filmed a documentary about a brothel
in India and the ongoing problem of child slavery in
countries where it is still being practiced. The possibility
of death didn't scare him. Fear was better than the pain
he felt.

But once he'd returned to the States and completed
the book with Frank, he realized he wanted to face
Claudia. His determination grew when he saw her on
a TV show one day sharing how men make wonderful
"accessories." He wanted to show her that this man
wasn't going to accept being tossed away. He now had
that chance. He was coming full circle, back to his roots
in TV and to the woman who'd broken his heart.

Peter looked over at Claudia as her makeup artist
touched up her foundation. That was one thing he'd never
had to deal with before—a makeup artist. Fortunately,
Ashley Leroy was good and efficient—meaning she fit
their budget. She made Claudia look fabulous, which
wasn't difficult. Claudia had a gentle, exquisite beauty.
She was tall, with a willowy figure, just a little meatier
than those rail-thin models one sees on the runway,
with a perfect set of size 36Bs and a great pair of legs.
Her medium-length hair was cut in a fashionable style,
framing her face and emphasizing her almond eyes and
slightly turned-up nose. But her most alluring feature
was her perfectly formed lips. Her rosebud top lip was

smaller and darker than her full, fleshy bottom lip, and it always looked kissable no matter if she was wearing lipstick or just lip gloss.

Unfortunately, scheduling was critical, and they were nearly two days off because Claudia kept getting her cues wrong and forgetting her lines. And when she did get her lines right, she sounded stiff and rehearsed. If he didn't do something soon, Peter knew he was about to see years of effort disappear like a soap bubble.

He knew he was to blame. The kiss two days ago had rattled her. That hadn't been his intention. He hadn't even planned to kiss her. He'd rehearsed how nonchalant he'd be when he finally saw her again. He'd take his time and let her simmer until he was ready to turn up the heat. He would be slow, steady and patient. She wouldn't know she was his until there was no turning back. It was the perfect strategy.

And it would have worked if the lights hadn't gone out. That changed everything. Suddenly, in the darkness, his senses were on high alert. It was instinctual—a result of his experiences in the dark forests of Russia to when he'd gotten caught in the cross fire of warring ethnic tribes in a remote village in Gambia. The night could be dangerous, and you were only one of two things—prey or predator. He knew his prey, and that made him more attune to her. When she'd stepped through the door, the first thing he heard was the sound of her earrings and bracelets, clinking together like a wind chime, followed by the sound of her heels clicking against the tile.

The scent of her floral perfume came next: a heady mix of passion fruit and vanilla, which reminded him of how she used to smell after a shower, leaving the steamy bathroom behind her. But he'd steeled himself from that memory, determined not to be distracted. He had to maintain a calculated distance, but that night her fear of the darkness shattered his resolve. It was a weakness he had yet to master. Her fear had always been a trigger for him, and it still was. That's when he'd made his mistake and touched her. The feel of her damp skin sent an electric shock of awareness through him. When she'd refused to sit because her clothes were wet, he had to steel himself from acting on his impulse to pull them off her.

But the image stayed, even though he covered her with a blanket. He thought of her wet body underneath, pictured the fabric of her blouse clinging to her chest and imagined being a raindrop sliding down her stomach and disappearing in her panties…

He managed to stay in check. He was determined not to sacrifice years of preparation for an impulsive desire. And it would have been fine if Claudia hadn't used her clinical tone with him. That's when he didn't care about risking his plan. His only goal was to make her as aware of him as he was of her. His kiss made it certain. Her voice may have been neutral, but her body wasn't. He could sense how quickly she responded to him, and it was an intoxicating drug.

He'd had to use all his strength to pull away and keep his gaze on her face instead of the outline her bra made through her still-damp shirt. But the moment he left her, he knew he'd made a tactical error. He shouldn't have kissed her so soon. He should have waited a few days. Because of his haste, he couldn't stop thinking about the feel of her lips, the touch of her hand on his chest, silently begging her to go lower. The attraction was stronger than he'd expected, but he wouldn't let it rule him.

He was going to prove that he was completely over

her by using every trick in the book that had made him famous. This time he'd be the one to walk away.

But he had to fix his current problem. He'd come on too strong, which wasn't like him. He wanted Claudia to be aware, but not at this price. It was bad for business, and he needed this show to work. Few knew that he was the money behind Frank's production company, Productions Unlimited Inc. It was only one of his investments in an industry filled with risk. His father thought he was wasting his time, but he would show him. If this show was a hit, Peter knew he'd be able to segue into other projects that mattered to him and use his celebrity status to raise money to fight curable childhood diseases.

But right now he had to make his selection of the cohost, Claudia Madison, work. Luckily, the screen lit up every time the camera had her in view. She had the perfect "it" factor, a special innate quality that drew viewers to her. From her bob haircut and lithe body, to her dazzling smile and bright brown eyes, she gave a person the feeling that good times were ahead. That was the quality he'd fallen in love with all those years ago.

Peter looked away and frowned. Thank God he wasn't still in love with her. His love for her had made him as weak and pliable as wet cardboard. She'd used it to her advantage to humiliate him. He was glad they hadn't married. He would have been miserable. He hadn't known who she really was until that night in the Las Vegas chapel where she'd left him standing at the altar. He'd waited there for hours, called her cell phone until his battery went dead while he sat in a pew watching other couples start a life together as his fell apart.

But he wouldn't think about that now. She wouldn't

hurt him again, and he would make sure this project worked.

Peter patted Frank on the back. "Give me twenty minutes."

"But—"

"Do you trust me?"

"Certainly," Frank said with some apprehension. "But—"

"Claudia's a woman, right?"

"Yes, but not just any woman."

Peter held up a hand. "Watch and learn."

Frank's unease didn't leave his eyes, but he began to smile.

Chapter 4

"Walk with me."

It was a command, not a suggestion, but Ashley didn't care. She rested a hand on her hip and narrowed her eyes at Peter. "Can't Claudia walk with you later?" she said, annoyed. "I have to get her ready."

The set became quiet. The crew members knew that Peter didn't like when people questioned his orders. Ashley didn't care. A petite woman sporting a series of close-cropped twisted dreds, she liked to keep Claudia on schedule. The energetic makeup, wardrobe mistress and overall "gopher" was responsible for making sure the hosts looked great in front of the camera. She had no trouble working on Peter. He just needed powdered makeup to keep the shine off his forehead. And only once in a while, she would need to substitute his tie selection when he inadvertently selected a hideous color or pattern. But because he'd spent a lot of time on TV sets behind the camera, he knew what was expected. Claudia was the one who needed more attention. She wasn't one to wear a lot of makeup, and when she did, she did so sparingly. She had no idea the time it took to get her ready for a shoot, and she couldn't understand the two hours needed to make her look "natural."

"Must you use that much foundation?" she complained. "I'm going to look like a clown!" But when Claudia started to break out after only two days of filming, Ashley was forced to hold back a little on the foundation.

Ashley had familiarized herself with the hectic schedule planned over the period of seven weeks in four different countries. Thankfully, the entire crew would have either a week or several days off between the first three places, before having to travel to another location. This provided Ashley plenty of opportunities to shop for any additional items she needed. But she didn't like interruptions, and she didn't take kindly to Peter's suggestion that Claudia go for a walk with him. At least, not at that moment.

"This won't take long," he said in an indulgent voice that made everyone relax.

Claudia cast an uneasy glance at Ashley then looked back at Peter. Since their kiss, she'd done her best to avoid being alone with him. Distance was her best defense. It's what she'd told her friend Tamara, who was one of the few who knew about her past with Peter, a month ago when she'd asked how she would handle him.

"Are you sure you want to do this?" Tamara asked, unsure after Claudia told her about the project. "I know the money is good, but I have several exes I don't want to see, let alone work with."

"It will work out. He won't want to deal with me, and I'll stay away from him."

"But you're going to be cohosting a show with him!"

"I know."

"Just remember to be careful."

She thought of her friend's words now as she looked at Peter's face, which gave nothing away. "I know I keep screwing up, and I'm sorry. I—"

Peter shook his head. "That's not why I asked you to walk with me. Come on." He left.

"I guess you'd better follow," Ashley said, resigned.

Claudia jumped out of her chair and did just that.

Once she'd caught up with him, she tried not to bite off her carefully applied lipstick, but she couldn't imagine what Peter had to say. She knew she was awful. The thought of the past two days galled her. She was used to being a success, of wowing a crowd. But recently she produced only eye rolls and groans from some of the crew members. Peter hadn't spoken directly to her since that first night. The past couple of days, he'd gone to bed late and gotten up early, and except for a cursory hello or good-night they didn't converse. Claudia gazed down the stretch of white beach with its sparkling aquamarine water and powder blue sky, amazed she could feel miserable in paradise.

The silence seemed to deepen as their distance from the crew grew. Claudia took a deep breath. "Before you say anything, I know you're disappointed in me and you have every right. Putting me on TV was a gamble, and so far it's not working out. Everyone has been patient, and I really appreciate that. So—ow!" She glared at him, rubbing her arm where he'd pinched her. "What did you do that for?"

"I told you, that's not why I wanted to walk with you."

"Then why?"

"I want you to tell me why anyone should visit here."

Claudia threw out her hands. "That's obvious."

"Not to me. I've come here so often, it doesn't mean the same anymore."

She wasn't surprised he'd been to Hawaii before. She knew he enjoyed life's luxuries. "The women and the wine aren't enough?"

Peter ignored her comment and said, "Why should people—single people—come?"

"This beach is gorgeous."

He shrugged. "I've been to a lot of beaches."

"You cannot ignore the sugar white sands and gorgeous weather."

"Sure I can."

"It's the perfect place to show off one's figure."

"So?"

"To enjoy the sensuous smell of the many varieties of tropical flowers found on the island. Listening to the cry of native birds. The—"

He pointed at her. "That's it!"

She halted. "What?"

"That's what we need on camera. That passion. Be yourself—natural, fun, friendly. You're talking to the women who've bought your books and made them bestsellers. They want to connect with you. Give them that chance. Be their friend. Can you do that?"

"Yes."

"Good. Also, don't memorize your lines. Believe them. Own them. Make them yours."

Claudia nodded. "Okay."

Peter reached into his trouser pocket and took out a tiny digital video camera and focused it on her. "Okay, you're on."

"What?"

"Talk to me."

She blinked but said nothing.

He let his hand fall. "Pretend that the camera isn't there. Just talk to me." He held up the camera again. "Now, begin!"

"What am I supposed to say?"

"Anything you think is interesting."

Claudia looked out over the beach. "Hawaii is an island of secrets and mysteries—" her tone was calm, yet forceful "—with tales of gods and goddesses that could rival those found in ancient African and Greek stories. As I look out at the calm waters, I think of a story. Want to hear it?"

Peter nodded and continued filming. Then Claudia told him a story about a Hawaiian princess and her love, betrayal and death. It mesmerized him. He no longer heard the sound of the ocean or felt its breeze. Her words kept him spellbound. They both moved and angered him. How could *she* tell him a story about a woman betrayed by the man she loved?

"The end," she said.

Peter stopped filming and shoved the camera back in his pocket.

Claudia rested her hands on her hips with a smug grin. "Will that work?"

"Yes," he said curtly. He walked up to her, cupped her chin and studied her face. His gaze, which had once caressed her with tenderness, was unreadable. "Tell Ashley to soften your makeup, and be careful of your expressions." He let his hand fall and tilted his head. "You show too much emotion. You have to be more guarded. The camera catches everything—especially fear. Be an actress."

She raised her eyebrows in protest. "But I can't act."

"Sure you can. You're excellent at showing emotions you don't really feel."

Claudia scooped up a fistful of sand and threw it at him.

Peter wiped his face and glared at her. "What the heck was that for?"

"How dare you say that to me. I've always been honest about my feelings."

"You certainly fooled me." He pointed at her as she scooped up another fistful of sand. "You'll regret doing that a second time."

"I regret a lot of things when it comes to you. But it won't be this." She threw the sand.

Peter stood still a moment then rushed forward. Claudia turned and ran, but she couldn't outrun him. He grabbed her from behind and swung her up into his arms and walked toward the water. "I should throw you in."

"Ashley would kill you."

"It would be worth it."

Claudia struggled to release his hold. "Put me down."

He continued toward the ocean. "I know a few myths of my own, including the ocean god Kanaloa."

Claudia wrapped her arms around his neck. "He's also the god of death, so if you let go I'll take you down with me."

Peter met her eyes. "I don't doubt it."

"Is it your guilt that makes you want to see me dead?"

He abruptly released her so she could stand. "My guilt?"

Claudia stumbled but steadied herself. "Yes, after what you did to me?"

Peter raised his eyebrows, stunned. "After what *I* did? Are we talking about the same night? I wasn't the one who didn't show up on our wedding day. You left me standing there and I waited for…" He stopped and shook his head. "You could have told me you changed your mind the day before or the week before, but you waited until one of the most important days in a man's life to let him know that he wasn't good enough for you."

Claudia frowned, confused. "What are you talking about? I thought I made myself clear."

"Yes, you made yourself very clear. I'd actually thought something had happened to you and checked all the hospitals. You didn't even make it on the flight. But I still had hoped that maybe you'd missed the day. Even when I returned to our apartment and found all your things gone, I still didn't think you'd left me. Then I found your note where you explained that you'd made a mistake and didn't want to see me again. That our love affair was over. And…what is it?" he asked when Claudia gasped. "What's wrong? Did you get bitten or something?"

"Yes," she lied, pretending to rub a bite on her leg. She straightened. "We'd better go." She turned.

Peter grabbed her arm, making her face him. "You didn't get bitten, did you? What's wrong? Am I missing something?"

Claudia pulled her arm away and kept her face averted. She couldn't allow him to read her thoughts. Not now. She couldn't bear it. Her mind raced as she tried to fathom the magnitude of the truth. All this time Peter hadn't known the real reason she hadn't shown up, and she couldn't tell him. "No, you're right. What I did was cruel and thoughtless." She took a deep breath then finally turned to look at him. "You can see me as a selfish bitch or a pathetic wimp. Either way, I panicked and you're better off without me." When his dark eyes continued to search her face, she forced a smile. "Look how successful you are now, and you can have any woman you want and still stay a happy bachelor. You're living every man's dream." Before Peter could probe deeper, she turned, eager to escape into the safety of a crowd.

But Peter stopped her. "I said I wouldn't let you run away from me, and I meant it."

Claudia took a hasty step back. "Please, Peter, don't. Not here."

He stared at her, surprised by the fear in her eyes. Not weariness. Not unease. True, glittering fear. Of him. It shook him. He reached out to her, but she moved away. "What aren't you telling me?"

"Nothing." She held up her hands in surrender when he opened his mouth to argue. "You win. I regret everything and I'm sorry. I don't expect you to forgive me."

He hadn't anticipated this. She was supposed to be haughty. Fight him. Not surrender with tears gathering in her eyes. And for one wild moment he just wanted to hold her. He gripped his hands into fists. What the hell was going on? Why was she still able to get to him? Was this another trick? A way to manipulate him?

Claudia brushed the clinging sand from his shirt, desperate to divert his attention. "I'm sorry—"

Peter grabbed her hand. "I promise if you're hiding something from me, I'm going to find out."

She didn't reply.

He let her hand go. "Let's get back to work," he said, then walked past her.

Claudia briefly shut her eyes, relieved that her secret was still safe.

Chapter 5

All Roy Fitcher wanted was a cold beer and a hot woman. Preferably both at the same time. He leaned against a palm tree, waiting for the shooting to restart. He'd been to Hawaii lots of times and was bored. He couldn't understand how Warren could marvel at the same location each time. He frowned. Peter Warren—what an annoying prick. He hated the guy and his smug smile, arrogant commands and perfect clothes. Unlike everyone else, he rarely wore T-shirts. No, Mr. I'm-Better-Than-Everyone always wore dress shirts, crisply ironed and never wrinkled. The guy was unreal.

But he'd grown up with money, unlike Roy, who had to fight for everything. Although he was a successful cameraman, he'd always held a secret desire to be in front of the camera one day like Warren had managed to do. But that wasn't a surprise, everything seemed to come easy to the guy. He wouldn't even be here if Frank hadn't called him. Roy liked Frank. He was a man's man and treated people fairly and paid well. And the money for this assignment was good enough to help him with some gambling debts. But aside from the money, the job had another perk— Claudia Madison. He watched her laugh at something Ashley said and smiled. He planned to get to know her better. Although she'd turned him down for drinks earlier, he was undeterred. He had plenty of time to change her mind.

Roy paused when he saw Peter go over to Claudia. He waited for Claudia to dismiss him, but instead she followed him down to the beach. They should be getting ready for the next shoot. Why was he leading her away? He looked at Frank, but he didn't seem concerned. Roy folded his arms, resisting the urge to follow them. Peter wasn't trying to make a play, was he? He turned again to Frank and saw that Ashley had joined him and they were both watching Peter and Claudia. Roy decided to find out what was going on.

"What are you two up to?" he said, trying to sound more casual than he felt.

"Watching the master at work," Frank said, gesturing to Peter.

"What's he doing?"

"I don't know, but I hope it works."

"I don't know what the big deal is." Roy frowned, still amazed by the other man's appeal. "I mean, what's he got that I don't?"

Ashley sniffed. "I hope that's a rhetorical question."

He shot her a glance. "Okay, so he's good-looking and rich, so what? He's shallow."

"You sound jealous."

"I'm not jealous. I just thought women wanted more."

"The thing about Peter is his contradiction. There's a part of him you want to rescue and a part of him you want to tame. Plus he's sexy. It's a tempting package." She paused. "What on earth? If he throws her in the water, I'll kill him."

"Relax," Frank said. "It's just a ploy."

Ashley breathed a sigh of relief when Peter set Claudia down. "I wonder what the argument's about?"

"He's probably trying to give her pointers on how to be more natural in front of the camera."

"She might not like what he has to say," Ashley said.

"So far her performance has been…" Frank faltered.

Ashley filled in for him. "Stiff."

"That's a good way to put it."

"I'm sure she'll improve."

"She has to."

Ashley watched them more closely. "It's funny how good they look together. I wouldn't have expected that."

Frank straightened. "What do you mean?"

"Look at them—how their gestures seem to complement each other. How her artsy dress makes him look more casual, and his classic style makes her look less flamboyant. It's strange." Ashley looked at her handiwork, pleased with the outcome. Claudia looked stunning in a pale blue, off-the-shoulder cotton blouse and a white pair of wide-legged silk pants. She had pulled back Claudia's hair, which was held in place with a heavy dose of hair spray, and her outfit was set off by coral-shell earrings and a necklace. Peter looked equally ravishing in a dark purple, finely woven cotton shirt that showed off his muscular physique and a pair of loose-fitting khaki trousers. Together they made a very handsome pair.

Frank clapped his hands together. "It's great." He stood. "I just got an idea," he said then left.

"Oh, they're heading this way," Ashley said. "Back to work." She returned to her station, which was situated off to the side under an oversize bamboo umbrella.

Roy didn't move but kept watching Peter. "He's a fraud," he muttered. "And one day I'm going to prove it."

"No."

Frank held up his hands. "Just hear me out."

Peter and Frank sat in Frank's suite. The shoot was over and they'd just finished dinner.

"I heard you the first time," Peter said, "and the answer is the same. I'm not doing scenes with her."

"I know she's not your type. You like your women a bit more…" He hesitated, searching for the words.

Peter sent him a sharp look. "A bit more what?"

"Classy."

"Claudia's classy."

"Not in the usual way."

"In the usual way?" Peter said in a soft voice that was indistinguishable.

"You know…the big hoop earrings and long necklaces. That artsy style. We like our women more understated, right?" he said, suddenly unsure of Peter's mood. "I'm not saying she's not a very attractive woman."

"I know what you're trying to say, and the answer is still no."

"Okay, so you don't like her." When Peter looked surprised, Frank shrugged. "It's obvious. We all saw you nearly toss her in the ocean."

He shrugged. "I was just making a point."

"There's something else."

Peter shifted in his seat. "What?"

"She gets under your skin. I can't help but notice it, because I know you. You're cordial to her, but not in your usual way. Typically, you get a woman to smile, then you get her to laugh, then you get her into bed."

Peter began to grin. "There's still time."

Frank shook his head. "You won't be able to get her with your typical charm. The biggest problem is she's a female version of you."

Peter's grin vanished. "She's not a female version of anything, and certainly not me. She's no different from any other woman."

"If you believe that you'd be making a mistake."

Peter drummed his fingers on the table. "I understand her more than you know."

"Probably and I don't know why she rubs you the wrong way, but it works."

Peter stopped drumming and flattened his palm on the table. "What?"

"When I saw the two of you on the beach today, my mind went crazy. Because she's not your type, it makes things more interesting. You're more unassuming. I don't know what it is, but something sparkles when you're together."

"Sparkles? What is this, a disco?"

Frank grimaced. "Bear with me—I couldn't think of another word. This is a great idea."

Peter shook his head. "No, there's no reason to change things. She was flawless in her last shoot. I've finally got her on track."

"I know. Whatever you said worked. She was natural and friendly and great to look at. But together, you're dynamite. The camera will love you. You want a hit? I know how to give you one."

"We have different audiences," Peter said, knowing he was fighting a losing battle.

"You'll blend them together. The guys will love looking at her, and the ladies will love looking at you. It's the perfect combination. It's TV gold!"

Peter looked away.

Frank leaned forward. "Besides, combining scenes in the various locations will save on costs and put us back on schedule."

"I can't argue with that."

"Don't argue at all. Just tell me if you want a hit or not." He held out his hand.

Peter stared at Frank's extended hand, conflicted. He wanted this to work, but he'd made another mistake this afternoon. He shouldn't have touched her again, but he hadn't been able to help himself. He remembered the way the sun touched her hair, the way the wind caressed her skin, how her face glowed as she told him about her impression of the beach. She'd stirred something deep within him, and for one wild instant he pictured her naked on the beach with the waves washing over her smooth brown body, making her legs look sleek and wet and her nipples hard. Then he imagined himself as the wave completely covering her…

Peter silently swore as the vivid image rose again in his mind. He'd found nothing wrong with her makeup, but he had to say something to help dampen his dangerous attraction to her. It was more potent than he'd realized, and now he couldn't stop thinking about the brief look of fear he'd seen on her face. What did it mean? It wasn't just sexual unease, and it reached him at his core. He had to find out what she was hiding. But now wasn't the time.

He knew Frank understood what worked, and fortunately no one suspected how he really felt about Claudia. The situation was complicated enough.

Peter shook Frank's hand. "Don't make me regret this."

Chapter 6

He didn't know. All these years she'd hated him for the wrong reason. But Claudia knew she needed to let him believe what he had to. His bitterness kept her safe. Their kiss was just a salve for his bruised ego. She had no doubt that their relationship couldn't be saved.

Fate had intervened for a reason. And the truth, while it freed her and allowed her to heal, would devastate him if she told him now. No, she'd never tell him.

But thoughts of what might have been assaulted her and wouldn't let her enjoy her environment or relax. That evening she'd eaten a meal by herself. Their personal chef, Samson, who came with the villa, had made an excellent dish of garlic shrimp, eggplant and tomato pilaf, and for dessert frozen tarragon mousse with strawberries and fresh-sliced Hawaiian pineapples. She was still getting used to the extravagant accommodations. She'd taken several pictures of the grand ten-foot, solid-wood dining table and the handblown-glass, ceiling-mounted chandelier, which had a dimmer switch to create a specific dining ambience. Tonight, she'd put it on a low light.

A spectacular view of the ocean and sunset blazed in the distance and could be seen from the patio. She had hoped for a quiet, restful evening, but that wasn't to be. Outside on the patio, the crew spent the rest of the evening trying to capture one of the island's exquisite crimson-and-scarlet sunsets.

Claudia tried to read and then watch TV, but neither could calm her thoughts, even after a twelve-hour workday. It was still early evening, so she called the concierge and within five minutes a taxi arrived and took her to an exclusive nightclub just a few blocks away. She felt wired. After Peter had walked away from her on the beach, she'd gone in front of the camera and nailed every line and hit every cue. She shocked everyone, but Peter only looked smug. She didn't care. She was going to make this project a success no matter what he thought of her. He'd broken her heart, but he'd also healed it.

"Can I buy you a drink?"

Claudia turned and saw Roy take the seat next to her at the bar. She liked his attractive, loose-limbed style. Unlike the others, he didn't make her feel nervous and had rooted for her through her gaffes. She gestured to her half-finished martini glass. "I'm fine, thanks."

"Good job today."

"I bet I had you all nervous."

He shrugged. "It takes getting used to. I knew you'd get the hang of it eventually."

She took a sip. Then a song came on and she rocked back and forth to the beat.

Roy held out his hand. "Dance?"

"Sure."

Claudia followed Roy to the dimly lit dance floor and let him draw her close. He was a smooth dancer. It had been a while since she danced with a man. She'd had a casual affair four months ago that had ended amicably, but none of her affairs was ever serious.

"Watch out for Warren."

Claudia laughed, surprised by his warning. "You don't have to worry about him."

"I thought so," Roy said, pleased. "He's not like us."

"Like us?"

"He's not what he seems. I'm not fooled by that clean-cut style of his."

"Hmm."

She stiffened when she saw Peter enter the club. Their eyes met, but she was the first to turn away. Roy sensed the change in her and looked over his shoulder. "Don't let him bother you. He doesn't own us."

"No," she agreed, watching Peter take a booth with Frank.

"Besides, give him ten minutes and he'll have a woman at his side."

It took five. Soon two very attractive women were giggling with him. Claudia tried to look away, but her gaze kept returning to him. She fought not to notice how one woman leaned into him and that he didn't move away, and that the second woman let her long black hair brush against his shoulder.

"Poor Frank," she said.

"Don't feel sorry for him. He likes taking Warren's leftovers."

Claudia frowned, not liking Roy's words but understanding his meaning. However, she hadn't come to the club to talk about Peter. She wanted to erase him from her mind and disappear into the dim lights, crush of bodies and loud music.

She closed her eyes and let Roy take the lead, but when a faster song came on she allowed herself to be consumed by the pulsing drumbeats and quick-paced sound.

She pulled away from Roy and lost herself in the music, undulating her torso, swaying her hips in a sensual rhythm. She gasped in surprise when she backed into someone and turned her head to apologize until she realized it was Peter.

"You should watch where you're going," he said in a teasing voice over his shoulder.

"Maybe you should just move out of my way."

"Or maybe you shouldn't take up so much space. There's enough room on the dance floor for both of us."

Claudia wiggled halfway down to the floor, pressing her body against his, feeling the heat of his back and the soft curve of his butt. "Really?" she said, making her way up again.

Peter turned to face her. "Yes. Otherwise, you have to make room because I'm not going anywhere."

Claudia boldly faced him, their bodies dangerously close but not touching. He didn't back away and her pulse quickened, but she accepted the challenge and the heady jolt of excitement. "Neither am I."

One of Peter's newfound companions grabbed his arm before he could reply. Claudia waved her fingers in a triumphant motion of goodbye, but Peter leaned forward, this time making sure that his chest brushed against her shoulder. His warm breath caressed her ear when he said, "Don't think you've won," before he let himself be led away.

Roy came up next to her. "Did he upset you?"

"No, it was nothing," she said, her spirits plummeting as she saw the two women fawning over Peter. "But I'm ready to go."

"That's a good idea."

They went outside where the air was cool and walked back to their villas. Roy stroked Claudia's arm. "The beach is nice at night."

"Yes, I can see it from my villa."

He took her hand. "It's better up close."

She drew away. "Not tonight."

"I read one of your books and I like your premise. I'm not up for anything serious. I wouldn't put any pressure on you, but I'd like to be with you."

"I'm flattered Roy, but I need to focus on my work."

"It will get easier. We have lots of weeks we'll be working together." He stopped in front of her door and smiled. "Let me know when you change your mind."

Claudia couldn't help but notice the confidence of his words—not if, but when.

She shook her head, amused. "Good night, Roy."

He kissed her on the cheek. "Good night."

Claudia entered the villa, took a hot shower and changed into a set of silk pajamas then slipped into her ultralush pillow-top bed, wondering if she should have taken Roy up on his offer so that she wouldn't keep thinking about Peter. She didn't want to think about him. She needed to fall straight asleep. She wouldn't wait up and listen to hear if he'd brought home a companion or imagine him using his sexy smile and velvet voice to lure a woman into bed. What he did was none of her business.

It didn't matter that when he'd looked at her across the room as she was dancing with Roy, that all other men fell away. Claudia pounded her pillow. *No, I'm not doing this again.* She had too much at stake. She would act the role she needed to play. He saw her as a runaway bride, and that's what she'd be. Besides, it fit her public image.

It suited his public image, too. Peter was a natural in front of the camera. He never missed a line or cue, could ad-lib with ease and was immensely fun to watch. Not many people could transfer between radio and television with such ease. But he did most things well. Even before their talk on the beach, Claudia knew she was failing miserably. She was too aware not to notice how anxious everyone had been getting because of her. She lived her life watching people and gauging their reactions. She was an observer. People were something she understood. She liked to make sense out of things, because she'd grown up in a house of quiet chaos.

On the outside they were an ordinary family—a mother, a father, two girls and a boy. But if one were to remove the first layer, it would reveal a mother who had obsessive-compulsive tendencies. Everything had to be right according to her standards. The second layer would reveal a father who had stopped trying to do anything and had become emotionally dead. The last layer would show a sister who struggled with bulimia and a brother who failed at everything he tried, including three marriages. Claudia excelled by knowing what people wanted. She couldn't fix her family, but she was determined to help others.

In elementary school she'd spent most of her time with the school counselor instead of in a classroom. She'd been anxious all the time. Then in middle school she'd blossomed once she'd found out what her mother liked most: achievement. And Claudia made sure she did. She got straight As, ran for student-body president and won, organized fundraisers and excelled in sports. She had her whole life planned. A medical degree by the time she was thirty and her own practice by thirty-five.

Peter Warren hadn't been part of her plan.

They were opposites, but somehow they'd clicked. Strange how it was her friend Tamara looking for a good time and a nightclub that had brought them together.

Chapter 7

"He's mine," her friend Tamara said the moment she saw the two men enter the club.

They sat at a table that gave them an unobstructed view of the entry.

Claudia stifled a grin, not surprised by her friend's words. The two women shared an apartment and sometimes clothes, but never men. It was a promise they had made between themselves. Fortunately, it had never been an issue, because their taste in men was so different.

Claudia studied the two men, doing her best to guess which one would soon be in her friend's clutches. The first man looked like a possible regular in a brown leather jacket and sporting a diamond stud earring. His friend, on the other hand, stood out not only because he was tall and as light-skinned as his friend was dark, but his clothes branded him an outsider. His conservatively

cut jacket and dark trousers didn't blend in with the
ethnic flavor of the club.

"I bet I know which one is yours," Claudia said.

"Go ahead."

"You like the one who looks like he belongs on a
campaign trail or could take over a corporation."

Tamara grinned. "I've been working on him for two
months now. It took me forever to get him to meet me
here at the club. I only convinced him because I said I'd
have someone for his friend."

Claudia pointed to herself. "That would be me."

"Yes. Keep his friend suitably entertained while I
work on becoming the next Mrs. Peter Warren."

"You're that certain?"

"He's perfect for a woman with my aspirations. He
comes from money and has prominent parents, even
though they're divorced. He's studying film and radio
for his bachelor's degree, but I'm sure with the right
guidance he can be persuaded to enter a more suitable
career. And his father's business is very profitable."

"And what if he doesn't want to follow in his father's
footsteps?"

"He will. He's rich, handsome and full of potential."
Tamara lightly tapped her chest as though her heart were
fluttering. "I'm in love with him already."

Claudia laughed. "You hardly know him. I've never
seen you like this."

"I know. That must mean he's The One."

Claudia resisted rolling her eyes. "How come I've
never met him or heard you talk about him?"

"You've always been out when he's stopped by, and
I didn't want to mention anything just in case nothing
developed. Now things have changed."

Claudia believed her. No man was safe when

Tamara was on the prowl. Even she wasn't immune to her friend's influence. She wouldn't have come to the Virginia nightclub if Tamara hadn't forced her.

"You've got to learn to live a little," she'd said when Claudia had settled in for another night of studying. "You're doing great in all your courses. Don't grow old before your time."

Her friend was right. Claudia buried herself in medical school and her job as a research assistant in a prestigious science lab near the university. Going out was a good break and would put her newfound knowledge about observing people to work. The Kalahari, a West African-themed jazz club known for its fine cuisine and music, was a great place to push worries aside. Its popularity came solely from word of mouth through the immigrant college crowd at the local university and colleges in the area.

"Looks like they won't even make it in," Claudia said, noticing how the bouncer was hassling the two men and checking their IDs.

"Yes, they will." Tamara slipped out of her chair and weaved her way through the crowd until she reached the pair. She immediately claimed the one she wanted when she slid her arm through Peter's and kissed him. Claudia didn't know what she said to the bouncer, but moments later the two men were heading toward their table.

"There was a minor misunderstanding with their IDs," Tamara explained.

"Misunderstanding?" Claudia asked.

"Yes, he thought they were fakes," she said, flashing Peter's ID, which said he was a lot older than he looked, before handing it back to him. "But it's been cleared up." She brushed something from Peter's jacket. "He's probably just jealous that your shoes cost more than he makes in a month."

Peter's jaw twitched, but he didn't reply.

The expression came and went in an instant, but Claudia couldn't ignore the meaning: he didn't like the mention of his money. She glanced at her friend but could see that Tamara hadn't noticed anything. His friend, however, did. Claudia decided to ease the tension with a smile. "I'm glad you both made it. Hi, I'm Claudia."

Tamara turned to her. "Yes, where are my manners? Claudia, this is Darius and Peter."

"A pleasure," she said, shaking Darius's hand then Peter's.

Darius met her eyes and smiled; Peter also met her eyes, but he held her hand in a warm, solid grip a tad longer than she'd expected.

"How come he didn't hassle you?" Darius asked.

"Because Tamara's cousin owns the club," Claudia said, quickly trying to recover from the sensuous touch of Peter's hand.

"That's good to know. Can I get you ladies anything?"

Claudia and Tamara gave him their orders, then Peter said something to him in a low voice before he left to get their drinks at the bar.

"I'm so glad you could make it, Peter," Tamara said as he draped his jacket on the back of his chair. When he sat down, she looped her arm through his again.

Claudia noticed the slight jaw twitch again and inwardly groaned. *You're overdoing it, Tamara,* she wanted to say. *He doesn't like to be grabbed at. Be more subtle.* Her friend was cute, petite and bubbly, and that usually worked with men. But Claudia knew her friend would have to try a different tactic with Peter. When he glanced away, Claudia nudged her friend then mouthed "Let go."

Tamara did, and she saw Peter relax.

"This is your first time here, right?" Tamara asked in an anxious voice.

"Yes," Peter said and rested his arms on the table.

His terse reply wasn't a good sign. Claudia saw the desperation on her friend's face. If she didn't do something soon, the evening would be a disaster. Claudia glanced down and saw something peeking out from under his shirtsleeve. The sight of it stunned her. "Is that a tattoo?" Before he could respond, she reached over and pushed his sleeve back, revealing a Japanese character. "It's beautiful. Not every artist can make the symbol look so smooth and clean." Claudia traced the pattern with her finger. "It means *peace,* right?"

"No, it means *harmony.*"

She shot her head up, stunned by the mesmerizing sound of his deep voice. "Oh," she said, unable to manage anything more interesting.

"I bet you have a tattoo also."

She nodded, still captivated by the sound of his voice.

"Can I guess where?"

She swallowed, a hint of anticipation shooting through her. "Try your best."

Peter's gaze lazily roamed over her figure then returned back to her face. "Your ankle."

Claudia widened her eyes, surprised by his accuracy. "How did you know?"

Peter nodded to her leg, and she glanced down and noticed that her short skirt and crossed legs had made the tattoo on her ankle visible. She laughed. "So much for guessing."

He grinned. "It was the first thing I noticed when you sat down."

"You obviously have an eye for detail."

"I have an eye for a lot of things." His eyes captured hers.

Claudia nearly stopped breathing. He stared back at her with depthless, dark brown eyes that hid a mystery she wanted to solve. She soon became aware of how warm his skin felt beneath her fingers. She hadn't stopped touching him. She yanked her hands back. "I'm sorry," she said, quickly remembering how his jaw twitched when Tamara touched him.

Tamara grabbed Claudia's arm and pulled her out of her chair. "We're going to go freshen up," she told Peter, dragging her friend away.

Once in the restroom, Claudia said, "What was that all about?"

"I told you he's mine."

Claudia laughed. "That was pretty obvious the moment you pounced on him."

Tamara looked in the mirror and touched up her lipstick. "I didn't pounce. I staked claim." She turned back to her friend. "Hands off, Claudia."

"But I didn't do anything."

"You were flirting." She mimicked Claudia's tone. "Oh, wow, it's beautiful. It means *peace,* right? You obviously have an eye for detail."

"He was the one who asked about my tattoo. I was just trying to get him to talk. I didn't expect the tattoo. Don't tell me that the sight of it didn't surprise you."

"Yes, it did, but let *me* be surprised. Not you."

"He's not my type anyway. Besides, I like my men older."

"He's two years older than we are."

"You bought that ID?"

"Yes. He can't help it that he's adorable."

Claudia thought about his tattoo and his eyes. Puppies and babies were adorable. Peter was something else.

"This is my chance. Don't mess it up for me."

"I wouldn't dare, but I'd be careful. Still waters run deep."

"I like them strong and silent. Honey, when I grabbed his arm, you wouldn't believe the muscle I felt there. I bet his thighs are just as solid."

"I wouldn't keep squeezing him if I were you, and don't keep mentioning his money."

Tamara narrowed her gaze. "You think you know him better than I do? I've studied psychology too, you know."

Claudia shook her head. "I'm only trying to help. I want to see you happy."

Tamara smiled. "I am happy, and I'll be as naughty or as nice as I need to be to keep his interest." She finished touching up her makeup and combing her hair then got three condoms from the dispenser on the wall. "It's going to be a fun night."

And it was. Claudia danced with Darius but didn't want to monopolize him, so she encouraged him to mingle with other women while she danced with an exchange student from Sweden and then a guy from California. The music was booming, the crowd rocking and the drinks flowing.

Claudia returned to the table happy and exhausted, surprised to see Peter there alone. "Where's Tamara?"

He gestured to the dance floor, where Tamara was

dancing sandwiched between two men. Claudia laughed then sobered when she remembered her companion. "She really likes you. I'm telling you this so you don't have to be nervous or anything. It's like discovering there's a pop quiz. No matter what you do, you'll get an A. So all that—" Claudia waved toward her friend in a dismissive gesture "—is nothing serious. She's just having fun and trying to impress you."

Peter pushed a glass aside and rested his arms on the table.

"But you're not having fun, are you? This isn't your kind of place."

He shrugged. "I'm open to new experience," he said, handing her a napkin.

"Oh, thanks," Claudia said, wiping the sweat from her forehead and then her neck. "I love to dance, but I always have to go home and take a shower." Claudia dabbed her chest then stopped when she felt him go still. He probably found her coarse. The women he probably went out with wouldn't dry themselves off with a bar napkin. She crunched up the napkin and cleared her throat. "I hope you haven't been designated to guard the table. If you want to dance, I can keep watch."

Peter bit his lip then said, "No, I'm fine."

"You don't want to dance?"

He shook his head again. "Not yet."

Claudia stifled a groan. *The strong silent type.* Tamara could keep him. She turned her attention to the dance floor, hoping she could spot Darius. "What a crowd, huh?" she said just to fill the silence between them. "I like to study people." She surveyed the crowd then pointed. "See that woman over there? She's going to wake up tomorrow regretting her decision if she leaves with that man. He's married. Want to know how I know?"

She glanced at Peter expecting him to look bored. Instead, she found his intense gaze focused on her. He nodded. She swallowed, suddenly unnerved by his attention. "I've met his wife." She gestured to a man near the back wall. "Now that guy is out of his league. He needs to go to some place quiet. He's probably like you. You're only here because of Tamara, right?"

Peter shook his head then offered her a sudden arresting smiled.

Claudia caught her breath. He was a lot more than adorable. He was gorgeous. *He's mine,* she heard Tamara say. Claudia clenched her hand into a fist and stared down at the table. He wasn't her type anyway.

"Okay, now it's your turn. You try to read people."

"I won't be as good as you."

She fell forward, again enchanted by his voice. "It's like a secret weapon."

Peter blinked. "What?"

"That voice. It's beautiful. Why don't you talk more often? No wonder you're studying radio and film. You'll be perfect."

"Tamara thinks I'm doing it as a hobby. She's not the only one."

"Don't worry. She'll get used to the idea. You have to follow your passion."

"Even at my age?"

"You're what? Twenty-seven?"

He nodded.

"That means you're seasoned. Besides, you could easily pass for much younger. A lot of students enter college because they don't know what to do or because they have to. You know why you're here, and it's better late than never." She smiled at him, letting all her preconceived notions drift away. He wasn't a snob or dull. He was wonderful. "I admire you. It takes courage to do what you want when others don't approve."

Peter leaned forward. "My parents still hope it's a phase. I've already done some voice-over work, and in high school I interned at a local radio station. They actually offered me a job. I also have a successful podcast."

"Why are you even in school then?"

He lowered his eyes. "Degrees mean a lot in my family. I thought if I had to get one, I might as well get one in a field that interests me." He met her eyes. "But enough about me. Why did you choose psychiatry?"

"Actually, I did a double major in both psychology and psychiatry. I wanted to make sure I had the medical training of a psychiatrist so that I could prescribe the best medications for my patients. And a psychology degree allows me to not have to rely on a big practice, but to spend part of my time doing research and writing articles. People fascinate me."

Peter rested his chin in his hand. "Do *I* fascinate you?"

In every way, Claudia thought, falling into his melting brown eyes. She blinked, realizing the danger of her thoughts. "Yes. I mean no."

"Which is it? Yes or no?"

"Yes, but in a purely speculative way."

Peter's eyes brightened with amusement. "Of course." He glanced at something behind her then stood. "Come on," he said, taking her hand.

"Where?"

"Where do you think?" he said then led her onto the dance floor.

"You want to dance?" He pulled her to him and she tried to wiggle away. "This isn't the way it works. You're here with Tamara."

"I don't see her with me right now."

"She really likes you."

"And you don't?"

"Not the way she does."

"Relax. I saw her dancing with Darius."

Claudia sighed with relief. "Okay." She held up one finger. "Just one song."

Peter only smiled.

Claudia danced with him the rest of the night. He was a great dancer. Whether the beat was fast or slow, with him she lost track of time. At times they danced together and other times apart, but she had a wild night with an unassuming man who made her laugh and feel wonderful. Then she raised her arm to wipe the back of her forehead and glanced at her watch. She swore.

"What?"

She tapped her watch. "That can't be the time."

"It's still early."

"It's nearly one o'clock. I've got work tomorrow." She swore again. "And I forgot all about Tamara." She briefly squeezed her eyes shut. "She's going to kill me." She began to make her way through the crowd.

Peter grabbed her arm and turned her to face him. "Claudia, we need to talk," he said, his voice urgent.

She held up her hand. "No, we don't."

"We can't pretend that—"

"Yes, we can, and if you won't, I will. This can go no further. You're good for her, she'll make you happy. Let's leave it at that."

"You don't mean that."

"Yes, I do."

Peter looked at Claudia for a long moment then let her arm go.

Claudia returned to the table, where Tamara sat steaming. She looked at Peter then glared at Claudia. Claudia held up both her hands. "I am so sorry. We lost track of time."

Claudia saw Peter's jaw twitch, but this time she didn't care.

Peter grabbed his jacket from off the back of the chair then took Tamara's hand in such a smooth, inoffensive gesture, both women were too surprised to protest. Claudia watched him take her friend over to a quiet corner. Tamara stared up at him with her arms folded defensively.

"He doesn't know what he's dealing with," Claudia muttered.

"Yes, he does," Darius said, coming up behind her. "Don't underestimate him."

He was right. As Peter continued to talk, Claudia saw her friend soften. Then smile.

Claudia whistled, amazed. "He's good." *I made the right choice.* Any man who could maneuver a woman like Tamara that easily was dangerous. She smiled at Darius, and they set up a date to go out for drinks. Once they'd exchanged numbers, Claudia looked at her friend again. "Tell Tamara I'll meet her outside."

Ten minutes later they were driving home and Tamara was laughing.

"What did he say to you?" Claudia asked, pleased by her friend's buoyant mood.

"I can hardly remember. One moment I was mad at you, and the next moment I was laughing. We've got a date for Saturday night." She winked. "I told you he was mine."

"Yes."

"He said you just felt sorry for him or something and that's why you were together."

That was the first reason, but as the evening progressed it had become something else. But Claudia wasn't about to tell her friend so.

Tamara suddenly looked pensive. "I don't know how you got him to dance."

"He probably said yes just to get me to shut up."

"Hmm. I can't wait to see him again. There's something special about him."

"Definitely," Claudia muttered.

"Hands off, Madison."

Claudia stiffened, knowing that Tamara jealously guarded whomever she thought was hers. And she had Peter. "I was just agreeing with you," Claudia said, trying to keep her voice light. "Don't worry. I'll stay far away from him."

Chapter 8

For the next several weeks Claudia did just that. She was cordial when she saw him and he to her when he came by the apartment to pick up Tamara. She maintained a safe distance, although his gaze said a lot more than his words ever did.

"I don't like the way you look at him," Tamara said one day after Peter had left their apartment.

Claudia sat at their dining table working on a term paper. "I don't know what you're talking about."

"You didn't have to come out of your room to study."

Claudia looked at her papers and laptop. She liked using the dining table because if offered more room than her desk. "I was here first."

Tamara folded her arms, unappeased. "You want him too, don't you?"

Claudia sighed, tired of her friend's suspicions. Yes, she

was attracted to Peter, but she'd never betray her friend. But no matter how much she tried, she couldn't seem to convince her of that. "I'm too busy for a relationship anyway."

Tamara pursed her lips. "So you're saying that you do want him and would take him if you had the time?"

Claudia shook her head. "No, I'm saying that I'm not interested."

"I've been cheated on before, so don't try any tricks with me. Don't call him, or meet with him or anything behind my back."

"Why are you saying this?"

"Because I want you to stay away from my man."

"Nothing will get in the way of our friendship. I'll stay away," Claudia promised.

And she would have if Levar Brown hadn't entered her life.

Claudia never guessed that accepting a walk home from her friend Levar would change her life. They'd studied together at the library, and both were going after their degrees. It was winter so it got dark early, and after her 7 p.m. evening class she'd felt comfortable having him walk with her across campus to the apartment complex she shared with Tamara. She didn't protest his insistence to take her to her apartment door, although she was a little uneasy stepping into the empty elevator with him. The moment the doors slid closed, her uneasiness grew.

"You don't like closed spaces?" he asked, sensing her tension.

"Sometimes."

The elevator jerked to a stop and the lights went out. Claudia pressed her hand against the wall to steady herself and tried to remember to breathe. Ever since she was a child she'd hated the dark.

"Don't worry," he said. "I'm sure they'll get it fixed soon."

"Yes."

"Until then, let's make the most of it." He abruptly grabbed her and pressed his mouth against hers. She fought to free herself, but his grip was too strong.

"You know you want this. You've been teasing me for months."

Claudia slapped him hard. He swore, pushed her to the floor and ripped her blouse. The sound of the tearing fabric made her struggle even more, her bare skin rubbing against the cold metal floor. She swung at him wildly, punching, kicking and screaming. But he banged her head twice hard against the floor. She saw stars and decided to go limp. She felt him straddle her as he unzipped his pants.

No. Oh God, no. This can't be happening to me. Claudia squeezed her eyes shut, trying to orient herself and figure out her next move. She needed to catch him unaware. She lifted her knee, but he anticipated her and moved quickly. He slapped her across the face then pinned her shoulders down. "You're lucky you missed."

He ground his mouth against hers and she bit his lip, drawing blood. He jerked back and suddenly the lights came back on. The elevator jerked and started ascending. Levar looked up at the camera and scrambled to his feet. He fixed his clothes. "Don't tell anyone," he warned as she gathered her things together. "Promise me you won't."

Claudia held her backpack and handbag close to her chest, forming a shield. She could feel the pain in her shoulder where he'd held her down, and her head ached.

"Promise me, Claudia. Don't say anything. Besides, nothing happened anyway." He smirked.

The elevator doors opened on the fifth floor. She hurried out, rushing down the empty hall.

He followed her. "It's your word against mine."

She didn't turn back.

"Remember, I know where you live," he shouted.

Claudia turned the corner and saw Peter leaving her apartment. He halted when he saw her. "What the—" His gaze darted to Levar then back to her. His eyes flashed with rage.

Levar held out his hands when Peter impaled him with a dark look. "Wait, brother, it wasn't like that."

Peter slowly walked toward him and said to Claudia, "Do you want me to break his arms or just his neck?"

Claudia looked back at her attacker with anger rising in her. "His hands."

Levar stumbled back and gestured to Claudia. "You're going to take her word over mine? You know how women change their minds."

Peter kept walking.

Levar turned and ran. Peter raced after him. Claudia followed them but couldn't keep up. By the time she reached outside they were gone. She rested against the wall then slid to the ground and drew her knees to her chest.

"Claudia?"

She shot to her feet, ready to fight until she realized it was Peter.

His face was grave. "You shouldn't be out here." He took off his wool jacket and draped it around her shoulders. "Here. Put this on." He watched her as she did then asked, "Are you all right?"

"He hurt me, but he didn't…" Her words died away.

Peter nodded, not forcing her to continue.

"Did he get away?"

"No," Peter said with grim satisfaction. "I got him. He won't hurt you again. Come on."

"Where?"

"We're going to the police."

"You don't need to come with me."

"I'm not going to let you do this on your own."

Peter didn't leave her all night. At the police station Claudia was assigned a female police officer, who was a member of the sexual assault team. She asked Claudia if she wanted to go to the hospital to be examined. Claudia declined but gave a full account of what happened and allowed them to take pictures of her injuries.

"Sounds like the same guy we've been trying to catch," the officer said. "He's committed at least three rapes over the past several months. Now we have a name, thanks to you." After she signed several papers, Peter took Claudia back to her apartment building. She felt weary, but also satisfied.

Before going inside, Claudia collapsed against the outside door. For a moment, she didn't know what to feel. Relief? Joy? Revenged? All she knew was that the man standing beside her had given her back the sense of safety Levar had stolen from her. "I'm fine now. You don't have to take me inside." She hugged him. "Thank you for everything," she whispered.

His arms encircled her and he held her close. For a long time neither said anything. But soon their embrace became more than an expression of gratitude or relief. It became more sensuous and tender. Claudia became aware of the soft feel of his shirt against her cheek, the solid feel of his muscular arms that could harm her but instead held her gently, the racing of his heart and the erratic rhythm of her own. Her face felt flushed, but when she felt the tantalizing touch of his lips against her forehead, she knew their feelings were forbidden.

She drew away. "Peter don't."

"I can't help myself," he said in a raw voice. "I can't pretend I don't feel the way I do." He shook his head before she could argue. "I'm not seeing Tamara anymore. We broke up tonight."

"It's too soon for us. She'd think something has been going on between us."

He lightly touched her face. "It was. The moment I saw you in the club that night, that was it. I tried to do it your way, but it didn't work."

Claudia went inside the building and saw the elevator, but she decided to climb the stairs instead. "I can't think about this right now."

Peter followed. "I won't pressure you, but I just want you to know how I feel."

"You don't have to follow me."

"Yes, I do." He held up his hands. "I won't say anything more about it."

"Good." They headed to her apartment in silence. Claudia unlocked the door then turned to Peter. "Thanks again for everything. Goodbye." She opened the door then stopped.

Peter took a step toward her. "What is it?"

Claudia opened the door wider. All her suitcases and boxes were stacked in the foyer. Tamara sat on the couch—her arms folded—waiting.

Claudia looked at the boxes then her friend, confused. "What's going on?"

Tamara leaped to her feet, her face a mask of fury. She glared at Peter. "I knew it! Now I know why you dumped me."

Peter shook his head, exasperated. "Tamara, this is beneath you."

"Beneath me? At least I'm honest. I'm not sneaking around with *your* best friend." She rested a hand on her hip. "Were you together all night? Did you think you could sneak in without me knowing?"

Claudia took a step toward her, her voice soft. "Tamara, that's not—"

She swept Claudia with a look of disgust then gestured to the coat she wore. "So you're wearing his clothes now?"

"He loaned it to me because my blouse is torn." Claudia removed his coat to show her. "I was attacked. We just came back from the police station."

A flicker of emotion flashed across Tamara's face then disappeared. Tears filled her eyes. "I'm sorry, but that doesn't change anything. For months I've had to see the way he looks at you and the way you look at him. I told you he was *mine,* and you still stole him from me."

"I understand you're upset and you want someone to blame," Peter said, "but blame me, not Claudia. I told you it wasn't working."

Tamara rolled her eyes. "Now you're going to defend her."

Claudia spoke up. "Tamara—"

She pointed to the door. "Get out!"

"Please."

She grabbed one of Claudia's suitcases and threw it into the hallway. "You're a liar and a thief and I want you out of my place. Now." She threw another suitcase, barely missing Peter.

Peter seized Tamara's arm. "That's enough."

She yanked her arm away. "You're lucky I didn't throw her stuff in a Dumpster." She flashed a bitter smile. "But of course, you could buy her anything she wanted."

Claudia looked at her friend in disbelief, stunned by her anger. Then she smelled the faint scent of liquor. "Tamara, I think you just need to sleep this off."

"Shut up."

Peter picked up some of Claudia's things. "Let's go."

Tamara held on to the door frame. "You broke my heart, you know that?" She shouted at him as he marched down the hall. "You bastard!"

Claudia picked up the rest of her things then walked out the door. She turned to look at Tamara. "You'll regret this in the morning."

"Go to hell." Tamara slammed the door in her face.

Claudia hung her head then followed Peter outside and found him putting her suitcases in the trunk of his car.

"This is not your fault," he said. "I noticed she had a jealous streak from the beginning." He took a box from her. "I'm just sorry it had to end this way." He finished loading all her things.

"What are you doing?" she asked when he closed the trunk.

"You're staying with me tonight." He walked around and opened the passenger door. "I have an extra bedroom. You're going to take a shower and rest. We can pick up your car tomorrow."

Claudia was too tired to protest and the offer sounded

inviting. She took out her cell phone and left a message for her sister so her family would know where she was. But she didn't take a shower that night; instead, she fell asleep on the way. She vaguely remembered being carried and the feel of satin sheets being pulled up to her chin, but nothing else.

Claudia woke up to the sound of something sizzling and the smell of toasted raisin bread. She looked around the room and was instantly hit by its masculine elegance. She wasn't in a guest bedroom. She was in *his* room. The walls were painted a muted brown with off-white trim. There was a tall wooden dresser with thick brass handles against one wall, a series of wooden boxes against another and a handsome valet, made out of teak, where a recently pressed shirt and tie neatly hung. Over by the window was what looked like a reading desk with an executive leather chair and a row of shoes, lined up next to a shoe-polishing stand that was positioned in front of a large, mirrored walk-in closet. Claudia noticed Peter had hung up her robe and set out some toiletries for her.

She hurried into the bathroom and washed her face, brushed her teeth and then retrieved some clothes from her suitcase and changed.

When she left the bedroom, she saw that his apartment was expensively decorated without being gaudy. Along with the sizzling sound, she heard low voices. She peeked her head around the corner and saw Peter cooking and watching a game on TV. He suddenly looked up and saw her. Their eyes met, and at that moment Claudia knew her heart would forever be his. "Did you sleep well?"

"Yes."

He waved her forward with a spatula. "Come on, I'm making brunch."

This is crazy, Claudia thought. It could never work. Their lives and temperaments were so different. She studied the sciences, he the arts. She liked to talk, he didn't. Perhaps their interest in each other was based on their attraction being forbidden, but now that it wasn't, their feelings would change. The researcher in her had to find out. She walked up to him and kissed him.

She imagined his kiss to be like him—quiet, reserved, guarded but simple and sweet—like French vanilla. What she got was rum raisin. Bold, daring and passionate. He tasted delicious and she opened herself to him in body, mind and spirit. She drew back and stared up at him with wonder. "I don't believe this."

"I do." He kissed her again.

Their attraction had been instant; their lovemaking combustible. They stumbled to the couch wrapped in each other, and Peter pulled down her top. The quick motion made Claudia stiffen as she imagined the fabric tearing and remembered another man's hands on her...

Peter sensed the change in Claudia and stopped. He captured her with his eyes. "It's okay," he said in a soft voice.

She nodded, unable to speak.

"Do you want me to stop?"

Claudia shook her head as tears gathered in her eyes, longing for the protectiveness of his arms.

His hand gently caressed her cheek. "I'd never hurt you," he said, his voice deepening with emotion. "And I'll never let anyone hurt you." He brushed a tear away. "You'll always be safe with me."

She believed him. Not because of his words, but

because at that instant she unlocked the mystery of his dark eyes and saw the soul of a man she could trust. She buried her fears and doubts and arched into him, letting him know what she could not express in words.

He groaned in response. "Did you know what you were doing to me with that napkin?"

"Napkin?"

"Yes, when we first met at the nightclub and you dried yourself with it. You made that simple act so sexy, I wasn't sure I'd be able to stand up for the next hour."

Claudia laughed, pleased by her effect on him. "I thought you might think I was crass."

His hand inched up her leg. "Far from it. I wanted to do this then."

"If you liked that, you should see what I can do with a loofah sponge."

"I plan to."

She kissed him again, and this time his lips tasted sweeter than the ripest berry. His hands were softer than silk, and when his bare flesh met hers, his body felt hotter than an inferno and together they burned. He made her senses spin and her body sweat, and soon she felt whole again and treasured. The pain of Levar's attack and her loss of Tamara's friendship became a distant memory.

Peter burned their brunch, but neither cared. All that mattered was being with each other. They didn't eat anything until dinnertime, which Peter ordered in. The next morning they snuggled on the sofa while Peter watched TV.

"Oh, wait!" Claudia said as Peter flipped through the channels. "I love this movie."

Peter frowned at the black-and-white image. "What is it?"

"*Love Affair.* A classic. They remade it as *An Affair to Remember* with Cary Grant, but I've always loved the original. It's about two people who meet on a cruise and agree to meet in six months at the Empire State Building. Tragedy and misunderstandings get between them, but their love never wavers. Can we watch it?"

Because he would have done anything for her, Peter said yes. Claudia cried at the same places she always did and sighed in others. When the movie was over, she rested her head on Peter's shoulders. "Thank you."

"She should have told him," Peter said.

"She loved him too much to be a burden to him."

He frowned. "If he loved her, she wouldn't be. I don't think love needs to be tested."

"Love is always tested."

He kissed her forehead. "Nothing could keep me away from you," he said then switched the channel to a crime drama and Claudia read the daily newspaper she'd picked up at the convenience store because Peter didn't have a subscription.

She gasped when she read the lead story.

"What?"

She sat up. "Early yesterday morning a man was found tied to a pole by his belt with his pants pulled down."

"Amazing the things that happen," Peter said without interest.

"They won't release his name, but he had to be taken to the hospital. He'd been badly beaten." She paused. "Peter, you didn't."

He raised his eyebrows in innocence. "I didn't what?"

"I wish I could have seen him."

"Me, too." They never talked about the incident again.

"You don't seem surprised about us," Claudia said weeks later when Darius came to visit.

"That night he told me he wanted you, but you turned him down. He tried to make things work with Tamara, but after meeting you, she didn't have a chance. You accept him as he is. You make him feel proud. He's still a little sensitive about his disability."

"Disability?"

"Yeah, dyslexia. He doesn't talk about it, but you won't catch him reading unless it's for work, and don't even try to read his handwriting. In a family of academics, he's the black sheep. He got held back twice in elementary school, and even after his diagnosis his parents expected better. His older brother, Thomas, was considered the smart one."

"Was?"

"Yes, but that's another subject. You'll have to wait to hear that story from him."

However, Peter never talked about his family. He preferred action to talking and took her boating, bowling, rowing, running and swimming. He treated Claudia to fine-dining restaurants she'd never been to where she tasted an array of culinary delights. They had weekend trips to New York, where they went to museums and the theater. He showered her with gifts—flowers, candy— especially her favorite, caramel chocolate—trinkets and expensive jewelry.

For Claudia it felt almost too wonderful to last, and it didn't after she got a call from her mother. Her sister's bulimia had landed her in the hospital and her mother needed Claudia's help to take care of her sister over the next couple of months.

"I wish I didn't have to go," Claudia said as she packed her things. "I love my family, but it's difficult being with them." She looked at Peter as he sat on the other side of the bed. "With you I don't feel so alone."

"You can have me forever if you want."

"What do you mean?"

"Marry me." He took her hand in his and drew her down next to him.

It was an impulsive declaration, but Claudia didn't hesitate when she replied. "Yes," she said without apprehension. She knew that he was the man she wanted to spend the rest of her life with, even though they'd known each other only a few months. "When?"

He gently cupped the side of her face. "I would marry you now, but I want to be my own man and not depend on my family's money. I want to be the man you deserve."

She smiled. "You already are."

His expression remained serious. "No, not yet. I still have a lot to prove, but in three months I'll have finished my degree. And I have a job lined up so I'll be able to support you while you finish your studies. You won't have to work such long hours." He bit his lip. "But I could work at my dad's place for a couple of months so that we could get a house and—"

Claudia shook her head. "No, I want you to follow your heart. I can wait."

Peter took both her hands in his, his eyes brimming with tenderness and love. "Okay, then. Three months from now, let's meet in Las Vegas at The Love Chapel at five o'clock and get married. I'll buy our tickets right now so that everything will be set."

Claudia held his hands against her chest. "Just like in *Love Affair?*"

Peter scowled. "No, not like that. You'd better show up."

"Oh, I will." Claudia threw her arms around him. "Nothing could keep me away."

He drew her close and kissed her. "Good. Otherwise I'll hunt you down."

"You won't have to. Three months from now everything will be perfect. You'll be working, my sister won't need me and I can finish my studies."

They'd laughed, basking in the glow of their love and a future filled with possibilities, not knowing that fate had other plans.

Claudia thought about that moment, aware of the irony of her life. She'd gotten Tamara back but had lost the man she'd loved. He was happy. He liked his freedom as much as she did hers. She wasn't the woman she used to be. Her life was perfect.

Yet when she closed her eyes, she felt the loss of what might have been, something beautiful and magical. She thought of her favorite movie, *Love Affair;* her life had mirrored it but without the happy ending, and tears seeped from under her closed eyelids.

Chapter 9

"Let's try that again. This time with a kiss," Frank said after he'd stopped the filming. They were in a perfect location for the day's shoot, with the azure ocean in the background and a pebbly cove off in the distance inviting one to swim, scuba dive or go snorkeling.

"What?" Peter and Claudia said in unison.

"It will add a nice spice to the scene."

Claudia sent Peter a nervous glance. "But I don't—"

"It's just for the camera," Frank said. "Trust me. It will work. Start with your closing remark." He gave the cue, and Peter looked at the camera and said, "A word of warning, fellas. This is a special place. Choose your lady with care."

Claudia opened her mouth to say her closing remark, but before she could Peter surprised her with a kiss that completely shattered her calm. When his tongue slipped into her mouth, a shiver of ecstasy swept through her, and soon his soft, wet lips were impossible to resist and she wound her arm around him, drawing him closer.

"And...cut!" Frank said. "That was fabulous. You two are on fire!"

Peter abruptly released Claudia, but not before sending her a smoldering look that caused her heart to race.

Claudia slunk into her chair, both exhausted and aroused. She knew that Peter was still her weakness and she'd have to work hard to stay away from him. She had to remind herself that she was here to work—nothing more. It had been several grueling days of shooting, and they still had one more.

She'd quickly learned how much work traveling with a film crew was. She'd been up since 5:00 a.m. and it was now nearly evening. Thankfully, they'd quickly become a tight group. Their five-person crew, shooting entirely using small cameras and photography equipment, had already gotten into rhythm.

Frank kept everyone on schedule by managing to include in their contracts that he would deduct from their pay if they were late getting to the set by more than fifteen minutes.

Ashley helped keep everyone sane. As the go-to person, she assisted the film crew making sure whenever they were going out on a shoot that they had the necessary items. Getting to a site with all their gear was an event in itself. For most of the locations, they rented either four-wheel-drive SUVs or minivans. They had to travel light and make sure that in addition to their camera equipment, they had their backup generators for lighting and sound equipment.

In her role as wardrobe mistress, Ashley was also responsible for selecting the clothes for the cohosts and props needed for each shoot. Every evening she would meet with Frank to discuss and work out everything that would be needed for the next day of filming.

At times there was a lot of tension among the crew. There was the "pain in the butt" part of the photo shoots. This included taking apart the equipment and putting it together again, setting up the lights in different settings and times of day and worrying about how the light reflected on the scene and the hosts. The soundman, Eugene Knotts, a quiet man with shaggy white hair, had to make sure the audio was captured, whatever the weather provided.

The two cameramen, Roy and Lance, were seasoned professionals and excellent at capturing scenes needed as fillers, and they were usually gone before dawn— only to return for the days scheduled shooting around 9:00 a.m. A compendium of footage was filmed at various locations, shot over time and on several different days to augment and supplement the final edited version. The primary philosophy behind the show was to provide a mix of escapism and excited curiosity—allowing viewers to escape from the humdrum regularities of their mundane lives. With this in mind, Frank, an award-winning director, knew he needed ample material to work with.

After recovering from the shock of learning that she would be shooting scenes with Peter, Claudia steeled herself to endure days of filming in exotic romantic locations and not being distracted by how good Peter looked in each of them. Everywhere they taped on the island, Peter's recognizable status came into play and a crowd of women would gather and watch him in awe, simpering when he smiled at them. Claudia tried to ignore the disruption by studying the local venues whenever she could, chatting with those fans who recognized her and planning her next book.

Claudia looked at the orange glow of the setting sun. The crew had just completed filming the two of them eating dinner on the lovely Hanalei Bay on Kauai's north shore. Behind the beach was a breathtaking backdrop of waterfalls and emerald mountain peaks wrapped in mist, soaring thousands of feet toward the heavens with large coral reefs at the end of the bay.

The clear waters, clean white beach and swaying coconut palms were a photographer's dream. The melodious sounds of tropical birds provided the perfect background noise for the scene. Samson, who had prepared and served up to three meals a day back at the villa, had difficulty relaxing in front of the camera. It was finally decided to let him prepare and cook the meals off-camera and only film him serving the dishes.

Claudia wished she'd had the opportunity to actually eat the food, instead of pretending she was, because Ashley kept touching up her lipstick between takes for the sake of continuity.

Yesterday they'd taped an episode on a secluded beach, which was accessible only by helicopter or landing watercraft. There they'd found a stunning panoramic oceanfront view. The sound of the waves lapping gently along the shoreline, which could be heard day or night, provided a soft rhythm. Following a sumptuous picnic, Claudia and Peter went for a walk along the beach. The powdered-sugar sand and sparkling turquoise water were sheltered by a wide, protective offshore reef providing ideal swimming conditions. But Claudia wasn't allowed to swim, because she couldn't get her hair wet since she had to quickly change for the next three scenes.

Peter didn't have that problem so he took off his shirt and trousers, revealing a perfect physique. He winked at her. "Like what you see?"

He didn't give her a chance to respond before he dived into the water and disappeared underneath.

To get him back for that teasing remark, Claudia had Ashley dress her in a sexy see-through sarong for their next scene. When she caught him looking, she whispered, "Try not to drool."

But he nearly had the final laugh when she learned about their last major shoot before flying home.

"A lava field?"

"Yes," Frank said. "It's a great place for stargazing."

"What's wrong with the beach?"

"We've shot enough beaches here. Trust me, it will be great."

"She's afraid of the dark," Peter said.

"I'm not afraid."

But she was. Later that evening, Claudia's anxiety grew as they drove to the location. For their adventure on the lava field, they had to wear proper shoes for walking on the lava and had to use flashlights so that they could find a flat area to sit down and do the shoot. Claudia pushed down any fear and went through the scene like a pro, but once the cameras stopped rolling her imagination took over. Viewing the stars from the stark darkness of the lava field gave her an eerie feeling.

She paused when she heard a sound behind her. Then someone grabbed her from behind. She screamed and began throwing punches.

"Whoa! Calm down," Roy said, backing away from her. "I was just playing with you."

Claudia hugged herself to keep from trembling, unable to speak.

"What are you afraid of?" He put his flashlight under his chin, the light distorting his features. "The bogeyman?"

"Leave her alone, Roy," Peter said, coming up to them.

"I was just having a little fun. You can take a joke." He tweaked Claudia's chin. "Can't you?"

"I said leave her alone."

Roy's playful tone change. "Plan to do something about it?"

"Only if I have to."

Frank spoke up. "Roy, help Lance pack the SUV."

Roy scowled then left.

Peter walked up to Claudia. "Are you okay?"

She threw her hands up in exasperation. "I feel like an idiot."

"That wasn't my question."

Claudia covered her face. "I've done hypnosis, acupuncture, aromatherapy, and I can't seem to fight this."

Peter removed her hands and forced her to look at him. "It's okay."

Claudia looked up at him, surprised by his tenderness. She'd expected him to be mocking or smug, but he was neither and she felt her embarrassment slip away. She looked down at the hands that held hers, her heart picking up pace.

"You know you never have to be afraid with me."

His voice sounded extra deep and magnetic in the dark stillness. "I know."

His lips brushed against her forehead, his breath warm against her skin. "The dark can't hurt you."

She gripped the front of his shirt, taking strength from his solid presence. Her embarrassment was gone, but somehow her fear wasn't. "But things in the dark could."

"I'd never let anything or *anyone* hurt you."

Even you? She wanted to ask him, but she licked her trembling lips instead. "Thank you."

Peter released a fierce sigh. "Claudia, I don't want your thanks. When I kissed you on camera I meant it."

"I know."

"So then you also know that I—"

"Come on!" Frank called. "We're ready to roll. Peter, I've got to talk to you."

Peter sighed then let her go.

Chapter 10

Claudia hardly slept that night, wondering what Peter would have said if Frank hadn't interrupted him. She could guess, and the power of her imagination kept her hot. She couldn't pretend that she didn't feel the same attraction he did. He wanted an affair, and she'd give him one. She just had to plan it to make sure that she didn't look overeager. The next day, they did a quick scene at the villa again then wrapped up the filming early, giving her a chance to explore. Claudia decided to go for a walk and deal with her warring feelings. She didn't want to be attracted to Peter, but she couldn't deny that she was.

She walked around the charming small town next to the villas, drinking in the sight of the lush tropical foliage. She stopped in one of the boutiques, looking for souvenirs. She thought of her friends Suzanne and Noreen and bought an eight-inch aquarium round plate, in cobalt blue, exquisitely made out of fused glass. She also bought a handblown glass piece depicting a conch shell with an image of the white-sand beaches and sea, and several items made out of bamboo for her niece Tess, godson Luke and Madame Curie.

Then she saw something she knew Peter would love—an acacia box. Acacia wood is prized for its beautiful grain and rich color and is usually hand-sculptured to create one-of-a-kind art pieces. She hesitated. She remembered he liked to collect boxes like this. He rarely talked about his family, but on one instance he did when she asked him about his collection.

"I like the order and symmetry. It's simple and yet can hold so many things. That one I made in woodshop when I was fifteen," he said, handing her a piece.

"It's very good."

He took it from her and replaced it. "It's passable, but not like master woodworkers. An uncle gave me my first one when he traveled to Ghana. He said he thought I would appreciate it and find it useful."

"Why?"

"Because it was a place where I could put my award ribbons, since my parents didn't hang them up."

"Why not?" she asked, surprised by that admission.

He shrugged then changed the subject.

Claudia studied the box now, thinking of that moment, then impulsively bought it. Perhaps she should tell him what really happened and why she hadn't shown up in Vegas. Not that it would change anything, but so that the feelings between them wouldn't be so strained. They should start their affair with the past buried behind them.

She returned to the villa with her bags of purchases and headed to her room. She had to tell him the truth.

She saw Peter's silhouette out on the lanai. She took a deep breath then went toward him.

"Yes, I miss you, too," he said in a gentle tone.

She stopped. He was talking on his cell phone. She wanted to leave, but she couldn't.

"It's going well." He was silent then said, "I know." He listened then nodded. "I wish you were here, too." He sighed. "It's not that simple." He paused. "I'll always love you. Now I've got to go. Uh-huh. Yes. Bye."

Claudia didn't move, feeling a searing pain as her hopes for an affair disappeared. She quickly brushed her feelings aside. He'd never been that casual with his emotions before. Perhaps he'd changed. By all appearances, whoever he was talking to was special to him and her traitorous heart was jealous. Who was the woman who had elicited such tender affection? What did she look like? Was she sophisticated and refined? What did she do? How long had they been together?

Claudia hated the questions but couldn't stop them from coming. It helped everything make sense. She had been surprised when he'd returned to the villa alone that night after the club. She'd assumed it was because they had a full workday ahead. Now she knew he was in a serious relationship. He'd kissed her out of spite because he could and he knew what it would do to her. But his heart belonged to someone else.

"Did you want me?"

It took Claudia a moment to realize he had disconnected and was talking to her. "Uh…no."

He put his cell phone away. "I guess a better question is *do* you want me?"

She swallowed. "No."

Peter took a slow step toward her, his tone deepening into huskiness. "Don't be coy, Claudia. I know you do."

"Who was that on the phone?"

He hesitated then moved closer. "How much did you hear?"

"Enough."

He sighed then shook his head. "It's not what you think and has nothing to do with us."

"Us?"

His finger traced a stirring path down her neck. "Don't fight what you feel." He placed his hands on her shoulders and drew her close. "Admit that you want me."

Claudia licked her lips, but her gaze never wavered. "You want me more."

His gaze dropped to her lips then returned to her face. "Maybe. What should we do about it?"

"Take a cold shower?"

"Together?"

She smiled. "No."

"You have another suggestion?"

"We can see where it leads."

"I like that idea." He bent to kiss her but stopped when his cell phone rang. He swore. When he saw the number, he swore again.

Claudia stepped back with a wry grin. "I guess that's our cold shower."

Peter held up his hand. "No, just give me a minute."

Claudia turned, knowing the mood was gone. "Good night," she said then left.

Peter swore again as he watched Claudia go, then answered. "Hello?"

"I saw that postcard you sent Thomas," his father, Lloyd Warren, said.

Peter groaned and walked back inside. "Do you know what time it is?"

"It's later here than there. What have I told you about getting his hopes up?"

Peter went into the kitchen and opened the fridge then closed it. "He wanted to see a picture, Dad. That's all."

"He said you'd take him there one day."

"Yes, maybe one day."

"It wouldn't be safe. He doesn't travel well. Why don't you find another hobby? You can do better than this."

Peter tapped his fist against his forehead. "Dad, let's not do this."

"You come from a long line of success. Professors, mathematicians, surgeons, and you've made a career out of a running gag."

Peter hung his head, knowing he couldn't stop the often-repeated lecture. He sat at the dining table and waited.

Lloyd Warren didn't disappoint him. "*Your Bed or Mine?: Tips from the Ultimate Bachelor.* What kind of title is that? When are you going to grow up and get a real job? Do something useful with that degree of yours. You certainly worked hard enough for it, but you haven't put it to good use."

"Let's forget about me for a moment. I'm worried about Thomas."

"He's fine."

"He wants more independence. Let him get a job or volunteer."

"How do you know he's unhappy?" Mr. Warren demanded.

"I spoke to him."

"He's doing okay. He probably was just in a bad mood."

"I can afford—"

"I can afford a lot of things too, so don't start throwing your money in my face."

"I was only trying to—"

"I don't care what you can afford. I've always taken care of him and I always will."

"He's not a kid anymore, and I think letting him move into the group home will build his confidence."

"You know what can happen in those places."

Peter kept his voice even. "I've been studying—"

"That's a surprise, when you barely managed to complete your degree. Do you have one of your women read the books to you?"

Peter ignored the barb. "As I said, I've been studying and researching the field and learned—"

His father laughed with derision. "Your field is pseudoscience, sound bites and hot women. I deal in the real world. Your next stop is Bermuda, right?" He didn't wait for a reply. "Send *us* a postcard." He hung up.

Peter gently set the phone down then pounded the table several times with his fist. He pounded out his rage, his frustration and his feeling of helplessness. He pounded the table until his hand ached, then he sat back and took a deep breath. His hand shook as the pain registered, but he didn't move.

"I know you don't want to talk about it," Claudia said in a quiet voice behind him. "But can I at least check to see if you've broken your hand?"

He sent her a look.

She sat down, unfazed. "You've done it before."

He looked away, in no mood to argue. Soon he felt

her long, smooth fingers gently touch his hand. He knew his hand wasn't broken, but he didn't mind her exploratory touch. With each gesture he felt his anger melting away. Soon his frustration followed, then his tension. He looked at her with wonder as she kneaded his entire hand.

This was what he'd missed most—her understanding. She read people well and understood him. It was why they had been so good together. She read his moods and left him alone when he needed to be. She wasn't like other women who would ask him what was wrong or try to force him to talk and open up.

He felt her begin to draw away, but he clasped her hand before she could leave. His grip wasn't strong, just enough to restrain her. He didn't look at her. He wanted her to stay, but he didn't want to talk. She understood the silent request and squeezed his hand. Once he knew she wouldn't go, he leaned back in his chair and stared out the window, trying to gain control of his conflicting thoughts.

She'd been there for him another time when he'd argued with his father and ended up in the hospital after smashing his hand through a wall. He hadn't told her what the call was about then, either. He'd wanted to keep her away from the ugliness of his family. He felt the same way now. Peter looked over at Claudia to see if she was as lost in thought as he was. She was asleep with her head resting on her folded arms.

He brushed her hair away from her cheek. "Claudia?"

She opened her eyes and smiled. "Guess what?"

He couldn't help smiling back. "What?"

"Your hand isn't broken."

His smile grew. "I never would have guessed."

Her expression grew serious. "How many bones did you break last time?"

"Three."

"Only three?"

He nodded.

She lifted his hand. "I bet it was this one." She kissed his index finger. "This one." She kissed his ring finger. "And this one." She kissed his thumb.

"I also broke my wrist."

She placed her lips on his inner wrist.

"And I once shattered my shoulder."

She raised an eyebrow then placed a kiss there.

"It was my right shoulder."

"Oh." She kissed his other shoulder.

"And my nose."

She shook her head. "You never broke your nose. Your face is too symmetrical."

"Some people wanted to."

"But they didn't."

"I have a scar on my thigh."

Claudia raised both eyebrows in feigned innocence. "Inner or outer?"

"Inner. On my right leg."

She lowered herself to the ground then pushed up one leg of his shorts. "I can hardly see anything."

"It's really faint."

She stifled a grin then kissed him there. "Is it this?"

"It's a little higher."

She kissed him again.

"A bit more."

And again.

"Higher."

She looked up at him with amusement. "If I go any higher, I won't be kissing your thigh."

"And you wouldn't hear me complaining."

She rested her hand on his front. "Funny, it doesn't feel broken. Have you been having trouble with it?"

It was a bold move, and for a moment he didn't speak. Then he said, "Yes."

Claudia glanced up, surprised. "Really?"

Peter pulled her into his arms. "Yes, it keeps leading me to you." His mouth covered hers in a wild, hungry assault.

When they pulled away for breath, she whispered, "Bedroom?"

"It's too far."

"It's only a few feet away."

"Right, but I want you now." He lifted her onto the dining table.

"This brings back memories."

He unzipped his shorts and put on protection, which he'd had in his back pocket. "Let's make some new ones."

They made enough memories to last the rest of their lives. Clothes lay discarded around them and Claudia welcomed his hard body against hers, her skin tingling at the touch of his hot flesh. They were passionate and reckless, not caring if they got caught—the possibility only heightening the thrill. The movements were hot, quick and primal.

"You're going to leave scars," Peter said as her nails dragged down his back. They'd left the dining table and continued on the bare floor.

"Something to remember me by," Claudia said, wrapping her legs around him, inviting him deeper inside her. Both experienced a pure and explosive pleasure that left them weak when it was over.

Peter rolled away then stared up at the ceiling. "Amazing."

"Thank you."

He laughed. "You're going to take all the credit?"

Claudia turned on her side and rested her hand on his chest. "I suppose I could give you some."

He lifted her hand and kissed the back of it with mock humility. "Thank you."

Claudia sat up. "I bought you something."

He stilled.

"Don't worry," she said in a light tone. "I know tonight doesn't mean anything. I just thought you would like it. I—"

Peter kissed her to keep her from talking. He couldn't let this night mean more than playful recreation. "What you just gave me was good enough."

"Aren't you even curious?"

"No." When she began to smile with knowing, he sighed, resigned. "What did you get me?"

She adjusted her clothing and left the room then returned and handed him a medium-size shopping bag. He reached inside and pulled out an extraordinary piece of artwork. It was a small box, made out of acacia wood. He knew just where to put it—next to a similar box he'd gotten in Brazil after his parents' divorce.

Damn. He was touched. He didn't want to be, but he was. He ran his hand over the decorated inlay. She knew him too well.

Claudia folded her arms. "You don't like it?"

He opened the box then closed it. "Why do you say that?"

She rubbed the muscle at his jawline with her thumb. "This tells me when something's upset you."

He stood. "It's nothing. I like it. Thanks." He cleared

his throat. He knew he sounded abrupt and cold, but he couldn't help it. "We'd better get to bed. We have a long flight tomorrow."

"Right." Claudia hesitated then looked away. "Good night."

"Night," Peter said in a quiet tone, knowing she didn't hear him as she headed for her bedroom. Peter watched her go, a part of him wishing she would stay.

Chapter 11

Peter went into his bedroom, placed Claudia's gift on the dresser then picked up his pillow and threw it across the room. He threw it with such force it hit the wall with a bang. *What was wrong with him?* He had her. He'd won. He could walk away from her now and let her feel the pain of it. Why didn't he feel better about it? Where was his sense of triumph and satisfaction? Victory? Why did his bed suddenly seem so large and empty without her? Why did he want to be where she was? Could he still have feelings for her like before?

Peter picked up another pillow and threw it on the ground. No, that wasn't it. He was just strained about the upcoming show and his family, and she helped him take his mind off things. If he hadn't had that talk with his father, he wouldn't be this vulnerable.

How much of his conversation had she overheard? Could she tell that it was him? Did she think he'd handled his father well? Peter briefly shut his eyes and swore. That was the problem. He still cared about her opinion.

He walked over to the window and stared out at the view. He took a deep, steadying breath. He had to focus on the goal. He had to ignore how one look from her took him back to when everything about her mattered to him.

He was older now. Wiser. But he didn't feel wise. Something wasn't right. She'd come to him too eagerly and let him go with the same compliance. He'd expected some protest, some anger. But just like on the beach, it was as if she expected him to hurt her, and it didn't make sense. Did she really feel guilty? She'd been eavesdropping on his first call and he'd seen the questions in her eyes, but she hadn't asked him anything. Part of him was glad, because he didn't want to answer questions right now.

He still wanted her. He wanted to fall asleep with her in his arms, to inhale the scent of her lotion, to feel her hair against his face. Peter groaned. *Oh, God. He was falling in love with her again.* He turned from the window. He didn't care. He wanted her too much to care. He'd have her again tonight and deal with the consequences later. He kicked a pillow out of his way as he walked to the door. He opened it then jumped back when he saw Claudia getting ready to knock. She let her hand fall.

He gripped the door frame to keep himself from grabbing her. She looked soft and cuddly in a short cotton nightdress. "Couldn't sleep?" he asked.

"No." She hugged herself, her eyes unsure. "My bed's cold."

He drew her into his room and kicked the door closed. "Mine's not."

"I didn't think so."

"Are you ready to sleep?"

"No."

They stripped down then fell on the bed, their actions less frenzied this time but no less intense. Afterward they lay in each other's arms but didn't speak.

Claudia lazily stroked his thigh then wrapped her hand around him, teasing the head with her forefinger. "How come Little Peter won't go down?"

"If you keep doing that he won't," Peter said in a husky voice.

She drew her hand away. "Sorry."

"Don't apologize. I didn't say he didn't like it."

She rested her chin on his chest. "No one can know about us."

"Why not? People have affairs all the time."

"We're different."

He shrugged. "All right." But he sensed something else bothered her. Like him, she could be quiet and patient when she wanted to draw out a secret from someone. He stroked her hair. "What else is on your mind?"

"I'm just thinking."

"There's no one else, Claudia."

"Hmm?"

He glanced away then sighed. "That first phone call…I was talking to my brother, Thomas."

"Oh, I see."

"I doubt it."

"You never talk about him."

"It's a painful subject."

"At first I thought he was dead."

"In my family, he is in a way." Peter hesitated. "He's developmentally delayed."

"So what was that second phone call about?"

Peter rested a hand behind his head. "My father and I don't agree on how to take care of him." He released a weary sigh this time. "Before his accident, Thomas was the smart one. He was an honors student. He had the most innovative ideas, and my parents were certain he'd create something that would change the world. Then I came along—the black sheep of the family—barely scraping by in school. I was a star athlete, but that didn't count. Any gorilla could throw a football—it took skill to solve an equation. I didn't mind the comparison much, because I was proud of my brother. He was heading places, and then in one moment all that ended." Peter swallowed.

Claudia touched his shoulder, sensing the memory was painful.

"And it was my fault. He wouldn't have gone there if it hadn't been for me."

"Where did he go?"

"The basement. I know it sounds stupid. I mean, what could be so dangerous about a basement. But it was for him, and I knew better. See, it had been raining for days, and I was getting antsy because I hated being stuck indoors. My brother was fine with his books and video games, but I wanted an adventure. So I decided to explore the basement. We weren't allowed to go down there, because it was damp and Mom was worried about mold, but I wanted to go some place forbidden. I was ten and didn't fear the consequences of getting caught. I'd gotten in trouble before, so I didn't care.

"Thomas was fourteen and didn't want to go. He didn't like to upset our parents. I called him a name or something—I don't remember—and said I'd go by myself and told him to keep watch. When I went down there, I found some boxes and trunks that I started going through. I didn't hear Thomas call out to tell me that my father was coming. Because he didn't want me to get into trouble, he ran down the stairs to come and get me. It took a while for him to find me. I was all the way in the back room."

Peter squeezed his eyes shut. "The wheezing started almost instantly. Thomas couldn't catch his breath." He opened his eyes and stared sightlessly ahead. "I recognized that he was having an asthma attack. I tried to help him up the stairs, but he couldn't make it and collapsed. I got my father and he carried him upstairs. My mother called an ambulance, but by the time the EMTs arrived, he'd suffered a stroke and he never fully recovered.

"The strain of my brother's care caused my parents' divorce. My mother eventually remarried. I have a stepsister who is a physicist and a stepbrother who is a neurologist. My father never remarried. He raised the two of us." Peter took a deep breath. "He'll never say it but my father blames me, and there isn't a day that goes by when I don't think about what Thomas could have been. I think about it most when it rains."

"Your brother is who and what he is," Claudia said softly. "I know you love him no matter what, and that's okay." When he didn't respond, she continued. "I had an aunt who came to stay with us for a while and one day I broke a beautiful teacup and desperately tried to put it back together so I wouldn't get into trouble. Of course that was impossible, and my aunt caught me. Tearfully I apologized, and she said that it was fine and left it at that. A few days later she showed me a mosaic-tile trivet she had made. She said this is a lesson about life. Sometimes in life things break and can't be put back together again as they were. They must become something else. I still have that trivet as a reminder. Don't see your brother as broken—see him as he is now. He is worthy now." She licked her lip, uncertain. "Why didn't you tell me about him before?"

"A number of reasons."

"Name one."

Peter opened his mouth then closed it. "It's complicated."

"No it's not. Did you think I would judge him or something?"

Peter looked away.

"I knew you were hiding something from me even back then."

"I wasn't hiding anything. I just didn't want my family to interfere with us. You don't know what my father's like."

"I don't know what any of your family is like. You never introduced me."

"You didn't miss anything."

"Your father couldn't be any worse than my mother."

Peter sent her a look but didn't reply. His meeting with Claudia's mother hadn't gone well. Although Mrs. Madison appreciated that he was working toward his degree, she wished he had more ambition.

"Now I see it wouldn't have worked out between us." Claudia rolled onto her back.

"Feeling validated now? You dodged a bullet. You don't have to deal with a man who has a damaged brother and father issues."

Claudia regretted her words. "That's not it at all. I—"

"Like I said, my family is complicated and I didn't

want you swallowed up in it. I knew you would try to get involved, and I didn't want that. Back then you thought you could solve everything. You were opinionated and stubborn. It would have been a mess."

"So I'm nosy, opinionated and stubborn, huh?" She sat up. "With a list of other faults you probably haven't shared. I'm surprised you wanted to marry me in the first place."

"Blame it on the idiocy of youth."

Peter meant to hurt her, and he succeeded. She pushed back the covers. "I knew this was a mistake."

"Wait. Dammit. Come back to bed."

She pulled on her nightclothes.

"I—I'm sorry."

"Don't be. We weren't meant to be together. I just regret it happened the way it did, but it was the right choice."

His gaze pierced hers. "Why did you say yes?"

"Because I loved you and I wanted to be your wife."

"But you ran away and I never saw you again. Who or what changed your mind?" He held up his hand when she opened her mouth. "Forget it. I don't want to know. You explained everything in your letter. Just tell me one thing."

"What?"

"Were you pregnant? Did you get scared and have an abortion or have the baby and give it up?"

"No. No, I'd never keep something like that from you."

"What would you keep from me?"

"Nothing. I've told you everything."

"Dammit! Then why do you keep looking at me like that?"

"Like what?"

"As if I've hurt you."

Claudia sat on the side of the bed and let her shoulders slump. "It's just a look of regret and painful memories."

"A good diagnosis, Doctor."

She straightened. "Don't mock me."

"I'm not." He sat beside her. "I won't hurt you if you promise not to run away from me again."

"I promise."

He lay down then drew her down next to him. "You're wearing too many clothes."

She took off her nightdress.

"That's better," he said. Then they both settled down into sleep, never believing they could. But once they closed their eyes they did, daring to believe in promises again.

Chapter 12

North Carolina

The first sign something was wrong was the dirty welcome mat. When Claudia entered her apartment, she sighed as she looked around at the wilted plants and the stack of papers on the floor. Madame Curie, a silver tabby American shorthair, came up to greet her with a look of rebuke.

Claudia stroked her. "I'm sorry, but she's family."

Madame Curie released a low meow. The sound surprised Claudia, because Madame Curie was usually a quiet cat who only made sounds when she was displeased—such as when Claudia's mother came to visit and referred to her as "that thing."

"At least you look well fed," Claudia said, continuing to stroke her cat to get her to purr.

Madame Curie blinked instead.

"Aunt Claudia! You're home!" Her twenty-year-old niece, Tess, barreled into the room and gave her a fierce hug. Her older brother's middle child was an exact replica of herself. She was tall but not as thin, with slightly ample hips, which she showed off by wearing painted-on jeans with a tight-fitting purple T-shirt that emphasized her perfectly sized bosom and exposed her midriff. Her hair, which was about the same length as Claudia's, was left in its natural state and looked like an out-of-control bush that needed to be tamed. Like her aunt, she was not one to wear a lot of makeup, but she loved putting on false eyelashes and wearing pink lipstick, which she outlined with a dark purple lip pencil.

Madame Curie meowed again, and Tess jumped back and scowled down at the animal. "You know, I think Grandma's right. That cat is the devil. She actually swiped at me when I took away her food."

Claudia picked Madame Curie up. "She's usually very gentle. Maybe she hadn't finished and you annoyed her." She set the cat down. "Just leave the bowl next time and wait until she walks away."

Madame Curie meowed again. This time long and loud.

Tess pulled a cat hair from Claudia's blouse, annoyed. "Fine. I hate when she does that. I fed her, so I don't know what she's whining about."

"She's not whining. She's just talking. Um...Tess—"

Her niece's face suddenly lit up. "You're right. Let's not talk about the cat." She hugged Claudia again. "I'm so glad you're back! I've been waiting to hear all about your trip! I made dinner. Well, actually I bought dinner. But I put the dinner on plates, so in a way I sort of made dinner, because I wanted everything to look nice when you got back. Here, let me take your bags." Claudia let her niece hustle her to the dining table, which at least was clean.

Claudia looked at her dry plants. "Tess, about the…"

Tess sat and uncovered Claudia's plate. "I hope you like shrimp-fried rice. They had regular fried rice, but I thought the shrimp would be a nice touch."

"Tess—"

"I can heat everything up if you want me to, but I think it's still warm. Did you have a smooth flight? I hate bumpy ones."

"Tess—"

"I'm always afraid the stuff in the overhead bins is going to fly out and hit us on the head."

"Tess!"

"Yeah?"

"The place is a mess."

Tess looked around, surprised. "Really?"

"Did you water the plants?"

Tess slapped her forehead. "Oh, yeah. I knew I was forgetting something."

"And the paper?"

"I started a stack and then got busy. I promise I'll do better next time."

Claudia opened her mouth then closed it. There shouldn't be a next time, but she knew there would be. Tess was Chester's baby, and he wouldn't be happy if Claudia fired her. Tess had a week to prove herself while she was in Bermuda. Otherwise Claudia knew she'd have to hire someone else before leaving for six weeks in Europe. Claudia scooped up her rice, too tired to think about it.

"Well?" Tess said.

"Well what? The shrimp is nice."

"No. I don't care about the food. How was Hawaii?"

"It was more wonderful than I expected," Claudia said, referring to the man she'd woken up to more than the island. He'd nearly made her miss her flight. "We were very fortunate the weather held up while we were there. The sky at night is breathtaking and—" She stopped when Tess shook her head.

"I mean how was *he?* What was he like?"

"Who?"

"You know who. Peter Warren, the host."

"Cohost."

Tess rolled her eyes. "Whatever. Is he as sexy in person as he seems?"

Absolutely. "Yes."

"Did you two—" her niece made a graphic gesture with her hands "—get it on?"

Claudia's mouth fell open. "Tess!"

Tess grinned. "Is that a yes?"

Claudia didn't reply.

"Come on, Aunt Claudia. You've never been shy about your men before, and now you might have hit the jackpot and you won't tell me? That's not fair."

"Nothing happened."

Tess leaned forward. "Not even a little something? A peck on the cheek, a pat on the—"

"Nothing happened," she repeated in a firm tone.

Tess sighed, disappointed. "Shame."

"I got you something," Claudia said, eager to change the subject. She took out a small package from her handbag and handed it to her.

Tess quickly opened the gift. "This is fabulous! Oh, I almost forgot. You got a special package." She disappeared into Claudia's bedroom then returned with a small brown package and set it on the table.

Claudia studied it, curious. It had no return address, but it had been sent by special delivery. Claudia opened it and pulled out a lacy black bra-and-panty set. She picked up the note inside and read "For Bermuda."

Tess picked up the lacy red teddy underneath the bra and panties. "Oh, it's gorgeous! It must have cost a fortune. Who is it from?"

Claudia took the teddy from her and closed the box. "A secret admirer."

"I bet you know his name."

Yes, she did, but she didn't want her niece to know anything about her affair with Peter. She didn't want anyone to know, especially her family, because of her past with him. It would make things too complicated.

Claudia only winked then finished her food in silence.

"What's his name and when will you see him again?" Noreen said when she saw Claudia.

Suzanne looked at Noreen with exasperation. "Tact is a lost art with you."

"We're friends. Claudia knows what I mean. She's glowing with happiness."

"That doesn't mean she's found a man."

Noreen sent her friend a look as if she was naive.

The three women sat in Suzanne's sunroom, having finished a light lunch of baked salmon with basil, hot wheat rolls and a fruit salad with whipped cream. The sound of saws, hammers and vacuuming could be heard as workers decorated Suzanne's house for her annual spring garden party. Suzanne looked very much like a woman of privilege in a pair of beige tailored trousers and a white silk blouse, while Noreen, wearing her signature black-framed glasses, with her unruly curly hair, petite frame and oversize top, looked several years younger than she was.

"Creating a TV show is more grueling than I thought it would be, but I still had a great time," Claudia admitted.

Noreen adjusted her glasses, her gaze shrewd. "Are you sure that's all?"

"What do you mean?"

Suzanne frowned. "Drop it, Noreen."

Claudia looked at them, curious. "Drop what?"

"We didn't want to say anything, but we both sensed that before you left there was something on your mind."

Yes, Peter had been on her mind, but she hadn't told her friends. "It's nothing. I've just never done something like this before, and I didn't want to screw it up. So far it's been going very well."

"Do you think you'll be able to attend my party? I know your schedule is hectic."

"I always make time for my friends. I should be back in time for it."

Suzanne smiled. "Well, we're thrilled to hear that things are going so well for you."

Noreen looked unconvinced.

Not wanting to go into details, Claudia opened the large bag she'd brought with her and handed both of them their gifts. "And this is for Luke," she said, giving Suzanne an extra package.

"I'm sure he'll love it." When Suzanne opened her gift—the handblown glass piece—she grinned. "I'll find the perfect place to put this," she said then looked up and pointed to one of the workers who was carrying a small, white wicker table. "That does not belong in the house. Will you please take it to the gazebo?"

"But Mr. Gordon said—"

"I don't care what Mr. Gordon said. *Mrs.* Gordon says it belongs in the gazebo." She then noticed one of her outdoor plants in an oriental vase near the base of the staircase and pointed. "Did Mr. Gordon tell you to do that also?"

He nodded.

Suzanne pursed her lips then slowly stood. She noticed her husband talking to another worker. She turned to her friends, keeping her voice neutral. "Excuse me while I go kill my husband," she said then left.

Noreen laughed as she watched Suzanne march up to her husband, Rick, who was giving their seven-year-old son, Luke, a piggyback ride. "You'd think he would know better than to interfere with one of Suzanne's beloved parties."

Even though he wore a pair of dark trousers and a pressed light maroon shirt, Rick looked more suited for a dark alley than a boardroom. There was an untamed energy to him, but despite his dark looks, he looked at his wife not with annoyance or amusement, but acceptance. At one time Peter had looked at her like that, Claudia thought as she finished her drink. "He knows, he just doesn't care." She watched as Rick listened to Suzanne then shook his head. "He's not a pushover."

"Who do you think will win?" When Claudia sent her a look, Noreen shook her head. "I know. Silly question." They watched the worker take the wicker table away, but the plant stayed. Noreen grinned. "Ah, compromise! The big word we married people have to live with." She turned to Claudia and rested her chin in her hands. "Something *you* don't have to worry about."

"Nope. One of the many benefits of being single."

Noreen nodded then said, "So?"

"What?"

"We've been here nearly an hour and you haven't mentioned your cohost. I saw his picture. He's definitely worth mentioning. What is he like?"

"You're a married woman."

Noreen fiddled with her glasses. "Just because I wear these doesn't mean I'm blind. Tell me about him. I write romance novels, remember? I can always consider this research."

Claudia smoothed her napkin. "He's very professional."

Noreen frowned. "He's obnoxious, isn't he?"

"No, he's easy to work with and—"

"You're lying."

Claudia stiffened. "What makes you say that?"

"I've never heard such a boring description of a man from you."

"That doesn't mean I'm lying."

Noreen was quiet a moment then sighed. "I know things have changed, but that doesn't mean we can't be completely honest with each other. I know how you feel. When Suzanne got married I felt a little lost. I don't want you to feel like the odd one out."

"I don't."

"A part of me used to envy how free you are with men. I could never be so bold. You live life to the fullest, and in a way I lived vicariously through your adventures."

"You're just being sweet. I know you have plenty of adventures with Michael."

"I guess I'm just trying to say that we don't want you to feel weird around us. We love you just the way you are. I'm so proud of you, and this TV series is what you deserve. Some of us are meant to settle down and some of us aren't. Don't change."

Claudia forced a smile then glanced at Suzanne, who was laughing at something Rick said. They looked the perfect picture of wedded bliss. "Don't worry. I never will."

Days later, Claudia thought of her reply to Noreen as she shopped for items for her upcoming trip to Bermuda. It was just an affair. Her involvement with Peter wouldn't lead to anything, so she was going to enjoy it while she could. She didn't need to get married. Affairs were a lot more fun. They were exciting and uncomplicated. As part of her shopping spree, Claudia decided to visit a small boutique just outside Durham, which specialized in the kind of eclectic fashion she liked.

She bought a wine-colored silk-cashmere wrap cardigan which was perfect, even in summer. She was always freezing on the plane, and the wrap was like a blanket and could also serve as a nice cover-up for any spills. She also found an expensive pair of fashionable sunglasses and an off-the-shoulder full-length exotic-print sundress with a ruffled trim, which made her look stunning. She was completing her purchase when another costumer said, "Oh, my goodness, it's you. Claudia Madison."

Claudia turned to the stocky woman with frizzy brown hair, who stared at her in awe. "Yes, it's me."

"You're a sign!"

She took a step back, unsure if the woman was sane. "A what?"

"A sign." The woman clasped her hands together. "Now everything is clear. I was just wondering if I should marry my boyfriend. He asked me three days ago and is still waiting for an answer, but I haven't been sure." She pulled out her phone and showed Claudia a picture. "See, that's him. Isn't he cute?"

The man was bucktoothed with large ears that reminded Claudia of a rabbit. "Yes," she said, thinking that rabbits were cute.

The woman looked at the photo with affection. "I call him my casino, because with him I feel like I've hit the jackpot."

"You look happy."

The woman's enthusiasm dimmed. "We are now, but what about in the future? With the divorce rate the way it is, is marriage worth the expense? Well, anyway, that's what I was thinking about when you walked in, and now I know my answer. I'm going to turn him down."

"Just seeing me made you decide that?" Claudia asked feeling uncomfortable.

"Of course! You believe in the independent woman and living life without the ring. You once said the only ring you want from a man is when he's trying to call you."

"Yes, but if you want—"

She looked at Claudia's items. "Oh, that looks great. Aren't you taping a show or something?"

"Yes, it should air in the fall."

"I'll be watching it."

Claudia watched the woman leave and shrugged. She wouldn't feel responsible for the woman's decision or her boyfriend's disappointment. When Peter had asked her to marry him she'd had no doubts, but she'd also been more impulsive then. Claudia put the hanger back. Was that how people really saw her? As antimarriage? It didn't matter anyway. The woman had already made up her mind and was only using Claudia as an excuse. Besides, she had better things to do.

She visited her favorite crafter—a jeweler who made one-of-a-kind jewelry from antique gold and silver and rare stones and gems. Luckily, she arrived just in time to select a magnificent set he had just made that included large drooping earrings, a necklace and a bracelet. When Peter saw her again, she knew he wouldn't be disappointed.

Chapter 13

Bermuda

The jock always got the girl. Roy watched Peter go for one of his morning runs and scowled. Just like the guys in high school, he was going after the golden girl. Roy had seen him being real friendly with Claudia lately. He knew he'd come back and try to show off his damn muscles for her; even Ashley cast glances at him. What was it about athletes, anyway?

In school Roy hadn't been able to do sports because he was small and suffered from allergies and asthma. Instead of being the one cheered for on the field or court, he'd been on the sideline taking pictures for the student newspaper.

By junior year he'd outgrown his allergies and gained some height, but that hadn't stopped the jocks from stuffing him into lockers or forcing him to help them with their homework. Warren was just like those guys. He wasn't that smart and just wanted to use Claudia as another conquest to brag about. He didn't deserve her. Claudia was a special woman. She shared his sense of humor and listened to him. She treated him like an equal. In Hawaii they'd gone out for drinks and she listened to his ambitions and encouraged him. She was the perfect woman for a guy like him. For now they were just friends, but he would find a way to change that...

"Did you get what I sent you?" Peter asked in a low voice as they prepared for their next scene.

They hadn't had much time to talk. Roy and Lance had missed their flight, costing them one full day of shooting. The past two days they'd spent trying to catch up. Peter and Frank made sure the necessary paperwork and legalities were taken care of before doing the first filming, showing Claudia and Peter on a rented boat, which also came with a hired skipper. The skipper, a man of about fifty, with broad shoulders and a warm smile, decided to take the crew to the east end of the island where they explored Castle Harbour, which is almost completely surrounded by islands, forming a protected lake. To avoid the powerful swells, the skipper had to drop anchor on the west side.

They spent several hours in that location, filming various scenes from different angles. Ashley had to retouch Claudia's hair several times, before and after a shot, due to the wind bouncing off the waves and tossing her hair in different directions.

"Don't use too much hair spray," Claudia told her.

She ignored her. "I have to when your hair won't cooperate."

The skipper then took them to one of the uninhabited

islands off Mangrove Bay, where they did a major shoot featuring native birds and unusual plants and flowers.

For this scene, Claudia wore a two-piece, formfitting linen skirt with a slit on the side, matched with a bold yellow front-tie blouse.

"I don't know what you're talking about," Claudia said with surprise as she moved her blouse aside to give Peter a peek at her black bra.

Peter grinned.

She leaned forward and whispered. "I left the panties at the hotel."

His grin faded while his heated gaze dipped down to her skirt then back to her face.

"Smile, we're on." She turned to the crew and said, "Welcome to another episode…"

The second the cameras stopped rolling, Peter took Claudia's hand and led her away.

"Where are you going?" Frank shouted after them.

Peter didn't slow his pace. "To discuss something." He led Claudia into the privacy of some overgrown trees then kissed her as if she was air and he a man starved for oxygen. "I'll get you for that one." He breathed against her lips.

"I thought you'd be pleased."

"Pull another stunt like that and our affair won't be a secret anymore."

She giggled. "I couldn't help myself."

"Were you telling me the truth?"

"Why don't you find out?" she challenged.

"You better not be lying to me," he said, slipping his hand under her skirt.

She hadn't been lying, and they didn't return to the set until they heard the crew searching for them.

The fifth day on the island, Frank decided to film Peter and Claudia following the Bermuda Railway Trail on horseback. The trail, which stretched for twenty-one miles, crossed the three interconnected islands that make up Bermuda. At the end of the trail, both hosts, feeling somewhat sore, were treated to the local cuisine at a fine white-tablecloth restaurant in the middle of town.

The selection included exotic dishes such as caramelized sea scallops and pecan-and-herb-crusted sea bass complemented with cassava pie and Bermuda rum punch. It was a smooth shoot, except when Claudia was bitten by a bug that left a large welt on her upper arm, which Ashley had to cover. Once filming was done for the day, the crew returned to the hotel. Claudia went to her suite while Peter followed Ashley to her room to discuss a location change.

Peter stood in Ashley's hotel room, surprised by the amount of makeup she had. He picked up one of the many small bottles of foundation. "Wow. You have a lot of stuff. Is she turning into a diva?"

"Claudia? No way. All that flash is really just a show. I love working with her, except—"

"Except what?"

Ashley hesitated. Just as a hairdresser knows a woman's real hair color, as a makeup artist she knew most women's flaws, and she'd gotten close to Claudia and they'd become friends. "I probably shouldn't say anything, but I feel like I can trust you."

He set the foundation down. "What are you talking about?"

Ashley lowered her voice. "Her scars. I wish she wasn't so self-conscious about them."

"Scars?" Peter furrowed his brows. "Claudia doesn't

have any scars." He hadn't seen them, and he'd seen a lot of her.

"Well you wouldn't see them, that's what the makeup's for. But to be honest, they're so faded you wouldn't notice them anyway. The one at the base of her neck is the worst. But the fact that she survived that accident is a miracle."

He stared at her blankly. "Accident?"

"Yes, her car accident. It happened years ago."

"When?" he asked, his voice hoarse.

"Eight years ago. I'm not sure she'd want me to tell you, but you might make her feel less self-conscious." Ashley lowered her voice to a conspiratorial tone. "This was when she was living in Virginia. She was racing to catch a flight to Las Vegas when the tire blew on her car and she crashed. They had to medevac her out and… Peter, what's wrong?" Ashley said when he turned and stormed out of the room.

Claudia lounged on her bed after a relaxing bath. She loved her suite, which was in one of Bermuda's luxury hotels. It was decorated with distinctive artwork, elegant fabrics and furnishings, stone and wood finishes and luxurious bathroom fixtures, including a stand-alone deep-soaking tub. Each bedroom had a mahogany queen-size bed and a waterfront view from a private, expansive balcony.

She was slipping into sleep when the pounding on her door startled her awake. She grabbed a robe. "I'm coming."

She opened it, surprised to see Peter. He pushed past her and slammed the door.

"You lied to me."

Claudia blinked. "What?"

"Why didn't you tell me about the accident?"

Claudia held up her hands to calm him. "I—"

"All this time you had me believe that you'd jilted me, and it was because you were in the hospital. Why?"

"Peter—"

"Why! You told me you weren't hiding anything. Why did you lie to me?"

"I didn't lie," she said quietly. "I told you."

"When? Before or after you cleared out of our apartment?"

"My brother did that. My mother thought it was best because we weren't sure when I'd fully recover. But I left you a note and she told me he left it for you."

"He did. But in the note you didn't say anything about an accident. You just said that you didn't want to see me. That it wouldn't work between us and that our love affair was over."

Claudia pressed a hand against her forehead. "That's not exactly what I wrote. You read it wrong."

"What?"

"When you…you read the words in the wrong context. I said we needed a break and I didn't want to see you. I was hoping that after some time had passed we'd have a chance to do our *Love Affair* over. I was referring to the movie. It was my fantasy that we'd eventually meet up in Las Vegas."

All color drained from his face. He stumbled back and hit a side table. A large vase fell and shattered, but he didn't notice. "You mean we've been separated all these years because of me? Because I misread your letter?"

"Peter," Claudia said in a soft voice. The devastation on his face was painful to see. "It was my fault, too. I should have had someone talk to you, but I didn't want you to worry and I thought my letter would be enough. I was a silly romantic, but I wanted you to live your life. I didn't want to be the one holding you back. I was in the ICU with serious injuries, and didn't want to become a burden. Now I realize that I was wrong and it was a mistake. I know how hard it is for you—"

"To read?" He cut in. "Yes. Your fiancé was too stupid to read a damn letter correctly."

Claudia reached for him, but Peter pulled away.

He didn't want to be comforted. He wanted to feel the pain of his stupidity. Feel the full effect of his loss. If he'd taken the time to read it correctly, everything would have been different. But he had been full of anger and hurt when he'd read the first few lines of her letter, and in a rush he had misunderstood every word before tearing it up.

"Love Affair," he repeated the title of the movie as if it were a curse word. "I told you I hated that movie."

"You never told me that."

"Well, I'm telling you now. I hated the fact that no one told him. I hated him not being there for her after her accident and that she suffered alone." Peter gripped his hand into a fist as a realization struck him. "That's why you didn't tell me. You discovered my mistake when we were on the beach in Hawaii, didn't you? How long were you in the hospital?"

"Peter, don't do this to yourself."

His tone hardened. "How long?"

"A few weeks, but—"

His voice broke. "God, I'm so sorry."

"Peter, please don't torture yourself. This is why I didn't tell you. You would have given up too much for me. Your sense of honor would have gotten in the way. You would have stopped going after your dream and taken a job in your father's business, just so that you could take care of me and you would have been miserable. I didn't want that."

"I wouldn't have been miserable. I would have had you."

"It wouldn't have been enough."

He turned toward the door.

"Don't go."

"How can you stand to look at me?"

Claudia rushed to him and wrapped her arms around him, resting her head against his back. "I forgave you."

"How can I forgive myself? My father was right. I—"

"He wasn't right." Claudia moved in front of him. "He *isn't* right. It was a mistake, and we both made ourselves miserable because we thought the worst of each other. If I'd given you a second chance or the benefit of the doubt—"

He gently pushed her to the side and opened the door. "I can't...I just need to be alone for a while." He raced down the stairs.

He was a fool. Peter walked aimlessly around the Royal Navy Dockyard, a tourist attraction sporting Victorian streetlighting, a terrace pavilion and a grand bandstand for concerts. He didn't notice any of it as he wandered through the Craft Market which was known to have some of the best local crafts on the island. He was in a fog. All this time he'd misunderstood. Why had everyone listened to her and not contacted him? Didn't they think she mattered to him? He'd once said that nothing would separate them, and he'd been wrong. Peter shook his head. Even if someone had called him, he might have been too drunk to register anything. Then he'd disappeared for a while so that no one could reach him. He'd run away like a coward when he should have confronted her.

He felt stupid, and the echo of those who had agreed in the past reverberated in his mind. He heard his aunt's words: "He's not going to amount to much no matter how much money you spend on him." His mother's words: "I don't care about the diagnosis. He's still not very bright." His stepfather's words: "With those grades, we'll be lucky if he gets a minimum-wage job." And his father's words: "He tries hard, but he doesn't make up for Thomas."

With Claudia, he'd thought he'd banished all those fears. She made him feel smart, viable and accomplished.

Even now she'd guarded his ego. She'd allowed him to hurl insults and taken his temper because she didn't want to hurt him with the truth. Another woman wouldn't have been so kind. He didn't deserve her. It would take a lifetime to make up for his mistake. But he would try. He'd convinced her to be his lover. Now he'd convince her to be his wife.

He stopped walking and went into a craft store to look at some souvenirs. He didn't want to go back to Claudia empty-handed, but nothing appealed to him—until he saw a small stone carving.

Chapter 14

Frank stared at him. "Are you out of your mind? A castle?"

Peter nodded. He sat on Frank's couch in his suite. "Yes, I want us to shoot our next location in a castle."

"In France?" Frank repeated just to make sure.

"Yes."

Frank rubbed his head. "Listen, I know your connections have allowed us to stay in these luxury places both in Hawaii and here, but a castle stay for our entire crew is going to really cost us—meaning you—a lot of money. Plus the food, travel expenses and getting permissions—"

"I don't care *how* much it costs. Just make it happen."

"But castles aren't very interesting."

Peter jumped to his feet and rubbed his hands together. "We'll make it interesting." He turned to Frank and held out his hands. "I want something big and impressive with lots of land." He snapped his fingers. "Oh, and a top-notch chef. It will be okay if the chef wants his or her restaurant featured. And please make sure to also get a top pastry chef. I want pastries."

"Pastries?"

"Yes, French pastries. Oh, and I also want flowers. In season, fresh."

"What has gotten into you? These are the kind of crazy things a guy talks about when he's getting ready to propose or something."

Peter nodded. "That's right."

Frank's mouth fell open. "You're going to ask a woman to m-a-r-r-y you?"

"I'm thinking about it."

"You want to get married?"

Peter sent a quick glance to the door. "Keep your voice down."

Frank lowered his voice. "Who is it? That nurse or that teacher you broke up with a year ago? I liked her. Are you going to have her flown in for the day?"

"That won't be necessary. She'll already be there."

"Really, she's traveling in France?"

"No, she'll be there with us."

Frank looked puzzled, then dawning slowly fell over his face. "Claudia?"

Peter nodded.

He stared at Peter, stunned. "You're going to ask Miss No-commitment-I'd-rather-be-shot-than-go-down-the-aisle to *marry* you? Do you need time away in an asylum?"

Peter sat back. "Relax. I'm just thinking about marriage." He rubbed his chin and mumbled. "I won't pop the question yet."

"You'd lose everything. Your fans, your sales, the radio show, *this* show, your sponsors."

"I know."

"People will turn on you and feel betrayed. If just one person found out you were even thinking about tying the knot, your reputation might never recover."

Peter hung his head, feeling the weight of the risk. "I know." An awkward moment of silence settled between them.

Frank clasped his hands behind his head. "I say go for it."

Peter looked at his friend, dumbfounded. "What?"

"Life's about taking risks. For the past couple of years, you've been playing it safe. You've done what you need to do to keep up the image, which, my friend, we both know isn't you." He let his hands fall and leaned forward when Peter started to protest. "It's true. You talk big, but that speech at my wedding was more than sentiment. You meant every word. I don't care if your plan succeeds or fails. At least you will have tried. And a woman like Claudia is worth it. I like her. She's good for you."

"Even though she's not my usual type?" Peter said with a grin.

"Exactly. A long time ago, you may not remember, you gave me a quote about love. Now I'm going to give you a quote about marriage from Ovid. *'If you would marry suitably, marry your equal.'*"

Peter drummed his fingers on his lap. "She's definitely that, but I'm not sure she'll have me. At least not yet."

"You know I'm a softie. I'll find you a castle that will have Claudia in your arms in no time." Frank grinned. "And don't worry, your secret's safe with me."

* * *

Claudia nearly tore the door off its hinges when someone knocked. It had been four hours since her talk with Peter, and she was anxious to see him again. Her hope shriveled when she saw Roy standing there.

"Oh, Roy."

He shifted unsure. "Were you expecting someone else?"

"Sort of, but that's okay. Did you need something?"

"Ashley, Lance and I are going to a local jazz club, and I wanted to know if you wanted to come along."

"I'm real tired, but thanks." She began to close the door, but he stopped her.

"Can I talk to you for a minute?"

Claudia hesitated. "Can it wait until tomorrow? I really just want to go to bed."

"All right."

"Enjoy the music. You'll have to tell me about it tomorrow."

"I will."

Claudia smiled then closed the door.

The memory of her smile stayed with Roy as he made his way to the elevator. It was warm and genuine. She would have talked to him if she hadn't been tired. He liked how her place smelled. Next time he had to find a way to talk himself in.

He nodded a greeting when he saw Peter walking in the opposite direction.

"Where are you off to?" Peter asked in passing.

"We're all going to listen to some music."

"Sounds like fun."

"Want to come?" Roy asked, just to be polite.

"No. I have to talk to Claudia about something."

"It'll have to wait. I just came from her suite. She's getting ready for bed."

"She'll talk to me."

Roy gritted his teeth, annoyed by his arrogance. "I spoke to her and she's really tired."

"I won't keep her up then. See you."

Roy watched Peter knock on Claudia's door. She opened it and he waited to see her turn Peter away, but instead she opened the door wider. Peter turned and waved goodbye to him then entered her suite. Roy clenched his fists. He wanted to sock Peter in the face. She probably let him in only because he mentioned the show and she wanted to impress a man like him. He had that kind of power. Men like him knew how to lie and cheat to get what they wanted. He'd warned her about him. It was time he told Claudia the truth.

When Peter entered they held each other for a long time.

"I was so worried," Claudia said finally. She'd changed into jeans and a blouse in case she had to go looking for him.

"I didn't mean to worry you."

Claudia drew away and looked at him. "Who were you waving to?"

Peter blinked. He hadn't expected that question. "Roy."

Her eyes widened. "He saw you?"

"Yes."

"He saw you come into my room?"

"Yes. Don't worry, I was in Ashley's room, too. He won't think anything. Why are we talking about him anyway?"

"I just don't want this to get out."

"We can't keep it a secret forever."

"We don't need forever, just a couple of months."

"A couple of months?"

"Yes, until we finish taping the show."

"Then it's over?"

"Yes," she said, annoyed that he was being obtuse. "Affairs always end. We couldn't make it last longer than that. We live in different states and have different lives—"

"Let's not talk about the future right now."

"Or the past."

"Yes, let's just focus on what we have right now." Peter lifted up the back of her hair.

Claudia pushed his hand away and hastily stepped back. "What are you doing?"

"I want to see the scar."

"How do you…? Who told you about it?"

"Let me see it."

"It's the worse one. Why would you want to see it?"

"Because it's part of you."

"It's ugly and disgusting. If you want to see scars, look at this one." She rubbed the makeup off her inner arm then held it out. "See, it's pretty faded now, but it's there."

"I need you to trust me."

Claudia shook her head and swallowed hard. "We've been together all this time without you knowing about them."

"Trust me, CC."

The sound of her nickname on his lips shook her. She couldn't remember when he'd given her that nickname or the reason why, but the rich timber of his voice chased away her anxiety.

Claudia turned around and lifted up her hair. "It's awful, isn't it?" she said when he didn't say anything.

"I don't see anything."

She lifted her hair higher. "Now do you see it?"

"No, I don't see anything ugly, disgusting or awful." He tenderly traced the raised, discolored skin with his finger then pressed his lips against it. "I just see you, CC."

Claudia let her hair fall back in place. "I'm not CC anymore."

"Yes, you are." Peter wrapped his arms around her waist and whispered, "If I could go back in time. I would have stayed by your bedside and read every poem you ever wanted me to read, even if it had taken me months. I would have filled your room with flowers and life-size stuffed animals. And I would have had the chaplain marry us right there in the hospital. Whether you have bandages or scars, I only see you as beautiful."

Claudia spun around and gripped the front of his shirt. "Don't—"

He placed a finger over her lips. "Now it's my turn."

"Your turn to do what?"

"To kiss your scars away." He pressed his lips against the curve of her neck. "You don't need to tell me where they are." He removed her blouse. "I'll find them."

She laughed. "I'll point to the ones you miss."

Peter swept Claudia into his arms and carried her to the couch. "You won't have to." He gently set her down. "I'll be very thorough." He unlatched her bra then covered her nipple with his mouth.

"That isn't a scar."

"Really?" he said with feigned surprised. "How about this one?" He covered her other nipple and toyed with it with his tongue.

"No. Do you want me to—"

"I told you I'll find them myself." He ran a delicious path down her stomach with his tongue then kissed her navel. "This has to be it."

Claudia held his head. "Let's forget about the scars."

"No. I like to finish what I start."

She reached for his trousers and pulled down the zipper. "We can finish this later."

Peter took off her jeans then skimmed his hands up her thighs. "I plan to," he said in a husky tone. He began to lower her panties then stopped. He raised his head and studied her face. "Do you really forgive me?"

Claudia wiggled out of her panties. "Let me convince you how much."

His eyes darkened with emotion. "I'm serious, CC."

"So am I." She cupped his face in her hands. "I wouldn't want to be with anyone else in the world but you." She kissed him, a little afraid that he wouldn't believe her, but he did. His tantalizing mouth left no doubt of his feelings for her.

She slid her arms around him, reveling in the feel of his hard nipples against her breasts. She wanted to melt into him, to feel him inside her once more. She wanted him close, knowing that he'd never be close enough. She fought back tears. "I wish we didn't have a week before we went to Europe."

Peter's hot gaze followed the path of his hand as he made his way between her thighs. "Me too, but I have a lot of work to do."

"Doing what?" She no longer cared but asked anyway. Her voice was barely a whisper as he stoked the liquid heat within her, his expert fingers making her think of nothing but him.

He slid inside her and a slow smile spread on his face. "Making some of your dreams come true."

Chapter 15

North Carolina

Claudia was floating on cloud nine when she left Bermuda. She hit earth the moment she stepped into her apartment. She had to fire Tess. She set her suitcases down. Madame Curie glared up at her and meowed in disgust.

"Okay, you're right this time."

"You're home early!" Tess said, coming around the corner dressed in one of Claudia's satin robes. She cast a nervous glance behind her. "I didn't expect you so soon!"

"You don't need to shout, and I'm not that early." Claudia took a step forward. "Uh…Tess? I—"

Tess slid into her path, blocking her. "Did the secret admirer meet you in Bermuda?"

"Tess—"

"Because I kept imagining that he did and that you snuck off on a secret rendezvous and had hot sex—"

"Tess!"

"What?"

"What's going on?"

She gripped the front of her robe, and Claudia noticed some scratches on her arm. "Nothing."

Claudia looked around her apartment at the empty pizza boxes and ring stains on her coffee table. Then her eyes fell on what she was looking for—a pair of male shoes.

"Aunt Claudia, wait!" Tess said when Claudia pushed past her and headed for her bedroom. She opened the door and saw a young man dart into the closet.

"Get out of there," she said.

The young man stretched his arm out and pointed to something on the floor. "I will if you'd hand me my pants."

"I'm not shy. You can get them yourself."

When he didn't move, Claudia turned away. "Okay, I'm not looking." She heard the closet door open, and she stood silent while the man quickly put on his underpants, jeans and a stained T-shirt.

"I'm finished."

Claudia turned to him and said, "And your name would be?"

"Josh."

Claudia looked at her niece, who hovered in the doorway. "An explanation would be nice."

"I didn't expect—"

"Me to come home early," Claudia finished wearily. "We've gone over this, Tess." She folded her arms. "What did I tell you about having strange people in my place?"

"Josh isn't strange. We've been seeing each other for a long time, and you can trust him."

Claudia walked past her. "That's it, Tess. You're fired."

"What?"

"You heard me. I can't use you anymore. Especially for an entire month."

"What? Why?" Tess held up her hands in surrender. "Okay, I'm sorry I used your clothes and let Josh come over."

"It's not that." Claudia motioned to her living room. "Look at my apartment."

"I watered the plants this time."

"But you left ring stains all over my coffee and side tables, and there are crumbs all over the floor." She looked into her bathroom. "And why are Madame Curie's things in here?"

"I had to lock her in there because she tried to attack Josh. She was fine," Tess said without concern.

Claudia sighed. "I'm sorry, Tess."

"I'll clean up the crumbs."

"No."

"You can't do this to me. I love your place. It's so cool being here. Please give me another chance." She lowered her voice. "Please don't fire me in front of Josh. He thinks it's so cool that I do this for you."

Claudia shook her head. "I'm sorry, but I'm sure you can find something else that he'll think is cool."

"You can't just fire me. We're family."

"Which makes doing this harder."

"Dad's going to be angry."

"I can handle your father."

"My dad was right," Tess spat out. "You think you're

better than all of us. You think because you have money and men, you can treat people any way you like."

"If you've finished throwing a tantrum, I'd like to have my keys back." Claudia held out her hand. She'd given her niece the keys to her apartment and her silver BMW sports car.

"I don't know where they are right now. I'll get them later." She stormed into the bedroom and closed the door. Claudia waited with Josh in the foyer for Tess to reemerge which she did five minutes later.

"I really liked you, Aunt Claudia. Just you wait. You're going to miss me and you're going to regret this."

When Tess and Josh had left, Claudia shut the door and sagged against it. "I already do."

"You look terrible," Noreen said.

Claudia took a sip of the cocktail she held. They were at Suzanne's spring party, which was always a grand event. Her entire back garden was dressed up for the occasion, with manicured trees sporting an assortment of colorful flowers, waiters in tuxedos, a live band and a wide assortment of dishes. There was trout baked in wine, oven-roasted potatoes with rosemary and garlic, grilled veal chops with salad and swordfish rolls stuffed with shrimp. And for dessert, guests were treated to tiramisu and warm chocolate tortes with raspberry sauce.

Suzanne looked the perfect hostess as she mingled with her guests, dressed in a soft green sheath dress with gold piping and a hand-embroidered necklace. Noreen looked like the ideal guest in a sleeveless rayon top and suede skirt, a pair of silver earrings and silver suede boots. Claudia looked her boldest yet, wearing dark lace stockings against a white pencil skirt, knotted navy blue sweater and a pair of jeweled leather heels.

"I just had a shouting match with my brother. And now I have to find a new house/cat sitter for the next month while we're filming in Europe. Who do you use when you travel?"

Noreen shrugged. "I'll do it."

"But it'll be for an entire month."

"I know. Michael's going on a special assignment, and I like to keep myself busy so I won't worry."

Claudia looked over at Noreen's husband, who was saying something to Rick. He didn't have Rick's dark looks, but he was as attractive, in a charming, easygoing way. "He writes travel articles," Claudia replied, startled by her friend's concern. "What could you worry about?"

"It's a job I didn't want him to take. Besides, traveling can be dangerous, and Michael's a magnet for trouble."

"You worry too much."

"Probably. Is that a yes or a no?"

"Yes or no what?" Suzanne asked, joining them.

"I'm hoping to be Claudia's new house/cat sitter." Noreen shook her head when Suzanne opened her mouth. "It's a long story."

"The job is yours if you're sure," Claudia said.

Noreen looked over at her husband. "I'm sure. Oh, no...why did you have to invite her?"

Claudia turned and saw Tamara looking glamorous in a sleek silk dress. She'd done well and had married a wealthy businessman who adored her.

"I know she's an ambitious social climber," Suzanne said, offering Tamara a polite smile. "But she's on the board of directors at the university and her husband is friends with Rick."

"You two don't know her like I do," Claudia said. "She really has a big heart."

Tamara saw Claudia and waved. Claudia walked over to her and they hugged. Tamara looked her over. "We haven't had a chance to talk since you started taping your show. How are you holding up?" She dropped her voice in concern. "Has he bothered you?"

"No."

"Really?" Tamara asked, intrigued. "Of course. I shouldn't be surprised. Once he's finished with a woman he never returns. And we both know how he is with the ladies. You're better off without him. He was never the man for you."

"I'm over him. We're just two professionals working together. You don't have to worry about me."

Tamara flashed a bright smile. "Good. Well, I'd better go mingle, and I don't want to keep you from your friends."

"You're free to join us."

Tamara glanced at Noreen and Suzanne. "Thank you, but no." She wiggled her eyebrows. "You know I feel more comfortable around men."

Claudia laughed then watched Tamara saunter over to her husband, who was having what looked like an intense discussion with Rick and Michael.

Noreen shook her head when Claudia returned. "Okay, I know she throws a lot of money around and has 'key contacts,' as Suzanne says, but I still don't know how she can be one of your oldest friends. You're so different."

Claudia looked at Noreen's outfit then her own.

"You and I are not exactly twins."

"It's not what's on the outside that counts."

Claudia shrugged. "Okay, so she's a little shallow. But in spite of that, she has a good heart. We've had our fights, but she was there for me when I needed her most." Claudia remembered Tamara being by her side throughout her stay at the hospital, cheering her on through recovery and helping her deal with her shattered heart. "I don't know why you don't like her."

"Aside from the fact that she's flirting with my husband?"

"Every woman is," Claudia said, noticing the other women gathering around him. She suddenly thought about Noreen's fears about Michael's travels. "Are you worried that he might stray?"

Noreen looked at her, surprised. "No, never."

"Sorry, I just thought that might be why you're worried."

"It's not that. I trust him."

Claudia looked at the men pensively then said, "How did you two know Rick and Michael were worth the risk of loving again?"

Suzanne looked at Noreen then shrugged. "I know that people analyze love, affection, loyalty and marriage, but it's not something you can dissect. You just know."

Claudia opened her mouth to ask her what she meant by that. Her scientific mind didn't like such a vague response, but then she felt something tugging at her skirt and looked down to see Suzanne's son, Luke. He looked up at her with wide brown eyes and a serious expression. Although only seven, he was already a miniature version of his father. She was surprised to see him, because he was dreadfully shy and didn't like crowds.

"Hi, Luke."

"Thank you for my gift, Miss Claudia."

"You're welcome."

"Where's your grandmother?" Suzanne asked.

Noreen motioned to an older woman by the side of the house. "Taking a cigarette break."

"She said I could come down," Luke said.

"Probably because she knows she can't smoke in the house."

"I wanted to give something to Miss Claudia," Luke said, reaching into his trouser pocket.

Suzanne held out her hand. "Wait. You make me nervous when you say things like that. Is your gift wet, slimy, sticky or breathing?"

He solemnly shook his head.

Suzanne sighed. "Okay. Go ahead."

Luke took out ten large green cotton balls glued together and sprinkled with glitter and dots. The three women stared at the object, none wanting to guess what it was.

"It's beautiful," Claudia said, taking the creation from him. "The best I've ever seen."

Luke beamed.

Claudia bent down and kissed him on the cheek. "Thank you, sweetie."

He giggled then ran away.

The three women were silent, then Noreen said, "What is it?"

"It's a caterpillar," Rick said, joining them. "He made six, but I convinced him to only give you one. He hasn't stopped playing with the bamboo train you got him. Thank you."

"He's worth it."

Rick turned to his wife. "Could I talk to you for a minute?"

Suzanne excused herself then followed him. Claudia

watched Rick affectionately rest his arm around her shoulders and Suzanne lean into him as they walked away.

Noreen cleared her throat; Claudia looked at her. "Yes?"

"I saw that."

"What?"

"That *look*."

"What look?" When Noreen raised her brows in a you-know-what-I-mean look, Claudia added, "I'm just glad Suzanne's happy with Rick and you're happy with Michael and I'm happy with my work. We're all happy."

"Uh-huh." Noreen rested her hands on her hips. "So are you ready to tell me what Peter Warren is really like?"

Claudia thought of Peter kissing her scars; their night together in Hawaii when he told her about his brother; his fantasy of how he would have married her in the hospital if he had known. She wanted to tell her friends how wonderful he was, and that he would make a great husband. She stopped, startled by the thought.

Husband? It wasn't like her to even consider marriage. She had no illusion about it; she'd studied its history and propaganda and was too smart to enter into such an institution.

On her own she'd achieved every goal and ambition she'd had, and she didn't want that to change. Her entire career was based on her single status, and she couldn't risk it because of the sentimental feelings of a woman she no longer was. Besides, she doubted he would ask her. He had just as much to risk as she. She would tell her friends about her brief affair once it was over. She hadn't even told Tamara how things had changed. For now, the secret kept their tenuous relationship safe and special. "I'll send you a postcard."

Chapter 16

France

The French countryside greeted Claudia with rich architectural treasures featuring historical chateaus, cathedrals and lavish palaces. But when the car she shared with Ashley and Eugene drove up to a magnificent structure, she could hardly breathe. The exquisite beauty and charm of the castle, which sat prominently on a large manicured estate, was the centerpiece in a small picturesque town in southern France. The castle's setting among a landscape of hills, woods and ponds provided excellent imagery for the film crew.

The exterior was gorgeous and the interior breath-taking. Claudia marveled at her room, which was decorated with sumptuous blue fabric wallpaper, gold-plated picture frames with images of France's history and superbly carved ornate furnishings. Claudia immediately set out to explore. Located on the first floor in one of the towers was a suite with a large living space and an enormous marble fireplace, a large double-size poster bed and a panoramic view of the French gardens below with a lily pond, filled with koi goldfish, gray geese and ducks.

On the second floor of the tower was another suite with a large living space, marble chimney and view of the surrounding countryside and woodlands. It had beautiful silver-gray damask wall fabric and antique furnishings. Claudia heard the door open below, went to the main staircase and saw Peter enter.

When he looked up and saw her, she wanted to rush into his arms, but she gripped the railing instead. Only a week had passed, but it felt like years. He nodded in greeting. No one would have suspected that over a week ago they'd shared a shower and created enough heat to melt plastic. Claudia knew now wasn't the time to get together, so she just smiled and turned away.

"Can you believe this place?" Ashley asked, coming to stand beside her.

"No. I can't believe we get to stay here."

"Thank Frank for that. He arranged everything. When he told me his idea to shoot an episode in a castle, my mind went wild with ideas. You won't believe what I selected for you to wear. I've been shopping. Come on."

Once in Ashley's room, the two women went through each of the items Ashley had selected. Claudia stopped when she saw a large garment bag hanging on a hook behind the door. "What's in here?"

"That's for the party," Ashley said, pushing it back out of sight. "I've scheduled a tailor to come the night before the party to fit you."

"Can't I have a peek?" Claudia asked with mounting curiosity.

"No, it's going to be a surprise."

Claudia didn't get to see Peter that day and was surprised when Frank scheduled a shoot for the next day featuring her, alone, taking a perfumery course. The classes were held in a sprawling eighteenth-century farmhouse just outside the town where they were staying. Claudia and the crew arrived early the next morning, traveling in one of the two minivans they'd rented. During the introduction the instructor, a tall sophisticated woman, told them what they would be doing and that they would concoct their own signature scent.

Following a full day of testing, smelling and sampling different fragrances, in the evening the instructor treated them to a full meal of roasted duck breast with pomegranate sauce, rice pilaf, steamed vegetables and a warm chocolate torte with wine from a nearby vineyard. Before leaving, each student was given a take-home sample of his or her creation in a carry-on container that met the airlines' requisite three-ounce limit. Claudia had hoped to share her creation with Peter, but she didn't see him that night or the next.

France was a whirlwind of long, exhausting days that kept Peter and Claudia apart, from taping them going for a scenic bike ride, to visiting an old cathedral and exploring a cave. Claudia declined to be part of the cave expedition. On the set, Peter and Claudia felt that all eyes were on them, and they didn't get a chance to be alone.

"Feel like running away?" Peter whispered while the

crew set up. He stood with his back to her so that others wouldn't notice.

"Yes. Sometimes I get the feeling you're avoiding me."

"I've been working with Frank. You can always slip into my room at night."

"By the time night comes, I'm too tired to move. I wouldn't leave until morning."

He turned and fingered a strand of her hair. "Sounds like a good idea."

Claudia brushed his hand away and glanced around in case anyone noticed. "No one can know about us," she hissed.

Peter grinned. "Don't worry. People *expect* me to flirt."

Two more days passed before Claudia had a moment to talk to Peter again. The crew was scheduled to film her and Peter attending a French-cooking class. She looked forward to the class because she knew this would probably be the one chance to get him alone. The class was held in the private town house of a renowned French chef, who had converted the ground floor into a professional kitchen for lessons. Unfortunately for Claudia, the three other female students who had signed up for the class were thrilled to be featured on a travel show from America, and two of them wouldn't leave Peter's side.

The course started early in the morning, following a 6:00 a.m. trip to a large open market to buy fresh ingredients. For the next several hours, they created three courses—a starter, main course and dessert. During the class Peter had a terrible time trying to measure some of the ingredients and following instructions, so Claudia helped him by completing the measurements. By late afternoon, they had finished cooking and prepared for a delicious lunch featuring their culinary creations. Outside on a large stone patio, the chef's assistant displayed their work, which consisted of asparagus and goat cheese tart, Vietnamese monkfish cooked in caramelized nuoc mam (fish sauce) and almond macaroon galette with strawberries. A green-leaf salad, cheese and a selection of French pastries including madeleines and *mille-feuille* drizzled with chocolate and a light vanilla icing, as well as a wonderful French wine, were added to the main dishes. While Lance and the other members of the crew focused on filming the delectable array of food, Claudia pretended to clear something and moved close to Peter.

"Will I see you tonight?" she said under her breath.

"You'll see me at the party," he said, referring to the fiftieth-wedding-anniversary party the residing owners of the castle would be having and were gracious enough to allow them to film.

"That's not the same."

"Do you like your room?"

"I'll like it better with you in it."

He smiled. "I'll see what I can do," he said then left.

The day before the party, a tailor arrived at the castle promptly at 8:30 a.m. along with his assistant, and spent most of the morning fitting Claudia with her gown, adding a touch of sparkle with a priceless set of jewels.

"I didn't order this jewelry," Ashley said, stunned by the selection.

"These were in my instructions," the tailor said, setting the items on the table.

Neither woman argued.

* * *

Peter was the first to see Claudia as she made her way down the majestic winding staircase wearing a shimmering hand-beaded gown that clung to her form like a second skin. Her hair was pulled back, forming soft waves that tapered off at the base of her neck, where a thin white-gold necklace hung above her cleavage. A pair of stunning diamond-pearl earrings and finely woven white lace gloves completed the outfit.

Peter's look of enchantment was just the response Claudia wanted. But when he walked up to her and reached out for her hand, she drew away.

"Careful, we're on camera," she said, motioning to Lance and Roy.

"They're just getting fillers of the guests and capturing the atmosphere. They're not paying attention to us."

"They will if you don't behave yourself," she whispered, removing his hand from around her waist.

Peter's gaze dipped to her cleavage. "I don't feel like behaving myself."

Claudia lifted his chin. "Try."

"You're not wearing a bra, are you?"

A slight smile touched her lips. "I'll tell you later."

"Claudia—"

"You look amazing," Frank interrupted, measuring Claudia with his eyes. "I couldn't believe how much Peter spent—umph," he said when Peter jabbed him in the ribs. He rubbed his side and coughed. "Uh, I mean you look amazing."

Claudia smiled. "Yes, you said that." She turned to Peter. "So I have *you* to thank for all this?"

"No, I just helped," Peter said in a gruff tone, but she saw his ears turn red and he sent Frank a sharp look.

Frank rubbed his head then cleared his throat. "Okay you two, let's get to work. I want to start shooting in the main entryway, the great hall and then with you celebrating along with the happy couple. Celebrating lasting love always makes for great television."

"I wish it hadn't been an anniversary party," Claudia said, following Frank.

"Anniversaries make you nervous?" Peter asked.

"No, I just…" She sighed. "Do you think lasting love really exists?"

Peter looked at the elderly couple as they gazed at each other with a glow of affection. He then turned his gaze to Claudia, and the light of desire illuminated his brown eyes. "When I look at them, I do."

Chapter 17

That evening Claudia lay in her bed and stared up at the ceiling, remembering the party and Peter. Yes, he'd looked amazing in his tuxedo, and his devilish grin was distracting. But it had been his words about love that had made it hard to focus. He believed in lasting love? And the way he'd looked at her had sent shivers of delight through her. Did that look mean he loved her?

Claudia sat up and ran a hand through her hair, shocked and frightened by her thoughts. *Love? Marriage?* Those were two words Claudia Madison never thought about. But she couldn't ignore them now. What she felt for Peter was more than infatuation or sentimentality. It was deep and real. Did she love him? There was only one way to find out.

She checked her watch. It was 2:00 a.m. and she hoped he would still be up. She quickly changed then grabbed her coat and peeked her head out to make sure the hallway was clear. Then she hurried to Peter's suite and knocked.

Peter opened the door and pulled her into his arms and welcomed her with a leg-weakening kiss. "I was wondering how long it would be before you came," he said.

"Why didn't you just call me?" Claudia asked, still recovering from the feel of his lips on hers.

"I like to play hard to get." Peter buried his face in her neck. "Hmm. You smell good."

"I made the scent myself."

"You liked your perfume class?"

"I love everything about this trip." She tugged on the buttons of his shirt. "Especially this."

He covered her hands. "Wait."

"What?" She turned to face Peter's front door. "Did you hear someone?"

"No. I want us to take our time and enjoy this."

"I always enjoy doing this."

"I know, but I think we should try a slower pace."

"Slower?"

Peter nodded. "Unbutton *slowly*," he said, emphasizing the word.

Claudia hesitated, feeling a little silly, then gradually began undoing one button then the next. By the time she reached the fourth button, she saw the benefit of a more leisurely approach to discovery. Her deliberate motions made their anticipation grow and heightened the atmosphere with an electrical charge. She watched his Adam's apple bob up and down as he swallowed. "Like this?"

His voice was raw. "Yes."

She pushed his shirt off his shoulders and let her gaze lazily skim over his broad shoulders and firm chest.

Claudia felt his muscles contract under her fingers, and her breath quickened. Her trembling fingers moved to the front of his trousers, and once they were undone she gradually dragged them down.

"Don't stop now."

"I don't plan to," Claudia said, and his underwear soon followed the same languid path. She looked up at him while still on her knees, her gaze soaking in the beauty of his naked form. She touched the sleek muscle of his thigh and the firm roundness of his calf. He was well made in every part. If things had been different, they would have been celebrating their anniversary. Claudia suddenly realized that her feelings for him had nothing to do with reason. She still loved him. Soon his image was blurred by her tears.

Peter pulled Claudia to her feet and searched her face. "Hey, what is it?"

She lowered her gaze, unable to face him. "Nothing."

He lifted her chin, forcing her to look at him. His eyes bore into hers. "There can't be any secrets between us, CC."

Claudia squeezed her eyes shut and hugged him, burying her face in his neck. "I'm just so happy. The last time I was this happy—"

Her words were cut off when he lifted her into his arms and cradled her close. "Nothing's going to happen to separate us. Not this time." He walked over to the bed then gently set her down. "I won't let it." He pressed a finger to her lips before she could protest. "Trust me," he said then undid her coat. His eyes glowed at the sight he saw underneath. He removed her coat then stepped back to let his gaze encompass every part of her. "You look better than I imagined." He slowly untied the sexy red teddy she wore. "And now I get to take it off."

Claudia caught her breath when the back of his fingers brushed across her breast, making her nipples hard. Her immediate response surprised her. He'd touched her many times before, but tonight her body was responding to him as if it was the first time.

He heightened her senses to the feel of the satin sheets at her back, his scent, the sight of the damask walls, the sound of his breath against her ear. When he entered her, it was in the same deliberate way he'd removed her clothes. He stirred her senses, surging her into ecstasy. In return she made love to him, letting her body say what she was too afraid to. She let her body worship his. She gave him honor and a pledge of faithfulness, with no thought of tomorrow.

He drifted off to sleep soon after, but Claudia stayed awake and watched him. She wanted to touch him—run her fingers along the stubble on his face; trace his full, soft lower lip—but resisted. How many women had seen him like this, looking as harmless as a little boy? Many, no doubt, but it didn't matter. She wouldn't think about them. She couldn't make this more than it was. She had to leave.

Claudia carefully removed the covers then began to slip out of bed, but Peter's arm shot around her waist and held her down like an iron grip. His eyes remained closed, but his deep voice didn't sound sleepy. "Stay."

"No."

He drew her to him and nuzzled her cheek. "Please."

"No."

He opened his eyes. "I could make you stay."

She lifted a brow. "But you won't."

Peter sighed and reluctantly released her, but not

before playfully swatting her on the butt. "You're too stubborn."

She only laughed.

He lay on his side, resting his head in his hand. "You don't have to go," he said as he watched Claudia change back into the teddy and button up her lightweight spring coat.

"I can't be seen leaving your room." *I don't want to be seen as just another one of your women.*

"We don't need to be secretive."

Claudia slipped her shoes on. "It's better this way." She bent down and kissed him. "Good night."

She checked the hallway again to make sure it was clear then left. As she turned the corner, she bumped into Roy.

Claudia jumped back and grabbed her chest. "You scared me."

"He got to you, didn't he?"

"What?"

"I don't want to see you get hurt."

"Roy, I can take care of myself."

"I know a lot more about Warren than you do. He's not all that he seems."

Claudia walked past and gave him a quick pat on the arm. "Go and get some sleep."

"He's a fraud and I can prove it."

Claudia stopped and looked at him, intrigued. "I'm listening."

"I always wondered how he can be friends with all the women he's been with, and why he's into a lot of art like the theater and galleries." He leaned forward. "Musicals."

Claudia shook her head. "Roy—"

"Haven't you wondered why he dresses so…" He raised a significant brow. "You know."

Claudia held up her hand, sensing where he was going. "Roy don't go there. He's definitely not gay."

"I overheard him on his cell phone telling some guy he loves him, and it sounded…you know…serious."

"It wasn't—" Claudia stopped, not wanting to burst out laughing. She could imagine Peter's response to the accusation, but she didn't know if he wanted people to know about his brother. "He's not gay."

Roy gave her a once-over full-body scan. She kept her coat tight and up close. "Just because he can 'seal the deal' doesn't mean he only likes women," he said.

Claudia grabbed the lapel of Roy's shirt. "In Peter's case, he's not pretending." She gave Roy a light kiss on the cheek. "But you're sweet to look out for me," she said then walked away.

Roy watched Claudia leave, his cheek burning where her lips had just been. He touched his face and sighed. Warren was a lucky SOB.

The next day Peter noticed that Claudia was edgy. "What's wrong?"

"Roy saw me leaving your room last night."

"So what?"

"He said he was worried about me. He's afraid you'll hurt me because…" She bit her lip.

"Because what?"

"He…he thinks you're gay."

Peter blinked then threw his head back and let out a peal of laughter.

"It's because you like the arts, and he thinks you dress too well," Claudia added, barely able to keep the amusement from her voice.

Peter laughed even harder.

Claudia started laughing, as well. She fell against him, and he wrapped his arm around her shoulder. "And he overheard you telling your brother you love him, and he thought—"

"That he was my lover?" Peter finished.

She nodded and they shared a look then burst into fresh peals of laughter.

"What's the joke?" Frank asked.

Peter waved his hand, begging to stop; Claudia wiped tears from her eyes, unable to respond.

"Well, I hope you two can get yourselves together. We're ready," Frank said in a stern tone.

Peter covered his mouth and nodded; Claudia drew in her lips and made a guttural sound indicating her acknowledgment.

Peter managed to control his amusement, but his eyes continued to dance. He glanced up and saw Roy and waved.

"What are you going to say to him?" Claudia asked, suddenly anxious.

"Nothing," Peter said then swept her into his arms and claimed her lips with a kiss that had her mind spinning. He then released her and smiled. "I think that says everything."

She stared at him, wide-eyed and shaken.

"This time I'm not doing it for the camera. Now our affair is no longer a secret." He strolled away, pushing his hands in his pockets.

Claudia stood speechless. So did all the crew members. Then they broke out into a loud applause.

Ashley rushed up to her. "Oh my God, that was amazing. You've got so much color in your face you hardly need any makeup," she said, dusting Claudia's face with a brush. "Somehow I knew something would happen between the two of you." She continued to smile.

"Hmm," Claudia said, not knowing how to respond.

"You two sizzle. That energy had to go somewhere. You lucky girl."

"Hmm," Claudia said again, feeling her heart sink. With that one action, her affair with Peter had lost its magic and wonder, and she knew it would just be fodder for gossip and speculation.

"Too bad it won't last," Ashley said bluntly. "I see this happen all the time."

Claudia groaned inwardly. It had been less than ten seconds and already she was getting advice she hadn't asked for.

"Especially on movie sets," Ashley continued. "And in the theater. They usually never survive the real world. I mean, how can a real relationship survive after traveling to exotic locations, wearing terrific clothes and staying in a castle?" Ashley swiftly inspected Claudia, tucking a stray hair behind her ear, then nodded. "You're all set."

Claudia looked at Peter. Ashley was right, of course. Their affair couldn't last. But she hadn't expected it to.

When something's too good to be true, it usually is. That's what her mother kept saying through Claudia's painful recovery from her accident. After weeks of no response to her letter, Claudia had begun to believe her, although she still had a faint hope that Peter would at least try to reach her. He didn't.

"I just knew he wouldn't stick around," her mother had said. "Handsome and with all that money? No wonder he didn't come back. He just wanted a good time and that was you, for a while. His type always has someone else waiting in the wings. I'm glad I had your brother get some of your things out of his apartment. It's time to move on, just as Peter apparently has."

"Maybe I should have told him about—"

Her mother firmly shook her head. "No, you did the right thing." She grabbed a tissue and tenderly brushed away Claudia's tears. "You didn't want him to marry you out of pity. You're young and you have so much ahead of you. This is a good lesson. You've got to depend on yourself. Don't expect anyone to take care of you or be there for you. You're my star. I'll never forgive him for not replying to your letter or trying to reach you, but it's best this way. You need to forget him. Look what love did to my life.

"But at least your taste is better than mine. Your father comes from a long line of losers, but I was in love and thought it didn't matter. Don't make my mistakes. Choose reason over emotion every time, and you won't regret a thing."

And Claudia hadn't, and wouldn't. As Ashley had said—it was the exotic locations and fascinating experiences they had that made the relationship work, but could it survive two careers or the harsh reality of deadlines, overdue bills and family? Eight years ago their relationship hadn't gone through the fire—it had had an almost fantastical, fairy-tale quality. Then fate snatched it away.

Chapter 18

Italy

It would end in Italy among the rich cultural heritage of undiscovered towns, fine baroque architecture, white sandy beaches, culinary delights and fine wine. With its typical Mediterranean climate—hot, dry summers and long days of sunshine—Italy allowed the crew to shoot some of the best scenes yet. They traveled through unforgettable landscapes blanketed with blooming flora and an assortment of trees including palms, olives, lemons and oranges.

After resting for a day, they filmed Claudia and Peter taking a hot-air balloon ride to visit a small hilltop town with a spectacular view of southern Italy's countryside. The streets were narrow and mazelike and whitewashed, providing excellent contrast and background imagery. That night, under a pitch-black sky punctuated with thousands of stars, the town awoke. Musicians of all ages appeared and played traditional music while some of the spirited residents shared their dances in the old ways.

An entire day was set aside to film Claudia and Peter learning about wines made from that part of the country. As they drove, they were met with rows and rows of grapevines stretching off into the distance. Since the time of the year they'd arrived was not the time of harvest, which was August to the end of October, Peter and Claudia were graciously given a private tour by the town's mayor, a tall, deeply tanned individual with a wonderful laugh, who in exchange for his time wanted to be featured in one of the episodes. Frank obliged. The crew was allowed to tour the best wineries and meet famous wine producers in the area and taste their best wines, all while exploring the beautiful countryside.

Disappointment struck twice, however, when Frank discovered that their next intended episode, featuring the making of Italy's finest olive oil, would not be possible because the olive harvest began in October and ran through February, and their filming would be completed by the end of summer. Both disappointments regarding the wine and olive oil were the direct result of Lance not attending to detail. He had relied on information pulled off a website instead of contacting the tourist board in the area. Frank knew then that he'd be letting Lance go, once they got back home. In addition to his role filming some of the scenes, and providing lighting, he'd been assigned the job of scheduling all locations, making sure everything went as planned. It was evident that he wasn't up to the task, and Frank was thankful the mishap had happened in only one location. Again thanks to Frank's genius, instead of filming the cohosts actually making olive oil, he decided to develop a skillfully narrated version using Peter's recognizable voice as the voice-over, explaining to the viewers the different techniques used. As a result of the mayor's influence, Claudia and Peter were filmed visiting and dining at some of the best and most ancient olive oil mills in Italy. Ashley had a lot to do, and she had to be creative with the wardrobe selections.

She was relieved to have brought along an assortment of accessories, because changing what the hosts wore was vital to avoiding stagnant scenes.

For a full dining experience, the meals had olive oil in or with everything. They particularly liked an array of tempting appetizers where olive oil was drizzled over nonpasta dishes, such as roasted peppers, marinated artichoke hearts and sliced eggplants. The day ended with an invitation to the mayor's house, where they were able to taste the light and fruity extra-virgin olive oil produced in the northern part of the area and compare it with the stronger and spicy oil produced in the southern part. Before the filming, none of the crew, including the hosts, had any idea that olive oil could taste so vastly different, and Claudia had been unsure that it would be interesting. She couldn't imagine why anyone would want to see olive oil being made, and she was pleasantly surprised by how fascinating the process was.

Early the next morning, Claudia sat on the terrace of the bed-and-breakfast, knowing she didn't want to leave. While the rooms were certainly not as opulent as those in Hawaii, Bermuda or France, they were bright and airy and furnished in the relaxing pastel colors seen all over that region. Plus, it was close to the Mediterranean Sea.

She especially enjoyed the owners, two white-haired

middle-aged sisters, Brigitta and Natalia, who were fluent in English and French as well as Italian.

Each morning, breakfast was provided on the terrace—and the guests got to taste several of southern Italy's famous breads, which were made in an ancient stone oven. Along with the bread were tasteful seasonal fruits: black and green figs, sweet pears and red oranges, grown by the sisters in their garden. Whenever they could, Brigitta and Natalia had breakfast, lunch and dinner with the crew and enjoyed telling them about life in the town. Claudia wasn't sure she'd keep her figure with all the eating they kept doing, but she never had the willpower to refuse what was offered. Besides, she could always work off several pounds by spending more time with Peter.

Natalia and Brigitta loved seeing them together. They told Claudia so one evening while she stood enjoying the setting sun under a tree where Peter had left her after a long stroll and a delicious kiss goodbye before he went to meet with Frank.

"A woman in love is one of the prettiest things in the world," Brigitta said.

"You're such a happy couple," Natalia added.

Claudia smiled, because she knew people liked to say that even when they didn't mean it. All young couples appeared happy.

"I can see you don't believe me," Natalia said with a knowing look. "It's because you think too much up here." She tapped the side of her head. "Instead of in here." She tapped her chest.

"I don't mean to offend you."

"I take no offense. You're young and you don't know as much as you think yet."

"That Peter," Brigitta said. "He is a good man. Sturdy, strong." She winked. "Rich."

Claudia couldn't stop a smile. "Yes, but I have money, too."

Brigitta waved the thought away with a quick motion of her hand. "It's always a lot more fun to spend a man's money. It's even better when he spends it on you."

Natalia nodded. "That Peter of yours reminds me of my Giuseppe."

"Giuseppe?" Claudia asked, surprised. She knew the two sisters had never married. "Was he a nephew or brother?"

"He was my heart. The man I was to marry. We were engaged and would have married right away, but I wanted to wait until the war was over. I was a practical woman and thought it was the right choice. He never came back. I've always regretted that." She clasped Claudia's hand. "Grasp a chance when it comes. You may never get another opportunity again."

Claudia took Natalia's words to heart and seized every opportunity she got to be with Peter both on and off the set. But she knew that opportunity would soon end. She had made a lifetime of memories with him and knew it would be hard to say goodbye. But she had no other choice.

She thought about their affair as she sat on the terrace and rehearsed how she would part with him.

Suddenly, Frank ran out onto the terrace. "Start packing."

"Why?"

"There's a storm warning."

"A storm? Why didn't they tell us earlier?"

"Brigitta just told me. She heard the warning on her shortwave radio. They are evacuating the entire area."

With so much going on with the project no one on the crew had bothered to turn on the radio, since most of the stations were in Italian and they hadn't seen a need to listen to English stations such as the BBC or the Voice of America.

Sirens pierced the air.

Brigitta came to the doorway. "It's going to be bad, very bad. Whenever you hear the sirens, you know it's going to bad. With Natalia's help, I was able to get all of your plane tickets changed." She handed them to Frank.

"Oh, here comes Natalia." The older woman's face reflected the sobering news.

"It's bad, bad. They are warning of pounding rain and extreme flooding. They are evacuating everyone. The last time we experienced a storm like this, the entire town was under water for over a week and twenty people lost their lives, including a family of four. You need to go right now, if you don't want to get stuck here before the airport closes."

The siren continued to wail.

"Where's Peter?" Claudia asked.

"He's with Roy and Lance getting extra footage for filler scenes. We're going to need them. It looks like we'll be losing a week out of the schedule because of this."

"But—"

"Don't worry. I sent a message to them. Ashley will be traveling with you. Come on. We don't have much time. You two will fly out on the first plane. The rescue team is sending a helicopter for Peter, Roy and Lance. They will fly out on the next flight right behind Eugene and myself.

Claudia stood, wanting to scream while looking up at

the clear sky, not believing that it would soon transform into gray storm clouds. Once again, fate would separate her from Peter without a formal goodbye.

He hated rain. Peter sat in the back of the SUV he shared with Lance and Roy as the torrential rain pounded the windshield. Roy drove in silence while Lance listened to the weather report. The day had started off well when he'd left the warm comfort of Claudia's bed to go get fillers with the two cameramen. Peter had heard about a tiny village up in the mountains from a local resident who'd told him that it was rarely visited by tourists and had a unique artist community. Frank agreed to the excursion, always eager to make sure they had as much footage as possible. Peter's interest was piqued further when he heard about the village's long tradition of making papier-mâché, known as *cartapestra,* and the area's examples of *cartapestra* dating back to the seventeenth century. The location was also known for exquisite stonework carved into the churches and palaces, using an unusual rock found in the formations in the hills surrounding the village.

By the time they arrived, the town center was beginning to come alive with artisans, and Peter didn't want to miss a thing.

"Don't forget the stonework," he told Roy.

Roy shot him a glance. "You got everything else— you want to take my job, too?"

"What's that supposed to mean?"

Roy shrugged. "Nothing. I wouldn't want anything I say to get me fired."

"Come on, I'm sure he didn't mean anything by it," Lance said, hoping to defuse the tension between Peter and Roy.

Roy ignored him. "What are you even doing here, Warren? Isn't it enough that you're hosting the show? You have to manage us filming it, too?"

"I like being involved in every aspect of production. I wasn't criticizing," Peter said, trying to be fair. "I just know what to look for because I used to be behind the camera." Peter rested his hands on his hips. "But you don't like me for another reason, right?" He raised a brow and a slight smile touched his lips. "Is it Claudia?"

Peter's smug expression made something in Roy snap. He'd seen that smile on the boys who'd stolen his lunch money, who'd made fun of his hand-me-down clothes. But he was bigger now and wanted to wipe that smile from Peter's face. He set his camera down. "Yes, it's about Claudia," he said then punched him.

Lance rushed forward. "Are you crazy?"

Peter stopped him with an outstretched hand. "It's all right," he said then tentatively rubbed his jaw. "What's on your mind, Fitcher?"

"You're a fraud," Roy said, further angered by Peter's calm. "You're a user and you're using Claudia to cover for you."

"I'm not—"

"I know you're not gay, but you're something. I just haven't figured out what yet. What I do know is that everything comes easy for you and you take it all for granted, but I won't let you treat Claudia like all the others."

Peter sniffed. "And how do you plan to stop me?"

Roy saw the challenge and took it. He rushed at Peter, but at the last moment Peter moved aside then gripped him in a choke hold. "You're right. I'm not what I seem," he whispered in his ear, his voice dark with menace. "And I don't care what you think of me, but when it comes to Claudia stay out of my way." He shoved Roy from him and Roy stumbled forward holding his neck. "Now go shoot the stonework."

Roy glared at him but knew better than to say anything. Lance opened his mouth to comment but stopped when Peter's cell phone rang. That's when their plans changed. Frank told him to start for the airport ASAP because a major storm was headed for the town. He'd packed their suitcases and everything would be there when they arrived.

Now the three men traveled down a steep winding road and could see that the rain battered the embankment. The immense volume of water raging down the river as a result of the torrential rain from up north was flooding the low-lying areas. Lance had speculated they could risk driving the SUV along the rugged country roads, and after a harrowing forty-five minutes, they finally drove onto a main road leading to the airport. But they still had twenty miles to go.

Peter heard Lance suddenly swear. "What is it?"

"The announcer said that a strong southerly wind was expected to push the Mediterranean deep on land. He expects the flood to be like the disastrous ones which have struck the south of Italy eight times in eleven years."

Roy pulled the car over to the side. "I need to stop for a minute."

"Can't it wait?" Peter said, in no mood to get stuck in mud on some country road.

"You want to go out in this weather?" Lance said, also stunned by Roy's request.

Roy did not answer. He got out of the SUV and walked toward a field. Thankfully, the heavy rain had lightened, but Peter and Lance didn't understand their companion's strange behavior.

"If it's a nature call, he could use one of the bottles in the back of the van." Lance looked at his watch. "We need to get going if we are going to get to the airport on time, especially in this weather."

Peter did not respond. He was looking at Roy with growing concern.

Lance looked over at Roy as well. "What do you think is wrong with him? It's like he's having some sort of attack," he said when Roy doubled over.

Peter shot out of the van and raced over to Roy. Roy gasped for air with the palm of his hands on his knees. The pallor on Roy's face and the wheezing sound from his chest ignited Peter's temper. "Why didn't you tell us you have asthma?"

"I…I…need…" Roy turned and grabbed the cuff of Peter's shirt, fear evident in his eyes. Peter could feel Roy's panic begin to rise, and Roy's heightened emotion made him start to cough while his breathlessness and wheezing increased. He fell forward, and Peter caught him before he hit the ground.

An unrelenting curtain of rain soaked through their clothes and softened the earth beneath them, making the path slippery and treacherous. Peter switched into automatic. After his brother's attack, he'd learned all he could about first aid so that he could be prepared for any event. On the football field he'd helped a fellow player suffering from heatstroke. As a volunteer firefighter he'd performed CPR on a heart attack victim, reset a broken arm, even aided a choking child. But never this. He hadn't dealt with a severe asthma attack since his brother's years ago, and for a second his mind went blank and he was a helpless ten-year-old watching the brother he'd idolized slip away from him. If he didn't act fast enough or do the right thing, Roy could die or end up like his brother.

He remembered the white walls of the hospital ward where they'd kept Thomas, the Asian nurse who always smiled at him but would never give him straight answers to his many questions. He remembered his brother's physical therapy to help him walk and talk again and how they'd applauded when he'd been able to use a spoon again. He remembered the arguments his parents would have at night that would always leave his mother in tears.

I'm not going through this again, Peter thought, pushing back those memories as he registered the heaviness of Roy's limp body. He wouldn't let Roy's family go through it, either. Let this be his redemption for what he hadn't been able to do then.

"Roy, where is your medicine?" Peter demanded, shaking him.

Roy didn't respond. He was drifting in and out of consciousness.

Peter yelled to Lance. "Bring me Roy's backpack."

"What's going on?" Lance said, anxious.

"Just get me his damn backpack," Peter snapped.

Lance reached into the back of the SUV, grabbed Roy's backpack then rushed over to where Peter was.

"Roy's having an asthma attack," Peter said. "I need his medicine fast or this guy's going to die." He nodded to the backpack. "There should be an inhaler in there somewhere."

Lance searched the bag. "I don't see it. What does it lo—?"

Peter grabbed the backpack and swiftly searched through its contents until he found it. He adjusted

Roy's position. "Lance, I need you to support him." He saw the fear on the other man's face and said, "He'll make it," knowing that Lance needed the assurance. He understood how frightening it was to witness someone struggle to breath and basically have their own lungs suffocate them, but he needed Lance to focus. "It's probably a stress-induced attack brought on by the frightening storm conditions. His medicine will help." Peter slapped Roy's face hard.

Roy's eyes briefly fluttered open, and Peter administered the medicine.

"Breathe, Fitcher. Breathe. It's going to be okay." When Roy's eyes opened again, Peter could still see the panic and fear in them. "I'm not going to let you die. You're going to be okay. I'm right here with you. You're going to be fine." Peter continued to talk to Roy while administering the medication, and soon Roy's color started coming back and his breathing returned to normal.

Lance released a sigh of relief.

"We need to get out of here," Peter said. "He's going to be weak from this. Help me get him to the van."

The two men carried the half-conscious Roy to the SUV and put him in the backseat.

"Hey man, how are you with driving an SUV in this rain?" Peter asked, jumping in the backseat with Roy.

"This will be easy. I used to be a long-distance truck driver before I decided to go into film. Buckle up. U.S.A., here we come."

The medication was taking effect. Peter saw Roy's color return, and he was no longer fighting for every breath. Roy closed his eyes.

But when they were within five miles of the airport, they saw a blockage ahead.

"I'm sorry, sir," an Italian officer said, "but you cannot continue on this road."

"We are with a film crew from America, and we need to get to the airport right away to catch our flight. We don't want to be stranded here. My colleague just had a serious asthma attack and needs to get home and see his personal physician," Peter said.

The officer looked at Roy.

"Okay, you can go. Drive slowly and instead of driving through the water, try to drive on the edge of the puddles. Good luck."

"Thanks."

At the airport, Peter picked up all three tickets and they were soon getting into a small plane. Roy had recovered enough to sit up, but the attack had exhausted him.

"How did you know what to do?" Roy asked, his voice barely audible.

"I have a brother with asthma," Peter admitted with some reluctance. Then he bit his lip. "Can I tell you about him?"

Roy nodded and Peter told him the story of his past that he no longer wanted to keep secret or be ashamed of.

And as he spoke, Roy's image of Peter as a calculated ladies' man floated away, followed by his picture of him as a self-serving jock, rich jerk and arrogant bestselling author until all that was left was an ordinary man. He'd misjudged him on every level. When Peter was finished, Roy shook his head in admiration and disbelief. "I was right, you are a fraud."

Peter laughed. "Thanks," he said without rancor.

"No, in a good way," Roy clarified, not wanting to cause offense. "You play a role that's not really who you are. You're smarter and deeper than anyone thinks. I'm sorry I didn't see it before."

Peter shrugged, brushing aside his praise. "It works for me."

But Roy refused to let Peter dismiss him. He seized Peter's hand, and when he spoke his voice shook with emotion. "I owe you my life. I didn't have any brothers until now. Until you. If you ever need anything, let me know."

A brother. Not to replace the one he had, but to add to his life. Someone he could depend on and trust. Peter gripped Roy's shoulder and said, "I will."

The scent of freshly polished wood and her favorite linen-and-sky scented carpet deodorizer greeted Claudia when she entered her apartment. "Thank you, Noreen," she whispered while squatting down to pat Madame Curie, who had come up to welcome her. She sat down on the couch and didn't realize she'd fallen asleep until a soft knock on the door woke her. She saw that it was dark. Opening her eyes, Claudia squinted at her watch then opened the door. Peter stood there, red-eyed and exhausted. She didn't ask him why he was there. She just hugged him.

"I was worried."

"You thought a storm and an ocean could keep us apart?"

Claudia caressed his face with her two hands, feeling the day-old stubble of his beard. "You look as tired as I feel. Come on." She took his hand and led him into her bedroom. They didn't speak. They got in bed, pulled up the covers and fell asleep, happy to be together.

Several hours later, Peter woke up with a start. "What's that?"

Claudia yawned. "What's what?"

He glanced at the door on alert. "I heard a noise."

"It's probably Madame Curie." Claudia turned back over to sleep.

"Madame who?"

"My cat—I never let her hear me call her that—it annoys her. She only responds if you call her by her name."

Peter didn't respond. He was focused on what he perceived to be a danger. "No. The sound's larger than what a cat, excuse me, Madame Curie could do." He stood, tense. "Give me something."

Claudia quickly grabbed a wooden clothes hanger out of her closet and handed it to Peter.

He waved it in the air, exasperated. "What do you expect me to do with this?"

"I couldn't find anything. Wait." She disappeared into the bathroom then returned.

Peter frowned. "A curling iron? Never mind. Stay here." He exited and quietly closed the door.

Claudia waited by the door, and seconds later she heard a piercing scream. She ran into the kitchen and saw Noreen holding up a butcher knife.

Peter pushed Claudia behind him. "I told you to stay in the bedroom."

"It's okay. I know her. Noreen, he's with me."

Noreen kept her grip on the knife. "You're not supposed to be back yet. What are you doing here?"

"We came back early."

"It would have been nice if you'd told me." Noreen looked somewhat relieved, but she still held the knife out.

"You can put the knife down." Claudia came out from behind Peter.

Noreen returned the knife to the slot in the butcher-block holder on the counter then folded her arms, waiting for some sort of explanation. "You weren't supposed to arrive back for another week," she said, annoyed.

"I know. It's a long story. But let me introduce you. Noreen, this is Peter. Peter, this is Noreen."

Peter held out his hand. "Nice to meet you."

Noreen briefly shook his hand. "You scared the s—"

"Noreen," Claudia warned.

Peter grinned. "I'm sorry about that."

Claudia turned to Peter. "Darling, why don't you go and get changed so I can talk to Noreen?"

Peter took his cue and left.

Noreen watched him go, then whispered, "Talk about taking your work home with you. No wonder you've been keeping him a secret. He looks even better in person."

"I can explain."

"You don't have to explain anything to me. I'm just surprised he's the so-called Mr. I'll-Never-Marry."

"What do you mean?"

"That guy isn't a player. He's got 'commitment' written all over his face."

"No, he doesn't. He's like me. We both don't want to get married. Ever."

Noreen shrugged, unconvinced. "If you say so."

Claudia loved her friend, but sometimes she could grate on her nerves. "Besides, how can you know that?"

"I know men, and he's the serious sort. Funny, he looks younger than his photos. Is there something you're not telling me?"

"No."

"Just don't break his heart, okay?"

"I'll try not to."

"Be gentle. Try not to get too serious."

"When have you ever known me to get serious about a man?"

"You have a point. But he's a smooth liar."

"What do you mean?" Claudia said bewildered.

"He said it was 'nice to meet me.' It's never nice to meet a woman with a knife aimed at your chest. But with that voice, I almost believed him." Noreen looked down at her watch. "Well, I'd better go."

"Sorry for the mix-up. Thanks for looking after things for me."

"It was fun, but Madame Curie doesn't like to be left alone. Twice when I came back I saw papers moved and once a box knocked over."

Claudia frowned. "Madame Curie is usually careful. Perhaps something frightened her."

Noreen began to grin. "She won't be left alone now." She turned to the door.

"Wait." Claudia rushed over to where she'd dumped her luggage. She reached inside a large paper bag. "Here. This is for you."

Noreen pulled on her coat. "Thanks, you shouldn't have." She picked up her handbag and walked to the door. "Just a word of advice."

"What?"

"Whatever he asks for, say 'yes.'"

"I didn't realize you had such dangerous friends," Peter said as they ate breakfast in Claudia's kitchenette.

"We surprised her. She didn't expect anyone to be here."

"She's a little thing, but she's lethal."

Claudia laughed. "Noreen? Never."

"Hmm," Peter said, doubtful, then he reached into his pocket. "Oh, Roy sent us these," he said, placing pictures of them on the table. "He also sent soft copies."

Amazed, Claudia picked up the photos of her and Peter in the different countries they'd visited—one with them on the beach, another walking along a street, a third kissing behind an olive tree. "Roy took these? Why?"

"Blackmail?"

Claudia looked up and frowned. "That's not funny."

"I wasn't trying to be funny." Peter picked up one photo and studied it. "He thought he was protecting you."

"Then why did he decide to give them to you?"

"It's a long story. Let's just say it's done now."

"I'm glad he did," Claudia said with a slight shudder. "Especially this one."

Peter took the picture from her. It was of them in a jewelry store. "What's so special about it?"

"This one looks like we're buying an engagement ring. In the wrong hands this picture could get us into trouble."

Peter looked at the photo with renewed interest. "Would that be so bad?"

"I'm going to blame that kind of talk on your jet lag." She paused. "How long can you stay?"

"Just a few days, then I have some work to do back in Georgia."

"Great." She would accept whatever time he could give her. *Don't get serious*, she heard Noreen say. She wouldn't. Claudia knew that the more casual their affair was, the safer she was.

But during the next two months, she felt less and less casual about him. Peter would drive up for the weekend, and they filled the days going hiking, visiting a local art gallery which was featuring the art of Jacob Lawrence and riding their bikes around a lake near her apartment. One weekend they went in-line skating. Although Claudia enjoyed Peter's visits, she still felt that there was more to him than he let her see. So she decided to turn the tables on him.

Chapter 19

Claudia checked the address again to make certain she was at the right place, then she looked at the heavy oak-paneled door of his town house. Surprising Peter might not be a good idea, but after driving for six and a half hours it wouldn't make sense to turn back. The drive down had been a breeze. No construction, no accidents, which was amazing. And with the weather in the low nineties, Claudia had been able to really enjoy her convertible—and topped eighty miles per hour at times—though always on the lookout for the police.

But now she was here, and there was no going back. She took a deep breath then knocked. Peter took a while to answer and when he did, he didn't look shocked—he looked thunderstruck.

"Claudia!"

"Yes." She forced a smile. "Surprise!"

"That it is." He glanced behind him. "Um…"

Her smile faltered. "Is this a bad time?"

"Hurry up, Peter," a female voice called out to him. "I want you to stay hard."

Peter briefly shut his eyes. "I'll be right there."

Claudia took a step back. "Obviously it *is* a bad time."

Peter grabbed her hand. "You know me better than that. Come on." He yanked her in then closed the door. "I've got my brother for the weekend." He helped her remove her coat and took her suitcase. "Right now we're doing crafts."

Claudia followed him into the kitchen and saw three people sitting at the table with an assortment of colored paper, scissors and glue spread out everywhere. The young woman looked up and smiled. "Everyone, say hello to Peter's guest."

"Hello!"

Peter did the introductions. "This is Penelope. She's an art instructor. And this is Trevor. And this is my brother, Thomas."

"Trevor is my best friend," Thomas said with a grin. He was a tall man with large hands and, like his brother, boyish features. "Do you know how to make lemon meringue rice pudding?"

"No," Claudia said.

"Peter and I can show you."

Claudia sent Peter a look and he mouthed "It's okay" before he disappeared with her suitcase into another room. Claudia went over to the sink and washed her hands then stood next to Thomas. He walked over to a pantry and took out a flowered colored apron and put it on Claudia. By the time Peter returned his brother had all the ingredients laid out. "We need brown sugar, cornstarch, ground cinnamon, low-fat milk, cooked rice, margarine, eggs, lemon peel." He took a breath and then continued, "And lemon juice, sugar, vanilla and sliced almonds."

Thomas held up a stained recipe card. "We're using a recipe, and I'm reading it because I can read better than Peter."

Claudia glanced at Peter, uncomfortable with Thomas's remark, but Peter didn't seem bothered by his bother's comment. He looked proud.

"Yes. Thomas is a really good cook," Peter said. "I'm just his assistant."

Thomas continued with his instructions. "We have to mix everything together and then put it in the oven to cook," he said then proceeded to carefully measure each ingredient, referring back periodically to the instructions. While waiting for the dessert to cook, Thomas and Trevor showed Claudia their other crafts. After baking in the oven, the dessert was ready for the final touches. Thomas proudly spooned the meringue over the center of the pudding and sprinkled it with almonds, then he baked the dish uncovered for another ten minutes before serving it.

"This is delicious!" Claudia said, licking her spoon in an unladylike fashion. "Thomas, I've never had anything so good." Trevor, Pamela and Peter agreed. Thomas beamed. Claudia didn't wait to be asked and offered to wash the dishes while Trevor and Thomas completed the craft they'd been doing earlier.

Before Trevor and Penelope left Peter instructed the two men to clean up and put everything in a large blue plastic bin.

Claudia picked up her handbag. "I guess I should be going, as well."

"You mean you drove over six hours just to spend a couple of hours?"

Claudia flushed. *If only he knew what she had packed in her overnight bag.* "No, I…" She looked in Thomas's direction.

Peter rubbed his upper arm. "You don't have to go. You won't be in the way."

"What else do you have planned?" She hadn't considered that Peter might have company.

"The park or a movie," Thomas shouted, not looking up from what he was doing.

Claudia still felt awkward and a little foolish for her impulsive decision to come.

Peter took her handbag. "You won't be in the way. This is such a fabulous surprise and treat for us, and I want you to stay."

Claudia looked at Thomas. "Do you mind if I stay?"

"Can we still go to the park?"

"Yes."

"Then I don't mind."

"Great, let's go."

At the park, Thomas monopolized Claudia and showed her all his favorite places, including the jungle gym, which he'd grown too big to play on; an artificial pond where they sometimes went fishing; a wooden bridge and Japanese gazebo; the petting zoo with a handful of pigs, sheep, goats and a pony; and his favorite—the carousel. Although she didn't want to, Thomas convinced Claudia to ride the carousel with him, at least two times, before they all sat at a picnic table eating large waffle ice-cream cones.

That night Peter tucked Thomas in bed then joined Claudia on the sofa, draping his arm over her shoulder.

"This was a great day. Thank you. You really made him happy." He leaned over and kissed her gently on the forehead.

"He's fun to be with."

"Yeah."

"And he likes to talk about a lot of things."

Peter nodded.

"He even told me his birth date."

Peter focused on the TV. "Really?" He pushed a button on the remote.

"Yes, including the year he was born."

Peter stilled.

"I was surprised. It was the exact same year you were born. It started me thinking. How could that be? You're not twins and he looks older than you. So I figured you took his birthday because you wanted to emulate him. But that leaves me with one important question. How old are you?"

"You know how old I am."

"I know how old your driver's license says you are. Wait! Your brother and I are nearly the same age. So that means you're younger than me?"

"Claudia."

"By how much?"

"Let's—"

She covered her mouth. "The bouncer was right all those years ago. You *were* underage!"

"It's not like that."

"You've always looked so young. It was staring me in the face, and I slept with you. Tell me the sex was legal."

"Yes, it was. I was over twenty."

"By how much?"

"Enough."

"How much?"

"A year."

"You were twenty-one! Oh, my God, you're still in your twenties?"

"I don't know why you're making such a big deal out of a four-year age difference."

"Six."

"What?"

"It's really six." Claudia looked away.

"You mean you're—"

"Don't say it. I'm just closer to mid-thirty than early thirty," she said, unable to look at him.

"Why?"

"My mother wanted to put me in a certain program, so she fudged the numbers and never changed them back."

He laughed.

"It's not funny." She lowered her head, embarrassed.

He nuzzled her neck. "I always knew I'd gotten myself a sexy older woman."

Claudia shook her head in disbelief. "Even Noreen saw how young you are just from her brief encounter at my place."

"I may look young, but I'm man enough for you, so let's not make this an issue." Peter pulled her closer and lifted her chin up.

"It's the voice that makes you appear older." She looked into his eyes.

He rested his head back. "Claudia."

"All right, all right. I won't mention it again. So what do you have planned for tomorrow?"

"Dinner at Stephano's."

"Great." Claudia stifled a laugh. "Kids eat half price."

Peter sent her a glance but didn't reply. However, he got his revenge that night by proving he was all man, and she never teased him again.

That Saturday, Peter decided to treat Claudia and Thomas to a day trip on a private boat he rented. They drove out of town to a small lake, where he showed off his boating skills while she took pictures and Thomas watched the birds. In midmorning, Peter anchored the boat and they dined on a packed picnic basket that Peter had purchased from a local deli, which included one of Claudia's favorite wines. After arriving home, they rested then went to a movie and later to Stephano's for dinner.

"This has been one of the best weekends ever," Thomas said as Peter helped his brother prepare for bed.

"I'm glad."

After saying his prayers, Thomas got into bed. "I really, really like Claudia."

Peter picked up the worn copy of *Robinson Crusoe* lying on the table beside his bed and handed it to him. Even when they were children, Peter had enjoyed listening to his brother read adventure tales. Those memories held special significance to him now. "I like her, too." He nodded and opened the book. "Okay, what chapter are we on?"

Thomas set the book aside. "So are you going to marry her?"

Peter sighed. "The first girlfriend I introduce to you, and you already have us walking down the aisle?"

He nodded happily. "I *really* like her."

Peter opened the book and flipped through its pages. "I know you do."

"And she likes me."

"Yes." He handed the book to his brother and tapped the page. "I think we stopped here."

"I don't want her to go away."

"She won't go away."

"Promise?"

"I promise."

Thomas closed the book. "She'll make a pretty bride. Remember when Mom got married? Wasn't she pretty, and Yvette?"

Peter nodded, remembering his stepsister's wedding.

"Can I be your best man?"

"Only if you'll read the next chapter," Peter said, determined to change the topic.

Thomas grinned, opened the book and began to read.

That night Peter stared at the ceiling, unable to sleep. His brother made everything sound so simple. But it wasn't. Claudia would have to give up a lot to be with him. He couldn't leave Georgia. He needed to be close to his brother. Would she be willing to give up her life in North Carolina? It would be a risk for both of them, but she fit into his life. He liked how well she got on with Thomas. If he asked her to marry him, at least he'd know how she really felt about him.

The next morning Peter woke to the smell of cinnamon and sugar. He left his bedroom and found Thomas and Claudia preparing breakfast. Thomas gingerly put icing on a tray of hot cinnamon buns.

"Hmm, something smells good," Peter said.

"We're making breakfast," Thomas replied.

Claudia patted him on the back. "He's a great helper."

Peter saw the pride on his brother's face and then gazed at the woman who'd put it there, his heart buoyant. "Thanks for doing this."

"I don't mind."

He bit his lip, gathering courage. He'd ask her now. He took her hand, although his trembled a little. "Claudia?"

"Yes?"

He swallowed. "Will you—"

"Aaggh!"

They jumped apart and turned.

Thomas held his arm. "I didn't mean to," he said, his eyes wide with fear. Hot sticky icing was all over the front of his apron and on his forearm.

Claudia quickly rushed over. "It's okay, Thomas. Let me see." Without realizing it, Claudia's medical training kicked in. His skin was already a bright red and turning purple—she knew it was probably a second- or third-degree burn that would blister. "We need to take him to the nearest hospital."

Chapter 20

Lloyd Warren stormed into the emergency room, only to find his son Thomas sitting on a hospital bed with his arm wrapped in a large bandage. He was a large man, whose athletic build his two sons had inherited, with white hair and a matching mustache.

He glared at Peter. "What happened?"

"It was just a kitchen accident."

"What was he doing in the kitchen?"

"Cooking."

"He doesn't cook. Kitchens are dangerous."

"He loves to cook. He's not a kid."

"He's close enough. You should have been watching him."

"I was. I turned my back for one second—"

Mr. Warren sent Claudia a cursory glance. "Are you sure you weren't distracted?"

Peter's jaw twitched. "It was an accident."

"Should I even bother to introduce myself to her? I know by the next time I see you again, you'll have another one."

Claudia stepped forward. "My name is Claudia Madison. And Peter's telling the truth. It happened so fast it couldn't have been stopped."

"This proves my point. Thomas is safer with me. I can watch him better than anyone."

Claudia turned and saw Thomas watching them, tears forming in his eyes. "Couldn't we talk about this another time?" she said. "You're upsetting him."

Mr. Warren ignored her and said to Peter, "You're so irresponsible. You can't even look after him for one weekend."

"Don't be mad at Peter," Thomas begged. "It was my fault. All my fault."

Mr. Warren softened his voice. "I'm not mad. Just worried about you. When the doctor comes, I'll take you home."

Peter tightened his hand into a fist. "Dad, I have another whole day—"

"You've had him long enough. You and Claire can go home."

"Her name is Claudia," Peter said through clenched teeth.

Mr. Warren lifted Thomas's arm. "Does it hurt?"

Peter stared at the back of his father's head for a long moment then stormed out.

Claudia touched Thomas's knee. "It was wonderful meeting you."

"You're going away?"

"I have to go home, but I'll see you again another time."

"Don't lie to him," Mr. Warren demanded.

"I'm not lying."

Just as he did with Peter, he ignored her and addressed his next question to Thomas. "Would you like some ice cream later?"

Claudia bit her tongue and started to walk away then stopped. She looked back at him. "There's something pathetic about a man who won't admit that he's afraid."

Mr. Warren spun around.

"I'm glad I got your attention."

"I'm not afraid of anything."

"When Peter told me about you, I'd expected a great, imposing figure, but all I see is just a scared little old man."

"Old? Scared? I'll let you know that I have a PhD and one hundred papers published in the best scientific journals."

"I too have a college degree. Two, to be exact, and an M.D. But this isn't a contest. I know you have a successful business and you're a pillar in your community."

He looked at her with renewed respect. "You're not like Peter's others."

Claudia dismissed the comment. "Taking care of Thomas must be a lot of work."

"I manage."

"What happened today was an accident. It was no one's fault." Claudia braced herself for what she was about to say next. "It wasn't your fault that the basement was moldy or that Peter had gone down there. Keeping Thomas as a child won't take your fears away. It will only make them grow. He's a wonderful cook and he loves doing it. There are a lot of opportunities out there. He could become a baker's apprentice."

"A baker's apprentice? He could have been—"

Claudia's voice was firm. "He's wonderful as he is."

Mr. Warren let his gaze fall, and his bottom lip trembled. "Do you know what it's like to lose everything you'd ever hoped for?"

"Yes."

He looked up, surprised, but he could tell from her expression that she was telling the truth.

"I learned that living in the past doesn't make living in the present any easier. Mr. Warren, right now you have two wonderful sons." She lightly touched his arm then left.

Moments later Claudia found Peter pacing in the waiting room. He stopped when he saw her. "What did he say to you? Is he still convinced that it's my fault?" He shoved a hand in his pocket. "I wouldn't be surprised. He'd blame me if Thomas stubbed his toe or if it snowed in July. He only points out what I do wrong. I can never please him. I'm sorry you even had to meet him."

"It's okay," Claudia said softly, knowing he was more hurt than angry. "I didn't mind. Like Thomas, he's part of your life."

"My brother may be delayed, but he's not a child—he's a man. He deserves the dignity of being treated like one. My father won't let him work, won't let him volunteer or do anything. He just keeps him locked away at home with him."

"He's a frightened man."

Peter laughed in disbelief. "My father's not frightened of anything."

"Peter?" Mr. Warren said.

He turned and folded his arms. "Yes?"

"Come by my house tomorrow."

He nodded.

"Good," Mr. Warren said then returned to Thomas.

Peter frowned once his father had gone. "I wonder what he wants."

"Maybe he wants to talk."

"My father doesn't talk. He lectures or he shouts." Peter shook his head. "I'm sorry, but I won't be good company tonight."

"That's okay. It's time for me to head home anyway."

"You know you wouldn't have to if…" He glanced at the door leading to the emergency room then shook his head.

"If what?" she urged him.

Peter turned to her. "Nothing. I'm glad you surprised me."

"Me, too," she said, but her tone was sad.

Peter took a deep breath before ringing the doorbell. He rarely visited his father's house and wasn't keen to do so now. His father's housekeeper, Kinsey, answered.

"I'm glad you came by," she said.

Peter stepped in. She closed the door behind him. "What mood is he in?"

"You'll see," she said, taking Peter's coat.

"How's Thomas?"

"He's fine, but the pain medicine makes him drowsy, so he's taking a nap." She suddenly grinned. "He told me he's going to be the best man at your wedding."

Peter pinched the bridge of his nose and groaned. "My brother has a big mouth."

"Your father says he likes your girlfriend, too. When will I get to meet her?"

Peter was saved from answering her question when his father called out to him, "Peter, is that you?"

"Yes," he said then walked into the living room. He

halted and stood paralyzed. "What are you doing?" he asked, watching his father wrap up one of Thomas's science fair trophies. Three cardboard boxes sat at his feet.

Mr. Warren gently placed the trophy in one of the boxes. "Burying my son." His voice cracked, and he cleared his throat then took down a framed photo of Thomas holding the trophy. "Something I should have done a long time ago." He swept his hand over the image.

"You don't have to do this."

"Yes, I do," he said with a sad sigh. His eyes met Peter's. "And I want you to help me if…if you want."

Peter kneeled down and picked up a ribbon his brother had won in a spelling bee. "Sure."

His father was silent a moment then said, "I've been hard on you, and I'm sorry."

"It's okay."

"No, it's not. Your mother and I were unfair to you. You deserved better than that. I hope you'll forgive me."

"Sure," Peter said again, feeling uncomfortable with his father's confession.

"Blaming you felt so much easier than letting go. I wouldn't have seen it if it hadn't been for your girlfriend."

Peter couldn't help but smile. "She can't help analyzing people. She's a psychiatrist. No, psychologist. Actually, she has a medical degree in one and a graduate degree in the other. An overachiever."

"That explains it."

"My complete opposite."

"No, you've achieved a lot of things. I just didn't take

the time to notice." He smoothed down his mustache. "Thomas told me you're planning to marry her."

Peter glanced up at the ceiling with exasperation. "I didn't say—"

"I don't care what you wrote in that book of yours, I'd be honored to have her as a daughter-in-law. She's quite a woman." He patted his son on the shoulder. "You've done well for yourself, and I'm very proud of you."

Peter swallowed hard, fighting back tears. He'd never realized how much he'd wanted his father to say that to him. His gaze fell as he tried to gather control of his emotions.

Mr. Warren saw the effect of his words and decided to change the subject. He pointed to the wall. "You work on those pictures and I'll handle the trophies."

Peter nodded, and together they packed away the past.

Chapter 21

"Claudia, don't look at today's newspaper, watch the news or go online," Suzanne said a week later.

"What?"

"It's only going to upset you."

"What are you talking about?"

"Your affair with Peter is everywhere. There are rumors that you're getting married."

"What!"

"Yes, and pictures, too. Call your publicist right now," her friend said, then hung up.

Claudia did just that and her publicist, Kaneeka Watkins, confirmed her worst fears.

"Someone close to you leaked the story."

"But there's no story to leak. Okay, so we had an affair, that's all."

"That's not all this source said. I don't know who

betrayed you, but I would watch my back if I were you."

"But it's not true."

"Doesn't matter. I heard from the executives, and they're shelving the TV show until this firestorm dies down. We need to do a strategic attack with Peter's people. I'll get back to you."

Claudia searched her mind. Who would want to do this to her? Noreen? Suzanne? Tamara? No. She glanced down and saw Madame Curie licking her paw and suddenly remembered the scratch marks on Tess's arm when she was leaving the apartment. She thought of her missing keys, which Tess returned two days later. Madame Curie getting locked in the bathroom, and Noreen saying things had been fiddled with in her apartment. *You're going to regret this.* Tess must have made a copy of her keys then found Roy's photos in her apartment. Claudia swore. She looked at Madame Curie. "You knew all along, and I didn't listen. It's time to get to the bottom of this." Madame Curie let out a loud, high-pitched meow and then trotted off to her favorite place on the windowsill.

"Where's Tess?"

"She's in her bedroom," Claudia's brother, Chester, said. "What's this about?" he asked when Claudia pushed past him.

"She knows," Claudia said, heading to her niece's room. She flung open the door.

Tess jumped up from her computer. "Damn, don't you know how to knock?"

"Of course I do, but privacy obviously isn't a high priority with you."

Tess sat back at her desk. "I don't know what you're talking about."

Claudia pulled Tess's chair from the desk and wheeled it around. "Sure you do."

Tess folded her arms. "I don't have anything to say."

Chester appeared in the doorway. "What is going on here?"

"You'll find out in a minute."

"You don't have any proof."

Claudia grinned. "So now you know what I'm talking about?"

Tess frowned and looked away.

"I don't care how you leaked the story or why. I'm here to congratulate you on your success."

Tess turned to her, surprised.

Claudia nodded. "Yes, what you've done is impressive, and I've always appreciated a woman who can hold her own, even at my own expense."

Tess looked wary. "You don't mean that."

"Sure I do. A young woman like you giving my publicist a near coronary is not something to be ignored. You wanted to get back at me, and you did. You win. You not only defeated me, but this guy." Claudia held up a picture. "This is Frank Brady. He's the producer of the TV show we just finished filming, and he's worked his butt off these past three months—no, actually an entire year, if you include writing the script—to make the series work." She held up another picture. "This is Eugene Knotts. He has two kids in high school he has to support. He's a widower. His wife died from breast cancer a year ago."

Tess's lip trembled and she turned away.

Claudia turned her head back around. "Don't be shy. This is your time to triumph." She held up Roy's picture. "This is Roy Fitcher. He nearly died taping one of the scenes for the show, and he was just getting back on track after a series of bad projects. And this is Ashley Le Roy. She relocated from Arizona just to get on this project.

"And, of course, there's Peter Warren, who probably won't get a contract for his next book because, thanks to you, he'll be busy defending himself against his critics, who have been waiting like hyenas, ready from the beginning to tear him apart. Congratulations on hurting them all! Of depriving them of the victory they'd worked so hard for. Congratulations on being a selfish, petty, mean-spirited brat."

Tess wiped away a tear. "I knew you'd be angry."

"I'm not angry with you, I'm ashamed of you."

Claudia turned.

"I didn't know," Tess said.

Claudia looked at her.

"I didn't think it was that big of a deal. I was angry at how you embarrassed me when I worked so hard—"

"No, you didn't work hard. My apartment was a mess, you let my plants die and you mistreated Madame Curie."

"I didn't think it would get this far. I'm sorry."

"I forgive you, but unfortunately your apology won't fix anything." She took a step back. "You can throw away the copy of my key you made. I changed the locks." She left the room.

Chester followed her down the stairs. "You didn't need to be that dramatic!"

Claudia shot him a glance. "I guess going through my things is a habit she picked up from you. All those years ago, I never realized you took *everything* out of the apartment I shared with Peter. No wonder he thought I left him. I just wanted you to take a few of my things so he wouldn't think of me too much and have you leave him my note."

"I didn't."

Claudia halted at the front door. "Didn't what?"

"I didn't go. Something else came up and I couldn't make it, so Mom had someone else do it."

"But she told me you did."

He shrugged. "She probably forgot because so much was going on."

"Right," Claudia said softly. *Either that or she lied. But why?*

"It was my niece."

"It was my brother."

"You shouldn't have come here," Claudia said, ushering Peter inside.

"I had to see you," he said, patting Madame Curie when she brushed against his leg. "What were you saying about your niece?"

"You first."

He picked up Madame Curie, who instantly began to purr, and walked over to the couch. "My brother may have told some people at the day center he goes to that I was getting married, and the story spread."

"It wasn't your brother. The idea is too far-fetched. Why would he think we were getting married when he barely knows me?"

Peter stroked Madame Curie. "Well, the thing is—"

"This whole fiasco is my niece's fault," Claudia interrupted.

"Maybe, but there's something you should know. You can't be certain—"

"I am. She admitted it." Claudia told him about her

discussion with Tess. "She's young and spoiled. She apologized, but that doesn't change anything."

He sighed. "I know. Frank told me the show isn't in the fall lineup."

Claudia went over to the large bay window in her dining room and looked out. "It was risky for you to come here." She glanced at him. "If anyone sees us together, it will just fuel the fire."

Peter gestured to the space beside him. "I know. I've thought about that, but I don't care."

Claudia sat down next to him. "You're right. We have to do something about this. This may be the last time we get to see each other for a while and…wait a minute. You don't care? Are you mad?"

"I have the solution." He set Madame Curie down.

"What?" she said with eagerness.

"Marry me."

Claudia laughed. "I'm sorry, but I didn't hear you correctly. I thought I heard you say—" She shook her head. "Never mind. What's your solution?"

"Marry me."

Claudia gaped at him, her voice barely a whisper. "You want me to marry you?"

He nodded.

She jumped to her feet in anger. "No, absolutely not. Why would you even ask that?"

"That's fear talking. Listen to your heart."

Claudia tapped her chest then the side of her head. "My heart and my head say 'this is a bad idea.'"

"It's what we both want to do," he said quietly.

"No, it's not. We're happily single. That's our brand. That's everything."

"No, it's not everything."

"Our reputations, our source of income, our very livelihood doesn't mean anything to you?"

"No."

"Oh, I forgot. You don't need the extra money," she sneered. "Peter, this isn't like what happened when you kissed me on the set in front of everyone. I'm not going to be one of your women."

His jaw twitched and he glanced away.

Claudia noticed his tension and hugged herself. "I apologize. That wasn't fair."

Peter stood and reached for her arms. "You were willing to marry me once."

Claudia drew away from him, determined not to weaken. "That was a long time ago." She held up her hands before he could speak. "I cannot risk all that I've struggled to build—"

"What you've built is a lie."

She lifted her chin. "It is not a lie."

"Really? Then why haven't you admitted in any of your books or articles that you were about to get married once? Did you ever tell your family what we'd planned to do in Las Vegas? Do any of your current friends know about me? Why must I be kept a secret?

"I don't know about you, but I don't want to live like a fraud anymore, no matter how much it costs. The money, the fame, the women don't matter when my life feels meaningless. I want to talk about what's important to me. Fighting for my brother's rights. Being with a woman I care about. The rest can go to… Don't you see we may lose some things, but we'll gain much more—each other."

"There are women out there who depend on me. If I marry you, it will be like I betrayed them. I can't let them down."

"Women like your mother?"

Claudia's gaze drifted away, and she moved her shoulders in a restless motion. "My mother has nothing to do with this. I'm a symbol of independence."

"Maybe that's the problem. You think of yourself as a thing—a symbol, a brand, a marketing object. You're a woman first, Claudia, with the right to change your mind and have your own hopes and desires." His eyes searched her face. He lowered his voice, which cascaded over her like velvet. "I'm not asking you to marry me to make a statement or prove a point."

"Then why?" she demanded.

Peter shook his head in disbelief. "In case you haven't noticed, I'm in love with you."

Claudia lowered her gaze, unable to face him. "If you truly loved me, you wouldn't ask me to do this."

Peter was silent for so long that Claudia had to look at him. She saw the pain in his eyes. "Somehow I'd thought you'd say you loved me, too," he said.

"I do love you," Claudia said, a cold knot forming in her stomach. "I just can't marry you. The woman who was willing to run off on an impulse died in the accident. I can't bring her back. I can't give up the life I've built for myself."

"I wasn't asking you to give up your life. I was asking to share it with you." Peter walked to the door. "At least this time is different."

Claudia blinked back tears but kept her voice steady. "Different?"

"Yes. This time we get to say goodbye." He moved in and tenderly touched her face. "Goodbye, Claudia," he said then walked out of her life.

Chapter 22

Traveling Single was a ratings success. Claudia didn't watch it. She couldn't. At first she'd been happy that her separation with Peter had squashed the rumors and allayed the fears of the executives, who then decided to put the series back in. But now all that success felt empty. The TV show had increased her fame and she'd received a lucrative two-book contract, fan mail from women all around the world and a cable talk show developed just for her.

Claudia sat in her home office with Madame Curie dozing in her lap, as a light November rain tapped on the window. She opened a magazine that was sitting on a side table and saw a recipe for a lemon meringue pie and thought of Thomas. She wondered if his father had given him more freedom, but most of all she kept thinking about Peter. He had disappeared from sight. He'd resigned from his radio show, and his publicist had made an announcement in a recent online feature that he was working on several independent projects and going in a totally different direction. To continue the *Traveling Single* series, executives had scoured the country looking for a replacement. But no one had the chemistry she'd had with Peter, so she bowed out and didn't renew her contract.

"You turned him down, didn't you?" Noreen said when Claudia told her about the search for a new cohost. They sat in Noreen's home office.

Claudia stared at her friend, amazed by her perception. "How did you—"

Noreen shook her head, her smile a little sad. "Claudia, it was written all over his face how much he loved you."

Claudia let her gaze fall. "You think I've made a mistake."

"It's not about what I think."

"Noreen?" Michael called from another room. "Do you know where my gray shoes are?"

Noreen briefly glanced at the ceiling in exasperation. "That man and his shoes."

Claudia grinned at her friend's annoyance. "I bet you're happy he's back safe and sound."

Noreen returned her smile. "Absolutely." She stood. "I'll be back in a minute."

After Noreen left, Claudia walked around her friend's office, letting her gaze sweep over the framed book covers of Noreen's romance novels. Claudia thought the embracing couples were cheesy. But that hadn't stopped her from reading every one, because the stories went beyond salacious sex, handsome men and beautiful women. They were stories about relationships and lasting love and happy endings. She was glad Noreen was living her own now.

She thought about Suzanne in her grand house with Rick and Luke, and soon Noreen and Michael would escape to their island getaway for the winter. Her friends were building new lives without her.

Claudia picked up a picture of Noreen's island retreat and turned it over. Written in Michael's handwriting was a message that read, "For my Angel." She couldn't help but smile at the extravagant gift he'd given her friend.

"You're welcome to visit any time," a male voice said behind her.

Claudia jumped and spun around. "Oh, I didn't mean—" She quickly returned the picture to its rightful place. "I wasn't prying."

Michael shrugged, unconcerned. "I didn't think you were."

Claudia liked Michael, but she felt like a child caught by the principal and she didn't know what to say to him. "Did you have a good trip?" she finally managed.

"Yes, thanks," he said with an easy smile that made Claudia relax. "It will make a great story."

"Noreen was worried about you."

Michael ran a hand down his face and groaned. "I know. I'm still getting used to having someone worry about me." He shoved a hand in his pocket then studied Claudia a moment. "You know, I never thought I'd get married. I'm older than your man Warren, so I could have given him a few tips of my own—and you, too."

Claudia toyed with her necklace and narrowed her eyes in a teasing glare. "Did Noreen put you up to this?"

"No," Michael said, but he nodded "yes" and gestured to the door, where Noreen was likely listening in.

Claudia covered her mouth to keep from laughing.

Michael's eyes sparkled with humor then just as quickly grew serious. "You know her. She worries about everyone she cares about. In the end, she just wants you to be happy. Really happy."

Happy, Claudia said, recalling his words as she gazed at the recipe. Sometimes happiness had a high price.

A knock on the door awoke her from her thoughts, and someone called out, "Claudia, it's me."

She sighed, recognizing Tamara's voice. She wasn't in the mood for visitors, but saying no to Tamara was never a choice. She opened the door to find Tamara grinning and holding up a bottle of champagne. "I'm here to celebrate."

"What?"

"You and all you've accomplished." Tamara waltzed past Claudia and went into the kitchen. "After only four episodes, your show has everyone buzzing. Have you seen it yet?"

"No, I don't need to."

Tamara took down two long-stemmed glasses from one of the overhead cabinets. "I don't blame you. Working with Peter must have been enough of a stress. I'm so glad your publicist was able to clear up that awful gossip about you two. For a minute, I was scared you would have to end another love affair, like you said in your letter."

Claudia paused. "I never wrote that."

Tamara popped the cork. "You didn't? Oh, I must have just thought it then." She poured the champagne into the two glasses.

"Funny, because that's what Peter said I wrote,"

Claudia said, choosing her words carefully. "I just thought it was his dyslexia."

"It probably was. You know there's no cure, right?"

"But maybe the mistake wasn't his," Claudia said, putting together a story she didn't want to believe. "I could understand him not understanding the reference, but you knew *Love Affair* was my favorite movie. I remember when I was in the hospital, my mother wanted to get in touch with him and you offered to help. I dictated my letter to you, but you never let me see it."

Tamara handed her a glass then walked into the living room and sat down on the couch. "You had so much on your mind and besides, you were recovering from your injuries and I was taking care of things for you. I doubt you can even fathom all that needed to be done."

Claudia sat in front of her. "Like getting rid of Peter?"

Tamara leveled Claudia with a look. "Are you accusing me of something?"

"*You* were the one who cleared my things out of his apartment, just the way you cleared my things out of yours. You wanted me out of his life."

Tamara sipped her drink.

"My parents didn't know about the fight I had with you. They still thought you were my dearest friend so you were the one my mother called when I ended up in the hospital. And when you came running, I was grateful."

Tamara took a sip of her drink. "I was there for you." She set the glass down. "I listened to you go on and on about Peter and how wonderful he was, even though you'd stolen him from me. I never said a word."

"I always thought it so admirable of you to forget

our last fight and forgive me for what you'd thought I'd done. But you never did, did you?"

Tamara crossed her legs. "I did. At least at first, but when you told me what you'd been planning to do in Las Vegas, I lost it." She toyed with the large ring on her finger, her eyes dark. "I could take you dating him and sleeping with him, but the thought of you marrying the man *I* should have married made me sick. I couldn't stand it. So I switched some words around." She leaned back, unrepentant. "Besides, if he'd really cared and loved you so much, he would have called you. He didn't even try. Luckily, you found out the kind of man he really was."

"Because he didn't know," Claudia said. "He told me if he had known, he would have married me right there in the hospital."

Tamara sniffed. "He's just telling you what you want to hear."

"Were you ever going to tell me?"

Tamara stayed stubbornly silent.

Claudia sat back, stung. "You married a man who adores you and you've gotten all that you want, and you didn't feel the slightest guilt—"

"Guilt?" Tamara's lip curled with a sneer. "What do I have to feel guilty about? You've had a great life. You've had plenty of men who've adored you. What do you need a husband for? Don't blame me for what happened between you and Peter. If you'd really wanted him, you could have told him the truth instead of making us all part of your stupid deception. But you were afraid. Even back then the thought of marriage frightened you."

Claudia shook her head. "That's not true."

"Really? Then why didn't you tell him about your accident?"

"I didn't because—"

"Because you didn't want to stop his success?" Tamara scoffed. "You had a gorgeous, rich man ready to give up everything for you, and you didn't tell him because you cared too much about him?"

"I was afraid he might have rejected me."

Tamara waved her finger. "I don't think so. You were stalling. You barely knew him six months and you were scared of making that commitment. You were afraid that you'd end up in an unhappy marriage like your mother did. And that you would destroy all the hopes your parents had put in you."

Claudia turned away. "It wasn't like that."

"I did you a favor. I got him out of your life, helped you get over him and then helped you write your way to this life." Tamara gestured at Claudia's large and expensive condominium and all of the custom-designed furniture. "You don't need marriage, Claudia." She lifted the glass again as though in toast. "Millions of women agree."

Claudia stared at her friend, unable to speak. *You're just a symbol.* Peter was right. She'd become a prisoner of her own propaganda. Claudia, the free-spirited one. Claudia, the achiever. But she was also Claudia, the woman who had the freedom to make a choice. *Whatever he asks of you, say yes,* Noreen had said without judgment. Her friend knew the desire of her heart, a desire that she'd been too afraid to see for herself. She looked at the recipe for the lemon meringue pie. "That's the trouble. I'm tired of living for millions. I just want to live for me."

"He's gone," Frank said when Claudia called him after being unable to reach Peter for three days.

"Gone?"

"Yes. He does that sometimes. He'll resurface in a month or two."

"A month?" Claudia repeated, feeling like a puppet.

Frank sensed the desolation in Claudia's voice and added, "His father might know where he is."

"Thanks." She hung up then quickly called Mr. Warren, but got his answering machine instead. She began to leave a message then stopped and disconnected. Claudia sunk into her chair and rested her head back. Peter was probably in some foreign clime enjoying the attention of attractive women in skimpy skirts. He never had to be alone if he didn't want to.

Claudia tossed her phone aside, depressed by the thought. Perhaps this was a sign that she should leave him. Maybe he wouldn't want to see her. She should let things be. No. She sat up. That defeatist attitude had gotten her into trouble all those years ago. Even if he'd changed his mind, at least she would know and wouldn't have to speculate.

She stood and paced as a wild idea formed in her mind. Maybe they'd just gone out. Suddenly she wanted to be with them, because they were a part of him. She packed up a few things and Madame Curie and said, "Let's go for a drive."

Hours later Claudia stared at Mr. Warren's dark house. Frank had given her his address. She rang the bell, hoping someone was home. No answer. She returned to her car, defeated, and sat in the driveway. Her mother was right. Reason was always better than emotion, and she'd just made a fool of herself. Worn and depressed, she closed her eyes.

She woke to the sound of someone tapping on her window and jumped when she saw a man's face pressed against the frosted glass until she recognized it as Peter's. She rolled down the window. "Hi."

He frowned. "What are you doing?"

"I came to see your father and Thomas, but no one was home."

"They're on a trip. I'm looking after the house. Come on in, it's freezing out here," he said, his tone just as cold. He turned and walked to the front door.

Claudia took Madame Curie's carrier and got out of the car then rushed up to him. She grabbed his arm before he walked inside. "I lied."

"What?"

She set the carrier down. "Frank told me you were away for a month or two, and that bothered me so much that I thought being with your family would be close to being with you." She hurried on before he could interrupt. "Over these past few months I've realized that you've never needed me to be anyone but myself. Then when I spoke to Tamara and found out what she'd done—"

"Tamara? You still know her?"

"Yes, she was there for me after the accident."

"What did she do?"

Claudia took a deep breath. "She's the one who took all of my things from your place. She wanted you to believe that I'd left you. And you didn't misread my letter. She changed it. So it wasn't your fault. She told me the whole story and I got the rest from my mother, who admitted that she'd lied to me because she didn't want me to get married."

Peter's face hardened with anger. "You mean they deliberately kept us apart?"

"You know how my mother is, and Tamara couldn't imagine us getting married. But it's not all her fault. I—"

"Dammit." Peter spun away and pounded the front door with both of his fists. "I could break her—"

"She's not worth it. Besides, I'm to blame."

Peter turned to her. "What do you mean?"

Claudia took a steadying breath. "I made a decision for you that wasn't mine to make." She briefly glanced down, his intense gaze too much to bear. "I should have told you the truth." She raised her eyes to his. "Can you forgive me?"

"You know I do. Come on. It's cold." He walked to the door.

Claudia rubbed her hands together, feeling the cold air seeping through her gloves. "I'm not really asking you to forgive me. I'm asking you to marry me."

Peter halted.

Claudia swallowed and stared at his still form, determined not to lose courage. "I want to share my life with you if you'll—"

Her last words were smothered by his lips. When he finally drew away, her heart was filled with so much joy and love that she laughed. "We're going to surprise a lot of people."

"I don't care," he said, his eyes dancing with humor. "We'll have a big wedding. If we're going to do this, we might as well do it in style."

"Sounds like fun."

Peter took out his keys and opened the door then picked up the carrier. "Now let me get you inside before you freeze," he said, and they entered the dark foyer.

"Let me go turn on the lights," Peter said, putting the carrier down in the foyer.

Claudia held him still. "No, just wait." She took a step forward and searched the darkness, surprised she didn't feel a knot of anxiety or tug of fear. Instead, she felt a warm sensation flow through her. She felt calm, and everything felt right. Her decision to be with Peter and their future ahead. She laughed in surprise. "At last, I'm no longer afraid."

Noreen Vaughn and Suzanne Gordon couldn't believe the envelope that arrived in the mail.

"I can't believe this is really happening," Suzanne said when she spoke to Noreen over the phone. "But I just got the wedding invitation."

"Me, too," Noreen said, tracing the elegant silver windswept style. "She's having the biggest wedding of all of us."

"In a French castle, no less. Of all of us, I can't believe she's getting married like this."

"She never does anything halfway. Did you see the note?"

"I'm looking at it now," Suzanne said then read the note attached.

Dear Suzanne and Noreen,
As you can see, Peter and I are getting married. I know it seems crazy, but at last I'm willing to take the risk. As someone once said, *Success in marriage is much more than finding the right person; it is being the right person.*

I've finally become the woman I want to be. I know that love needs to be tended, troubles need to be shared and trust needs to be given. Marriage may be the end of one adventure, but I'm ready for the new one and what's in store.
    Love,
    Claudia

* * * * *

REQUEST YOUR FREE BOOKS!

2 FREE NOVELS PLUS 2 FREE GIFTS!

KIMANI ROMANCE ™

Love's ultimate destination!

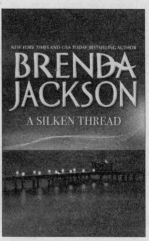

Jude asked. "You already owned the ranch, so what was your reason for going after me? Did you think you could use that hot body of yours to control me? Well, here's your chance. Try it now that I know what you are and what you want!"

"You don't know one single thing about me, Jude Emory!" Margret lashed out at him. "I had no idea that I was going to be left the Double Diamond!"

His expression showed no signs of softening. "Somehow, I find that hard to believe."

She glared up at him. "What's the difference, anyway? You're going to think the worst of me, no matter what I say."

"You're darned right I am," he flashed back. "I have thirty-three years' worth of blood and sweat invested in this place, and I don't intend to let you steal it from me."

Dear Reader,

It's May—spring gardens are in full bloom, and in the spirit of the season, we've gathered a special "bouquet" of Silhouette Romance novels for you this month.

Whatever the season, Silhouette Romance novels *always* capture the magic of love with compelling stories that will make you laugh and cry; stories that will move you with the wonder of romance, time and again.

This month, we continue our FABULOUS FATHERS series with Melodie Adams's heartwarming novel, *What About Charlie?* Clint Blackwell might be the local hero when it comes to handling troubled boys, but he never met a rascal like six-year-old Charlie Whitney. And he never met a woman like Charlie's lovely mother, Candace, who stirs up trouble of a different kind in the rugged cowboy's heart.

With drama and emotion, Moyra Tarling takes us to the darker side of love in *Just a Memory Away.* After a serious accident, Alison Montgomery is unable to remember her past. She struggles to learn the truth about her handsome husband, Nick, and a secret about their marriage that might be better left forgotten.

There's a passionate battle of wills brewing in Joleen Daniels's *Inheritance.* The way Jude Emory sees it, beautiful Margret Brolin has stolen the land and inheritance that is rightfully his. How could a man as proud as Jude let her steal his heart as well?

Please join us in welcoming new author Lauryn Chandler who debuts this month with a lighthearted love story, *Mr. Wright.* We're also proud to present *Can't Buy Me Love* by Joan Smith and *Wrangler* by Dorsey Kelley.

In the months to come, watch for books by more of your favorites—Diana Palmer, Suzanne Carey, Elizabeth August, Marie Ferrarella and many more. At Silhouette, we're dedicated to bringing you the love stories you love to read. Our authors and editors want to hear from you. Please write to us; we take our reader comments to heart.

Happy reading!

Anne Canadeo
Senior Editor

INHERITANCE
Joleen Daniels

Silhouette
ROMANCE™
Published by Silhouette Books New York
America's Publisher of Contemporary Romance

To Lynn Byer and Judy Jacobs, who took time out of
their busy schedules to answer my questions;
To Linda Reiling and Brenda Parks
for putting up with me for so long;
And to Joel Schimek because I love him.

SILHOUETTE BOOKS
300 East 42nd St., New York, N.Y. 10017

INHERITANCE

Copyright © 1993 by Gayle Malone Schimek

All rights reserved. Except for use in any review, the reproduction or utilization of this work in whole or in part in any form by any electronic, mechanical or other means, now known or hereafter invented, including xerography, photocopying and recording, or in any information storage or retrieval system, is forbidden without the permission of the publisher, Silhouette Books, 300 E. 42nd St., New York, N.Y. 10017

ISBN: 0-373-08939-2

First Silhouette Books printing May 1993

All the characters in this book have no existence outside the imagination of the author and have no relation whatsoever to anyone bearing the same name or names. They are not even distantly inspired by any individual known or unknown to the author, and all incidents are pure invention.

®: Trademark used under license and registered in the United States Patent and Trademark Office and in other countries.

Printed in the U.S.A.

Books by Joleen Daniels

Silhouette Romance

The Ideal Wife #891
Inheritance #939

Silhouette Special Edition

The Reckoning #507
Against All Odds #645

JOLEEN DANIELS

lives in Miami, Florida, where she tries to juggle a full-time job, a part-time writing career, an unmanageable husband and two demanding children. Her hobbies include housework and complaining to her friends.

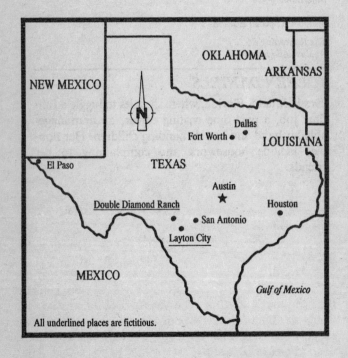

NEW MEXICO

OKLAHOMA

ARKANSAS

El Paso

TEXAS

Dallas

Fort Worth

LOUISIANA

Austin

Double Diamond Ranch

Houston

San Antonio

Layton City

MEXICO

Gulf of Mexico

All underlined places are fictitious.

Chapter One

Margret Brolin's head hurt, and she was colder than she'd ever been before in her life. She groaned and tried to roll over, one hand fumbling for the elusive bedcovers. Then she felt something wet lapping at her ear. Her eyes snapped open to focus on the gloomy interior of the car. What she saw there make her heart lurch in terror. She was in water up to her neck!

A wave of blind panic threatened to overwhelm her, but she fought it down by sheer effort of will. Slowly she lifted her head and looked out the window, dreading what she would see. But the water level outside and inside the car was roughly the same. Her worst fear was unfounded: the car wasn't underwater, yet.

Then she noticed that the passenger door was open, and a series of images flashed through her brain: the sound of the tire exploding, her head striking the windshield, the icy water pouring in as the car plunged into the creek. Her consciousness fading even as she fumbled the gearshift into park and told Todd to go get help. Please, God, let her son be safe!

She was twisting around to look out the back window, when a sharp stab of pain from her left foot made her gasp. Bending beneath the water, she let her hand slide down her leg. Her fingers encountered a piece of metal at ankle level. Gingerly, and then more forcefully, she tried to shift it, but it refused to budge.

Margret surfaced, wiping frigid water droplets from her face with a shaking hand. Panic tried to claim her again as she realized the gravity of her situation. She was caught like an animal in a trap, and there was no way she could free herself. No passing motorist was going to come to her aid—the creek wasn't visible from the road. Her only hope of rescue was a seven-year-old boy who wasn't allowed to walk to school by himself.

At the thought of a cold, scared Todd wandering around in the fast-approaching darkness, she nearly sobbed aloud. What if he hadn't even gotten as far as the creek bank?

She squeezed shut her eyes and clenched her fists so hard that her nails dug into the palms of her hands. Somehow the pain seemed to steady her. She had to think positively. She had to hang on.

Her characteristic optimism had almost reasserted itself when there was a flash of lightning and a crack of thunder. The sky seemed to open up, and the rain changed from a trickle to a deluge. As full darkness fell, the water around her gradually began to rise.

Margret stared unseeingly at the fractured windshield as the numbing effect of the frigid water spread from her body to her spirit. Was this it then? Was this how her life was going to end?

Once more her thoughts turned to Todd. If she drowned in this godforsaken Texas creek, there would be no one to take care of him. She'd been twelve years old when her own parents had been killed, and she'd grown up in a series of foster homes without ever having a family of her own. Now her son was being condemned to the same fate. It just wasn't fair!

Suddenly she heard a noise that was louder than the rain. It sounded like . . . like a man's voice shouting above the wind!

Margret hastily rolled down her window, praying that the voice wasn't just some illusion born of her own desperation.

She heard splashing sounds, then a string of angry curses directed at the freezing water of the creek. They were followed by a single, terse question. "Is anyone in the damned car?"

A sob of relief escaped Margret's throat, and she raised her chin out of the water. "I'm here!" she yelled as loudly as she could. "My foot's caught. I can't get out!"

There was a moment of silence as if the speaker hadn't really expected anyone to respond to his question. When he spoke again, his tone was almost gentle. "Okay, lady. You just take it easy now. I'm on my way."

She heard more splashing, and then a man materialized from behind the curtain of rain outside her window. She could tell that he was wearing a wide-brimmed Stetson, but it was too dark for her to be able to make out his features.

The creek surged around his waist as he bent to peer inside the car. "Are you alone in there? Did anyone go for help?"

"Todd . . . my little boy. You must have passed him on the road!"

She could hear the desperate insistence in her own voice. Logic told her that if this man had found her son, Todd would have been with him still. Emotionally, she clung to the hope that it was Todd who had told the cowboy where to find her.

Jude Emory wished that he could see the woman's face. She sounded as if she was on the edge of losing control. And the last thing he wanted to deal with was some hysterical female. It would probably be better to let her think her son was safe—at least until he could get her out of the car. But then he remembered how it felt to trust and be betrayed. The lie died on his lips.

"I didn't see a soul," he told her gruffly. "Just your car sticking up out of the creek. And even that was pure luck in this storm."

What little warmth Margret had left seemed to seep out of her body into the chill water surrounding her. The thought of her son out lost in the storm was almost more than she could bear.

"Listen, lady... what's your name, anyway?"

"Margret... Margret Brolin."

"Well, listen, Maggie, my brother has been riding in this area all afternoon. He was supposed to meet me by the creek at sunset. It's well after that time, and he's still not here—probably because he picked your kid up and needed to get him back to the house as soon as possible."

His use of her childhood nickname might have coaxed a smile out of Margret under better circumstances. Now all her thoughts were focused on Todd. She stared up at the cowboy's shadowy figure, wishing for just a glimmer of light so that she could read the expression in his eyes. His tone was low and controlled, his voice a reassuring lifeline in the darkness. She wanted very badly to believe what he was telling her, but she just wasn't convinced.

"You can't be sure that my son was found by anyone."

He didn't move or speak for several seconds. When he finally replied, his voice was intense. He leaned so close that a drop of rain slid from the dripping brim of his Stetson onto her upturned face. "Bottom line, Maggie. If I don't get you out of there soon, you're either going to drown or freeze to death. Your little boy's probably safe in a warm bed already. The best thing you can do for him right now is to take care of yourself."

Margret considered his words, and then put them aside. She grabbed his hand with nerveless fingers, her voice pleading. "Please, you have to look! I have to be sure!"

Jude had to force himself not to jerk away from her touch. He was cold, but she felt like a living ice sculpture. Cradling her smaller hand between both of his, he noted the softness of her skin, the delicacy of her bone structure. Her inner strength wasn't as tangible, but he recognized it just the same. "I'll look for him," he told her grudgingly. "*After* I get you out of there."

Margret accepted the compromise, knowing that there was no way she could force him to do her bidding. "Then hurry! You've got to hurry...."

Jude already knew he had to hurry—for her sake as well as her son's. She couldn't last much longer now that the temperature had dropped.

Reluctantly he released her hand, hiding his concern behind a smoke screen of annoyance. "Hold your horses, lady. This isn't something that can be done in a New York minute. I need to find out what's got ahold of you."

He opened her door and, muttering fiercely under his breath, sank into the water until he was submerged up to his shoulders.

Although Margret would have sworn that every nerve had been deadened by the cold, she jumped at the sensation her rescuer's lightly callused palm created as it moved down the length of her bare leg.

"Easy, Maggie," he murmured, his hands and his voice touching her gently. "Just take it easy. I'm not going to hurt you."

His comforting tone brought an unexpected lump to her throat. She'd been the recipient of too little no-strings-attached kindnesses in her life to remain unaffected when she did happen to encounter one. Her thoughts were interrupted when he spoke again.

"You're wedged in there pretty tight. Is your foot giving you any pain?"

Margret shook her head, then realized that he probably couldn't see the gesture. "No," she said aloud. "It only hurts when I try to pull free."

He grunted a noncommittal response and squeezed her knee reassuringly before moving away. "I don't know if I can haul your car out of here with just a horse and a rope, but there's no time for me to get more help. When I sing out, you put her in neutral and make sure the emergency brake is off. Can you do that?"

Margret took a deep breath and willed herself to answer in a steady voice. "Of course I can."

"Good."

She felt the brief caress of his hand on her cheek and the words seemed to rush out of her. "Tell me your name."

"What?"

Before she put her life into this man's hands, it seemed important that she know at least that much about him. "Please, could you tell me your name?"

"Emory," he said, his tone one of amused tolerance. "Jude Emory."

He turned and walked away, and she had to bite back a protest. She knew the feeling of abandonment that settled over her was foolish, but she couldn't seem to shake it. Anxiously she waited for his signal. Then, suddenly, it came.

"Now, Maggie!"

Obediently Margret shoved the car into neutral. To her horror, the vehicle began to roll forward.

"Jude!" Even as she screamed his name in an agony of fear and betrayed trust, the rope snapped taut and the car came to a tenuous halt.

"Hold on, Maggie! Just hold on!"

She heard him urging his horse forward, but still the car remained stationary. After a moment he called to her once more. "Set the brake."

There were more splashing sounds, then Jude was at her window again. "I'm afraid to put any more strain on that rope, Maggie. I'm going to try to push her out. Zack ought to be some help even without me in the saddle—he's trained to pull back on a rope if it goes slack."

"And if he doesn't?" Margret asked, picturing Jude pinned beneath her car.

"Then I'll just have to push harder," he answered after a pause that stretched out a beat too long to be considered comfortable.

Before Margret could formulate any more objections, Jude was gone. Seconds later she heard his shout above the wind. "Let her go!"

With a silent prayer, Margret released the brake. She braced herself for the inevitable lurch forward. When it didn't come, she knew that she had Jude to thank.

For one heart-stopping second, the car remained motionless. Then slowly but surely it began to move backward.

When it gained purchase on a higher section of the streambed and the water receded to waist level, Margret expelled the breath she'd been holding in a whoop of triumph. A moment later the car was once again on dry land, and she hastily rammed it into park. Then she leaned her head against the headrest, closed her eyes, and drew in a deep lungful of cold night air.

"We did it, Maggie! Damned if we didn't do it!"

The door opened again, and Margret saw Jude's indistinct form bending close to her. Without stopping to think about her action, she threw her arms around him and hugged him tightly. "Thank you," she whispered.

In the almost total darkness, her sense of touch came into full play. She felt the slightly abrading texture of new beard stubble against her cheek and reveled in the rough sensation, overjoyed that she was still alive and able to experience it. Her hands, shaking with cold, reached his back, and she traced the hard contours of his muscles through the barrier of sodden cloth.

After an initial start of surprise, she felt his hands touching her in return, rubbing her shivering shoulders with firm circular motions. He drew her even closer, and the heat from his body seeped through their wet clothing to touch her with a warmth that seemed to burn to the depth of her being.

Then his fingers closed around her upper arms, and he gently set her away from him. "Let me get you out of there, Maggie—before we both catch our deaths."

The last thing she wanted was to leave the warm haven of those arms, but she was forced to yield to the logic of the situation. Feeling bereft, she handed him her car keys and listened as he rummaged in the trunk.

As she sat there cold and alone, waiting for him to return, she began to wonder how she had become so emotionally dependent on this man so quickly. She had always considered herself to be a self-sufficient woman, yet ever since the cowboy had arrived on the scene she'd been acting like the proverbial clinging vine. She was out of danger now, so why couldn't she shake the feeling of utter vulnerability that had been haunting her since she'd regained consciousness?

"Here, put this on."

Margret reacted to the sound of Jude's voice with a rush of relief that only deepened her dismay. He pulled her forward and helped her into a large, heavy jacket. It was nearly as wet as her own clothing, but it was one more barrier between her and the wind.

"But—" she began to protest as she realized he was giving up his own jacket for her.

"You need it more than I do right now," he said simply.

Tears of gratitude welled up in her eyes, and she knew then how shaky her emotional state really was. With a resigned sigh, she forced herself to concentrate on separating Jude's words from the sounds of the raging storm.

"All I could find in your trunk were a couple of waterlogged suitcases and a tire iron. I'm going to see if I can use the iron to pry you loose."

He went down on one knee beside the car, and Margret shivered involuntarily as his fingers explored the metal and flesh that were so closely entwined.

"Let me know if I hurt you."

She heard a scraping sound as he wedged the tire iron between the frame of the car and the protruding metal that held her captive. But all she felt was the miserable cold.

There was a grunt of effort as Jude pushed down on the iron, and a curse when it slipped from his grasp and fell to the muddy ground. "Hell and damnation!"

Margret wiggled her foot experimentally and surprised herself by pulling it free. "It worked!" she exclaimed in astonishment. "Jude, it worked!"

Overjoyed at her sudden liberation, Margret swung her feet to the ground and tried to stand. She felt a sudden, sharp pain an instant before her ankle gave under the strain. She would have fallen if Jude hadn't caught her and lifted her into his arms.

Somehow he had expected her to have a pencil-thin body that was all jutting angles. Instead he was pleasantly surprised to find softly rounded flesh beneath his hands. Yet she was light enough that he could carry her easily. He decided that this was one woman he enjoyed having in his arms—even with a freezing rain pouring down on him.

He found himself wondering what color hair and eyes she had, what her face looked like. Then he dismissed the speculation from his mind. The few women that he had known since Anne had been only warm bodies to him. He couldn't clearly recall a single face or even one last name. And that was exactly how he wanted it. Besides, this one wouldn't be around long enough for it to make any difference to him whether she looked good with the lights on or not.

Margret began to shudder in the cold wind and rain. "I c-can walk," she told him, her teeth chattering. "You don't have to c-carry me like a b-baby!"

"It's quicker this way," Jude informed her without slowing his stride.

Unable to argue with his reasoning, Margret let her pride die a quiet death. Despite the jacket, her wet clothes felt like a layer of ice against her body. By the time they'd covered the short distance to where Zack stood patiently waiting, she was so miserable that it no longer seemed important who carried whom as long as they got where they were going.

Jude pushed her up to sit sideways in the saddle, and she groaned as she discovered that it was even colder without his body shielding hers. How must he be feeling with nothing between him and the storm but a thin, wet shirt?

Before she could change her mind, Margret slipped out of his coat.

"What do you think you're doing?" he demanded as he swung up behind her.

"P-put it on, and I'll show you." When he had obeyed her instructions, she half turned and huddled against him, shivering uncontrollably. Quickly getting the idea, he wrapped both the flaps of the coat and his arms around her. Hunching his larger body over hers, he gave her all the protection he could.

Pressed against her rescuer, Margret couldn't help but notice the solid feel of his broad, masculine chest and the crinkly hair that rose up above the top button of his shirt to tickle her nearly numb nose. Fleetingly, she wondered what color it was.

Then she heard the horse's hooves strike the asphalt of the road, and the course of her thoughts shifted abruptly. Reluctantly she turned her face into the biting wind and began to call Todd's name.

They rode on through the driving rain until Margret's voice grew hoarse from her efforts. But there was no response.

"You rest, Maggie," Jude ordered finally. "I'll take over for a while."

He guided her head back to its former resting place. Cursing her weakness, she allowed him to. She felt the vibrations of his throat as he called out her son's name, and she burrowed even closer against his neck. She was still so cold that she couldn't stop shaking. And she was so tired. If only she could sleep—just for a few minutes. Slowly she let her eyes drift shut.

"Wake up, Maggie. We're here."

Margret pulled her face away from the sanctuary of Jude's chest and squinted at the dark, deserted-looking cabin in front of them. She felt like sobbing in relief at the prospect of food, warmth and shelter. But then she realized that something was wrong. "Todd! What about Todd?" she demanded as Jude dismounted.

His hands reached up and settled on either side of her waist. "I covered as much of the road as I could, Maggie. The ranch house is the nearest place with a phone, and even that's too far for us to go in this storm. Now, come on. We've got to get inside."

Her son was in danger, and this man wasn't going to do anything to help him! It was in her mind to fight free of his grasp and ride away to continue the search on her own. But she found that she was now so weak she could hardly sit up without his support. When he tugged on her waist, she fell out of the saddle. He staggered under the impact as he caught her in his arms, and she realized that he was close to exhaustion himself.

"No!" She wanted to grab him and shake him, to make him listen to her. But all she managed to do was grasp the flaps of his jacket with about as much force as a week-old kitten. Her head sagged against his shoulder in a temporary admission of defeat.

Jude kicked open the cabin door, venting some of his own frustration. A few steps inside the dark interior, he deposited his shivering burden on the foot of a narrow bed. "Maggie, there's no electricity or heat in here. You've got to take those wet clothes off."

"I've got to find Todd!"

Her voice was barely audible, but her words ignited his anger. "Lady, I tried."

"If anything happens to him . . . Oh, God, I'll blame myself forever!"

For Jude, her words revived old accusations, old guilts. Memories that were better left undisturbed. Silently cursing himself for getting involved with the woman in the first place, he grasped her arms and hauled her up to a sitting position.

Leaning her against his shoulder, he began pulling her dress up with both hands. She tried to prevent it. Her efforts depleted the last remnants of his control.

"Stop that right now!" he hissed in her ear. "Or, so help me, I'll leave these on you and let you freeze!"

With a surge of energy Margret hadn't known she possessed, she pushed his hands away and stood up. She took one step forward and promptly collapsed in a heap on the floor.

Swearing profusely, Jude expended most of his rapidly dwindling strength getting her back up on the bed.

Margret lay limply against his chest, no longer capable of either resistance or cooperation.

Peeling her dress over her head, Jude threw it to the floor. He tried repeatedly to open the fastener of her brassiere with fingers that were almost totally numb. Finally he gave up the effort and tore the annoying garment apart. In the process, his hand accidentally brushed the tip of one breast.

To Margret the contact was not only shocking, she was so stiff with cold that it was actually painful. She gasped softly.

That small sound of distress defused Jude's anger abruptly. Muttering an apology, he laid her down on the bed and carefully stripped away her underpants. Then he retrieved a blanket and a heavy quilt from a nearby chest.

Margret sighed as she felt the blissful warmth of the thick covers spread over her. But she couldn't stop thinking about her son. He might be without even this amount of comfort.

A callused hand stroked her cheek, and Jude's voice came out of the darkness. "I'll get a fire started, and then I'll try to make it to the ranch house. If Todd's not there, I'll call the sheriff. But you, lady, are going to stay right here in this bed."

Any resentment Maggie may have felt at that order was canceled out by the other words he'd said. "You're going back out?" she gasped, struggling to a sitting position. "But you're just as cold and tired as I am!"

"Worried about me, Maggie? I appreciate your concern, but you can't have it both ways." He paused while she pondered that thought. "Is there anyone else I should call? Parents? Husband?"

"No, my husband's dead. Todd's the only family I have left."

"Sorry to hear that," Jude told her with polite insincerity. He realized with mild surprise that his rescue of this woman had left him feeling strangely possessive. Somehow he didn't like the thought of her belonging to some other man.

Maggie felt his weight lift off the bed and heard his footsteps as he walked away from her. There was the dull clunk of wood, the crumpling of paper, and then the sound of a match striking. Suddenly she could see water dripping from the leaking roof and the indistinct silhouette of a man squatting in front of a brick fireplace.

"Well, I'll be damned."

The softly muttered curse alerted Margret. "What's the matter?"

The silhouette stood and crossed back to the even darker corner of the room where she lay in shadow. Something that felt like a piece of paper was thrust into her hands.

"It's a note from my brother. He tacked it to the fireplace—must've figured I might stop here. He found your son hours ago. The note says that they were going to go on and try to make it to the ranch house before the storm broke."

Margret shuddered in relief, clutching the paper to her chest. "Does . . . does it say Todd is all right?"

"It doesn't say one way or the other," Jude admitted reluctantly. "Look, if your son was hurt, I'm sure Rob would have mentioned it in the note."

Jude waited for a response, but none came. He had a feeling that the woman was finally on the verge of tears, and he didn't know what more he could say or do to comfort her. Muttering something about seeing to his horse, he took the coward's way out and escaped into the blinding rain. Maybe by the time he got back, she'd be asleep.

But when he finally reentered the cabin after settling Zack in an adjacent shed, he was too cold and too tired to care about any woman's tears. Stumbling over the threshold, he leaned against the door and pulled off his wet boots. His socks, coat and shirt followed. After a second's hesitation, he discarded the rest of his clothes and wrapped himself in a thin blanket from the chest.

Treading carefully in the dark room, he made his way to the bed. She was so quiet, he assumed that she must be sleeping. But when he slid beneath the covers and slipped his arms around her, she tried to pull away.

He could see next to nothing in the darkness. But even through the blanket that separated his body from hers, he could feel the full, tempting curves of her breasts pressed against his chest. The vivid picture his imagination insisted on painting would have succeeded in arousing him if he hadn't been more than half-frozen. And if the woman in his arms hadn't been so totally vulnerable.

"I'm only trying to keep warm," he explained, in an attempt to calm her fears. "That fire's not even going to take the edge off the cold."

Suddenly the tremendous physical and emotional pressures of the day demanded a release. Margret began to sob quietly. She buried her face in his shoulder, unable to believe that this was happening to her. She had nothing but contempt for women who dissolved into hysterical tears!

Jude stroked her wet hair awkwardly, feeling like the world's biggest heel. "Cut it out, will you? I'm not going to jump on you!"

"I know that!" she told him, gulping in a breath of air.

Jude frowned in the darkness. She seemed so sure she was safe with him that it was almost an insult to his virility. "Then what are you crying about?" he asked more sharply than he'd intended.

"I want my son!" Margret wailed. Her anguished cry echoed in Jude's heart, tearing away layer upon layer of scar tissue until his wound was as raw and as painful as it had been on the day he'd screamed those identical words.

"Maggie," he said when he could trust himself to speak, "if I tried to get you to the ranch house in this storm, odds are you'd catch pneumonia on the way. And that sure as hell wouldn't do your son any good."

"I know that," Margret whispered. "But that doesn't stop me from worrying about Todd. If you had a child, you'd understand what I'm feeling!"

Jude thought about telling her just how well he understood. They were pressed close together in the narrow bed, two cold bodies desperate for warmth. He suddenly felt a compelling urge to reach out to her for emotional solace as well. He had almost made up his mind to confide in her, when her even breathing told him that she had finally drifted off to sleep.

His mouth curved in a cynical smile. It was just as well. He should have learned by now that he was every bit as alone lying in a woman's arms as he was in a solitary bed. No one could give him absolution for what he had done because he could never forgive himself.

One hand tangled in Margret's still-damp hair, Jude closed his eyes and allowed the welcome refuge of sleep to overtake him.

Chapter Two

Margret stirred restlessly inside her warm cocoon and slowly opened her eyes to focus on the sunlit interior of the cabin. Her breath caught as she realized she wasn't alone in the small bed. A man was lying half on top of her, an arm draped across her bare breasts and one long leg thrown over both of hers. His lips were so close to her ear that every exhaled breath tickled sensitive nerve endings.

All she could see from her limited vantage point was a lock of glossy, coffee-colored hair and the thickly muscled arm that was resting on her chest. She watched it rise and fall in time with her breathing, unable to comprehend either the complete intimacy of their embrace or her own easy acceptance of it. Her husband had been the only other man she'd slept with, and he had never wrapped himself around her like this. Yet with this man it seemed . . . natural.

Then he shifted slightly, and she discovered that their embrace was rapidly becoming even more intimate as she felt the most masculine part of his body press against her abdomen insistently.

Heat flooded her face, and her skin took on a rosy hue. To her utter mortification, she felt herself begin to respond to his arousal. Her nipples swelled beneath his arm, and she felt an ache deep inside that made her yearn to move her hips against his.

As if he could read her thoughts, Jude began to waken. His hand dropped unerringly to the apex of her thighs. Cupping the soft mound of golden curls, he gave it a possessive squeeze.

A jolt of pure desire surged through Margret's body, and she groaned aloud. An answering sound came from Jude as his mouth moved toward the throbbing peak of her breast.

Then the rational part of Margret's mind took over. Hastily she shielded her breasts with one arm and lowered her other hand in an attempt to dislodge the warm fingers that were resting on her lower body so intimately.

A growl of frustration issued from Jude's throat, and Margret gasped when she felt his tongue slide between her fingers, searching out the curve of her breast.

"Jude, stop!" She had intended the words as a firm command. Instead they came out as a breathy whisper that seemed more encouragement than deterrent.

At the sound of his name, Jude opened his eyes. Awareness dawned, and suddenly he realized where he was and who he was with. Apparently the blanket and his good intentions had both come undone during the night.

Reluctantly he turned his head away from the tempting sight of a creamy, fully curved breast that Maggie's small hand couldn't begin to cover. Resting his cheek against her trembling fingers, he tried to regain some control over the portion of his anatomy that was pressing into the soft skin of her belly with a will of its own.

Despite her protest, he could feel her response. He knew that he could probably overcome her resistance with a lot of reassurance and a few slow kisses. But he couldn't shake the nagging thought that that would be taking advantage of her. He'd undressed her and climbed into bed with her on the pretext of helping her. She'd trusted him to protect her. How could he betray that trust by trying to seduce her?

Cursing himself for an idealistic fool, Jude rolled away from Margret's enticing body and got out of bed. His back toward her, he gathered up his scattered clothes and began dressing.

Margret's mouth went dry, and the ache in her middle intensified. She knew that she should look away, but her gaze seemed to be riveted to the form of the man standing so unself-consciously nude before her.

He was tall, with broad shoulders, narrow hips and an all-over golden tan that was augmented by a liberal sprinkling of dark brown hair. And he had the most sensual backside she could have imagined on a man—firmly muscled, yet deliciously rounded.

He was so close to the bed that she could easily reach out and touch him. She wanted to, and she wanted him to touch her—as deeply and as completely as a man was capable of touching a woman. Instead she watched regretfully as the magnificent body before her was covered up by dreary white briefs and a seasoned pair of jeans.

Jude wondered what she was thinking. The way he saw it, there were two possibilities. Either she was angry that he'd given up so easily and left her unsatisfied. Or she was sitting there pouting, the picture of outraged virtue, waiting for him to grovel at her feet and beg her forgiveness. Well, she'd have a long wait before she heard an apology from him.

"I'm sorry."

Jude paused in the process of buttoning his shirt, unable to believe what he'd just heard. Slowly he turned to face her, and what he saw all but took his breath away.

She was sitting up, the quilt draped demurely over her breasts. Her eyes were downcast, and her cheeks were flushed. And she was absolutely the most beautiful woman he had ever seen. With wildly curling yellow-gold hair that fell all the way to her waist, a cover-girl face, and a generous bustline, she was the average man's sexual fantasy come to life.

He had pictured her as pretty, but serious looking—a woman whose appearance was marked by dignity and intelligence. At first glance most people would credit this woman with about as much real substance as a cone of cotton candy. But then most people hadn't been through hell and back with her.

Anne had taught him to equate beauty with deceit and betrayal. But the hours he'd spent with Maggie had convinced him that she wasn't like Anne. She was warm and honest and caring.

Pushing aside his instinctive distrust of her appearance, Jude amended his mental picture of the woman he'd just spent the night with and continued buttoning his shirt.

"Why are you apologizing to me, Maggie?"

"I didn't mean to lead you on like that," she said, keeping her gaze lowered. She just couldn't bear to see Jude wearing that familiar glazed expression. The look that told her more clearly than words that she wasn't being seen as a person with a mind, a soul and a heart, but as an object specifically designed to provide maximum sexual gratification.

Jude found what she had to say even more surprising than her looks. Her words dissolved his resentment and left him feeling downright ashamed of the way he'd behaved and of his jaded attitude toward women in general.

He cleared his throat self-consciously. "Well, I had no right to grab you the way I did. When I got into bed with you last night, I wasn't even thinking about—I didn't know that I was going to wake up..." He let the sentence trail off into nothingness, feeling all tongue-tied and red around the collar. He hadn't thought there was anything left that could embarrass him anymore. Obviously he'd been wrong.

Margret was astounded. Since she'd been old enough to buy her first brassiere, men had been grabbing at her without waiting for an invitation. When she dared to tell them that their attentions were unwanted, they'd angrily accused her of being a tease. Now instead of a temper tantrum and insults, she was finally getting an apology.

Margret raised her gaze, suddenly wanting very much to see what this man's eyes had to say. But nothing could have prepared her for the sight that awaited her.

She had imagined a handsome, appealing face, a countenance that mirrored the compassion and gentleness of his actions. But the tanned, weathered face before her could only be described as harsh. He had a square, beard-stubbled jaw, thin lips, a prominent nose—and a jagged ridge of white scar tissue that bisected the right side of his face from temple to chin.

His eyes were the only feature of that forbidding landscape that showed any potential for tenderness. They were long-lashed and wide set, with sweeping, finely arched brows. But the irises were so dark they appeared black, and they gave away nothing of the feelings behind them.

Jude watched Maggie's big, jade-green eyes widen in surprise. He felt the impact of that look like a punch in the gut. Somehow in the time they had been together he had forgotten about the scar—maybe because in the darkness it had ceased to matter. Not that he had ever been handsome, not by a long shot.

When he was young, girls his own age had been intimidated by his rugged appearance. But there were some older women who had seemed to find it fascinating—for a night or two. Jude might have felt lonely growing up, but frustration had never been one of his problems. Even after the accident there had been women—women who were drawn to the dark and the dangerous. But this woman wasn't that kind. Tensely he waited for some visible sign of the revulsion she was probably feeling.

Margret was ashamed of the apprehension that her first view of Jude's face had evoked. She knew that he was a good man. And her own looks had made her realize long ago how misleading appearances could be. It was just that her mental image of him had been so different!

Awkwardly she wrapped the quilt around herself and got to her feet. She winced as her injured ankle twinged in protest.

Instantly Jude was at her side, a supporting arm curved around her waist. "What are you trying to do?" he demanded, forgetting all about his appearance in his concern for her.

"This." Before he could react, she had raised her face to his and pressed her lips against the scar.

"What the hell was that for?" Jude rasped, not sure whether he should be angry or pleased.

Margret hesitated, a little embarrassed by her own impulsiveness. "I guess I wanted to prove to you that I like you—just the way you are."

A slow smile curved Jude's mouth, and the expression in those midnight-black eyes turned warm and compelling. "I like you, too. Is there anywhere that you'd like to be kissed?"

His other arm went around her waist, and suddenly she was being held close against his chest. Her heart began to pound, and her gaze was drawn inexorably to his lips. She hadn't meant her kiss to be a sexual overture, but now she was caught up in this man's magnetic field again. Wondering what his lips would feel like on hers, wondering . . .

Resolutely she pushed against his chest with one hand, clutching the quilt with the other. "I'd like to leave as soon as possible. I want to see my son."

"We'll go in a few minutes," Jude said soothingly. He understood the reason for her withdrawal. What he didn't understand was the feeling of loss it seemed to evoke in him. "Sit down and let me look at that ankle first."

She tried to move away from him, but he moved with her, supporting her. She sank to a sitting position on the bed, flustered by his nearness, but grateful for his help.

Then he went down on one knee in front of her, and she felt his hands on her injured ankle. As he lifted her leg toward him the quilt parted unexpectedly, giving him a glimpse of the downy nest where his fingers had been resting only moments before.

Margret hastily rearranged the coverlet, blushing to the roots of her hair. Her gaze skittered away from his—but not before she saw the naked desire in his eyes. Her own pulse began to race crazily. She'd never reacted to a man this way in her life before. Now, when she should have been thinking only of her son, her hormones were running wild. What was wrong with her?

Jude felt his body go taut in reaction to what he'd just seen and expelled his breath in a hiss of exasperation. What the hell was the matter with him? It had been years since his jeans had gotten so tight so fast with so little provocation.

Margret clamped her lips together as his fingers probed her bruised flesh. But his examination was so swift and gentle that, to her surprise, there was hardly any pain.

"You've got a cut on top here, and it's pretty swollen. But I don't think anything's severed or broken." He wanted to run his hand up the entire length of that smooth, shapely

leg. Instead he carefully set her foot back on the floor and
crossed to the small kitchen area.

Pumping cold water into the sink, he splashed it over his
face and rinsed his mouth. He made a determined effort to
put the woman in the bed out of his mind, and slowly his
body began to relax. By the time he had finished drying
himself with a slightly musty towel, he decided he was once
again more human than animal. It would take a shave and
a cup of hot coffee to complete the transition. He'd have to
wait for those, but he knew he'd have them soon enough.
Just as he'd eventually have Maggie.

When he returned to Margret's side, she accepted with
murmured thanks the wet cloth and the tin cup full of water he brought her.

He tossed her clothes on the bed beside her. "Mine are
still a little damp, too, but it's better than nothing at all."

Their gazes locked as each remembered the details of the
other's body and questioned the validity of that statement.

Margret was the first to look away. "Could you... Could
I have a few minutes alone?"

Jude wondered what she would say if he were ungentle-
manly enough to refuse her request. If it weren't for the situation with her little boy, he'd be tempted to find out.

"Sure thing. I'll go saddle Zack. Just be careful where
you walk. In some places the floorboards are as rotten as the
roof." Grabbing up his boots and his semi-dry socks, Jude
retreated to the front porch before he had a chance to
change his mind.

By the time Margret had dressed and managed to hobble
to the door, Jude had the horse ready and waiting in front
of the cabin. He looked up to see her framed in the doorway and couldn't help but stare. It was hard to believe that
this was the same woman he'd seen just moments before.

The wild blond mane had been pulled back and pinned
into a severe-looking bun. Her dress was an attractive shade

of green that emphasized the color of her eyes, but its loose-fitting lines managed to camouflage her figure quite effectively. And even those gorgeous legs had been minimized by a calf-length hem and low heels. She was still obviously a pretty woman, but enticing was no longer a word that could be applied to her.

Jude thought he understood her motivation in downplaying her sexuality. An intelligent, sensitive woman like Maggie wouldn't enjoy being hit on by every witless fool who thought that the cover was the whole book. He understood, but he still felt a pang of very masculine regret.

Margret stood in the sunlight, unable to believe that such a clear, beautiful morning could follow such a stormy night. The spring air was warm, and the rain had coaxed out every imaginable shade of green. And she was lucky to be alive.

She blinked, shading her eyes against the sun, and finally succeeded in focusing on Jude. With a shock she realized he was glaring at her in disapproval.

"Where'd you find the pins?"

"What pins?" she asked, unable to comprehend what he was referring to.

"The ones you used to put up your hair."

"Oh, those. They were still in my hair from yesterday. They just got a little ... misplaced during the night."

Margret knew then what had given rise to that forbidding frown. He was mad because she'd done away with Jiggles. That had been the pet name her late husband had used to refer to her whenever she'd allowed her natural appearance to shine through. She hadn't liked it, but she'd known that the slightest negative comment from her could send him into a week-long sulk. Besides, her annoyance had seemed petty. Paul had been so good to her. And he had given her Todd.

The thought of her son recalled Margret to the present. She looked down at Jude and cleared her throat delicately.

After all the embarrassing moments she had shared with this man, there still seemed to be no end to her humiliation. "I...uh...I couldn't seem to locate the bathroom."

His frown was replaced by a grin. "Old Pete had a real dislike for modern conveniences. I'm afraid it's out back."

Margret suppressed a groan. "What kind of a man would choose to live without electricity or indoor plumbing?"

Jude's smile turned a little sad. "When Pete retired, my daddy had this cabin built for him. But even Ben Emory couldn't talk that old codger into installing any 'newfangled' conveniences. Pete was the last of the old-time hands. Must've been over ninety when he passed on—no one knew for sure. That was more than a year ago, and I don't think this place has been used since. Until last night."

Margret shifted uncomfortably at his reference to the time they had spent together within the shelter of those walls. She had to remind herself that there was no reason to be self-conscious about what had happened. They had shared nothing more intimate than the physical closeness necessary for survival. Why did she feel as if they had given each other so much more?

She looked away from his searching gaze before she could be tempted to seek the answer to her question. Too much time had been wasted already. She had to confirm her son's safety.

Resigning herself to the inevitable, she limped painfully across the porch only to find Jude at her side once again. This time she suffered his support in silence.

When Margret was finally up on the horse, she breathed a sigh of relief. Her ordeal was over at last. But she'd failed to consider the five-mile ride that loomed ahead of her.

Even though Jude kept the horse to a slow walk, the gait seemed to intensify the throbbing in her ankle and her head. Yet somehow she found his closeness even more disturbing than the pain. Folded in his arms, pressed against the hard wall of his chest, she was made more aware of the scent, the texture, the presence of the man. The heat of his body seemed to stoke a passion in her that she had never known before.

Why hadn't she been able to feel that way about her husband? From her first night with Paul, she had realized that something was wrong. She had felt no desire for him, only a strange guilt when he touched her. She'd loved him like a brother, but before long she'd begun to doubt that that kind of love could be a firm foundation for a marriage.

He had been so desperate in his frantic efforts to please her, that he had only increased her anxiety. Finally, to spare his fragile ego, she had pretended a pleasure she didn't really feel, vowing that she would learn to enjoy his caresses. But instead she had become trapped in a vicious cycle of pretense and frustration.

Now a stranger seemed capable of arousing her with only a glance. It didn't seem right. But was Jude really a stranger? Hadn't the crisis they'd passed through last night taught her more about him than she could have learned in weeks, or even months, of casual acquaintance? Gentleness, strength, consideration, courage. He'd displayed all those qualities and more. What difference did it make where he'd been born, or how he liked his coffee? Things like that were just insignificant details.

"Do you and your brother live on your ranch alone?" she asked, trying to fill in some of the gaps in her information.

"My mother lives with us. Daddy had a stroke and died about ten years ago. My wife—"

Margret turned her head so fast that the resulting jolt of pain temporarily blurred her vision. "Your *wife?*" She knew that she was gaping at him stupidly, but suddenly that didn't seem important. She had just realized how significant insignificant details could be.

Jude's face was unreadable. "Does the idea of my having a wife bother you?"

"Yes!" Margret blurted. Then she realized how much she'd revealed. "I mean, you certainly didn't act married. If I had known..." She let the words trail off, unwilling to disclose the depth of the disappointment she felt.

"Don't tell me you've never slept with a married man before."

"The only married man I've slept with was my husband," Margret told him indignantly. "And he was married to me at the time!"

Jude looked into her face, assessing the truth of her declaration. Then he nodded, accepting it as fact. "You interrupted me too soon, Maggie. I was going to say that my wife died in a car accident three years ago."

Margret was bombarded by an assortment of diverse emotions: empathy for his suffering, anger that he hadn't corrected her misconception at once and relief at finding out he was single after all.

"I'm sorry to hear that," she murmured awkwardly. After a moment's consideration, she decided to leave it at that. Apparently Jude had intended his questions as some kind of character test. She wondered if she'd passed or failed.

Jude was pondering the same subject. He disliked playing verbal games, but he'd needed to be sure of how this woman thought. She obviously believed in honesty, fidelity and the institution of marriage. And, unless he was reading her wrong, she saw him as a potential bed partner. Now what was he going to do with what he'd learned?

When he'd pulled her from the creek last night, the past had seemed irrelevant and the future something they might not live to see. The present had seemed the only sure, the only important thing. In the isolation of the cabin, it had been easy to forget that any other reality existed.

But now that brief interlude was over. The word *respon-sibility* was beginning to make itself heard. Of course he could ignore it. He could invite Maggie to stay at the ranch until she was fully recovered. And once things were re-solved with her son, he could see to it that they picked up right where they'd left off this morning.

But Maggie was a very special lady, and he had nothing to offer any lady—special or otherwise. Women like her deserved a relationship, not a roll in the hay. And his desire for love and commitment, his belief in permanence, had ended with Anne's death three years ago.

Even if that hadn't been the case, any long-term relation-ship between a woman who looked like Maggie and a man who looked like him had the deck stacked against it from the start. If common sense wasn't enough to tell him that, his marriage to the beautiful Anne had certainly convinced him of it.

Margret could feel Jude begin to distance himself from her. It was there in his silence, his refusal to meet her gaze, in the way his arms gradually loosened their embrace until he hardly seemed to be touching her at all. She didn't un-derstand the reason for it. What had she said? What had she done?

But before she could ask him, they came to the top of a hill, and she was confronted by a view that commanded her full attention.

"This is my ranch," was all Jude said. But Margret heard a world of pride in those quiet words.

And he had something to be proud of. She gazed at the sprawling Spanish-style hacienda, the corrals, the barns, the whitewashed outbuildings and the fertile, grass-rich land that stretched as far as the eye could see.

"It's beautiful," she said, realizing for the first time how inadequate that word was.

Then she noticed the small towheaded boy sitting on the fence of the main corral, and her heart seemed to stop beating.

"Todd..." she whispered, unable to believe what she was seeing. Then she yelled as loudly as she could. "Todd!"

The boy's blond head turned toward her. He jumped off the fence and began running in her direction.

A cry of relief and happiness came from Margret's throat as Jude urged his horse down the hill toward her son.

Chapter Three

"What was that poem by that guy, Frost? You know, the one about two roads...?"

Margret looked across the dinner table into Rob Emory's dark eyes and recognized their seductive gleam. But it was tempered by a teasing smile so full of good humor that she couldn't take his flirting seriously, much less take offense. "You mean 'The Road not Taken'?"

"That's the one! If Jude had gone east yesterday, and I had gone west, I would have been the one who pulled you out of the creek. Now I'll probably never get a chance to be your knight in shining armor."

Margret ignored the derisive snort that came from the direction of Jude's chair and returned Rob's smile. "As far as I'm concerned, you're already my hero. I can't ever thank you enough for saving Todd the way you did."

Her son, seated on her right, smiled up at her as she laid an arm across his shoulders. When she turned back to Rob, she was amused to see that a blush had crept up the side of his neck. For once, Jude's talkative younger brother seemed at a loss for words.

Margret let her gaze sweep over his handsome features, from his full, sensual lips to the dark, long-lashed eyes now focused firmly on his dinner plate. If it hadn't been for those eyes, she would never have believed he and Jude were related.

Even in temperament the two were worlds apart. Jude seemed to resemble the dark, brooding hero of a tragedy while Rob was like a charming, devil-may-care cavalier from some romantic adventure. Of course, he couldn't have been more than twenty-two or twenty-three. Maybe Jude had been the same at that age. Maybe, but somehow she couldn't picture it.

At any rate, Rob seemed hopelessly immature next to Jude. But Rob had been sweetly attentive to her since they'd first been introduced. Jude, on the other hand, seemed almost unaware of her existence.

"Well," Rob responded at last, terminating her speculation, "all I really did was give Todd a ride home. And all the way he kept yelling that I should go back and get you. But I knew Jude was headed toward the creek, and Todd was already soaking wet and shivering. With the storm on its way..."

He looked at her beseechingly, as if begging forgiveness for his lack of gallantry.

"You made the right decision," Margret assured him. "And even if Jude hadn't rescued me, the sheriff would have."

After coming to the ranch, she'd learned that Rob had notified the sheriff's department of her predicament as soon as he'd returned home. Within half an hour of her arrival this morning Sheriff Dawson himself had stopped by to see her, bringing her waterlogged luggage and the purse she'd left behind in her car.

He, too, had apologized for not coming to her aid quickly enough. He'd arrived on the scene sometime after Jude had pulled her from the creek. Then, while he was in the process of searching for her, the storm had brought a tree crashing down across his car. By the time his deputy had managed to get the necessary equipment in place to free him from the wreckage and clear the road, it was morning and Margret and Jude were already on their way to the ranch.

Margret had understood the limitations of the sheriff's tiny, rural department. But she hadn't been prepared for his blunt pronouncement that she might as well sell her car for scrap. At a time when she'd had to count every penny, purchasing full insurance on that old jalopy had seemed like a waste of money. Although she'd finally agreed to let Sheriff Dawson dispose of the car for her, she couldn't afford to replace it.

She kept telling herself that she should be thankful. Both she and Todd were safe, and that was all that mattered. Still, she couldn't help worrying about the future. A new job and a new apartment were waiting for her in El Paso, but she couldn't claim either for at least a week. She had enough money to pay for food and an inexpensive motel for that amount of time. But she hadn't planned on having to buy bus tickets back to El Paso as well.

The sound of Nilda Emory's soft, faintly accented voice broke into her reverie. "Where is your pretty smile, my dear? Surely no problem can be that insurmountable."

Margret looked up and smiled self-consciously. Had her worry been that evident, her expression that transparent? She looked into the dark Spanish eyes that the Mexican woman had bequeathed to both her sons, and knew that the answer was yes.

This morning, when she'd first met the elegant, imposing woman with her severely styled ebony hair and seemingly ageless olive skin, Margret had been a little in awe of

her. But Mrs. Emory had anticipated all her needs and had
seemed quite capable of moving both heaven and earth in
order to fulfill them.

The older woman and a shy young housemaid had gotten Margret undressed and into bed with a borrowed nightgown and a breakfast tray before she quite knew what was
happening.

Just as she'd been finishing that delicious meal, the elderly, blustering family doctor arrived. After an examination that had made her long for Jude's gentle hands, Dr.
Hooper had diagnosed a sprained ankle. Although he'd
tried to badger her into a trip to his infirmary in nearby
Layton City for X-rays, Margret had managed to escape
with only a bandage on her forehead, a firmly wrapped ankle and a tetanus shot.

She'd dozed the afternoon away, waking from a vague,
but disturbingly sensuous, dream to the reality of a dimly lit,
deserted room. Then she'd heard the door click shut and
had realized that someone had been there, watching her as
she slept. A tauntingly familiar, citrusy fragrance had lingered in the air. It was the same scent that had permeated
her dream.

Her thoughts returning to the present, Margret looked
across the table at Jude. Had he been the one in her room?
She doubted it. Since they'd arrived at the ranch, he'd been
cool and distant. She wondered what had happened to the
intimacy they had shared in the cabin. Maybe the truth was
that the closeness that had seemed so special to her had only
been a result of the excitement and danger they had shared.
A natural but temporary result.

But even as that thought skimmed the surface of her
mind, Jude's gaze met hers. She felt its incredible heat. It
seemed to burn away every defense, every trace of civilized
restraint, until the core of aching, pulsing need inside her lay
naked and exposed.

Abruptly his gaze moved away as he turned his attention to something his brother was saying. Margret felt hurt, deserted and frustrated. But mostly she felt foolish. It had been lust she'd seen in his eyes, nothing more. And there wasn't anything special about that. She'd seen the same look in countless masculine glances. The only difference lay in her response. For the first time in her life, she burned with the same fire. She wanted Jude as much as he wanted her.

Frightened and a little ashamed of her realization, Margret took a sip from her water glass and tried to concentrate on the conversation going on around her. She was surprised to find that Mrs. Emory was addressing her again.

"Todd told us that you were from El Paso, but he couldn't give us the names of any relatives there."

It was evident to Margret that although Mrs. Emory had freely offered the use of her home to a stranger in distress, her continuing hospitality depended upon the information that Margret supplied her with now. Margret didn't blame the other woman for her caution. She considered it to be justified under the circumstances.

"We really don't have any family," she replied easily. "My late husband and I were both orphans." That was stretching a point in Paul's case. But since he had always referred to his abusive parents as being dead, Margret saw no reason to resurrect them now.

Nilda murmured a condolence and continued her tactful probing. "But from what we were able to gather from Todd, he had a grandfather who passed away recently. He said that you were on your way to the funeral when the accident occurred."

"Ed wasn't really Todd's grandfather. He was my employer. He was a writer, and I worked as his live-in secretary in El Paso. During the months we stayed with Ed, he and Todd did grow quite close."

She noticed the chill silence that descended on the group at the table, but she didn't understand the reason for it.

"Ed *Tanner?*" Jude finally asked, his black eyes totally unreadable.

"Yes," Margret confirmed, puzzled and disturbed by the strange tension in his voice. "Did you know him?"

Jude opened his mouth to reply, but his mother spoke first. "He was very close to our family. In fact Ed's funeral and burial will be taking place here tomorrow. Surely you were told that?"

"Then this must be Double Diamond Ranch!" Margret exclaimed, relieved—and somewhat amazed—that she had managed to reach her intended destination purely by chance. "Ed's lawyer sent me a letter with the date and time of the funeral and directions to the Double Diamond. I thought I was pretty close when I went off the road. But with everything that happened, it didn't even cross my mind to ask the name of your ranch."

Rob nodded in confirmation. "You *were* close. The creek forms the western boundary of the ranch."

Nilda Emory was silent for a moment, the slender fingers of her right hand smoothing an all-but-invisible wrinkle from the linen tablecloth. Then the same hand reached out to cover Margret's. "Please, put all your worries aside. As friends of Ed, you and your son are more than welcome to stay here with us. Tomorrow, and for as long as you wish."

Margret was as surprised by the other woman's obviously sincere offer as she was hesitant to accept it. Over the years she had learned that many people went out of their way to look for reasons to justify the negative first impression that her appearance tended to inspire. Though she didn't think that the Emorys fell into that category, they must have been Ed's friends for years. She, on the other hand, had known him a relatively short time. To them, she was a virtual stranger. She didn't want to give them any cause to believe that she intended to take advantage of their generosity. On the other hand, the loss of her car and her limited resources gave her little choice.

"Thank you," she said finally, accepting the older woman's offer. She breathed a mental sigh of relief, feeling more gratitude than those two little words could ever express.

Nilda Emory nodded in acknowledgment and gestured to the maid who was refilling the wineglasses. She gave the woman a whispered instruction, then turned back to Margret again. "I'm amazed that Ed would agree to hire a young woman with a child as his live-in secretary, Mrs. Brolin. He guarded his privacy fiercely, and he was very set in his ways."

"Frankly, I was surprised, too," Margret admitted. "I truly think he hired me because he felt sorry for me. My husband had just died, and . . . well, I wasn't in very good shape emotionally or financially. I know he didn't expect that we'd all come to mean so much to each other."

Her eyes grew misty as the memories came rushing back. When she'd first met Ed a little over a year ago, she'd been at the lowest point of her twenty-seven-year existence—a new widow with an eviction notice, a young son to provide for, and a savings account with a zero balance. She'd responded to his ad for a live-in secretary out of sheer desperation, but there had been something special between them from the time of that very first meeting—a liking and a respect that had only strengthened with time.

She'd enjoyed working with the old writer, transcribing the tapes he dictated and helping him to turn them into a finished manuscript. When his biography of Edgar Allan Poe had finally been completed, she'd been as proud as if she'd written it herself.

Mrs. Emory's voice broke into her thoughts again. "And you stayed with him until the end?"

Margret nodded, not trusting herself to reply with words. She remembered her concern about Ed's weight loss and his worsening cough. After weeks of nagging and cajoling on her part, he'd finally agreed to be examined by a doctor. The diagnosis of terminal cancer had devastated her, although she'd tried to be strong for his sake.

"Ed was a very kind, very special man," she said huskily. She smiled down into Todd's upturned face, willing him to remember the good times they'd all shared instead of the final sadness. Then she glanced at Jude, and her smile faltered and died.

The hard lines of his face looked as if they'd been carved from stone, and the expression in his eyes made Margret's breath catch in her throat. Then his chair scraped against the wooden floor, and he was gone.

She stared at the doorway he'd passed through for several seconds as though the wood itself held the answer to the riddle of his behavior. Then she looked to Rob. But he was staring at his plate, his lips pressed together in a grim line.

Mrs. Emory's softly spoken words broke the tense silence. "Please forgive Jude's rudeness, Mrs. Brolin. I believe your unfortunate accident revived some unhappy memories for him. His wife, Anne, was killed in a similar way three years ago. Jude was thrown clear, but Anne drowned when their car plunged into Layton Creek."

"What a cruel coincidence," Margret murmured, chilled by the revelation. Jude must have been at the wheel of the car, so he blamed himself for his wife's death—just as she had blamed herself when she thought Todd might be hurt. Yet was that the real reason for Jude's sudden departure? He hadn't seemed upset until she'd mentioned Ed Tanner.

Rob's voice took up the story. "Jude was hurt real bad, but he left the hospital against doctor's orders and just disappeared. We all thought he was dead until a few weeks later when we found out he was up at old Pete's place."

He looked up at her, pushing the food on his plate around with jerky, purposeless motions of his fork. "That's why he has that scar, you know. He had the best plastic surgeon money could buy. But after he left the hospital, his face got infected. He's lucky he didn't die. Or maybe that's not true. Maybe the luckiest thing would've been for him to have died in that accident."

"Roberto!" his mother protested.

"I'm sorry, Mama, but it's the truth! Sometimes it hurts me just to watch him trying to hold all that pain and guilt inside. After all this time—"

"We have guests," Mrs. Emory said, her voice a soft reprimand. "Please, let's not speak of unpleasant things tonight."

The maid stepped forward to clear the dinner dishes and serve dessert, signaling an end to the disturbing conversation. Rob excused himself and left to check on an expectant heifer, taking his plate of apple pie with him.

It was Nilda Emory who broke the ensuing silence. "I must apologize for Jude's rudeness, Mrs. Brolin. I assure you that our household is not always in such an upheaval."

Margret hastened to reassure her. "I'm very grateful for your hospitality, Mrs. Emory. And I have nothing but admiration for both your sons. If it hadn't been for them..."

She glanced at Todd and altered her statement slightly. "If it hadn't been for them, I don't know what would have happened."

The other woman smiled at her, obviously approving of what she'd said. "Please, you must call me Nilda. Mrs. Emory makes me feel much too old. And may I call you Margret?"

"I'd like that."

To her surprise, Margret actually found her appetite returning. When Nilda questioned her further about Ed, she answered freely, attributing the sadness in the other woman's eyes to the friendship she had shared with the late author.

Finally Margret noticed Todd's head nodding and realized that it was way past his bedtime. Excusing herself, she picked up the heavy cane that had materialized by her bedside earlier and used it to push to her feet. Bidding Nilda a reluctant good-night, she roused Todd and began to hobble away in the direction of their rooms.

Her son threw an arm around her hips in an attempt to help her, and she came close to tripping over his small body at least half a dozen times. But she didn't mind a bit. She was glad he was there to get in her way.

"How long are we going to stay here, Mom?"

"Why?" Margret asked. "Don't you like it?"

"I'd like to stay here forever!" Todd enthused. "Nilda baked cookies for me today, and she rocked me to sleep last night because I missed you. And Rob promised to give me a riding lesson if we stayed long enough, and if you said okay. Can I, Mom? Please . . ."

Margret felt torn. Todd hadn't displayed this much interest in anything since Ed's death. But she didn't know how much longer she could impose on the Emorys. "We'll see," she told him noncommittally. She softened at the sight of his dejected face. "I really don't think we're going to be here very long, but I don't see why you couldn't have one lesson—if Rob has the time."

Todd gave her a hug that almost sent her sprawling. "Thanks, Mom!"

They entered Todd's bedroom together. Margret flipped on the light and pulled out a dresser drawer, searching for something Todd could wear to bed. To her amazement she found all his clothes, freshly laundered and neatly folded. Her respect for Nilda Emory increased even more.

After her son had gotten into his pajamas and had washed up, Margret tucked him in and sat on the side of the bed.

Dimming the light, she reached down and smoothed back his hair. She had been concerned that yesterday's experience might still be troubling him, but he seemed to have taken it all in stride—one more debt she owed to the Emorys.

"What about Jude?" she asked curiously, wondering what her son's response would be. "Do you like him, too?"

Todd yawned and snuggled deeper into his pillow. "When you went to sleep today, he let me help him feed the horses. He told me all their names and a lot of other good stuff about them. And he didn't even yell when I tipped a bucket of water over. He's okay to be around once you get to know him," Todd concluded with authority.

Margret stared at him, surprised that he'd had no trouble at all seeing past Jude's intimidating appearance to the gentleness hidden beneath. Her child was more perceptive than she'd ever imagined.

Todd fell asleep almost at once, and Margret made her way next door to her own room. There she found that her clothes had also been washed and put away. Thankfully, she no longer owned any expensive, dry-clean-only items. Even the few pairs of shoes she'd brought seemed to have survived their immersion and still appeared wearable.

She washed, brushed her teeth and changed into a sheer black nightgown that Paul had insisted she buy. Most of her nightwear and lingerie were sensuous almost to the point of embarrassment. Paul had wanted her body on display for him. It was only when other men had noticed her figure that he'd minded.

Not that he'd criticized her, of course. Instead, he had complained about the men who looked at her and the way that it had made him feel. And he had subjected her to hurt, reproachful looks whenever any other man seemed to derive pleasure from her appearance. She hadn't ever been a flamboyant dresser, but she had enjoyed wearing high heels and clothes that flattered her figure. And she'd worn her hair loose and free. But Paul had ruined all that for her. She'd never been truly comfortable with her appearance, but her husband had actually made her feel guilty about it.

Gradually she'd begun to tone down her looks—loose clothing, long hems, low heels, no makeup. And her husband's silent approval had been her reward. That and his private lust. She'd been as ill at ease with his taste in intimate feminine apparel as she had been with her dowdy public image. Neither extreme was really her. But she had learned to live with it because it pleased Paul. Because Paul had always done everything in his power to please her. He'd even died because he'd wanted to please her.

Too restless to sleep, Margret slipped into a pretty, but modest, quilted robe that she'd purchased recently and opened the sliding glass door. Cane in hand, she stepped from her bedroom onto the dark-shrouded patio that ran the length of the house. Carefully she negotiated the few feet to the nearest lawn chair and sat down. She leaned back and closed her eyes, enjoying the quiet night.

For the hundredth time she wondered why Ed had chosen to be buried on a ranch in the middle of nowhere, instead of in a cemetery in El Paso. Since he'd lived quite modestly during the year she'd known him, she had concluded that the reason might have been financial. But now that she knew the Emorys, she felt Ed's motivation went further than just a free burial plot. He had wanted his final resting place to be near people who had loved him.

"Hello, Maggie."

Margret jumped at the sound of Jude's familiar voice. She'd thought she was completely alone, when actually he'd been sitting close beside her all the time! As her eyes adjusted to the darkness, she could barely discern his outline in the shadows. They were both seated beyond the range of dim illumination created by the lighted outdoor pool.

"You scared the daylights out of me!" she told him accusingly.

"I never scared anyone in the dark before, Maggie. It's when the light's on that I tend to run into problems."

After what had occurred at the dinner table, Margret had felt a bit uncomfortable when she'd realized Jude was on the patio with her. But when she heard his self-derisive comment, things quickly returned to their former perspective.

"Don't talk about yourself that way! It isn't funny. And it isn't true, either."

Jude was surprised by her passionate defense and by the warm feeling that rushed through him in response. On the ride home from the cabin, he'd promised himself that he would stay as far away from her as possible. Her mention of Ed at dinner had only reinforced that decision. Now here they were, so close he could reach out and touch her.

He should tell her the truth now. Tell her and then ask her the question that had been haunting him ever since he'd heard her speak Ed's name. But he told himself it didn't matter. Ed had been nothing to him. Less than nothing. And he had no intention of putting his hands on this woman again. Ever. Then he heard the low, husky sound of his own voice and knew he was a liar.

"Do you like what you see when you look at me, Maggie? Did you enjoy it when I touched you?"

Margret felt desire course through her in a pulsing, electric current as she remembered how his hands had felt on her body. Her throat swelled with emotion, making the single word she uttered sound strained and distorted. "Yes."

Jude was out of his chair and bending over her in the space of a single heartbeat. To hell with good intentions! He had to have this woman no matter what the consequences.

His hands framed her face, and his mouth found hers. Gently, reverently, he caressed her lips, molding them be-

neath his own. Then he heard her moaned response, and he
forgot about both the past and the future.

Intoxicated by a depth of passion he had never known
before, Jude tilted her head and plunged his tongue as far
inside her as it would go. She was all softness, all give,
opening to him and absorbing the force of his kiss until his
mouth seemed to sink into hers and become a part of it.

He was used to women who knew how to take from a
man, who demanded as much from him as he demanded
from them. He would teach Maggie how to take, too. But
for now her sweet submission was the most potent aphro-
disiac he had ever known.

Continuing his exploration of her mouth, he parted her
heavy robe with hands that trembled as if they were touching a woman's body for the first time. He encountered a
nightgown that was so insubstantial it was more of an in-
centive than a barrier.

Margret almost cried out as his hands discovered her full
breasts. He cupped one in each palm, his thumbs stroking
her hard nipples with a slow, circular motion.

"You're beautiful, Maggie."

"So are you!" she whispered, lost in a haze of arousal.
"Oh, Jude, so are you!"

It was as it had been with them at the first, both flaws and
attributes hidden by the darkness. Neither his scar nor her
beauty mattered in the private world they shared. A world
where feeling was more important than fact.

His head lowered to hover over one breast, while his
thumb continued to tease the other. She felt his warm breath
through the nylon, and then the hot wetness of his mouth
claimed her eager flesh.

Margret buried both hands in his hair to pull his head
closer, and arched upward to meet the most exquisite sensation she had ever known. Her hips moved restlessly in the

chair, and she longed to press against him, to wrap her legs around him.

Jude lifted her breasts and buried his face in the midst of their soft warmth. He was so hard that it was almost painful to him. He wanted to lift Maggie in his arms, carry her to his bed and plunge into her again and again. To touch her, taste her and take her until he was free of the spell she had cast over him. Until he was a sane man once more.

He wanted to move forward without thought, without delay, but the unasked question stood in his way. No matter what he told himself, he knew he had to hear her answer. He had to know.

Slowly, reluctantly, he pulled back. It was like tearing away a layer of his own skin.

"Maggie," he began, looking down into her shadowed face, "there was nothing personal between you and Ed, was there? Todd isn't my... isn't Ed's son, is he?"

Margret came back to earth with an almost audible thud. Her body still tingled where Jude had touched it, it still ached for him, but her heart withdrew behind its protective shield. This was like her husband's accusations all over again.

She'd often wished that Paul had spoken his aloud so that she could have denied them. But Jude's words were so ugly, so hurtful, so unfair, that she wished she'd never heard them.

"I knew Ed for just a little over a year," she told him as calmly as she could. "He was very special to me, but not in the way you mean. He was a truly good man. Someone who cared about other people."

Jude's laugh was totally devoid of humor. "Ed Tanner? Lady, you've got to be kidding!"

Margret didn't recognize the angry, bitter man who hovered so near to her. Yanking her robe closed, she pushed away from him. "I don't want to hear any more!"

Jude was incensed at her withdrawal. "What? I don't even get a chance to tell you my side of things?"

"I . . . I still miss Ed terribly. I couldn't stand to listen to you criticize a man I admired, a man I loved as if he were my father!"

To Jude, Margret's statement was the final irony—and the last straw. Then a new thought occurred to him, one that made his blood run cold with horror. It couldn't be! But then, Ed had known countless women in his day, and he *had* been blond and fair. . . .

Jude's fingers gripped her shoulders so hard that Margret cried out in surprise and protest. "Was Ed your father, Maggie? Tell me! I have to know!"

"Are you crazy?" Margret shouted, trying to follow the logic of his reasoning and failing miserably.

"Answer my question!"

"Ed wasn't my father!"

"Swear it!"

"I swear!"

He released her as suddenly as he had grabbed her, and she huddled in her chair, on the verge of tears.

Jude sighed in relief, feeling the terrible tension drain out of him. Then he looked at her and realized how he must have sounded, what she must think of him.

"Maggie?"

He reached out a hand to touch her face, but she recoiled defensively.

"Go away!" she told him fiercely. "Go away and just leave me alone!"

Swearing with great feeling, Jude hesitated for a moment. Then, without another word, he turned and walked away from her.

And when he had disappeared through the door leading to his room, the patio was so still and quiet that Margret could almost believe that the whole episode had been some horrible dream. But she knew that it had been real. She knew because the citrusy scent of his after-shave still mingled with the cool night air.

Chapter Four

"No, Jenny, I don't understand. Just why can't we see each other anymore?"

Hearing Rob's voice, Margret came to an abrupt halt in the doorway that led to the kitchen. Jude's brother was talking on the kitchen phone, his back toward her. It was obviously a very private conversation.

She had started to move away when he turned and saw her. His mouth twisted in a pathetic attempt at a smile as he waved her forward.

Reluctantly Margret stepped into the kitchen.

"Yeah, well, I'm sorry, too. When you *are* ready to talk about it, you know my number."

Margret watched him hang up the phone. The anguished expression he wore was such a contrast to his usual bright smile that her heart went out to him.

"Excuse me," she said awkwardly. "I didn't mean to eavesdrop. I was just looking for Todd."

"Jenny and I were supposed to get married," Rob whispered, as though she hadn't spoken. "As soon as she graduated from college. Now she calls me long distance to tell me she wants to break things off. Guess that's better than a Dear John letter, right?"

Margret felt a pang of sympathy for the younger man, but had no idea what she could say to comfort him. "Rob...I'm so sorry."

Rob visibly gathered himself together. He walked over and put his arm around her shoulders. Once again he was a carefree young man—if one didn't look too closely at the expression in his eyes.

"Don't worry about it, pretty lady. This is just my romantic technique. One sad story and I have you weeping and falling at my feet, begging to comfort me. Clever, huh?"

Margret felt her mood lift at his gentle teasing. Her lips curved upward until she was smiling, too. "Very clever. Much better than the way your brother handles things."

Rob lifted one eyebrow. "You had a fight?"

"I'm not even sure you could call it a fight," Margret confessed.

During a long, nearly sleepless night, she had tried to think of an explanation for Jude's behavior. She had even found herself wondering if Jude might be suffering from emotional problems as a result of his wife's death.

But he'd given no indication of instability the night he'd pulled her from the car. She was alive now because of his strength, determination and compassion. It was those qualities that had first attracted her to him, that continued to attract her.

She shook her head, frustrated by her inability to understand what had triggered Jude's outburst the night before. "Everything was going along just fine. Then suddenly Jude started asking questions about my relationship to Ed. From the things he said, I think he actually despised Ed Tanner."

"I don't want to disillusion you, Maggie," Rob told her softly. "But that pretty well sums up my own feelings toward the man."

Margret looked at him in astonishment. "Why? Why would you feel that way?"

"Because of what he did to my mother."

"What did he do?"

A veiled expression settled over Rob's finely drawn features. "I hate to deny you anything, Maggie, but I'm afraid you're going to have to get that answer from Jude."

She opened her mouth to issue a protest. But before she could voice it, a small body launched itself at hers. Her legs were clamped in a viselike grip, and only the cane she was leaning on kept her upright. "Good morning, Todd."

"Good morning, Mom! You sure woke up late. I already had my breakfast, so can Rob take me riding now?"

"Well . . ." Margret paused, debating the best way to prepare him for what was to come. She still wasn't sure that she should take Todd to Ed's funeral. But then the whole ranch was participating, so who was there to leave him with? She really had no choice.

Rob's voice interrupted her thoughts. "I can give Todd a riding lesson this morning, if you like."

Margret looked at him in confusion. "But—"

"I meant what I said a minute ago. And feeling the way I do, I'd really rather take Todd riding."

Margret thought about it, and decided her first instinct had been correct. Todd had already said his own personal goodbye to the man he'd called Grandpa. He didn't need to go through a long, trying ceremony on top of that.

"Okay," she agreed, wishing for a chance to finish the discussion that her son had interrupted. But Todd had Rob by the hand and was already pulling him toward the door. "Do you think Jude will decide to go out riding this morning, too?" she called impulsively.

Rob looked back toward her and shook his head. "He'd like to, but he won't. It's different for Jude."

It's different for Jude.

Rob's words replayed themselves in Margret's head a few hours later as she sat at the big oak table in the sunlit library of the ranch house. She couldn't seem to forget that conversation or the questions it had raised in her mind. Those questions had plagued her throughout the surprisingly crowded funeral service.

As Rob had predicted, Jude had been present for the ceremony. Yet Jude had spoken of Ed even more negatively than Rob had.

Of course Jude was the oldest Emory son, the male head of the family. He was probably obligated to put in an appearance. But Margret couldn't shake the feeling that Rob's words held some greater significance.

She glanced at the old clock on the library wall, wondering when Ed's lawyer would arrive. The letter she'd received from him with the funeral information had also asked that she be present for this reading of Ed's will. As far as she was concerned, it seemed a great deal of trouble to go through just to collect some memento that Ed could have given to her himself, weeks ago.

For an instant the thought crossed her mind that he might have bequeathed her something of real value. That farfetched idea brought a small, sad smile to her lips. Even if Ed could have afforded to give her the Garden of Eden and Shangri-la all rolled into one, it still wouldn't make up for the loss of a man who had come to mean so much to her.

"Is this seat taken?"

Margret started at the sound of Jude's familiar voice. She'd been so preoccupied, she'd failed to even register his approach. He stood by her chair with his jeans-clad legs braced wide; a navy-blue jacket and a string tie his only concessions to the formality of the occasion. Although she'd caught glimpses of him earlier at the crowded service, this was the first time they'd been within speaking distance. Now she could actually feel her heartbeat accelerate as her gaze met his.

Shaken, she forced herself to look away. "You're free to sit anywhere you like," she told him, her voice as cool and as steady as she could make it under the circumstances.

She was determined to keep her emotional and physical distance until Jude explained his actions of the previous night. But when he slid into the seat to her left and casually draped his arm along the back of her chair, her resolve began to weaken.

Her senses registered the familiar scent of him, the warmth of his body so close to hers, and memories of last night's accusations seemed to dim. Suddenly she could only recall the gentle touch of his callused hands, the soft caress of that ruthless mouth, her own eager response.

She laced her trembling fingers together in her lap, struggling to maintain an appearance of indifference. Thank goodness Jude wasn't able to read her mind! Then she sneaked a glance in his direction and saw that one corner of his mouth had curled up in a knowing smile as if he could indeed read her thoughts and thoroughly approved of their content.

A faint blush stained Margret's cheeks, and she hastily averted her gaze. Such images just didn't seem appropriate on the day of Ed's funeral. But she found it difficult to dwell on the end of life while sitting in the warm sunlight of a beautiful spring morning—especially when Jude was only inches away. And besides, she had the strangest feeling that if Ed could see her now, he would heartily approve of her attraction to Jude Emory.

That was one thought she would have enjoyed sharing with Jude—but she knew he wouldn't want to hear it. Just as she hadn't wanted to hear his side of things last night. Now she was ready to listen. She needed to know why Jude felt the way he did, why he had spoken to her the way he had.

She was trying to find the words to tell him how she felt, when Jude suddenly leaned close. "I'm sorry about last night, Maggie," he said in a low voice. "Forgive me?"

Margret felt a surge of relief and happiness at his words. She looked into his eyes and wanted more than anything to give him the answer he sought. But she forced herself to hold firm. "I don't need an apology, Jude—just an explanation."

Jude had sworn to himself that he was going to apologize and back off before he fell into temptation again. Looking into her eyes, he realized it was already too late for that. "There's not enough time to talk it out now. After the will is read, you'll understand part of it—something I started to tell you last night. You weren't ready to hear it then. Maybe you still aren't. But no matter what happens, bear with me for a while. There'll be plenty of time for explanations later."

Despite the feeling of apprehension that came over her at Jude's words, Margret had no opportunity to pursue the subject. At that moment Nilda entered the room accompanied by a middle-aged man carrying a briefcase.

The man approached and shook hands with Jude. Nilda made the official introduction. "Margret Brolin, this is Sam Perry, Ed's attorney."

The lawyer was fiftyish, stocky and distinguished looking. He gave her a smile full of country charm and fatherly concern as he took her hand in his large, warm grasp. "Margret and I aren't exactly strangers. I visited Ed's home in El Paso several times in the past few months. Sorry to hear about your accident, my dear. It's lucky you weren't seriously hurt."

Margret returned his smile. "That wasn't luck—that was Jude. He saved my life."

Perry's gaze flicked from her face to Jude's, then to Jude's arm which still rested along the back of her chair. "Strange how things work out sometimes," he murmured enigmatically. "Well, time to get down to business."

The lawyer closed the door and seated Nilda in the chair across from Margret. Then he took a seat at the head of the table. Opening his briefcase, he removed a sheaf of legal-sized papers and placed them on the table in front of him. He shut the case, lowered it to the floor and adjusted his glasses.

"We are gathered here to read the last will and testament of Edward Tanner...."

Margret sat back in her chair, bracing herself for a boring marathon of obtuse legal phrases. She hoped it would be over soon. Then she could finish her talk with Jude and hear his explanation of what had happened last night. She wanted so much for things to be right between them again.

"To Nilda Emory, I bequeath all of my personal effects, and all rights to my one hundred and ten mystery novels and my Poe biography."

Margret's head swiveled back toward the lawyer, her mouth slightly open in surprise. *One hundred and ten mystery novels?* Even when she'd heard Ed eulogized as a "famous author" at the funeral, she had assumed it was just polite exaggeration. And she'd had no idea he wrote mysteries.

Sam Perry read on, oblivious to Margret's reaction. "To Nilda Emory, I also bequeath the Double Diamond Ranch manager's house and all its furnishings."

Margret searched Nilda's composed features, puzzled by the words that had just been spoken. How could Ed give Nilda title to the manager's house on her own ranch? Had it been in Ed's name for some reason? Before she could speculate any further, she heard something that shocked her even more.

"To my only son, Jude Emory, I leave the sum of twenty-five thousand dollars and a guarantee of lifetime employment as the manager of the Double Diamond Ranch."

All warmth seemed to leave Margret's body as she watched Jude begin to rise from his chair. The questions he'd asked last night echoed in her mind. Now they made sense. No wonder he'd been so concerned about the possibility of her being Ed's lover—or Ed's daughter. Jude Emory was Ed Tanner's son!

"To my devoted secretary, Margret Brolin, I bequeath all rights to my unpublished work, entitled *The Legacy*, on the condition that she prepare it for publication herself. I also leave her the property known as the Double Diamond Ranch, including its buildings, machinery, livestock and any profits which accrue from its operation. This bequest is subject to the condition that she reside on said property for twelve consecutive months. If she becomes deceased or chooses to leave the ranch before the twelve-month period of residency is completed, the ownership of the Double Diamond Ranch will revert to Jude Emory."

Jude's fist came crashing down on the gleaming wood, and the heavy table shook under the impact. "Are you saying that son of a bitch went back on his word and gave her my ranch?" He turned on Perry, his eyes revealing his anger. "You know that the Double Diamond was promised to me from the day I was born. That old man had to be out of his mind when he made this will. I'm going to break it if it costs me my last dime!"

Perry leaned back in his chair, his arms spread wide in a gesture of helplessness. "Jude, I don't blame you for feeling the way you do. But I got to tell you, this is one will that's airtight. Ed paid to have two psychiatrists examine him on the day he drew it up." He removed two documents from the stack in front of him and held them up. "I have their statements right here. They say he was as sane as any man in Texas."

The papers slid across the smooth wood and came to rest directly in front of Jude. Margret watched him skim their contents with a feeling of sick apprehension. The whole puzzle had finally come together for her. This wasn't the Emorys' ranch at all. They had only been managing the place for Ed. They were *employees*. Except that one of those employees was Ed's son—a son who had expected to inherit the Double Diamond.

She remembered the pride on Jude's face when they'd come riding over the hill the morning after he'd saved her life. "This is my ranch," he'd said. No piece of paper could alter the simple truth of that statement. It was his because he'd earned it and because he was Ed's flesh and blood. She had no right to take it away from him, no matter what Ed's will said.

She opened her mouth to tell him so, but he looked down at her, and the expression of pure loathing on his face froze the words in her throat. "And *you*, the 'devoted secretary,' with your innocent and grateful act! I knew what you were the minute I got a good look at you. But your grit and determination, your love for your son—those things had me doubting the evidence of my own eyes. Well, it didn't take long for the truth to come out. You're nothing but a scheming little tramp!"

Margret hardly registered Sam Perry's sound of disapproval or Nilda's shocked protest. She felt as if every drop of blood had suddenly drained from her body. If Jude had drawn back and hit her with all his strength, he couldn't have hurt her one-tenth as much as he had with his cruel, concise assessment of her true worth.

She had been so sure that he saw past the sadly inappropriate facade of her appearance to the real Margret Brolin.

She had thought he understood. But he'd only seen what every other man had always seen. He'd only wanted what every other man had always wanted. She'd been a fool! Tears stung her eyes, but she refused to cry. She wouldn't show him any weakness.

Pushing away from the table, she took hold of her cane and, head held high, walked slowly from the room. Too proud to let anyone see her hurt, she retreated behind a shield of dignity and cool reserve. She maintained that shield until she was safe behind the closed door of her own room. Then she half hobbled, half ran to the bed and flung herself facedown across it.

But before she had a chance to even try to absorb what had happened, the bedroom door was thrown open. It rebounded off the wall with a crashing sound that vibrated through every nerve in Margret's body. Alarmed, she rolled over and tried to sit up. A heavy weight landed on top of her, knocking the breath out of her and flattening her body against the mattress. A big hand circled her throat, forcing her head up and back. Eyes wide with apprehension, she stared up into Jude's fury-filled countenance.

"Why, Maggie?" he growled. "You'd already manipulated Ed into forking over the ranch, so what was your reason for playing innocent and going after me? Did you think you could use that hot body of yours to control me, to get me to accept Ed's will and agree to keep running the ranch for you without a fight? Well, here's your chance, baby. Come on. Try it now that I know what you are and what you want!"

Margret struggled to draw a breath beneath the crushing weight of his body. It was Jude who had taught her how gentle a man's touch could be. But now his gentleness was gone, replaced by an unreasoning, barely leashed rage. Her mind was telling her that she ought to be terrified of him. But the predominant emotion coursing through her at that moment had little to do with fear. She was feeling the same simmering anger she saw reflected in Jude's dark eyes.

"You don't know one damned thing about me, Jude Emory!" she informed him in no uncertain terms. "I had no idea that you were related to Ed or that he intended to leave me the Double Diamond!"

Jude's expression showed no signs of softening. "Somehow I find that hard to believe."

Margret glared up at him. "I didn't know that Ed owned anything at all of value, let alone a ranch! The only book of his I knew about was the one I worked on. That was a biography of Edgar Allan Poe, and I'm sure that it will never become a bestseller."

For an instant Jude appeared to consider her explanation. Then he dismissed it with a shake of his head. "A woman like you? You're trying to tell me that you didn't know exactly how much Ed was worth?"

A woman like you. Obviously she would never succeed in convincing him that she was innocent. He wasn't capable of seeing past his own prejudices. "You're going to think the worst of me no matter what I say," she told him, her voice rising. "I just wish Ed were alive to tell you himself the way it was!"

"I'm sick of listening to you talk about Ed like he was some kind of saint," Jude growled. "He was a gambler, a drunk and a womanizer. He never gave a damn for anyone but himself!"

"That's not true!" Margret protested.

Jude gave her a smile that was more of a sneer. "I'm living proof, honey. While Ed was engaged to one woman because he wanted her money, he got Nilda Vasquez—a girl half his age—pregnant. He went ahead and married the first woman, anyway, then talked his ranch manager, Ben Emory, into marrying the girl he'd knocked up. I was that baby, Maggie. So don't try to tell me anything about Ed Tanner's character. I already know all there is to know.''

Margret squeezed her eyes shut, wishing she could shut out Jude's words as easily. She just couldn't reconcile his ugly description of Ed with her own memories of the man who had been so good to her and Todd. But she could see that Jude's pain was real enough. "People change," she ventured. "Maybe in later years he regretted how he'd lived, what he'd done."

"So he decided to make it up to me by leaving the ranch to you? Save the fairy tales for Todd, Maggie. We both know why and how you got the Double Diamond. Now let me make my position crystal clear.''

His gaze bored into hers. "Ed hardly ever set foot on this ranch. He didn't know what went on here and he didn't care—any more than he cared about me. Ben Emory, the man I consider my real father, ran the ranch and me after him. I have thirty three years' worth of blood and sweat invested in it, and I don't intend to let you steal it from me. So you can either leave now and let the ranch revert to me, or you can stay and try to earn it from me the same way you earned it from Ed—in bed, flat on your back.''

Margret's hand seemed to raise of its own accord, but the blow never connected. She gasped as Jude seized her wrist and shifted his weight so that his body lay completely atop hers. The evidence of his arousal was unmistakable.

Her gaze meshed with his as images of the previous night filled her mind. For an instant she forgot her anger and remembered only the pleasure his touch could bring. But she couldn't forget the words he'd spoken only moments before. *A scheming little tramp.* That's what this man thought of her. Well, it wasn't true, and she wouldn't let him treat her as if it were. Determinedly she turned her face away, breaking the spell of attraction.

Margret's silent rejection caused Jude's anger to burn even hotter. This woman had snatched away his birthright like a thief in the night and played him for a fool. He wanted to punish her, to make her pay for every acre of land she'd stolen and every half-truth she'd told. If she were a man, he would have beaten her senseless. But she was a woman, and there was only one way he knew to express his anger against her. His eyes as dark as midnight, Jude lowered his mouth toward hers.

Margret clamped her lips tightly together and endured his relentless, grinding kiss. Inevitably she compared it to the way he had kissed her only a few short hours before. She remembered the magic that had flowed between them so effortlessly then and the ugliness of the present moment nearly brought tears to her eyes.

Before the reading of the will, she had dared to hope that there might be a future for them—even if it only consisted of a few days of loving and sharing with a man who was attracted to her real self and not just her appearance. All she had wanted was a memory that she could cherish, a talisman against the lonely days ahead. Now even that modest dream had been crushed.

She could talk until she ran out of words and not convince him of her innocence. She could fight him to the limit of her strength, but there was no way she could win. Suddenly she felt unutterably weary. She just wanted to get the ugliness over with, to put it behind her. Let him do his worst. It didn't matter anymore. There was no way he could hurt her more than he had already.

Giving up the unequal battle, Margret let her body go limp.

Jude took full advantage of her sudden surrender. His tongue thrust into the undefended softness of her mouth, ravaging its depths with enough force to make Margret gasp. For one terrifying instant, she was truly afraid. Then, gradually, his strokes became softer, slower. Within seconds his aggression had become seduction, his battering invasion a reverent exploration.

Margret could have wept with relief. The angry, violent stranger was gone. But now she faced another, more dangerous challenge. She had endured Jude's black rage, but could she withstand his devastating tenderness?

His lips seemed to devour her resistance bit by bit even as she struggled to remain impassive. His fingers softly stroked the sensitive skin of her throat, stilling her words of protest before they formed. Then the hardness of his body began to move against the softness of hers in a rhythm as old as creation.

Trembling, Margret closed her eyes and felt the last of her resistance slide away. She knew that her heart would soon have to pay the price for this temporary pleasure she was taking in his arms, but it was worth the cost. Disregarding the danger, she returned his kiss with all the passion she possessed.

Jude groaned, excited by her response. He could feel the pulse in her neck racing beneath his fingers, her whole body quivering with need. Her arousal was as obvious as his own. He delved deeper into the hot depths of her welcoming mouth, forgetting suspicion and anger—forgetting everything but how good this woman felt in his arms.

But even as his body urged him to even greater intimacy, a warning began to sound in some higher level of his mind. His head reeling, he forced himself to draw back and look into Margret's flushed face. He had just intended to go far enough to frighten her—to scare her so much that when he let her up, she would run away and stay gone.

But instead of struggling and pleading, she had yielded to his strength, absorbing the violence of his intent and gentling it, transmuting his anger into pure desire.

He knew what she was, and she could still make him want her. She could still make him want her with an intensity that shook him to the core.

"Damn you, Maggie," Jude rasped. "Damn you to hell!"

A masculine voice, cold with warning, cut across his words. "Let her go, Jude."

Startled, Margret looked up to see Rob standing in the doorway. Her reaction was a jumbled mixture of embarrassment, relief and frustration. Before she could even begin to sort out those feelings, the weight above her lifted, and Jude was on his feet.

"What's the matter, *hermano?* You want her for yourself?"

Rob gave his brother a disgusted look. "Mama told me about the will. I know how you feel, but I'm not going to stand by and let you punish Maggie for something that was Ed's doing. If he hadn't given the ranch to her, he'd have given it to someone else. He wanted to hurt you, and he used her to do it. She's just a pawn, Jude. Can't you see that?"

"I see that she has the ranch, and I don't. And I see that she already has a white knight fighting on her side. To me that sounds more like a queen than a pawn."

Jude pointed his finger for emphasis. "Take my advice, little brother. Stick to girls your own age. Because this poor, helpless woman you're trying to defend doesn't need your help. She could swallow you whole, spit out the bones, and never lose a minute's sleep over it."

Margret sat up, her anger coming back in a rush. But before she could think of a suitable retort, Jude was gone.

Rob took a step closer to her. "Are you all right? Is there anything I can do?"

Shaking with repressed emotion, Margret clasped her hands together in an effort to steady them. "No, not now. Please, I just want to be alone."

For a second Rob looked as if he might protest. Then he shrugged. "I'll be around if you need me," he told her as he left the room.

Slowly, not sure just what she would discover, Margret scooted to the end of the bed and confronted her reflection in the dresser mirror. Her hair was tumbling down around her face, her cheeks were flushed, her lips swollen from Jude's kisses. Jude had been right, she thought resignedly. She did look like a tramp.

She buried her face in her hands, hurt, anger and disgust raging through her. How could she have responded to him after the things he'd said, the way he'd treated her? His only intent had been to use her and humiliate her, to punish her for a crime she hadn't committed. She ought to run as far and as fast as she could. Yet her heart was inexplicably drawn to the source of the danger.

Margret stared into the mirror until her image blurred and became indistinguishable from the reflected forms surrounding it. She'd grown up in a series of foster homes, places where she wasn't really wanted, places where she was emotionally and physically vulnerable to people who didn't care for her or respect her. Now here she was in the same situation. But this time there was a difference. This time she didn't have to stay.

She'd pack and take a bus back to El Paso today. And when she got there she'd... She'd what? Her new apartment wouldn't be ready for occupancy for another week. And if she used the money she had for bus fare, there wouldn't be enough left for her and Todd to live on until she got her first paycheck. She could probably find temporary work through an agency, but it was spring vacation. Todd would need day care, and that certainly wasn't free.

Suddenly her dismal speculations were interrupted. Her son came racing through the open doorway and jumped onto her lap. "I rode a horse, Mom!" he said, bouncing up

and down in excitement. "I really, really did. Rob said I'm
a natural cowboy."

Margret forced a smile, wiping at her eyes. "That's
great."

"Why are you crying, Mom?"

Margret felt her son's small arms close around her neck,
and her counterfeit smile became genuine. "I was just feeling a little sad, I guess."

"Don't be sad, Mama. I love you."

Margret held his body close to hers, desperately in need
of some unconditional caring. It didn't matter a bit to him
if she looked like Miss Universe or was as plain as mud. To
him she was just Mom.

All at once her priorities came into sharp focus. Todd was
the center of her life. He came first. And for the first time
in her life, she had something other than love to give him.
Ed hadn't just left the ranch to her, he'd left it to Todd as
well.

Margret remembered all the hours Ed had spent with
Todd: helping him with his homework, watching television, playing cards and other games. The old man had loved
her child as if Todd were his own grandson.

And she was the one who had cared for Ed after he became ill. The Emorys hadn't even bothered to come and see
him before he died—not even Nilda. And Jude had despised Ed. All he cared about was getting the damned ranch.

Margret felt something hard and cold settle in the region
of her heart. No wonder Ed had changed his will. The
Emorys ought to be grateful for what they had received. She
had earned the ranch from Ed—not in the way Jude had
suggested, but through her love and devotion. She had
earned it for her son, and she would fight to keep it for him.

"Are you through crying, Mom?" Todd inquired.

"Yes, baby, I am," Margret told him, meaning it. It was
the last time she'd let herself be that weak, the last time

she'd let her attraction for Jude come between her and her son's best interests.

Jude might think he was tough, but compared to her he'd been raised in the lap of luxury. She knew more than he would ever have to learn about the fine art of survival. Let him *try* and get her off this ranch. She wasn't about to walk away from the best thing that had ever happened to her. Margret Brolin was going to stay and claim her inheritance whether Jude Emory liked the idea or not.

...
...
...
...

Chapter Five

The bright noon sun pierced Jude's skull like a high-powered laser. Cursing the whiskey he'd drunk the night before, he pulled the door of the ranch house shut and forced himself to walk out into the yard.

Every step he took seemed to increase the burning agony in his head until he had to bite his lip to keep from groaning aloud. He was sure that nothing could make him feel worse than he felt at that moment. Then he saw *her.*

The new owner of the Double Diamond was reaching over the corral fence to feed his horse a carrot. She had a smile on her face as wide as Texas, and Jude was sure that if Zack had been human he'd have been smiling just as wide. The huge bay gelding was rubbing his head against Maggie's hand like an overgrown puppy dog begging for a caress.

The sight of her was enough to revive Jude's feeling of helpless rage—the same rage that had caused him to retreat to his room with a bottle of whiskey the day before. He was a man who rarely drank, but last night anger had driven him to it. Anger and fear of what that anger might lead him to do to Maggie if he stayed conscious and within touching distance of her. Or was it really fear of what she might do to him?

Against his will, sensory impressions invaded his mind: the satin of her skin gliding against the roughness of his palms; the heavy, silken fall of her hair; the sweet woman-scent that lingered between her soft, full breasts.

Forcibly he reminded himself of what this woman had stolen from him. He let the memory of her betrayal sear through him, burning away the foggy residue of his hangover. For the first time in hours, his head cleared, and his thoughts began to arrange themselves in coherent patterns.

He vaguely remembered making the decision to leave the ranch last night, but fortunately he'd passed out before he'd finished packing. Now that he was stone-cold sober, leaving remained an option, but everything in him rebelled against taking that course of action. Dammit, this was his ranch, no matter what any piece of paper said! His earliest memory was one of trailing behind Ben Emory, begging to be allowed to help feed the stock. He'd been working on the place from that day to this. The ranch had become his only reason for living after Anne's death. It meant more to him than any woman ever would.

But how could he stay on as manager day after day, year after year, knowing that he wasn't really the one in charge? That he didn't have any more say in what went on than Maggie was willing to give him? And knowing that he never would.

Jude's steps slowed as he drew closer to the scene. His gaze ran over her as if it had a will of its own. She had her hair pulled back and confined in a thick gold braid that fell almost to her waist. She was wearing shapeless jeans and a blouse that was so loose it looked like a maternity top. But as she leaned over the top rail of the fence to stroke Zach's arching neck, the baggy material was pulled tight across her breasts and buttocks, outlining a set of curves a man would have to be blind not to notice.

The group of ranch hands that had given up even the pretense of work to gawk at her certainly weren't blind. They weren't deaf, either, if the slack-jawed, slightly dazed expressions on their faces were any indication. They were listening to Maggie's sweet, velvet voice crooning silly endearments to Zack, and every man of them was imagining she was talking to him. Jude was sure of that, because for just a second he'd been tempted to close his eyes and pretend, too.

He remembered the way she had of looking at a man—as if he were everything that was strong and good and desirable in this world or any other. She'd made him want to be all that and more for her—right up until the second she'd snatched the ranch away from him.

His lip curling with self-disgust at the memory, he kept walking forward. He knew the exact instant the men became aware of his presence. The ranch yard became a sudden beehive of activity as interrupted chores were resumed and men swung onto horses that had been patiently waiting for them since the end of the lunch break.

He knew the exact instant Maggie became aware of him, too. She didn't turn her head, but her voice went from soothing to quavery, and he saw her whole body tense as if she were anticipating a blow.

He didn't see any reason to disappoint her. "Does it turn you on to have men drooling over you, Maggie?"

Margret's head whipped around in his direction, and she looked at him with a mixture of anger and astonishment. She fought for control even as the echoes of the past aroused an all-too-familiar feeling of guilt.

Backing away from the fence, she tugged at her shirt in an attempt to reassure herself that it wasn't clinging too closely to her figure. "What men?" she demanded, glancing around the all-but-deserted yard in bewilderment.

Jude stared into a pair of guileless green eyes—eyes so big and so green a grown man could drown in their depths. The woman seemed to have an absolute gift for defusing his anger and replacing it with an emotion that was just as hot, but infinitely more gentle. He found himself wondering if she really was sincere—if things between her and Ed had really happened the way she claimed.

Then he reminded himself that it didn't really matter whether she was a saint or old Jezebel herself. The one thing he knew for sure was that she had his ranch, and she obviously wasn't about to give it up without a fight. It was one battle he didn't intend to lose—no matter how down and dirty the tactics he had to use.

"What men?" he echoed derisively. "Your employees, boss lady! The ranch hands who've been standing around for lord only knows how long, watching you and wondering what it would be like to—"

"No!" Margret raised her hands to her ears to block out his accusations, accusations that were a painful repetition of those that had been echoing in her mind with increasing frequency since her husband's death.

She turned to run, but although her ankle had felt well enough this morning for her to dispense with the cane, the highest speed she could manage was a fast walk. Before she had taken three steps, Jude's hand circled her upper arm in a grip that was just short of painful. She voiced a wordless exclamation of protest as he swung her around and hauled her up against his hard, unyielding form.

She was conscious of apprehension, outrage—and shame at the hot surge of desire that shot through her as his arms went around her, pinning her lower body against the proof of his arousal.

She raised her hands to his chest, pushing to free herself from his grasp. But he held her easily, drawing her closer and closer until his lips were only inches from hers.

Exercising her last bit of willpower, she turned her face aside. She felt his lips press against her hair then delve between the shining strands to search out her ear. She gasped as his tongue traced the outer rim and moved lower to lave the sensitive lobe. He teased the plump nodule of flesh with his teeth, his breath a warm, unconscious caress that sent delicious sensations coursing through her.

She tried to recall all the reasons she had to fear and mistrust the man who held her, but not a single one came to mind. Despite all that had passed between them, she felt more secure in his arms than she had ever felt in her life.

His husky whisper dispelled that fragile illusion as surely as a hurled stone shattering a pane of glass. "I'm giving you fair warning, Maggie. Pack up your things and go back to El Paso."

A chill moving over her skin, Margret leaned away from him to look up into his face. "Or what?" she asked, fighting to keep her voice steady.

She could still feel the heavy beat of his heart, the rise and fall of his chest, the hard press of his body against hers. But his face was expressionless, his dark eyes shielded against her. "Or I'll do whatever I have to do to convince you to leave."

Margret's lips pressed into a thin line, and she glared up at him defiantly. "I grew up in foster homes, Jude. I never had anything of my own, not the clothes I wore or the food I ate. I swore that when I had children, they'd have the best that I could give them. This ranch is a home for Todd—a real home and a future that's better than anything I could ever provide for him."

"I'm all for mother love," Jude growled mockingly. "But it's my home and my future that you're giving him!"

Margret felt a twinge of guilt. If she'd had only herself to consider, she might have relinquished the inheritance. But that wasn't the case. "I didn't give it to him," she said defensively, ignoring her wavering resolution. "Ed did."

Jude's eyes narrowed, and rage flashed through him at the thought of her and Ed together. "Sure he did, Maggie. And we both know what you gave him in return."

Margret's ambivalence disappeared in a wave of anger. "I gave him all the things you never gave him! Caring, consideration, love... That's why he left the ranch to me and not you. It's your own fault you lost out, so if you think I'm going to step aside you'd better think again!"

"Oh, you'll leave," Jude told her, with quiet conviction. "You'll leave before the year is up. Maybe the isolation of ranch life will drive you back to the city. Or maybe you'll leave to get away from me."

"You may not be the most charming man I've ever met," Margret said with false bravado. "But I think I can stand living on the same ranch with you."

"Can you?" Jude asked. "Because if you stay, you may own the ranch, but I'll own you."

"What are you talking about?"

Before Margret realized his intent, Jude had her against the corral fence. He held her in place with the pressure of his own body, his hands rising to capture her face between them.

Margret squeezed her eyes shut, her whole being tensing in anticipation of a punishing kiss like the one he'd inflicted on her the day before. Instead she felt the hot caress of his open mouth against the leaping pulse in her throat. Her eyelids flew open only to drift closed again as he turned his attention to the earlobe he had favored earlier. His tongue and teeth tormented it expertly until she shuddered in his arms.

Jude buried his face in the sweet-scented glory of her hair, feeling the heady thrill of an inevitable victory. Her trembling body was mute testimony to the fact that the passion he'd aroused in her was real. The desire that had threatened to overwhelm them both from the first moment he'd awakened, holding her in his arms, was no lie. The flame was burning even hotter than before. But could he use its power against her without being consumed himself?

The whisper of self-doubt angered him. Sure, he wanted her now. What man could see her and not want her? But once he'd had his fill of her, once the physical itch was well and truly satisfied, he'd be able to walk away with no regrets.

Slowly, deliberately, he arched his aching body against hers. Her half-smothered moan brought a smile to his lips, and he closed his eyes in response to a wave of pleasure so intense it bordered on pain.

"I may not be a joy to wake up to in the morning," he said with grim determination, "but I'll make all your dreams come true after the sun goes down. You stay, and I'm going to make you my woman, Maggie. And I'll make sure that everyone around here knows it."

A shiver ran down Maggie's spine—a shiver that was equal parts anticipation and apprehension. Everything that was instinctive and female in her craved the sweet release that Jude was promising. And everything that was sensible warned her against it. Her desire for him was a weakness. A weakness he would use to exploit and destroy her.

Her resolve of the previous day slowly began to reassert itself and with it came resentment and anger. How dare he try to manipulate her this way? And how could she have let herself respond? Men had been trying to use her before she'd even been old enough to recognize the fact. Jude Emory was just one more.

Gathering all her strength, Margret flattened both palms against his chest and shoved.

Caught off guard, Jude stumbled backward. "What the hell?"

Margret quickly stepped away from the fence and retreated to what she considered a safe distance. Then she whirled around to face him again. Her cheeks were flushed and the expression in her eyes warned against pursuit.

"You egotistical jerk! Do you think I've been waiting around all my life to be seduced by you? Well, think again, Mr. Wonderful. I wouldn't sleep with you if you came with a pocketful of diamonds and a money-back guarantee!"

Jude watched her limp off, too surprised to think of following. Had he been wrong about her response to him? Had she been pretending about that, too?

A soft, low-pitched chuckle sounded behind him and he swung around, murder in his heart. He saw his brother's grinning face and held on to his temper with an effort. "You get an earful?" he asked sarcastically. "Or should I repeat it all for you?"

The grin faded from Rob's features, and his tone became as cold as Jude's. "I was hoping she'd slap your damned face."

Anger combined with the pain in Jude's head and the ache in his groin to consume what little restraint he had left. "If you feel like you're man enough to do it for her, little brother, you come right ahead."

Rob's gaze traveled from Jude's eyes to his clenched fists and back again. He shook his head, his disgust obvious. "I used to respect you, Jude. Now for the first time I'm seeing you for what you really are—what you have been ever since the accident. A bitter, empty excuse for a man."

A red mist seemed to descend in front of Jude's eyes. He took a step toward Rob before he realized what he was doing and stopped himself. "Leave it be," he growled. "Stay out of what's between me and Maggie."

"You may be my brother, but I'm not going to stand by and let you hurt her, Jude. No matter what the consequences."

Eyes narrowed, Rob fixed Jude with one last defiant look. Then he turned and walked away.

Jude stared after him, his anger escalating the pounding inside his head to nearly unbearable proportions. How could Rob side against him? Couldn't he see what Maggie really was and how she was using him?

Now he had one more score to settle with Margret Brolin. She'd done what he hadn't thought possible. She'd somehow managed to come between him and the younger brother who'd always looked up to him. And that was something he could never forgive.

Margret slammed the bedroom door and leaned back against it, struggling to catch her breath. This time she'd stood toe-to-toe with that arrogant cowboy and given as good as she'd got. She ought to feel very good about herself right now. So why did she feel like crying?

"Why, Ed?" she asked her empty bedroom. "Why did you leave the ranch to me?" Was it because she had taken care of him when he was sick while Jude had never visited? Or was there another, deeper reason?

There was, of course, no answer to her questions. Now that Ed was dead, there would never be an answer.

Her gaze centered on the office chair, the transcription machine, the laptop computer, and *The Legacy* tapes that Sam Perry had had delivered yesterday after the reading of the will. She'd spent the morning setting everything up, then she'd gone outside for a walk rather than face hearing Ed's voice on the tapes. Now she had no more excuses left.

Margret settled into the big swivel chair and rolled it up to the desk that Nilda had ordered the hands to move into her room. She turned on the computer, inserted the DOS disk, and within minutes she was prepared to start transcribing. Slipping the earphones on, she depressed the foot pedal to start the tape cassette marked Chapter One.

"This is the story of my life as I lived it. Like any other life, it is a tale of achievement and failure, laughter and despair. But looking back on it now from the brink of eternity, the emotion I feel most strongly is regret."

Margret lifted her fingers from the keyboard and stopped the tape. Then she sat back in her chair, fighting the urge to give in to grief. She had to focus on the words and not Ed's voice if she ever expected to get this project done.

The portion she had just listened to was far different from the Poe biography she had transcribed for Ed before. It didn't seem to be a mystery novel, either. In fact, it sounded as if he had intended it to be an autobiography. And what better place to discover the truth of Ed's feelings and motivations than in a book about his past? Maybe it would be possible to find the answers to her questions after all.

But was she strong enough to face those answers if it threatened to destroy her memories of a man who had meant the world to her? There was only one way to find out.

Margret took a deep breath, sat up straight in her chair and started the tape again.

"Jude?"

Jude raised his head from his inspection of a corral post that would soon need replacing. He felt the movement all the way to his toes. First Maggie, then Rob. Now Todd was after him. He had the worst hangover of his life. Why couldn't everyone just leave him alone?

He turned toward the boy, on the edge of verbally lashing out at Maggie's son like a wounded bear. The sight of the child's face made him choke back the words. Todd's expression contained all the sweetness and innocence he'd thought he'd seen in Maggie, minus the guile he knew lay beneath her pale, flawless skin.

Jude sighed against the pain in his head, resigning himself to enduring the endless questions the child would inevitably throw at him. "Yeah?"

"Can I help you feed the horses again, Jude? Please?"

Jude tugged his hat brim down in an attempt to block out the merciless glare of the sun. It was as futile as trying to block out the memories that assailed him. Himself as a boy, trailing behind Ben Emory, asking the very same question. Rob at seven, a tag-along pest, imitating his big brother's walk and his cussing with equal enthusiasm—and dire results for both of them. His own son who hadn't lived long enough to plague anyone with questions.

Jude blinked back the sudden moisture in his eyes. "The horses have already been fed," he said, his voice husky. He cleared his throat and started toward the barn.

"Will you teach me to be a cowboy? A real cowboy like you and Rob?"

Jude glanced down to find the boy trotting along beside him like an overeager puppy. He began to frame a lecture in his mind about how being a cowboy was hard, unrelenting work. A job short both on pay and prospects for the future. Then he looked into Todd's green eyes and knew all that would be as irrelevant to the boy as it had always been to him.

"Go find Rob. Maybe he'll give you another riding lesson."

Jude entered the cool, shadowy interior of the barn with a feeling of profound relief. He retrieved his bridle and saddle from the tack room, then turned to retrace his steps. He nearly fell over Todd in the process.

"Damnation!" The curse was out of his mouth before he even realized he'd intended to say it. Unable to call it back, he pressed onward. If he didn't make an issue of it, maybe the child wouldn't, either. "I thought I told you to go find Rob."

"He already rode away."

"Then go play with the other kids," Jude instructed, gesturing to where some of the ranch hands' children and the offspring of the domestic help were playing a noisy game of tag.

He walked back toward the corral, annoyed to find his small shadow in determined pursuit. Ignoring the child, he swung the saddle to the top rail and climbed up after it. Zack came trotting up, shaking his head and whinnying a greeting. Jude lowered himself into the corral and slipped the bridle over the gelding's head as the big horse playfully nibbled the front of his shirt.

"They don't like me."

Jude looked at Todd's despondent little face peering up at him from between two fence rails and couldn't help but feel a pang of sympathy. "That'll wear off. They just don't know you yet."

Todd stared down at the toe of one sneaker and proceeded to twist it into the dirt. "They called me a wimp."

Jude threw the saddle blanket over the gelding and carefully smoothed the wrinkles out, fighting down the surge of protective anger that seemed to have come out of nowhere. "Why'd they do that?"

"They said anyone who didn't know how to saddle a horse and ride it by himself was a real wimp."

"They all grew up around horses. You didn't. They'd feel just as out of place in a big city as you do out here."

"I guess so."

Jude turned away from the boy, but Todd's wistful expression stayed in his mind. He told himself that he wasn't going to get involved. Todd would work it out with the other kids a lot faster without any adult interference.

He hefted the saddle and swung it up onto the gelding's broad back. Of course if Todd *was* going to learn to ride, Zack would be the perfect choice for the boy's first horse. He was even-tempered and as steady as a rock. But, he reminded himself, it wasn't simply a matter of giving the boy the horse. Someone was going to have to put in a lot of hours teaching him and supervising him. And if he gave Zack to Todd, that chore would become his responsibility. He wondered why that suddenly seemed more of a challenge than a burden.

Jude opened his mouth to make the offer, then closed it before he spoke the words. He had suddenly realized what a fool he was being. How could he give the horse to Todd? The boy's mother already owned the ranch and every head of stock on the place. And as for him teaching Todd how to be a cowboy, he could just imagine what she'd have to say to that.

He might have been mistaken about her desire for him, but he knew for a fact that she loved her son more than her own life. He knew how protective she was of Todd. How would she feel if she thought her baby boy was in danger of growing up to be a rough-and-tumble cowpoke? Wouldn't that just put a burr in her britches!

A vindictive smile came to Jude's lips at the thought. But it was Todd's miserable expression that finalized his decision.

He hooked the stirrup over the saddle horn and reached a hand beneath the horse's belly to snag the cinch. "Well, I taught Rob how to be a cowboy," he said matter-of-factly. "I guess I can teach you. But only if you're willing to work hard at it."

Todd's eyes and mouth turned into three round circles of surprise. "You really mean it?"

"I said it, didn't I?"

Todd climbed up and over the fence with a whoop that caused the normally unflappable Zack to toss his head and snort. Before Jude knew what was happening, the cinch had been jerked out of his hand and he was on the receiving end of a hug that threatened both his balance and his objectivity.

Slowly he let his hand drift down to tousle Todd's thick, blond hair. The boy looked up at him with a trusting smile that went straight to his heart.

Jude couldn't have put a name to what he was feeling, but he knew it had nothing to do with vengeance. With a belated sense of apprehension, he wondered just what he had gotten himself into.

Gently he set the boy away from him and reached for the cinch again. "Watch me now, son, because next time you're going to be doing this yourself."

Margret was jolted from her concentration and half blinded by the sudden flood of light that entered her dimly lit bedroom. Squinting against the glare, she saw a small form come bursting through the doorway. She barely had time to stop the tape she'd been transcribing before Todd swooped past her, dropping a kiss on her cheek that knocked her earphones askew.

"Nilda said to tell you dinner's ready," he announced, leaping onto her bed and attempting to use the mattress as a trampoline.

"Don't jump on the bed," Margret said automatically.

She couldn't believe so much time had passed while she'd been working on the tapes. When she stood up, her protesting muscles told her that she had indeed been sitting for several hours without a break. She stretched, grimacing at the mild discomfort it caused.

Then, careful of her still-sensitive ankle, she made her way to the door.

Todd jumped down from the bed and grabbed her hand. "Come on, Mom! Hurry up!"

They entered the dining room together and found Nilda and Rob already seated at the table. Jude was nowhere in evidence. Still smarting from this morning's confrontation, Margret wondered if she would be lucky enough to be spared his presence tonight. She quickly squelched the small inner voice that told her she longed to see him again despite the pain that would inevitably result.

Smiling a greeting, Margret settled into a vacant chair. She was just taking a sip of iced water when Nilda began to speak.

"Since you're the new owner of the Double Diamond, I wanted to let you know that I'll be leaving my position as head housekeeper in a few weeks."

Margret barely avoided choking on her water. The workings of the ranch were so far removed from her thoughts that it hadn't even occurred to her that Nilda was a salaried housekeeper. Of course, it made perfect sense to her now that she considered it.

She looked at the older woman, hoping that the panic she was feeling didn't show in her face. "But why would you want to resign?"

"Yes, why?"

The sound of Jude's voice made Margret tense in her chair. She avoided his gaze as he took a seat at the table. Why couldn't he have come in a few minutes later? All she needed was to have him here to gloat over her difficulties.

Nilda placed her napkin in her lap, apparently unaware of the turmoil she had fomented. "I haven't been home to see my family in Mexico for years. And I've always wanted to see Europe."

Jude looked as surprised as Margret felt. "But, Mama, in all these years you never said anything about wanting to leave the ranch!"

Nilda gave her oldest son an indulgent smile. "It was never possible before."

To Margret it seemed that Nilda's two sons were having as much trouble coming to terms with their mother's announcement as she was. She was relieved when Rob voiced the question that she'd longed to ask.

"If you leave, who's going to take your place around here?"

Nilda turned to Margret. "You might want to manage the household yourself," she suggested. "There are only the maid and the cook to supervise. Of course, during the summer the situation is different."

"Of course," Margret murmured, although she didn't understand at all.

Rob took pity on her. "During the summer this is a dude ranch. We rent out rooms to people who pay to experience ranch life. And we provide meals and activities. But don't worry, we never have over ten guests at one time."

Aware of Jude's amused gaze, Margret tried to project an aura of confidence—knowing all the while that she was definitely out of her depth. "I think I could handle that—if you could work with me before you leave."

Unimpressed by the adults' conversation, Todd tugged on Margret's sleeve. "I'm hungry," he whispered loudly in a not-very-successful attempt at subtlety. "When do we eat?"

As if by some mysterious signal, the maid chose that moment to enter from the kitchen, carrying plates laden with food. Margret was astounded by the huge amounts of po-

tatoes, vegetables, biscuits and chicken—until the men began to load up their plates with double helpings of
everything.

She had filled Todd's plate and her own and was about to
lift the first forkful of food to her mouth when Nilda closed
her eyes and bowed her head. Margret hastily followed suit.

"...and may we learn to think not of what has been taken
from us, but instead be thankful for all the good things we
have received."

Sensing someone watching her, Margret looked up in time
to meet Jude's accusing stare.

"Amen."

Turning her attention to her dinner, Margret willed herself not to let the man intimidate her. She ate a few bites of
the delicious food, then defiantly launched into a topic she
was sure he wouldn't approve of.

"I started transcribing Ed's tapes today, and—"

Todd chose that moment to tip his milk glass over. Re-
flexively Margret reached out to right it. Todd caught it
first, but not before most of the contents had spilled.

"Damnation!"

Margret froze in the act of blotting milk off the tablecloth with her napkin and looked at her son in disbelief.
"What did you say?"

"Damnation," Todd repeated obligingly.

A strangling sound escaped from behind Jude's hastily
raised napkin, and Margret was suddenly sure it was laughter, not food he was choking on.

"You taught him that deliberately!" Margret accused, her
face red with anger.

Jude lowered his napkin, all signs of amusement gone.
"You think I'd deliberately teach a child to swear?"

Margret's eyes narrowed, and she leaned forward in her
chair. "You tell me."

Jude returned her stare. "Well, I'm sorry to disappoint you, lady, but it was just something he happened to over- hear. You'll be lucky if that's the worst thing he picks up living around a bunch of ranch hands."

Margret opened her mouth to reply, but was distracted by Todd's frantic tugging at her sleeve. "I'm sorry I said it, Mom! I won't ever say it again—I promise. Just don't fight anymore!"

"We're not fighting," Margret said, lowering her voice to a more normal level.

She glanced at a grim-faced Rob and an equally solemn Nilda in sudden embarrassment. She was about to voice an apology for disrupting dinner when Jude returned to the fray with a smile that didn't quite reach his eyes.

"Cowboys have a lot of unattractive habits. I was twelve when I first tried chewing tobacco. How old were you, Rob? Thirteen, wasn't it?"

Margret's eyes widened in horror at the thought of Todd chewing tobacco. How could Jude discuss the habit in front of her son as if it were something worthy of admiration and imitation?

The big lummox was sitting there looking at her now, daring her to take up the argument where they'd left off. Margret longed to tell him exactly what she thought of him and what he'd said. But Todd had been so upset when they'd exchanged words before. Maybe it would be better to restrain herself now, and "discuss" the matter with Jude later, after Todd had gone to bed. She was still trying to de- cide what to do when she heard Nilda make a sound of dis- gust.

"Chewing tobacco is a filthy habit," the older woman declared. "I would never allow it in my house, so don't make up stories about it to provoke me."

Margret was surprised to see a hint of real amusement come into Jude's eyes. "I'm not making it up, Mama. I re-

ally did try it—once. I saw you coming and I was afraid I
was going to get caught, so I swallowed the whole wad. I'd
never been so sick in all my life—and I sure never had the
urge to chew again!"

Rob laughed and shook his head. "It didn't last long with
me, either."

Jude gave him a questioning look. "Make you sick, too?"

"Nope. I just found out that girls don't like it. That was
the end for me."

Nilda looked on in disapproval while Jude and Rob
grinned at each other like co-conspirators.

Margret was so glad to see at least a temporary cessation
of hostilities between the two brothers that she forgot her
anger and breathed a sigh of relief.

Todd pushed back his chair. "I'm finished eating. Can I
watch TV now?"

Margret inspected his empty plate, wondering how such
a small boy had managed to eat so much food so quickly. "I
guess it's okay. I'll be in to check on you in a little while."

"What were you saying about Ed's book?" Nilda asked
encouragingly as Todd left the room.

Margret set her fork down, embracing the topic eagerly.
"It seems to be an autobiography, and I'm on the part where
he talks about his childhood. Contrary to what some people may believe," she said, throwing Jude a significant
glance, "he didn't have an easy life. As a matter of fact, he
grew up in a London slum."

Jude made a sound of disbelief. "Is that right?"

Margret's hands curled into white-knuckled fists. Apparently the all-too-brief interlude of smiles and pleasant-
ries had come to an end. "Why would anyone want people
to believe he came from a slum it if weren't true?"

"To buy sympathy—to play the poor boy who struggled
and made good. Don't make the mistake of believing that

every word on those tapes is gospel. The man was a born liar with no more scruples than a jackrabbit."

Margret was about to dispute that statement when Nilda interceded with an abrupt change of subject. "Margret, did you know that Layton City and Layton Creek were named after Drew Layton?"

Tearing her attention away from Jude, Margret forced herself to smile and respond to Nilda. "No, I didn't. Was he a friend of Ed's?"

Rob almost choked on his dinner. "You're kidding, right?"

When she continued to stare at him without the least bit of comprehension, he elaborated. "Ed Tanner was the biggest celebrity to ever own property in this area. Folks even voted to rename the town and the creek in his honor. They became Layton City and Layton Creek after Drew Layton, the main character in several of Ed's books and of the TV series that was based on them. Of course, all that happened a long time ago. Ed spent the last five years working on what he called 'a serious project.'"

Margret nodded absently. "The book I transcribed. His biography of Edgar Allan Poe." She still couldn't believe it. Even after she had learned that Ed had written over a hundred books, she hadn't dreamed he was *this* well known. She had never had any interest whatsoever in reading or in watching mysteries, so it didn't seem strange to her that she had never heard of Ed Tanner. But suddenly she understood why it had been so hard for Jude to believe that she was ignorant of Ed's fame or wealth—and she understood where Nilda was going to get the funds for her travels. Even though there wouldn't be any new works, the money earned on reprints of Ed's books would probably keep Nilda in style for the rest of her life.

She toyed with her napkin as another thought occurred to her. Ed had lived very modestly. And the only money mentioned in his will had been the twenty-five thousand he'd left to Jude. "If Ed's mysteries did so well," she asked, "what happened to all the money he earned?"

Jude paused in spooning out another helping of mashed potatoes and speared her with a look. "What do you think happened to it? He spent it!"

Margret felt her face heat at the derisive tone of his voice. It said "I told you so" plainer than any words. Doubt began to eat away at her idealistic image of the man she'd loved and respected. For the first time she questioned the accuracy of her own perceptions. Had she only known one side of Ed? Had there really been another, less perfect side?

She longed to excuse herself from the table and seek the comfort of her room, but she refused to give Jude the satisfaction of seeing her retreat under fire. "I don't know how it was between you and Ed, but if you'd just listen to the tapes maybe—"

Jude's voice cut through the warm room like a frigid draft of air. "I don't need to listen to any tapes—I knew the man. No one told me he was my father. When I was thirteen, I found that out by reading a letter he'd written to my mother. I called Ed Tanner up and asked him if what the letter said was true, if I was really his son. There was this long silence and then he said, 'Ben Emory is your father.' He never even gave me the chance to call him a liar. He just hung up the phone."

Margret shut off the tape and rubbed her eyes. It was no use. She couldn't concentrate on *The Legacy*. She wasn't seeing the computer screen in front of her, she was seeing the pain that had been etched on Jude's face earlier—the pain she'd put there.

Tugging off the earphones, she swiveled around to face Todd. "Okay, mister, enough TV. It's bedtime."

Her expression softened when she saw her son's sleeping form spread out across half of her bed. She moved to stand beside him and plant a kiss on his forehead. No matter how gloomy her mood, Todd could brighten it simply by being there. She started to wake him, then reconsidered.

For years she'd fought a constant battle with herself to keep from holding her son too tightly. She knew from her own experience in life that a person had to learn to stand on his own in order to survive. So she had been careful not to let Todd become too dependent on her, despite the emotional upheavals he'd been subjected to in his short existence.

Still, she had to relent once in a while. Maybe just for tonight he could sleep in her bed. It seemed ridiculous to disturb him now.

Margret carefully removed his shoes and worked the bedclothes out from underneath him. She covered him snugly, then switched off the lamp.

Standing back, she hesitated, uncertain of her next move. It was late, but she was too keyed up to sleep—or to work. Even the thought of reading didn't appeal to her. When she felt this way at home, she made herself a cup of hot chocolate, took a soothing bath and then tumbled into bed on the edge of unconsciousness. But here... Then she remembered that *this* was her home now. Surely she was entitled to some hot chocolate if she wanted it.

Margret switched off the TV and the computer and let her eyes adjust to the dark before stepping into the hallway. She followed its dim contours to the huge living room with its stone fireplace and high ceiling. Most of the room was in shadow, but one section was illuminated by a flood of light that appeared to be coming from an adjacent room—a room she had to pass in order to reach the kitchen.

She froze in place as she remembered what that room was. It was the ranch office, and Jude was its most likely occupant. Her first instinct was to slink back to bed, but she knew she'd never be able to face herself in the morning if she chose that option.

Rubbing her palms against her denim-clad legs, she gathered her determination. She should look at this as an opportunity. Perhaps it was still possible to ease the bad feeling between them—and her own guilty conscience. She could start by apologizing for upsetting him earlier. Then, if she played on his ego by deferring to his superior knowledge of ranch operations, maybe he'd agree to show her around the place and explain how things were run. Maybe they could work together instead of being enemies.

At any rate she had nothing to lose. Their relationship couldn't possibly get any worse.

Reminding herself of the old adage that the best defense was a good offense, Margret pinned a stray lock of hair into place and straightened her blouse. Then taking a deep breath and squaring her shoulders, she marched into the lion's den.

The room was everything she'd expected: wood paneling, dark leather furniture, an old mahogany desk. On the desktop an ancient typewriter, a phone and what looked to Margret like several months' worth of magazines dealing with horses and cattle competed for space with a pile of bills and a stack of worn ledgers.

The man behind the desk looked up at her, his surprise obvious.

Margret looked back at Jude, determined to get in the first word. She wasn't fast enough.

"What do you want?"

His tone brought Margret's hands to her hips. She almost snapped back at him before she remembered that she was here to negotiate a cease-fire, not to engage in another battle. "I came to apologize for upsetting you at dinner."

Jude stared up at her, wondering what her angle was. "Just the fact that you're on my ranch is upsetting me, lady. Haven't you figured that out yet?"

Margret managed to refrain from pointing out that it was *her* ranch. But, despite her best intentions, her voice rose perceptibly. "Rob mentioned earlier that this is a dude ranch. Is that all the land is used for?"

Jude's glare reached across the desk that separated them. "If you're implying that I'm a bad manager, don't. This used to be a cattle ranch until the seventies, when the federal government decided to put a price ceiling on beef. We had to open the place to guests in order to stay in the black. Now we only run a few hundred head of cattle so the city folks can have something to play cowboy with."

"You work with the guests?" Margret asked, unable to imagine it.

Jude made a sound that clearly indicated his feelings on the subject. "I work at avoiding them. The dudes are Rob's responsibility. I breed and train quarter horses, and we both work the cattle."

His tone still wasn't friendly, but at least they were talking. She searched for a question that would keep the conversation going. "So the ranch is making a profit?"

Jude stood up, and Margret took an involuntary step backward. "Is that what all this is about? How much money you can look forward to spending? The big payoff for your devotion to Ed?"

Her blood pressure rising, Margret tried to hold on to her temper. "I was devoted to Ed because he gave me a job and a place to live when I had nothing but a dead husband, an eviction notice and an empty bank account."

"You mean after you'd blown your husband's insurance money, right? Well, let me tell you something, princess. I'll see that you get an allowance for living expenses, but anything beyond that is out of the question. I'll run this place into the ground myself before I'll let you bleed it dry!''

Margret pressed her lips together to keep from blurting out the truth. She hadn't been able to collect on her husband's insurance policy, but, if she told him that, she'd have to tell him the reason why. And that was her guilty secret. She wasn't about to confide it to anyone—least of all to a man who had set himself up as her enemy.

Instead, she crossed her arms over her chest and stood her ground. "Stop threatening me! All I'm trying to do is find out how this place operates."

"Why?" Jude demanded.

"Because I have the right to know!" Margret yelled, her temper at the breaking point.

"Why don't you ask Rob? I'm sure he'd jump at the chance to be of service to you."

Gritting her teeth, Margret ignored his snide implication. "You're the one who runs this ranch. I want *you* to explain what goes on here. Is that beyond your capabilities? Or do you have something to hide?"

Jude walked around the desk and came toward her, halting only inches from where she stood. "I'm not trying to hide anything. I just don't have the time to waste. If you don't like that answer or the way I do my job, then fire me!''

"You know I can't," Margret fumed, his position forcing her to look up at him. "Your job is guaranteed by Ed's will!''

Jude gave her a smug smile. "Then I guess you'll have to live with it—or leave."

"When hell freezes over!" Margret shot back, madder than she'd ever been in her life.

She never saw it coming. One second she was shouting up at him, the next he had dragged her into his arms. His mouth covered hers in a kiss that demanded instead of asked. Margret bent under the force of it, too surprised to even protest.

Second by second the emotions flowing between them began to change and form new patterns like the colors in a kaleidoscope. Aggression shifted toward seduction; anger blended with passion. His arms became a cradle instead of a prison. The hand at her nape forgot to coerce and began to caress. Then, as suddenly as it had begun, it was over.

Jude released her, and Margret staggered back against the wall, disoriented and confused. She told herself that it was outrage making her hands tremble and her heart pound. Then she looked into his eyes and saw a reluctant desire that mirrored her own.

"You lied before," Jude said softly. "You *do* want me."

"Not on your best day!" Margret shot back, trying to control the tremor in her voice and failing.

"You want me as much as I want you. Admit it."

"No!" she insisted, clinging with dogged persistence to the only defense she had left.

"Isn't that why you really came in here tonight?" Jude asked softly, his fingers reaching out to trace the line of her throat.

"Mom?"

Margret started guiltily and turned to see Todd standing in the doorway of the office. "What's the matter, honey? What is it?"

"I heard you yelling. It woke me up. Who are you mad at?"

Grateful for the reprieve, Margret walked to the doorway and took her blurry-eyed son by the hand. "Don't worry about it. Let's just get you back to bed."

"Maggie..."

Reluctantly Margret turned back to look at Jude. His eyes held no malice, just a calm certainty that was more intimidating than any display of temper. "You stay here and it's going to happen, Maggie. You can bet the ranch on it."

Margret shook her head in negation, but in her heart she was afraid he spoke the truth.

Operating on automatic pilot, she got Todd undressed and tucked into his bed. Then she returned to her own room and sank onto the mattress. Leaning against the headboard, she tried to regroup her defenses.

It was a fact that she could no longer deny the attraction she felt for Jude. But nothing said she had to give in to that attraction. If she didn't provide him with an opportunity to seduce her, then it followed that no seduction could take place. She just had to avoid being alone with him again.

Feeling a little calmer, Margret undressed, turned out her light and settled down to sleep. An image of Jude as he'd looked moments before came into her mind. But it wasn't an image of anger, or fear, or even passion. It was an image of vulnerability. Just for an instant tonight, she thought she'd glimpsed a vulnerability in his eyes that fully equaled her own. Only the future could tell her if that image had been real or just an illusion. As she drifted off to sleep, she prayed that the price for finding out wouldn't be her own destruction.

Chapter Six

"*I* asked the heiress to the Reynold fortune to marry me because she was worth millions. She accepted because I was handsome, charming and good in bed—or so she told me. The word love never entered into the equation.

"Two weeks before the wedding, fate stepped in as it had so many times in my life. Playing a hunch at five-card draw, I kept the ace, king and queen of diamonds and took two new cards. Against all odds, they were the jack and ten of diamonds, and I won a ranch in Texas. A visit to check out the place seemed the perfect excuse to escape the incessant wedding preparations.

"On the ranch that I later renamed the Double Diamond, I met a beautiful young woman named Nilda Vasquez. She worked as a maid there and didn't have a penny to her name.

"She was very young and innocent, and for the first time in my degraded existence I tried very hard to cultivate the *qualities of restraint and nobility—qualities I'd scoffed at for years. Inevitably, I failed.*

"On the night before I was to return to New York for my wedding, I gave in to temptation and made love to Nilda. Afterward, she begged me to stay with her. I tried to tell her that she would only be miserable with a man like me, but she was too young to understand. I left her in tears to return to New York and the Reynold millions.

"When I finally came back to the ranch six months later with my wife in tow, it was obvious that I had left Nilda with more than just an unhappy memory. She was going to have a baby. My baby.

"I thought of doing the sensible, civilized thing and setting her up as my mistress. She might have agreed, but I knew she would have hated that life and hated herself for living it. For one brief, insane moment, I even considered leaving my wealthy wife to run off with that little Mexican maid. But I was still a womanizer, a spendthrift and a compulsive gambler. I would have made her life a living hell. And, of course, I would have missed my wife's money.

"Instead, I gave Nilda to another man. Ben Emory was the manager of the Double Diamond. He was clean, sober, honest, loyal and humble—the man every good Boy Scout aspires to become. In short, the ideal husband and father. I knew I'd made the right choice when I offered to pay him to marry Nilda and he refused the money.

"Staring down at me from the lofty height of moral superiority, he informed me he had already proposed to 'that poor little girl,' but she had turned him down.

"In the end, I was the one who persuaded Nilda that there was no hope for us, that she must marry Emory for the sake of the child. It was the hardest thing that I have ever done, and perhaps the only unselfish thing.

"Now as I look back on that day, I realize that it was the first time in my life I actually understood the concept of love."

Her throat aching with repressed emotion, Margret stopped the tape and removed her earphones. It had been Ed's voice, but the man he had been talking about was a stranger to her. A cynical, materialistic stranger whom she had never met. This was the Ed Tanner that Jude had known. Could that man still have been alive inside the compassionate old man who had befriended her? Had he only willed her the ranch to spite Jude?

At least now she knew the right person to ask.

Margret found Nilda sitting by herself at the kitchen table, thumbing through a well-worn recipe book.

The older woman looked up as she entered the room and gestured for her to come closer. "I'm helping the cook plan the menu for the party tomorrow night. Do you have any preferences?"

"Party?" Margret echoed, lowering herself onto a chair.

Nilda muttered a rebuke to herself. "Forgive me. I forgot to tell you. Once a month the local ranchers have a get-together. It's a combination social event and informal business meeting. This month it's the Double Diamond's turn to play host."

Margret, no social butterfly under the best of circumstances, felt only apprehension at the thought of being surrounded by a group of potentially hostile strangers. Her feelings must have shown in her face because Nilda reached over to pat her hand reassuringly.

"You already met most of the people on the guest list when you attended the funeral, but now you can get to know them as the new owner of the Double Diamond."

Margret leaned forward, letting her folded arms rest on the tabletop. "You've been so good to me, and I'm grateful for that. It's just that…well…I can't help but wonder why you don't resent me as much as Jude does."

Nilda closed the recipe book and looked at Margret directly. "I sincerely believe that Ed had the right to dispose of his property in any way he saw fit. I expected nothing, yet he left me the rights to all his works. He left Jude thousands of dollars. You cared for him when he was sick and made his last hours happy ones. Who am I to say what that was worth to him?"

"Jude doesn't seem to agree with you."

Nilda's dark eyes clouded with memories. "Years ago, Ed did promise my husband he would leave the ranch to Jude. And I know my son has considered it his ever since he found out about that promise. When Jude finally came back to us after the accident, he moved into the main house and he's lived here ever since."

"But you all live here," Margret pointed out, confused.

"No. Rob and I live in the ranch manager's house just as we did when my husband was alive. The only residents of the main ranch house are you, your son and Jude. I realize that you now own the ranch, but I doubt that Jude will agree to change his living arrangements."

"You've got that right."

The sound of Jude's voice turned Margret's head. She felt a thrill of anticipation that made a mockery of last night's resolution. The blood rose in her cheeks as she read the memories of their last encounter in his eyes—memories and an unholy amusement at her expense. Except for her son, she'd been alone in the house with Jude since the night she'd arrived!

Vowing to keep her bedroom door locked from now on, Margret ignored Jude's remark and focused her attention on the coffeepot. She got to her feet and crossed the room to pour herself a cup. Jude's hand reached for the pot at the same time hers did.

Margret hastily pulled back as his warm fingers brushed against hers—deliberately, she was sure. To her surprise, he poured two cups and held one out to her. Avoiding his gaze and taking care not to touch him again, she accepted the cup and carried it back to the table.

Jude held the remaining cup up and looked at his mother questioningly. She shook her head. He leaned back against the counter and took a sip of coffee.

The position did things to his jeans that Margret pretended not to notice. She sat tensely in her chair, wondering if she was safe, or if he would go so far as to make some embarrassing comment to her in front of Nilda. But when he finally spoke again, it was to his mother.

"I'll probably be late for dinner tonight. A coyote killed a newborn calf in the south pasture, and I'm going to try to track him down. Want to go with me, Maggie?"

Margret looked up, startled by the question. "No! I mean, no thank you."

"But didn't you say you wanted me to show you around the ranch?"

Margret saw the challenge in his eyes, but decided that, this time at least, discretion was the better part of valor. After last night's kiss, she had no illusions left concerning her immunity to his attempts at seduction. And she certainly had no intention of riding out alone with him.

The corners of Jude's mouth curved into a taunting smile. "Don't you trust me, Maggie?"

Margret would have liked to tell him just what she thought of his goading, but she respected Nilda too much to insult her son in her presence. "I want to work on the tapes today. Maybe some other time."

Jude's smile faded. "Still devoted to the great Ed Tanner. How touching."

"He earned my devotion."

"Wouldn't it be more accurate to say he paid for it?"

"Jude..." Nilda's voice held nothing stronger than a gentle rebuke, but it had the desired effect.

Jude pushed away from the counter and put his empty cup in the sink. "I'll see you later," he said, leaving by way of the kitchen door.

Staring after him, Margret wondered if his last words had been a threat or a promise.

At a loss as to what to say after Jude's display, she turned back to Nilda. "I'm sorry for bringing trouble to your family. Despite what Jude thinks, I never intended that. And I didn't know that Ed had left me the ranch until I heard the will read."

She looked at the older woman, trying to convey her sincerity. "I don't want to change anything here. All I want is a home, for myself and for my son."

To Margret's surprise, Nilda smiled. "After the accident, Jude walked around this house as if nothing would ever matter to him again. Then you came, and suddenly he is alive once more. Angry, but definitely alive. How can you call that bringing trouble? You've done something I thought couldn't be done—you've given me back my son. I only wish that you and he..."

Nilda paused and her smile faded. "But that is asking too much. His wife, Anne, was a very attractive woman. She was also an untrustworthy one. I spoke the truth that first night, when I said you had revived memories that are very painful to my son."

"I never meant to hurt him in any way."

"Pain is a part of healing. Jude must face the past before he can start to move beyond it."

Nilda's mention of the past gave Margret the opening she'd been hoping for, the chance to learn more about Jude's feelings for his natural father. "Jude seems to resent Ed bitterly, partly because of the way he treated you. I've transcribed the chapter that describes how you and Ed met and how you came to marry Ben Emory. And I have to admit that the man in the tape seems very different from the Ed I knew.''

Nilda sighed and nodded. "At the time, I hated Ed for insisting that I marry another man. I agreed to the marriage for the sake of the baby and because I knew Ben was a good man. Many years passed before I realized that Ed had been right. I loved him, but I would never have been happy with him. Eventually I grew to love my husband with a calmer, deeper love that I'd ever imagined was possible. Then I understood, and I thanked Ed for what he'd done.''

Her gaze focused on Margret. "Ed had many faults, but he was never intentionally cruel. And his nature was too generous to allow him to hold a grudge against anyone for very long.''

"Not even against Jude for not coming to see him when he was dying?''

"None of us here even knew Ed was ill—except for his lawyer, Sam Perry. And Ed swore him to secrecy.''

Margret shifted in her chair, more confused than ever. "Then why didn't Ed give the ranch to Jude as he'd promised your husband he would?''

Nilda clasped her hands on the tabletop, considering. "I honestly don't know. But I do know that he loved Jude.''

"Jude seems to hold a different opinion.''

"I am partly to blame for that,'' Nilda said with apparent regret. "From the very beginning, I meant to tell Jude that Ed was his father. But Jude and my husband were so close, I just couldn't bring myself to do it. Then one day I was out shopping and Jude found that letter and phoned Ed. By the time I came home, Jude had already turned to my husband for explanation and comfort. Ben filled Jude with all the pent-up bitterness and resentment he had been feeling toward Ed for years. I tried to tell Jude that Ed might have pushed him away because he didn't want to come between Jude and my husband. But by then my words fell on deaf ears. I have never been able to make Jude believe that Ed cared for him, any more than I could convince him that Ed once loved me."

The outside door opened and Rob entered the kitchen, putting an end to the intimate conversation. Todd was close on his heels, looking like a miniature ranch hand in a cowboy hat and boots.

"Where did you get those clothes?" Margret wanted to know.

"They're my old things," Rob explained. "Mama never could stand to throw anything out."

Nilda tapped his arm in a playful rebuttal as he bent to kiss her cheek.

Todd came over to the table to stand by Margret. He looked tanned and healthy, and suddenly she was glad she'd decided to stay on the ranch.

"We went all the way to old Pete's place today," her son told her, sounding very self-important.

"You did?" Margret looked at Rob.

The younger Emory brother opened the refrigerator and extracted two cans of cola. "When y'all were there the night of the storm, Jude noticed the leaky roof and the rotted floorboards. I went back today to look the place over so I could see exactly what materials I needed for the repairs."

He crossed the kitchen and handed a can of soda to Todd. "The old place may not be much, but it'd be a shame to let it go to ruin."

Margret automatically reached out to open the soda can for her son. To her surprise, Todd pulled away from her.

"I'm not a baby, Mom. I can do it myself."

Before Margret could respond, Nilda got to her feet, distracting her attention. "It's the cook's day off today, so I'm making lunch. Is everyone hungry?"

Rob and Todd chorused affirmations. Margret gave the only negative response. "I'm okay for now. I think I'll get back to work."

Nilda looked scandalized. "At least have a sandwich."

"No, I'm fine—really. After all I ate at breakfast, I'm good until dinner."

Nilda clucked like a mother hen. "You have to get outside more, get more exercise."

Grateful for the other woman's concern, Margret murmured a polite agreement. When Nilda moved away to begin lunch preparations, Margret turned back to Todd. But he was already on his way outside again.

He seemed different to her somehow. More mature, more distant. And she'd noticed a deeper drawl in his speech and a certain swagger in his walk that reminded her suspiciously of Jude. Or was she just imagining things?

Deciding that she'd have a long talk with her son later, she reached up and touched Rob's arm. "Would you walk me back to my room? There's something I want to discuss with you."

"Sure thing."

They were halfway to her bedroom before Margret asked him the same question she'd asked Nilda. "After the reading of the will, I heard you tell Jude that you thought Ed only left me the ranch in order to hurt him. Why would Ed want to hurt Jude?"

Rob hesitated, then gave her an answer. "Jude's hated Ed ever since the day he found out that Ed was his father—the day Ed rejected him. He made his feelings plain to Ed at every opportunity. My guess is the old man got fed up with Jude's attitude and decided he could be just as spiteful."

"Your mother doesn't believe that."

"My mother has always defended Ed. After all, she used to love him. It's hard to see the worst in those we love."

Margret realized he was trying to tell her something. "You think I'm looking for a deeper explanation where there is none. Just because I don't want to think of Ed as vindictive enough to disinherit his only son out of spite."

"That's entirely possible."

They reached the door of her room and Margret turned toward him, determined to ask the other question that had been weighing on her mind. "What about Jude's relationship with his wife? Were they happy together?"

Rob looked into her eyes, then slowly shook his head. "I'm sorry, Maggie. But that's not my story or my mother's story to tell. It's Jude's story. If you want to know more, you'll have to ask him."

"All right," Margret agreed, more determined than ever to get to the bottom of things. "I'll ask Jude."

"I'd advise you to put on a full suit of armor first. It's not his favorite topic of conversation." He looked at her speculatively. "You might just get him to answer, though. Since you arrived, he's done a lot of things I never expected to see him do again. Last night at dinner was the first time I'd heard him laugh in three years. You must be doing something right."

"Sure," Margret agreed, remembering her last confrontation with Jude. "I've given him a victim to torment."

Rob chuckled and kissed her cheek. "Just remember, if you need help, you can count on me."

Margret watched him walk away, her thoughts and emotions in turmoil. She felt as if her whole world had been turned upside down. Her rock-solid belief in Ed had been shaken, and Jude remained a dangerous enigma. Even her own feelings seemed to be shifting and changing more rapidly than she could comprehend.

It seemed that every path of the confusing maze she found herself in led straight to Jude. And, despite her brave words,

Margret wondered if she would ever summon the courage to confront him about anything again.

Margret sat in front of the computer for hours, trying to get some more work done. By late afternoon her neck and shoulder muscles were in knots. Nilda's comment about exercise kept coming back to her, and she wished she could go riding. But with Jude out and about, it was a risk.

Annoyed with herself, Margret got to her feet and began to pace. She already felt like a coward for backing down from Jude's challenge and refusing to ride out with him. Now she'd been reduced to hiding in her room. Was this the way she was going to spend the next twelve months?

Her mind made up, Margret quickly changed into jeans and a high-necked white blouse, then slipped out of the house and into the warm sunshine. She saw Todd at play with a group of other children and called to him to join her for a ride.

"Go ahead, Mom! I want to stay here."

Margret was a little disappointed at his refusal until she remembered that he'd been riding with Rob all morning. Tomorrow, she promised herself. Tomorrow they'd go out together. The last time she'd had access to a horse, she'd considered her son too young for serious lessons. But now that they were living on a ranch, maybe he ought to learn how to ride—if only for the exercise.

As she entered the nearest barn, a familiar nicker greeted her.

"Zack!" she exclaimed, walking up to his stall to scratch under his chin. "What are you doing here? Did that mean old Jude take someone else out to play?"

Looking the horse over, she didn't see any obvious injuries that would preclude riding him. Apparently, Jude had just felt like taking another mount. Since Zack was the only horse she was familiar with, Margret decided Jude's loss was her gain.

She retrieved the necessary gear from the tack room and made short work of saddling the gelding. Paul had given her riding lessons for Christmas one year and, after the lessons had run out, she'd continued riding for recreation. Of course, it had been a while since she'd ridden. After Paul's death there hadn't been enough money for groceries, let alone for renting a horse.

But Paul wasn't to blame for the way things had turned out—not really. Chastising herself for having unkind thoughts about a man who had loved her, Margret swung into the saddle. Once outside the barn, she turned north—the opposite of the direction Jude had said he was going—and urged Zack into a gallop.

In no time the wind had unraveled her carefully pinned hair. She laughed in delight as it streamed out behind her like a long, golden banner. For the first time in a very long time, she felt free.

She and Zack were both breathing hard when she finally reined to a halt beneath the sheltering branches of a huge oak tree. Unsure if the horse would stay put on his own, Margret led him some distance away where there was good grazing and fastened one rein to the lower reaches of a convenient bush. Then she returned to the shade of the oak.

Settling herself comfortably on the ground, she unbuttoned the high, constraining neck of her blouse. She leaned back against the wide tree trunk and closed her eyes. Her mind gradually emptied of thought as she let her worries go and relaxed completely.

The loud report of a rifle brought her back to reality with a jolt. She leapt to her feet, and the first object her eyes focused on was Jude. He was on horseback several yards away, holding a rifle that was pointed directly at her. For a fleeting instant, she went cold with fear. Then, almost at once, the fear began to dissipate. From somewhere deep inside came the certainty that this man would never harm her. She'd bet her life on it.

As Jude lowered the rifle and started toward her, she let out the breath she'd been holding and slowly slid back to a sitting position in the grass.

He was shouting at her even before his feet touched the ground. "What the hell do you think you're doing coming out here without telling me? You knew I was hunting that coyote!"

"You said you'd be riding south," Margret said, letting her head fall back against the tree to look up at him. "I didn't think you'd be anywhere near here."

"Did you stop to think that the coyote might lead me this way?" He slid the rifle back into the scabbard attached to his saddle, talking all the while. "He must've passed within ten feet of you. You're lucky I was taught to make sure of what's in the sights before I pull the trigger. Do you realize I could have shot you?"

"Yes," Margret said, meeting his angry gaze. "Believe me, I realize it."

For the first time Jude noticed her pallor and the betraying tremor in her hands. His eyes narrowed. "You thought that I was *trying* to shoot you, didn't you?"

"No! Yes... For a split second I guess the possibility occurred to me, but—"

Jude looked as if he might like to have her in his sights again. "Let me clear up any doubts. I was shooting at the coyote. What gave you the idea that I was capable of murder? Those damn tapes that old fool left you?"

"Ed wasn't an old fool!" Margret protested, pressing her hands against the tree behind her and pushing to her feet.

"He was worse than that."

"If you'd listen to the tapes yourself, maybe you'd understand him better. He cared about your mother and about you. That's why he insisted she marry another man—he knew that he'd make a lousy husband and father.''

"Is that how he'd justified it to himself?" Jude said with a smirk. "And you believe it?''

"Yes, I do.''

Jude took his Stetson off and slapped it against his thigh in frustration. "Are you really that blind? Or don't you want to see? Old, sick and dying, and the man was still collecting women.''

"If you're implying—''

"That you and Ed were lovers? I'm not implying anything. I'm saying it right out loud.''

"You don't understand the kind of caring we had between us, so you have to drag it down to your level, to make it something sordid and cheap!''

Anger flashed in Jude's eyes—anger and something even more dangerous. "Oh, you weren't cheap, lady. You sold for the price of a ranch. And to my way of thinking, I'm the one who paid that price.''

His cold gaze raked over her unbound hair and settled on the cleavage exposed by the open neck of her blouse. During their previous encounters, Maggie had gentled his anger and made an addle-brained fool out of him with a single kiss. This time it was going to be different. This time, *he* was going to control what happened between them.

A chill skittered along Margret's nerve endings. Instinctively, she took a step away from the tree, a step toward where Zack stood calmly grazing. But that was as far as she got. Jude threw his body against hers, forcing her to the trunk of the oak.

"Please . . ." she whispered, hoping against hope that he would relent.

"You don't have to beg for it, honey. I'm going to give you what you've been asking for since that first night. And when I'm finished, you won't even remember Ed Tanner's name.''

Margret read his intent in his eyes. They were a dark swirl of passion and anger, and her heart began to beat heavily. She was simultaneously repulsed and attracted, afraid and aroused. She wanted Jude, but she wanted the gentle man who had rescued her in the storm, not this rough, uncaring stranger. Torn between trying to fight her way free and remaining in his arms, she hesitated too long. And that moment of doubt sealed her fate.

Oblivious to Margret's revulsion, Jude buried his face in her neck, his teeth nipping at the soft skin of her throat. Since his wife's death, he had become used to experienced, jaded women—women who liked their sex rough and hard, hovering on the borderline between pleasure and pain. Now that he had finally come to realize the kind of woman Margret was, he knew that she was no different from the scores of other faceless, nameless females who had left him with claw marks on his back and a smile of complete satisfaction on their lips. The fact that this time he was angry and frustrated himself was just the icing on the cake.

Margret shut her eyes and fought a cry of protest. He was grinding his hips against hers, grinding her body into the hard tree with no thought of her discomfort. But why should he be any different than any other man she'd known? All her life the opposite sex had treated her like a creature with no feelings, no brains, no morals. This was simply the final degradation.

She told herself that regardless of what he did, he couldn't really touch her in any way that mattered, that afterward she could walk away as if nothing had happened. But he was hurting her on a level more significant, more lasting than the physical. The fact that it was Jude who was treating her this way sent the pain spiraling deep inside to burn to the depths of her soul.

Then, all at once, she felt him move away from her. Slowly, hesitantly, she opened her eyes and found him staring at her as if he'd never seen her before.

Jude watched the silent tears coursing down Margret's pale cheeks with a feeling of dull astonishment. Then he began to curse with great originality and depth of feeling.

Something in his expression broke down an invisible barrier inside Margret. She began to shake and to sob raggedly, gulping in air and releasing it in sounds that were hardly human. She closed her eyes, praying that he would have the decency to go away and leave her alone. Instead, she heard his cursing become louder and even more fluent. Suddenly he was gathering her into his arms.

Using the tree to brace himself, Jude slid down to a sitting position on the ground and settled an unresisting Margret on his lap. Not knowing what else to do, he began to rock her awkwardly, crooning soft, wordless syllables that had no meaning. Margret buried her face in his cotton-covered shoulder and cried until her supply of tears was exhausted. Then she simply clung to him as he moved back and forth.

Jude felt her body relax degree by slow degree until, finally, she lay against him like a trusting child. Slowly, carefully, he slid his hand beneath her chin and raised her face to his gaze. Beneath red, swollen lids, her green eyes focused on his. Reaching around with his free hand, he drew a handkerchief from the back pocket of his jeans and used it to wipe her face.

"Why the hell didn't you just say you didn't want me?" he asked her as softly as his anger would allow.

"I think I've wanted you since the night we first met. I just didn't want you...that way. I didn't want to be hurt."

"Then why didn't you tell me I was being too rough for you?"

She blinked up at him, bewildered by the question. "I thought hurting me was what you intended."

Jude started to explain his actions to her, then paused to think it over. Was she right, after all?

He looked down at the woman he held in his arms. Moments ago, he had seen only the hard, gold-digging witch who had stolen his ranch. A part of him had wanted to take that woman brutally and completely, to break down her defenses until he owned her. But now he wondered if that creature had ever really existed anywhere except in his imagination. And if he could brutalize any woman—even a consenting one—what did that say about the kind of man he had become?

Chilled to the bone, he knew he couldn't let this thing rest until he understood it completely. "Strange as it may sound to you, Maggie, I thought you were enjoying what I was doing." He took in the confused look on her face and knew she had no idea what he meant. "What I'm trying to say is, no woman would ever choose a man with a face like this if she wanted a night of sweet and gentle loving."

She frowned at him, more perplexed than ever. "What does your face have to do with anything?"

Her words and the look in her eyes touched him in places that he would have sworn had gone dead to all feeling years before. He shook his head, at a loss as to how to deal with the situation. "Ah, hell, Maggie! If you didn't like what I was doing, why did you just stand there and take it? Why didn't you do something, say something?"

"I didn't think I could say or do anything that would stop you."

"Well, you were wrong." He brushed a stray strand of hair off her forehead and thought that maybe he'd been entirely too right about her that dark night on the terrace. The urge to give was strong in her. Too damned strong.

His next words surprised even him. "Don't you *ever* sit back and let anyone treat you like you don't matter, Maggie. Not ever again. You hear me?"

Margret sat up abruptly and turned her back to him, suddenly needing the physical and emotional distance. "I guess," she said finally, "that I got used to being treated that way."

That simple statement had a red haze of anger floating in front of Jude's eyes. He wanted to shake her and demand to know who had dared to abuse her. But she'd already had enough temper and rough handling from him. Instead he took a deep breath and spoke quietly. "Tell me about it."

Margret didn't intend to. She certainly didn't want to. But somehow as she sat cross-legged on that sunlit patch of grass, the words came pouring out of her, like water breaching an overstressed dam.

"My parents died in a hit and run accident when I was twelve. The people at the first foster home I was sent to were very nice, but they already had a daughter of their own. Lisa hated me from the minute she saw me, although I didn't understand why at the time. To get rid of me, she stole money out of her mother's purse, then told her parents that I had done it. She said that I had threatened to beat her up if she told."

"Why didn't you tell them the truth?"

Margret's lips curled in a humorless smile. "Oh, I tried, but they didn't believe me—and neither did the social worker. I was sent to a home that specialized in 'problem cases.' I was doing okay there until the foster father began to show a special interest in me. I thought it was great at the time—I was starved for love and affection. Only he had a different kind of affection in mind. I realized that the first time he tried to put his hands on me."

Jude sat listening to the even, unemotional tone of her voice, outraged by what had happened to her and even more by her seeming accceptance of it. "And you let him get away with that?"

"When I realized it wasn't going to stop, I told my foster mother. She called me an evil little liar and threatened to have me locked up until I was eighteen if I told lies to anyone else. After what had happened in the first home, I didn't think anyone would believe me, anyway. But one of the other foster children had seen what had happened. He said he'd go to the social worker with me. We went, and we were both placed in other homes while an investigation was conducted."

Frowning, Margret toyed with a blade of grass by her knee while Jude waited impatiently for her to continue. After a moment the flow of words began again. "The foster father broke down and confessed. He ended up going to jail."

"Where he belonged," Jude reminded her, sensing her lingering guilt.

"Where he belonged," Margret echoed, as if it were an old lesson she hadn't quite mastered.

"And your husband?" Jude prodded. "How does he fit into all of this?"

Margret plucked the blade of grass, then let it fall back to the ground. "Paul was the other foster child—the boy who went with me to the social worker."

She smiled faintly, a mixture of affection and sadness. "The first time I saw him, I thought he was a pretentious fool. Then I realized that his bragging was just a cover-up for an inferiority complex that stretched a mile wide. He wasn't especially smart, or talented, or good-looking, so he made up stories in which he had all those qualities. But his favorite story was about how his wonderful parents had sacrificed their own lives in order to save him from drowning. One of the other kids at the home told me the truth. Paul's parents weren't really dead—they had abused him to the point that the state had taken him away from them and placed him in foster care. No one had ever really loved him.''

''And if there was one thing you understood, it was the need to be loved.''

Margret slanted a glance back over her shoulder, surprised by his perceptiveness. ''Yes, I understood that very well. I treated Paul Brolin like the brother I'd never had, and he gave me love and loyalty in return. We got separated after our foster father was arrested, and I never really expected to see him again. But we sent letters to each other and swore we'd remain friends.''

''The new home they placed you in, what was it like?'' Jude asked, already suspecting what her answer would be.

Margret shrugged as though it was a matter of little importance. ''I went to live with an older couple who had no other children in care. All they expected from me was the money they collected from the state. All I expected from them was room and board. We got along just fine.''

Her mouth tightened as she thought of the awful loneliness of those empty years, but she pushed the memory aside. ''When it came to the world outside the foster home, I guess I was too afraid of being rejected to try and make any friends. The girls at school seemed to want nothing to do with me, anyway, except to make fun of my secondhand clothes. I did get asked out by boys a few times, but they only wanted to park and wrestle. So I just stayed home. I got the heave-ho from foster care the day I turned eighteen.''

Jude traced the rigid line of her back with his gaze and tried to imagine being as alone as Maggie had been. He had been a loner, too, but he'd always had the warmth and security of a family to fall back on. She'd had no one.

Without really intending to, Margret found herself continuing her story. ''I was working as a secretary at a women's clinic and taking some night courses in accounting when

Paul decided to look me up again. For the first few minutes, he seemed to be as distracted by my appearance as most of the other men I'd met. Then the awkwardness disappeared, and we were just Paul and Margret again, two outsiders who had only each other to count on.''

"So you married him."

Margret stiffened at the hint of censure in Jude's voice. "He loved me and he understood where I'd come from. That was more than I'd expected to have. We wanted a family like the one I'd lost—the one he'd never had."

"Then you lost him, too."

The words hovered on Margret's lips. She wanted to tell him the whole story, but she was afraid to. Afraid that if she did, he would condemn her as she condemned herself.

It was Jude's voice that broke the silence. "And, somehow, for some reason, you blame yourself for his death. Just like you were to blame for your foster father going to jail and all the rest of the crap in your life!"

Stung by how close he'd come to the truth, Margret uncoiled her legs and twisted around to face him. "Just like you blame yourself for the death of your wife?"

Jude's voice was calm and level, but his eyes were a mirror of pain. "There's one difference between you and me, Maggie. She was leaving me for another man, and I wished her dead."

A wave of shock passed over Margret, and for a second she wondered if he *had* caused Anne's death intentionally. But something in her refused to believe him capable of that. Filled with pain for the betrayal he had suffered and with remorse for her hastily spoken words, she reached out a hand to comfort him as he had comforted her. But he pulled back.

She tried to sooth him with words instead. "Wishing for something in a moment of anger doesn't mean it's your fault when it happens."

"How about being behind the wheel of the murder weapon?"

The pain danced around him like an invisible aura, surfacing in his hoarse voice and his tense posture. Margret couldn't stand to see it.

"You intentionally drove your car into the creek?" She hoped he would correct her and talk about what had really happened. She hoped he would share his pain.

Instead he seemed to draw it back into himself. He took a deep breath and let it out slowly. "I told the story once, to Sheriff Dawson. I haven't talked about it since, and I don't intend to talk about it now."

Margret had shared her own deeply personal memories with him, and she was hurt by his refusal to share with her. She was about to get to her feet and leave when his arms circled her from behind. She tensed automatically, but his embrace was gentle, his breath warm on her skin as he nuzzled the hair at her temple.

"I don't want to talk about the past anymore. I want to concentrate on the present. And you." Jude let his hand smooth over the silky cloak of hair that covered her back. "It looks like spun gold in the sunlight," he whispered, not even trying to keep the awe out of his voice.

Margret smiled. "It's more like a rat's nest right now. The wind tangled it to a fare-thee-well."

"It's beautiful." He eased her back, intending to kiss her, but she pulled away.

"What's the matter?" he asked softly. "Am I still scaring you?"

Margret shook her head. "It's just that I'm not... I'm not very good at this."

"You're not?" Jude said, trying to hold back a smile.

"I..." Margret dropped her gaze. "With Paul, he tried, but...I just couldn't seem to respond. I didn't want to hurt him, so I pretended. Even that didn't seem to reassure him.

He was always so upset when other men noticed me. I changed the way I fixed my hair, the style of clothes I wore, but nothing seemed to satisfy him.''

"Dammit, Maggie, what about you? Didn't you have the right to be satisfied?''

Margret pushed the thought aside, uncomfortable with the long-suppressed feelings of anger and resentment that it threatened to arouse. "You don't understand. Emotionally, Paul just wasn't very strong.''

Jude reached out and took her into his arms again. "And what about the other men you've been with, Maggie? Didn't any of them give you the same kind of pleasure that you gave them?''

Margret felt a blush spreading its way across her cheeks. Self-consciously, she lowered her gaze. "Paul was the only man I've ever been with.''

Jude was glad Margret wasn't looking at his face. The expression of surprised disbelief there would probably have enraged her. He wondered if what she'd said could possibly be true. Despite Maggie's femme fatale appearance, there had always been a quality of innocence about her when he'd held her in his arms. Then he realized that he didn't give a damn if she'd been with one man or one thousand. Right now, there was no one else between them. For this small, finite space of time, she was his alone.

"I'm going to try and make love to you the way you want, Maggie—if I still remember how to be that gentle. I want you to tell me what you feel. I want you to tell me everything you feel.''

Margret felt the soft brush of his lips against her cheek. She sighed and closed her eyelids as he feathered butterfly-light kisses across them.

When he finally claimed her mouth, it opened beneath his like a blossoming flower. His tongue caressed the treasure he'd uncovered, learning its contours, its mysteries. Then, slowly, he seduced her tongue into reciprocating.

Margret no longer heard the sound of the wind or felt the heat of the sun. Her whole world was restricted to the sensations his mouth aroused, the feel of his body pressed to hers. She was barely aware that he had taken her down into the soft grass, that they were lying side by side. A hot, achy feeling spread from her breasts to her abdomen. She moved her hips, trying to get closer, trying to ease the ache.

Jude rolled on top of her, pressing his body against hers. "Better?" he whispered.

Margret bit her lip and arched against him, barely restraining a groan. "It's better," she breathed. "But it's not enough."

"No?" Jude smiled and nuzzled the hard peak of one breast through its cloth covering.

Margret started and clutched his shoulders, her nails digging into the cloth.

He slowly unbuttoned her shirt, his fingers straying to caress her breasts for a few seconds at a time before returning to his primary task. Finally there was nothing between her and the sunshine but a flimsy nylon brassiere.

Jude's tongue teased her earlobe, then his mouth engulfed it. Margret moaned in both pleasure and frustration.

"What do you want, Maggie? Tell me."

Margret capitulated, her desire taking her beyond her shyness. "I want you to do that to me here."

Shamelessly, she pulled his head toward her breast. He eased the scrap of nylon aside and obliged her. She whimpered as the exquisite sensation shot through her body, intensifying the ache tenfold.

Jude continued to oblige her until she was bucking under him and on the verge of tearing the shirt from his back.

"Better?" he asked, gritting his teeth against the demands his own body was making.

Margret looked up at him pleadingly, all modesty forgotten. "Please," she whispered. "Please..."

Jude moved his hand down between their bodies, his thumb rubbing against the most sensitive part of her. "Do you like this?" he managed to ask.

Margret was unable to form a coherent answer. Shock waves coursed through her, arching her back and curling her toes. Gasping for breath, she held on to Jude and moaned his name.

Jude looked down at her flushed, taut features, feeling a soul-deep satisfaction that went beyond sexual pleasure. He was giving Maggie something that no man had been able to give her before. Something to make up for all the times she'd been exploited and shortchanged.

Exercising his last tattered remnant of control, he continued to caress her until she stopped quivering and lay limp and sated in his arms. He was reaching down to unfasten his jeans when the sound of hoofbeats penetrated the haze of desire that surrounded him.

Sitting up, he saw one of the hands riding away from them, headed in the direction of the ranch house.

"Did he see us?"

"He saw enough to guess the rest." Jude turned and was transfixed by the sight of Maggie's pink-tinged cheeks, dazed green eyes and breasts that still bore faint marks of his possession. He had to fight the almost overwhelming urge to take her in his arms and finish what he'd started.

Silently cursing his own stupidity, he tore his gaze away from her and pushed to his feet. Making love to a woman in the middle of an open pasture in broad daylight. Just what the hell had he been thinking of? He knew the answer. He'd been thinking of Maggie and only Maggie. He'd always enjoyed sex, but he'd never been so totally absorbed in a part-

ner in his life. And now it had happened with a woman he'd
be a fool to trust. That thought was one he didn't care to
examine too closely. It made him far too uncomfortable. He
only wanted to remove himself from the primary source of
that discomfort as soon as possible.

"Get up and get dressed. Now."

Jude's harsh tone dissolved Margret's haze of content-
ment and completed her transition from warm fantasy to
cold reality. Bewildered and deeply hurt by his sudden
withdrawal, she gathered up her scattered clothes.

They rode back to the ranch without speaking, arriving
just as dusk was slipping into night. A group of ranch hands
was gathered around the main corral, smoking and talking.
Then silence fell as the men spotted them.

Margret felt her cheeks heat as she saw the hands begin to
nudge one another and grin. Holding her head high, she
rode by the men and turned Zack toward the barn. Then she
heard a masculine voice somewhere behind her.

"Is she as good as she looks, boss?"

Tears in her eyes, Margret pulled Zack to a halt in front
of his stall and waited for Jude's answer, waited for the
beauty of the experience she'd shared with him to die a final, ugly death. He'd threatened to seduce her and flaunt
their intimacy in front of the men, to make it impossible for
her to stay on the ranch. And now she'd given him the perfect opportunity to follow through on that threat.

"Mrs. Brolin is the new owner of the Double Diamond.
She's the one who'll be signing your paycheck from now on.
So if you want to keep your job, I'd advise you to watch
your mouth."

Margret slid down Zack's side and landed on legs that
nearly gave way beneath her. Grasping the saddle horn for
support, she turned her head to meet Jude's gaze. She saw
a reflection of her own surprise and disbelief in his eyes.

She watched as Jude reined his horse around and spurred the reluctant mare back out into the darkness. And for the second time that day, she cried.

Chapter Seven

Margret climbed down out of the pickup truck and shut the door. "Thanks, Rob," she said with a smile. "I really appreciate it."

Rob returned the smile and added a wink. "My pleasure."

They had spent the day together, riding over the ranch in the truck and sharing an easy camaraderie. Rob had shown her the land and the cattle, and explained more than she could remember about both. Stopping by the creek at noon, they had eaten a leisurely picnic lunch. Then the tour had continued for the remainder of the lovely spring afternoon.

Tempted by the prospect of a sympathetic listener, Margret had started to tell Rob about her experience with Jude a dozen times during the day. But she just couldn't bring herself to do it. It was really too personal and too painful for her to talk about. And she certainly didn't want to say anything that might lead to more trouble between the Emory brothers.

In spite of her brooding thoughts of Jude, she had enjoyed both learning about the Double Diamond and Rob's pleasant company. In fact, she realized that she had never had a better relationship with anyone than she had with Rob. He was kind and sweet-tempered, his sense of humor was wonderful, and he treated her like a person instead of a sex object. But, somehow, she wasn't attracted to him at all in a man-woman kind of way. No, she'd had to fall under Jude's dark spell!

She had lain awake a good part of last night thinking about yesterday's events. Jude's touch had made her feel like a complete woman for the first time in her life. The cool withdrawal that had followed had devastated her. And then he had come to her defense in front of the hands. Why?

All she could conclude was that he had been raised to treat all women with respect. At the crucial moment, that fact had made it impossible for him to humiliate her publicly—even as part of his plan to get her off the ranch. And now she'd be willing to bet that he was probably blaming her for his lack of resolve and resenting her even more as a result.

Margret pulled her thoughts back to the present and turned away from the pickup with a sigh. "See you at dinner, Rob."

"Dinner tonight's going to be the party buffet."

Margret swung back to face him, realizing that she'd forgotten all about the party. It was just as well—a party was the last thing she was in the mood for. "I have an awful lot of work left to do on those tapes," she said, hedging.

"If you think you're wriggling out of this one, think again. You're going to this party, and we're going to dance the night away."

Margret wondered what Jude would think of that. Most likely he wouldn't even notice. That thought rankled. But hadn't she spent years minimizing her looks and modifying her behavior in order to achieve that precise result? The thought of her actually trying to make any man jealous seemed so out of character that it was laughable.

"Well, do we have a date?"

Remembering all that Rob had done for her, Margret reluctantly gave in to his wishes. "I guess so."

"If only all my women were so eager."

Margret gave him the smile he expected and waved as he drove away. But before she could turn toward the house, she felt someone's gaze on her.

She looked toward the main corral and encountered Jude's disapproving glare. Her first impulse was to continue on into the house. Then she changed her mind. She hadn't done anything she was ashamed of, and she wasn't going to let him intimidate her anymore.

Jude watched Maggie approaching the corral and cursed under his breath. He had defended her last night simply because he couldn't help himself. He would sooner have taken a bullet in the chest than let anyone ridicule her because of what they'd shared together. He told himself that he would have done the same for any woman, but he was honest enough to admit that she'd affected him in a way no other woman ever had.

Maggie was the enemy—and she was also the first person he'd ever been emotionally naked with in his life. But she had been naked with him, too—or had she? Was she really as vulnerable as she seemed or just ten times more subtle and clever than he'd ever suspected? Act or not, she had gotten under his skin with a vengeance and he was afraid. Afraid that no matter what he did, no matter how hard he tried, he would never be able to completely exorcise her.

Now here she was, seeking him out again, trying to force the issue—after she'd been out gallivanting with his brother all day. Jude wondered just how they had spent those hours. The possibilities that came to mind made Jude want to punch something. Or someone.

The young filly he was working with sensed his anger and snorted nervously. Jude consciously relaxed his stranglehold grip on the lead rope and murmured to her reassuringly.

"Mind if I watch?"

"Would it matter if I did?" Jude didn't trust himself to look at her. All day he'd been remembering the soft warmth of her skin, what she'd looked like as she'd come apart in his arms.

Gritting his teeth, he picked up a grain sack. He let the hobbled filly sniff at it and generally absorb the fact that it was nothing that could hurt her. Then, moving slowly, he began to rub the sack over her face and head.

"What are you doing?"

Jude wanted to snap at her, but he was forced to keep his voice soothing for the filly's sake. "It's the first step in breaking a horse. I'm getting her used to being touched by a man."

"Breaking a horse? But I thought that involved climbing on and riding them to a standstill."

Working his way down the filly's neck, Jude looked up at Margret and wondered if she was trying to give their conversation sexual overtones. Her expression was all innocence, but she had given him an idea.

He let his gaze slide over her suggestively. "I don't force myself on her all at once. Too much chance of damaging the filly that way. I start off slow and easy, and I touch her everywhere."

Margret watched the grain sack's slow progress across the filly's chest and down one long leg. The liquid, velvety tone of Jude's voice brought the blood to her face.

"Once she knows my touch and gets used to the blanket and saddle, I start leaning my weight on her, preparing her for what's coming."

He passed the sack over the filly's back and under her belly. Margret clenched her fists, fighting the memory of Jude's hands stroking her own receptive body.

"When I finally do climb on top of her, she's ready and willing to take me anywhere I want to go."

"Then what?" Margret managed to ask.

Jude looked her straight in the eye. "Then I pass her on to the next man."

His words cut Margret to the quick. She held his gaze for several heartrending seconds. Then she turned her back on the corral and started toward the house, forcing herself to walk slowly.

Jude watched her until she opened the kitchen door and disappeared inside.

"Jude?"

Turning away from the now empty ranch yard, Jude saw Todd climbing through the corral fence.

"I finished grooming Zack. Can I help you with Prissy now?"

"Sure you can."

Jude continued to run the grain sack over Prissy's glossy coat, explaining to Todd as he went. But for once his mind wasn't on his work. He was thinking of the look he'd put in Maggie's eyes. It had given him none of the satisfaction he'd expected to feel. Instead he felt disgust. And for once it was directed toward himself.

Margret stared at the computer screen without really seeing it, her fingers automatically finding the right keys as Ed's voice droned on. Then abruptly the tape ran out.

She reached for the next tape and knocked the carefully arranged stack to the floor. Cursing under her breath, she bent over and scooped the tapes up off the carpet.

She could think of nothing but the cruel words that Jude had said to her earlier. He had seduced and humiliated her, just as he had promised to do. But the joke was on him. She was angry now and more determined than ever to retain the inheritance that Ed had left her.

Rubbing her tired eyes with one hand, she slipped a cassette into the transcription machine with the other and depressed the foot pedal. She had typed only a few words before she knew that the tape couldn't possibly be the next one in the sequence. She was about to switch it off, when she realized just what Ed was talking about.

"When news of the accident that killed Jude's wife reached me, I saw this as the opportunity I had been waiting for. I felt that, somehow, I had to reach out to him, to help him in his hour of need. Now that Ben Emory was dead and Jude was an adult who had made some mistakes of his own, I thought that we could talk about the past, that I could finally explain why I had acted the way I had.

"At the hospital I had to reveal our relationship in order to see him. The nurse took it upon herself to announce me: Mr. Emory, your father is here.

"Jude took one look at me, turned his bandaged face toward the wall and said four words that ended our reconciliation before it began: My father is dead.

"His rejection was utterly predictable, but I feel the pain of it even today. Yet I would not change any of my actions toward him. My refusal to acknowledge him as a child, my total lack of participation in his life, were the finest gifts that I could have given him. If I could only make him understand that, I think I would die a happy man."

Struggling against tears, Margret pulled off the earphones and laid them on the desk. At last she'd discovered something of importance. No matter how bad their relationship had been, Ed hadn't been bitter. He hadn't blamed Jude for rejecting him. So that couldn't have been his motivation for denying Jude the ranch.

She started to get up, to go to Jude and tell him what she'd learned. Then she realized she was being a fool. She owed him nothing—unless it was a payback for the pain he'd deliberately inflicted on her. Besides, he hadn't believed anything else she'd told him about the tapes. Why would he believe this?

"Aren't you dressed yet?"

Margret swiveled her chair around and saw Rob standing in the doorway. A particularly handsome Rob dressed in a Western-style shirt and slacks and a bolo tie. She couldn't help but smile in appreciation at the sight.

"I guess I'm just not in a party mood," she confessed.

"Neither am I, to tell the truth. But I decided I owe it to myself not to give in to that feeling. My former fiancée made her choice. I'm not going to spend my life mourning something I can't change."

Margret felt ashamed. In her preoccupation with her own problems, she had forgotten that Rob was suffering a recent hurt. And she realized that what he was saying applied to her situation, too. Jude wasn't worth it.

"Okay," she said with more determination than enthusiasm. "I'll be ready in a few minutes."

Rob nodded his approval and left the room, closing the door behind him.

Fifteen minutes later Margret stood in front of the dresser mirror, frowning at her reflection. On impulse, she had applied the makeup in the seldom-used bag of cosmetics she kept in her purse. The color of her red dress was a vivid contrast to her pale skin and blond tresses, but it was loose and shapeless. Her tightly coiled hair didn't look right, either.

Hesitantly, and then with more assurance, she began to remove the hairpins until long waves of gold hung free around her shoulders. She unbuttoned the neck of the dress and folded down the collar.

A knock sounded at the door just as she was spraying perfume behind her ears. "Come in."

Rob opened the door and she waited for his reaction. But she hadn't expected a terse, "Wait a second. Don't go anywhere."

She watched him disappear and wondered what on earth he was up to. He was back a minute later, pulling the maid with him. He gestured toward Margret and began speaking to the woman in rapid-fire Spanish that Margret couldn't begin to follow. This time it was the maid who disappeared.

Margret crossed her arms over her chest and tapped her foot. "What's going on?"

"I'm icing the cake."

Soon Margret was looking into the mirror again. A wide, red leather belt, gold hair combs, red lipstick and red high heels had been added to the picture. For the first time in a long time, she approved of her reflection.

She caught Rob's eye in the mirror and grinned. "Let's go to the party!" Suddenly she couldn't wait to show Jude just what he was going to be missing.

The first person Margret saw when she entered the crowded living room was Todd. He ran up to greet her, coming to a sliding stop that almost deposited a pile of guacamole dip on her dress.

Margret steadied the paper plate he held. "I missed you today, sweetie. How about a hug?"

"*Mom!* What if the other kids see me?"

Margret felt both pride and regret. Her son really was growing up. "Rob and I had a great time driving around the ranch," she told him. "I wish you had agreed to go with us. Just what was so important that you had to stay behind?"

"I got to help train Prissy," Todd told her with obvious satisfaction. "And I learned how to groom Zack."

Margret was about to ask who Prissy was, but her son was already turning away. "I'm going to get some soda."

"Don't have more than one can!" Margret called after him.

Frowning, she watched him move away. In the short time they had been on the ranch, she'd become so used to Todd's needs being met by Nilda and the maid that now she took the situation for granted. Her son was obviously thriving, but she missed the closeness they had shared when they'd lived alone. Was she being overprotective, or was she right to feel concerned by the sudden change in their relationship?

Feeling a touch on her arm, Margret came out of her reverie to find Rob at her side. "Maggie, I'd like you to meet Dan and Clara Jenkins. They own the Lazy J spread."

Margret acknowledged the introduction with a smile and a nod. After that, everything became a blur of unfamiliar names and faces as Rob escorted her around the room.

Grateful for his support, Margret stayed close to his side, nibbled at the food he brought her and tried her best to make small talk. She only hoped that her apprehension didn't show. She was certain that as far as the disputed ownership of the Double Diamond was concerned, these people were on Jude's side rather than hers. Everyone was outwardly polite, even friendly, but she could imagine what they were really thinking.

Some, like Sybil Perry, were more transparent than others. The wife of Ed's lawyer, Sam Perry, smiled at her. But the woman's faded blue eyes were as cold as her thin, blue-veined hand. While she said all the appropriate, acceptable things, her tone was full of disdain.

Margret was relieved when Rob led her away from the Perrys and out to the space in the center of the room that had been cleared for dancing. Someone brought out a guitar, an accordion appeared out of nowhere, and a third volunteer sat down at the piano.

Rob taught her the two-step while she laughed at her own lack of grace. "It's been a long time," she confessed.

"We'll make up for it tonight."

They danced to so many songs that Margret lost count. "This is fun, but these high heels are a little too tight," she said, hoping that Rob would take the hint and call a time out.

When he didn't respond, she looked up and found that his attention had strayed. She followed his gaze and felt a shock of recognition as she saw that Jude was watching her. She quickly looked away. "Don't you think we should sit this one out?"

"No way. I'm just getting warmed up."

The song ended and the dancers broke apart, applauding enthusiastically. Then the mournful notes of a popular love-gone-wrong number filled the air, and Rob took her into his arms for a slow dance. With a growing feeling of defiance, Margret followed his lead.

Jude watched Margret and his brother sway by and wondered how far things had gone between them. He had believed in her innocence when he'd held her in his arms yesterday, but he still couldn't bring himself to trust her completely.

Could she possibly be trying to make him jealous, or had she decided to concentrate on Rob now that her bid to control him had failed? She could use his brother to gain acceptance with the rest of the ranchers and to help her run the ranch her way. If she really was the schemer he'd believed her to be, going after his brother was the smart move.

Jude took another swallow of lightly spiked punch and told himself he didn't care. His handsome, idiot of a brother was old enough to choose his own path to damnation, and Maggie... Maggie was too hot to handle. She played havoc with his control and neutralized his common sense. She was an explosive that, if he let his guard down for even an instant, had the potential to blow him straight to hell.

Even now he wanted her so badly that he was aching. She looked better than any woman had a right to look in that damned red dress. It clung to every luscious curve. He wanted to run his hands over it, to trace all the secret places of that beautiful body. To watch her writhe in response to his caresses. To bury his face in her hair.

Jude watched his brother smiling down at Maggie and saw her return that smile. Then Rob lifted the hand that had been resting at Margret's waist and tucked one stray golden strand of hair behind her ear.

Jude set his cup down on the nearest flat surface and walked toward the couple in the middle of the dance floor. Neither of them looked his way as he approached. Were they so wrapped up in each other that they were unaware of his presence?

He tapped Rob on the shoulder, making no effort to be gentle about it. "I'm cutting in."

Rob looked at him and frowned in obvious annoyance. "It would be nice if you'd ask the lady if she wants to dance with you."

Jude remembered the last conversation he'd had with Maggie and thought there was damned little chance she'd say yes. She hadn't even deigned to look at him yet.

"I said, I'm cutting in," he growled.

Rob released Margret and turned to confront his brother. "You've been hanging around animals for so long that you're starting to act like one!"

Ignoring Rob's remark and Maggie's startled expression, Jude reached out to take her into his arms. But before he could follow through on his intent, a hand grabbed his arm and spun him around.

Incensed, he shook loose and stood facing his brother. He was dimly aware that the music had stopped and that the room had grown very quiet.

"I told you to *ask*, Jude. Do you remember what that means?"

"Get the hell out of my way."

Margret watched, horrified, as the two brothers stood, fists clenched, glaring at each other. Her numb brain groped for something she could do, something she could say before things went too far.

She took a step toward Jude, intending to agree to a dance—to ten dances—if he'd only move away from Rob. But her son was there before her.

Todd looked up at both of the men he had come to regard as his personal heroes. "Don't fight!" he pleaded, tears standing in his eyes. "Please, don't fight!"

Jude looked down at the child, fully realizing for the first time what he'd been about to do. He saw the same realization dawn in Rob's dark eyes. "No one's going to fight. Are they, Rob?"

Rob looked at the small, anxious boy and shook his head. "No, no one's going to fight."

Margret squatted down next to Todd and gave him a reassuring smile. "Brothers argue all the time, sweetie. Just like you and your friends do. But after they argue, they make up. And they still love each other and want to be together."

Todd looked at her and nodded, rubbing at his eyes. "I thought they were going to hurt each other."

"Well, they're not. Come on now. I'll tuck you into bed and tell you your favorite story."

"I'm too old for that stuff! I can go to bed by myself."

He walked through the crowd without a backward glance, leaving Margret staring after him. He *was* growing up—so fast that she couldn't keep pace. And it hurt a little to know he'd never need her in quite the same way again.

Straightening up, she turned to Rob. "Would you mind going with him?" she asked softly. "Just to supervise. I think he'd be more likely to accept that from you than from me tonight."

The expression in Rob's eyes told her that he understood her real motive—and disapproved. "You're sure?"

"I'm sure."

With a last warning glance at Jude, Rob turned and followed Todd out of the room.

"Maggie—"

Margret whirled to face Jude, her eyes flashing with anger. "Leave me alone! You don't want me—you made that plain earlier. You just can't stand the thought that your younger brother might be man enough to take me away from you!"

Trying her best to conceal the shame she was feeling, Margret walked away and joined the group that had gathered around Sam Perry. Jude was left standing alone in the middle of the dance floor.

Ed's attorney greeted her a bit too heartily, as though he wanted her to be sure of her welcome. "Well, Margret, how is your work on *The Legacy* coming along?"

Grateful for the opening he had given her, Margret responded eagerly. "It seems to be an autobiography."

"An autobiography?" Mrs. Perry echoed, her eyes glittering with interest. "How much more fascinating than those dull old mysteries. Was Ed really as wild and wicked as rumor has it?"

Margret hesitated, reluctant to talk about Ed's personal life to anyone outside of the Emory family. Although the tapes had been intended for publication, it seemed like a violation of trust. Before she could decide what to do, Jude's voice came from behind her.

"You'll never find out what Ed Tanner was really like by reading that book. It's just a sugarcoated whitewash job. And Ed picked just the right person to prepare it. Margret thinks the man was a paragon of virtue."

"That's not true!" Margret snapped. "In the tapes Ed is often very critical of himself and his actions."

Sybil Perry smiled maliciously. "You certainly did care for Ed, didn't you? I can see how the Double Diamond ended up as yours. And now the Emory brothers are fighting over you, too. Tell me, is there any man anywhere who's immune to your charms?"

For one of the few times in her memory, Margret didn't even try to hold back. "Lots of people are immune. The kind of people who are so full of greed and spite that they can see only *those* qualities in everyone else."

Sybil drew in her breath sharply, her eyes narrowing to mere slits. "Don't take that holier-than-thou tone with me!" she said, her voice carrying throughout the room. "It's obvious what kind of a woman you are. The kind whose greed has no limits. The kind men kill themselves trying to satisfy!"

The woman's words contained a truth that chilled Margret's heart. She had to get away. Away from all these people and their accusing stares.

Her face as pale as death, she made her way through the crowd, seeing only a mass of strangers' faces, wanting only to escape. After what seemed like an eternity, she reached the sanctuary of her bedroom. Like a wounded animal, she closed herself off from the rest of the world.

Huddled on the bed, she drew her pillow close and shut her eyes. The passage of time became irrelevant in the pitch-dark room. She had no idea how long she lay there, trapped in her own private purgatory of guilt and regret. Then, suddenly, she wasn't alone anymore.

Jude's body was pressed against the length of her back, his arms cradling her in warmth. She didn't even try to move away. There was no anger left in her, only despair.

"Whatever's wrong, Maggie, I want to make it better. I want to believe in you. I want to believe that your sweetness isn't just a mirage. And when I'm with you, I do believe." His body trembled as he pressed it against hers. "I still want you, Maggie. I thought I could let you go, but I can't—not yet."

Margret didn't hear any promises in his words, but she did hear the ring of truth. Because when he held her like this, she believed, too—in happy endings, in forever and, most of all, in him.

"What is it, Maggie? What are you hiding from?"

She took a long, shuddering breath. The words seem to come by themselves, with no conscious effort on her part. "After we were married, Paul wouldn't let me work. I took some college courses and did some part-time typing at home—that was it. But he always insisted that we have the best of everything."

She swallowed hard, fighting against the sense of remembered hurt. "One day I came home and found him on the floor of the den, the gun still in his hand. I couldn't understand why he'd taken his own life. I soon found out that he'd gotten himself so deeply in debt trying to maintain our luxurious life-style that we were about to lose everything we had. Rather than face me with the truth, he'd shot himself. Because it was suicide, I couldn't even collect his insurance. I was evicted from our house a few days after he died. If it hadn't been for Ed giving me a job and a place to live, I don't know what would have happened."

Torn between sympathy and outrage, Jude stroked one ice-cold arm. "You ought to be furious over what he did to you! Instead, you seem to hold yourself responsible for the wrong choices he made.''

Deep inside Margret agreed with Jude. She *did* have a right to be angry. Yet as soon as that thought surfaced, a tide of guilt rose up to overwhelm it. ''Paul loved me so much. He tried to give me everything he thought I wanted. I think he was somehow afraid that I'd turn to another man if he didn't because . . . of the way I look. He died trying to live up to my expectations, and I couldn't even respond to him physically. I wanted to, but I just couldn't!''

Jude felt her shaking with silent sobs, and his doubts about her suddenly seemed ludicrous. He believed in her pain. He wanted to ease it.

''Maggie, you didn't ask for all the things your husband tried to give you. You wanted to work and help out, but he wouldn't let you. Paul brought all his insecurities and problems to the marriage—you didn't cause them. If you'd never met him, he would have led the same life and come to the same end.''

Jude's words flowed over Margret like a balm. The fact that he could say them—and believe them—made her question the validity of her doubts and the guilt that had been part of her since her husband's death.

She turned into his arms, longing to help him as he had helped her. ''You shouldn't blame yourself for the accident, either.'' She felt his muscles stiffen with resistance, but she kept on talking. ''You need to let go of all the old guilt and pain you've been carrying around for so long. If you ever want to find any peace of mind, you've got to forgive your wife and you've got to forgive Ed. He regretted that he'd never been a real father to you. It's all in *The Legacy* tapes. If you'd just listen to them—''

She was prepared for a negative reaction, and he didn't disappoint her. He pulled away from her and sat up on the side of the bed. ''Maybe my mother needs to believe Ed gave a damn. I don't. If Ed cared about me so much, why didn't he leave me the Double Diamond?''

"That's the one thing I don't understand," Margret admitted. "But the answer may be in the tapes." Tentatively she reached out and touched his back in the darkness. "It really is a good book—and it's an honest book. I guess I did think Ed was a saint before I started transcribing those tapes, but I don't now. He was a man with some very big faults. Some that I might have even less tolerance for than you do."

"I doubt that!"

"Like you tried to tell me after the reading of the will, Ed was a womanizer, a heavy drinker and a compulsive gambler. He gambled his way out of a London slum and into America's upper class. He won this ranch in a poker game. When his wife finally cut off his access to her money, he even wrote his first book on a double-or-nothing bet that covered a huge debt to a very dangerous man. If he'd lost that bet, he would probably have lost his life."

"You're still defending him Maggie."

"If ever a man needs defending, Ed is that man. He was guilty of so many things. But he paid for his sins. He had nothing in the end, Jude. You were right about him losing his whole fortune—and a substantial part of his wife's as well. She ended up divorcing him. And he lost the respect of his only son."

Jude said a crude word and moved away from her touch. "He didn't lose my respect—he never had it! Ed Tanner passed himself off as someone who was worthy of admiration his whole life. The fact that he's still doing it now that he's dead is just too much for me to take."

Margret struggled to clarify her feelings, for Jude's sake and for her own. "I don't admire him anymore, but I don't condemn him, either. Because I think he was a different person from the man you knew. I think the Ed I knew was a man you never met."

Jude jumped up off the bed, his voice shaking with anger. "And he's a man I don't want to meet. Can you understand that? You can talk until you turn blue and it won't make any difference. I know all I need to know and I've heard all I intend to hear about Ed Tanner!"

As her bedroom door slammed behind Jude, Margret bowed her head in defeat. It seemed as if they would never have any real relationship until Jude resolved his feelings for Ed. And that would never happen unless she could discover the reason Ed had changed his will.

Wearily Margret got up and switched on the light. She sat down at her desk and booted up the computer. Her eyes blurry with fatigue, she continued to transcribe, determined to find the answer for Jude's sake—and her own.

Chapter Eight

Margret woke at her desk, stiff and discouraged. Despite hours of work, she still hadn't discovered why Ed had changed his will. She was beginning to doubt that she ever would.

The harsh glare of late-morning sunlight seemed to make a mockery of all the hopes that she'd allowed herself to entertain the night before. Jude's concern for her had appeared genuine, but his attempt to comfort her after Sybil Perry's verbal assault could have been a ploy. Perhaps he'd seen his influence over her slipping when she was with Rob at the party and decided to tighten his grip on her again.

He had said that he wanted her, but he hadn't made any promises or mentioned the future. He hadn't even talked of a truce between them. His sexual interest was real enough, but could she trust him with her heart?

With an oath of frustration, Margret crossed to the closet and pulled out a change of clothes. She slipped out of the wrinkled red party dress, still deep in thought. Ed's inheritance wasn't worth the pain it had brought with it. She ought to leave the ranch to Jude and go back to El Paso while she still had a job offer and a place to stay. At least there she'd have peace of mind. But something in her refused to give up. She had to see this through no matter where it led, no matter what the cost.

Once dressed, Margret made her way to the kitchen in search of a cup of coffee. As she entered the room, she saw that Nilda was its only other occupant. The older woman glanced up and nodded, then returned her attention to the silver she was polishing. "The only bad thing about parties is the cleaning up afterward."

Margret located a cup and poured her coffee, dreading the conversation that would follow. But it was best to get it over with. "I guess you heard about the fight Jude and Rob almost got into—and about what Sybil Perry said to me."

"I was busy in the kitchen, so I missed all the excitement. But, yes, I heard."

Nilda finished her polishing and began to return the silverware to its case. Margret watched her, slowly gathering her courage. "You might as well know the whole truth," she blurted finally. "My husband committed suicide."

Nilda looked up and met Margret's pain-filled gaze. "That must have been terrible for you."

Margret had expected condemnation, not support. The explanation she had been prepared to voice came out anyway. "I—I cared for my husband. I tried to do everything his way, but it didn't help. He still took his own life."

"I'm sure that you did everything you could," Nilda said, her eyes testifying to the sincerity of her words.

Margret blinked in surprise as the other woman started out of the kitchen. "But what about Jude and Rob? I have to explain—!"

Nilda turned back to look at her. "I've seen greedy people in my life, Margret. I've seen people who enjoy stirring up trouble. You aren't like that. Even my foolish son would see that if he wasn't afraid to open his eyes and look. But everyone has to come to the truth in his own way, in his own time."

Margret watched Jude's mother leave the room, deeply impressed by the other woman's hard-won serenity and wisdom. Feeling her mood lighten perceptibly, she finished her coffee and put the cup in the sink. She smiled at the cook who came in to check the various pots that were simmering on the stove and received a smile in return.

Sliding her hands into her jeans pockets, she walked over to the sink and peered through the kitchen window. The sky was overcast. Not a good day to go riding, but a perfect day to spend time with her son.

"Maybe I'll see if one of the pickups is available," she said. "Do you think that Todd and I could make it to Layton City and back before it starts to rain?"

The Mexican woman shrugged noncommittally. "Todd is out with Jude, as usual. But they should be back for lunch very soon."

Margret felt a chill of warning and tried to tell herself she was being foolish. "You must mean he's out with Rob."

The cook looked at her with a frown. "No, Todd is with Jude, always. He follows him like a small shadow."

Margret was suddenly sure that she was right to have doubts about Jude. If he was somehow using her son to get her to leave the ranch, she would never forgive him. Never!

Leaving the kitchen without a word of goodbye, Margret hurried out of the ranch house. She headed for the barn, determined to find Todd if she had to ride over every inch of the Double Diamond. But before she could even cross the yard, she saw a cloud of dust in the distance. Fighting a growing sense of impatience, she retreated to the porch to wait.

One of the hands came out of the barn and opened the corral gate. Minutes later the ranch yard was full of dusty riders and bawling cattle.

Margret's heart seemed to freeze in mid-beat when she saw Todd in the thick of things with the other hands, waving his hat and shouting to keep the heifers in line. As the cattle were being herded into the corral, Todd looked up and saw her watching him. He smiled proudly and raised his hand.

Margret waved back, even managing a shaky smile of her own. Just as she was beginning to believe that everything would be all right, one of the heifers decided to try to push by Zack and make a break for it.

Margret watched in horror as the big horse was slammed sideways. Todd, his attention on her, was caught by surprise. Even as he fought to maintain his precarious balance in the saddle, Zack recovered and swung back to head off the escaping heifer. That sudden move unseated Todd, and he went off the far side of the horse—out of Margret's field of vision.

She left the porch at a run, but Jude was there before her. Positioning his horse between Todd and the cattle, he kept them clear of the boy until they were all safely in the corral. By the time Jude had dismounted, Todd had already picked himself up off the ground and grabbed Zack's reins.

"Are you all right?" Margret asked breathlessly, as she ran her hands over her son, searching for injuries.

"The boy's fine."

Furious, Margret whirled around to face Jude. "How dare you put my son in danger this way?"

Jude's expression darkened with anger at her accusation. "I'm only teaching Todd to do the same things that Rob and I did at his age. Hell, if he was back in the city riding a bicycle, he'd be bound to fall off once in a while. A horse isn't any different."

"He could have been crippled or even killed!"

"Maggie, that could happen crossing a street in El Paso. You can't keep your son tied to your apron strings forever."

"I'm not hurt!" Todd shouted, his gaze shuttling between his mother and Jude.

Margret, aware that she was upsetting her already overstimulated son, tried to downplay the incident. "You'll just have to be a little more careful from now on," she said, patting his shoulder. "And no more riding unless I'm with you."

Todd jerked away from her, on the verge of tears. "I can ride by myself! I'm not a wimp anymore—I'm a cowboy just like Jude!"

Stunned and hurt by Todd's defiance, Margret turned back to Jude. "You did this! You did this so that I'd be forced to leave the ranch to get him away from you!"

Jude looked at her, willing her to understand. "The thought may have crossed my mind in the beginning, but that isn't the way it turned out."

Margret shook her head. She had risked her own well-being on the chance that Jude cared for her, but she wouldn't risk Todd's. "From now on, you leave my son alone."

"Mom, no!"

Ignoring Todd's protests, Margret turned away from Jude.

He grabbed her arm, forcing her to face him again. "Dammit, Maggie! You're overreacting to this whole thing."

"Take your hands off me!"

"What in the hell is going on here?" Rob asked, walking up on the scene.

Jude gave him a warning look. "It's none of your business. Go back to whatever you were doing and let me handle this."

Rob put his hands on his hips and held his ground. "Don't order me around like I'm a wet-behind-the-ears kid or some hired hand! I work just as hard as you do around here—plus I have to put up with your lousy disposition."

"I'm still the ranch manager here," Jude growled, "and what I say goes. If you don't want to take my orders, then pack up and leave."

He turned his back on Rob and, propelling Margret with him, started for the house. The last thing he expected was the hand that fell on his shoulder, jerking him backward. It provoked an instinctive reaction. He released Margret, clenched his fist, pivoted and swung.

Rob landed on his backside in the dirt. He sat there and looked up at Jude, his expression of astonishment almost comical.

Jude looked down at Rob, a feeling of sick disbelief gathering in the pit of his stomach. From the day his little brother had been born, he'd looked after him and protected him. And Rob had been there for him, too, holding up his end of the ranch work without complaint, always ready with a smile or a word of encouragement when it was most needed. During the last few years, Jude's only response had been a terse order or a snarled reprimand. Until today.

Filled with remorse, he held out his hand to his brother. "I'm sorry, Rob."

Ignoring Jude's proffered hand, Rob pushed to his feet. He gave his brother a pitying look that was more cutting than any angry glare. "I'm sorry, too, Jude—sorry for you and for what you've become." Deliberately he turned his back and walked away in the direction of the barn.

Jude felt the hurt caused by Rob's cool dismissal with every fiber of his being. Backing away, he grabbed up his horse's reins. He swung aboard and urged the mare into a gallop, knowing he could never outrun the memory of the things he had said and done, or the realization of the kind of man he'd turned into—the bitter, contemptible man he'd seen reflected in the mirror of his brother's eyes.

Margret watched him go, feeling torn. Half of her felt his pain and wanted to comfort him as he had comforted her. The other half recognized she'd be acting like a fool. The man had turned the only human being who loved her against her—and he'd done it purposely, maliciously.

Hardening her heart, she turned to Todd, but he moved away from her, tears streaming down his cheeks. Breaking into a run, he made for the house. Margret called his name and ran after him, but she was a second too late. He disappeared into his room and she heard the click of the lock.

She paused outside the door, her palm pressed against the wood. She felt like crying herself. Despite her unhappy marriage, Paul's suicide, Ed's death, Jude's resentment of her, she had always had Todd's love to fall back on. Had she lost that now, too?

"Todd," she called, trying to steady her voice. "Please open the door so we can talk things over."

There was no response. After a moment Margret reluctantly decided that the best thing to do would be to leave him alone until he was ready to come out on his own. Forcing herself away from the door, she crossed to her own room.

She sat down at the desk and turned on the equipment, but Ed's voice was only a meaningless annoyance. Her thoughts wouldn't let her concentrate on her work.

She ought to take Todd and leave the ranch right away, but something other than pride seemed to be holding her here. She felt responsible for the rift between Jude and Rob. And, now that she had calmed down, she had to wonder if she really *had* overreacted to Todd's cowboy activities. Was it possible that Jude really cared for Todd? That he cared for her? Or was she just being hopelessly naive?

Margret moved away from the desk and threw herself down on top of the bed. She'd gotten too little sleep last night. She was tired. Tired of trying to second-guess Jude's motives, tired of trying to decide the best path to take. Maybe if she could just rest for a minute, she'd be able to think more clearly. With a weary sigh, she closed her eyes.

Margret woke with a start. The room was dim with the shadows of approaching night. She knew that there was something she had to do, but for a moment she couldn't recall what it was. Then she remembered. Todd.

She rinsed her face with warm water and straightened her hair. At the door of her son's room, she knocked softly.

"Todd?"

There was no answer. Was he still that upset or had he, too, fallen asleep? Carefully she tried the door. It swung open without resistance.

She walked inside and called his name again. The only sound was the scrape of a wind-driven branch against the windowpane. In the dimness it took her a moment to register the fact that the room was empty.

A premonition began to dance along her nerve endings, demanding her attention. She tried to shake it off and found that she couldn't. Switching on the bedside lamp, she let her gaze sweep over the room. The first thing she noticed were the drawers that had been emptied of clothes and left open. Then she saw the note that was hanging from the mirror by one clumsily placed piece of tape. With a trembling hand, she reached out and tore it from its resting place.

Dear Mom—Im going away to live by myself so ev-ryone will stop fiteing.

Love Todd

Margret felt as if an icy band had tightened around her heart. She ran to the kitchen where she found the cook busy preparing dinner. The woman confirmed that she had noticed some food missing earlier, but she didn't know where Todd was.

In the barn Margret went from stall to stall. Zack, the horse she had seen Todd riding this afternoon, was missing.

Jude! She had to find Jude. He'd know what to do, where to look.

Margret was halfway to his room, when she remembered what had happened earlier in the day. Fighting down the panic that had almost overwhelmed her, she retraced her steps and went back out into the rising wind to look for Rob. She found him on the porch of the small house he shared with his mother.

"Hello, Maggie," he said, the melancholy in his eyes belying his smile. "Come on up and sit with me for a while."

Without even acknowledging his greeting, Margret poured out her fears.

He was by her side before she'd finished talking. "Don't worry, Maggie. We'll find him. You call Sheriff Dawson, and I'll get the hands together and start looking."

"I want to help," she told him, hurrying to keep up with his long strides. "I'll go crazy if I have to wait here!"

He paused in front of the main barn, his brow furrowed in thought. "Okay, you take my truck, and I'll go on horseback."

"Are you sure?"

"It gives me an advantage. A horse can go places and take shortcuts that a truck can't. And remember, Todd's on horseback, too. You're probably not going to find him on the road—unless he's following it so he won't get lost."

Margret prayed that was the case.

Minutes later she was in the truck, ready to pull away from the shelter of the ranch house and into the dark, wind-tossed night. She had just switched on the headlights when she heard someone call her name.

Nilda came up to the window and pressed a warm thermos into her hands. "Your son will be home soon," she said. "I'm sure of it."

"I hope so!"

"Everyone here will be praying for him."

Margret thanked her and drove out into the darkness. She drove slowly and carefully, the memory of her recent accident fresh in her mind.

She hadn't gone far when the beams of the headlight cut across the figures of a horse and rider. She jammed on the brakes, elation coursing through her. But her relief was short-lived. As the rider came closer, she saw that it wasn't Todd, after all.

"Is that you, Maggie?" Jude asked, bending in the saddle to peer inside the truck. "Where do you think you're going at this time of night?"

"Looking for my son!" Margret snapped. "Have you seen him?"

Jude looked at her as if she'd lost her mind. "No. Why would he—?"

"He ran away!" Margret shouted, unleashing her anxiety and her anger. "Because of the argument we had today and the fight between you and Rob. He thinks it was his fault!"

Jude cursed vividly. "Are the men out looking? Did Rob—?"

"Everything's been taken care of," Margret told him, her voice frigid. "You can go back home."

"The hell you say!"

"Stay out of this! If you hadn't turned him against me, none of this would have happened in the first place!"

Their gazes locked and they sat there in silence, Margret's eyes communicating her anger and hurt, Jude's shouting a denial that he never voiced. Then he pulled back on the reins and blended into the night.

Margret let her forehead rest on the steering wheel. She felt as if something very precious had died, and she longed to turn back time, to change what had happened. But she knew it was impossible. She had to think of Todd now. She had to worry about him.

Raising her head, she wiped at her eyes and thought about the note her son had left. He'd said he was going to go live by himself. Where could a child find shelter? A cave? A building of some kind? There were several outbuildings on the ranch, but Rob and the hands had finished searching those before she'd left.

She frowned in concentration. Where would she go if she were running away and needed a place to stay? Suddenly it came to her. Old Pete's cabin! Rob had taken Todd there once, on the night her car had plunged into the creek, then again to do a repair assessment. Todd would almost certainly remember how to get there.

As a light drizzle began to fall, Margret turned on the windshield wipers and sped off toward her destination.

The drive seemed endless. Inevitably her thoughts turned to the night when she and Jude had first met. They had ridden through the rain and darkness searching for Todd then, too. For a moment she longed for Jude's companionship and support. Then she dismissed the thought angrily. Whatever had been between them was finished. She and Todd would have been better off if they'd never come to the Double Diamond!

Lightning flashed across the sky, followed immediately by the resounding boom of thunder. Margret started at the noise, wondering if the bolt had struck nearby. Minutes later, she began to notice a strange glow against the dark sky. Her heart seemed to skip a beat when she realized it was coming from the direction of Pete's cabin.

She pushed down hard on the accelerator, taking the curves as fast as she dared and praying she was wrong. But the closer she got to the site, the brighter the glow became.

When she took the last turn, she saw that a tree and some brush behind the cabin were burning—perhaps ignited by the lightning she'd seen. Despite the drizzle, the fire had evidently spread to the cabin and set the back wall aflame. Half of the roof had already caved in.

Adrenaline pumping through her system, Margret swung the truck around to the front of the structure. Zack reared up in her headlights, fighting the tether that was keeping him too close to the smell of fire. Even as Margret watched, the railing on the porch gave way, and the terrified horse galloped off into the night, trailing rope behind him.

Slamming on the brakes, she shoved the truck into park, and jumped from the vehicle shouting Todd's name. She ran up the steps and threw open the door only to be met by a billowing cloud of black smoke.

Coughing repeatedly, her eyes tearing, Margret dropped to her hands and knees and crawled into the cabin.

"Todd! Answer me!"

Moving forward, she blinked in an attempt to clear her smarting eyes. She saw the fire licking at the remainder of the roof, consuming more and more of the old wooden cabin like a hungry predator. Desperately she called her son's name again, but there was no answer. Then, in the light of the flames, she saw him lying on the floor, pinned by a fallen beam from the roof.

Choking on the smoke and the searing air, bruising her hands and knees on the debris-strewn floor, Margret made her way to Todd. Finding his pulse pounding beneath her fingers brought a sob to her lips, but she couldn't rouse him.

She grabbed him under the arms and tried to pull him free. The beam held him fast.

Dizzy and gasping for air, Margret stood up and attempted to lift the heavy piece of wood. Despite repeated efforts, it refused to budge.

There might be something in the truck that she could use as a lever, but did she dare leave Todd in order to look? She glanced up to check on the progress of the fire. A wave of horror engulfed her. Above her head, the entire remainder of the roof was now laced with flames!

Frantic, feeling herself on the edge of unconsciousness, she forced her blurry eyes to focus. Her gaze came to rest on a splintered board. She snatched it up and wedged it beneath the imprisoning beam. Bearing down with all her weight, she prayed for a miracle. For a second she thought her prayer might be answered. Then the half-rotted wood broke under the strain. She fell forward onto the floor with a moan of defeat.

Her lungs aching, Margret fought for the oxygen necessary to hold back the encroaching darkness. But it was a losing battle. Exhausting her last ounce of strength, she crawled back to Todd inch by agonizing inch. Lying down beside him, she did her best to shield his body with her own.

Then she spiraled into the darkness, away from the heat and the pain. Down to where only thoughts and images existed. And regrets. She was as much to blame for this as Jude was. If she'd just given the ranch back to him, none of this would have happened. Why had she been so stubborn? It all seemed so unimportant now. The only thing of real importance was love. The love she felt for her son. The love she felt for Jude. Despite how he might feel about her, she wished she could have told him. But she'd been too proud and too scared to admit it before now, even to herself. And now it was too late. It was too late for everything.

A light appeared in the darkness, and Margret felt a feeling of peace and acceptance wash over her. She wanted to reach the light, to join with it. But just as she began to move toward it, she heard someone call her name.

Annoyed, she tried to ignore the voice, but it was familiar—and persistent. With a feeling of regret, she turned and walked away from the light, back toward the world of heat and pain.

Margret opened her burning eyes, groaning with the effort. She saw a silhouette against the flames, a man in a wide-brimmed Stetson. She couldn't see his face, but she knew who he was. It was his voice that had called her back.

Lying on the floor, unable to move, she watched him bend over her son. Flames were reflected in the silver of his belt buckle as he hunkered down and wedged his shoulders under the beam. Grunting with the effort, he straightened. In one fluid motion he lifted the heavy obstacle and cast it aside. Then he reached for her.

She tried to help him, but it was beyond her power. She had to fight to keep her eyes open as he half carried, half dragged her and her son out into the cool night air.

Just as they cleared the porch, what was left of the cabin roof came crashing down. There was a shower of stinging sparks, and then they were falling, falling into the cold, wet grass.

Margret tried to breathe, but she was seized by an uncontrollable spasm of coughing. Jude bent over her, his hands stroking her face and hair. She wanted to tell him that she was sorry, that she'd been wrong to doubt him. She wanted to tell him that she loved him. But before she could form the words, the darkness came up to claim her once more.

Chapter Nine

Margret pulled the blanket back up to cover Todd's sleeping form. Then she stood in the child's darkened bedroom, enjoying the pleasure and relief that came from knowing that her son was out of danger.

It would be dawn soon, and she knew she ought to be asleep herself. But it had only been hours since the fire, and she still found it hard to believe that she and Todd had escaped with just scrapes and bruises. Old Dr. Hooper had treated both of them for smoke inhalation and had X-rayed Todd at his infirmary in Layton City. The doctor had come to a conclusion she concurred with: they were both very, very lucky.

Yet Margret had been unable to sleep. She found herself leaving her bed at regular intervals, compelled to check on Todd's condition. He had been sleeping for hours, with a tranquility she sincerely envied.

As if he could sense her presence, her son stirred in his

sleep and then opened his eyes to look up at her. "I'm sorry, Mom," he whispered hoarsely. "I'm really sorry."

Margret moved forward to sit on the side of his bed. She smoothed his hair back with a hand that bore several small abrasions. "We both could have been hurt very badly, you know. I want you to understand that."

"I know," Todd said. "I didn't really want to leave. I just wanted everyone to stop arguing."

Margret straightened his blanket and knew it was past time she told him the truth. "The reason everyone has been arguing is because Ed was Jude's real father. Jude thought Ed would give him the Double Diamond, but Ed gave it to me instead."

Todd blinked as his sleepy mind tried to comprehend all that she'd said. "And that's what everyone's so mad at each other about?"

"Uh-huh. You were just one more excuse for us to fight. I would have explained before, but you wouldn't give me the chance."

"I will next time. Word of honor."

His eyes began to drift closed, and Margret got to her feet. She bent over to kiss his forehead.

"Mom? Don't you like Jude even a little bit?"

"I like him very, very much." She smiled at the confused expression in her son's eyes. "Go to sleep now. We can talk all you want tomorrow."

She stood watch as Todd surrendered to sleep once more. She knew her comment about fighting with Jude and liking him at the same time had been incomprehensible to the child. She had trouble understanding it herself.

With one last backward glance, she slipped out the door and crossed the hall toward her own room. Inevitably, she found her gaze straying to Jude's bedroom door.

If she were to be honest with herself, she would have to admit that her concern for Todd wasn't the only reason for

her predawn restlessness. Jude hadn't spoken a word to her
since she'd regained consciousness in Doc Hooper's infirmary. Her attempt to thank him had received only a grunt
in response. Todd's presence on the ride home had effectively prevented her from making any further efforts to
reach him. And as soon as they'd arrived at the ranch house,
Jude had disappeared into his bedroom, closing the door
behind him.

Now Margret couldn't help but notice the telltale sliver of
light beneath that closed door. Apparently Jude was up very
early—or he hadn't been able to sleep, either.

She hesitated, her hand on the knob of her own bedroom
door. The urge to go to him was strong. She was consumed
by a growing impatience, an overwhelming longing to tell
him how she felt, what she'd decided. A need to resolve the
issues that stood between them once and for all.

But there was another emotion inside her that was just as
urgent. Fear. She was afraid that if she intruded on Jude's
self-imposed solitude, he wouldn't want to hear what she
needed so badly to tell him.

Somehow she knew that on the other side of that door
Jude was grappling with emotions as powerful as those she
was experiencing, with urges as contradictory and compelling as her own. If she disturbed him now, before he was
ready to face her, there was no predicting what his reaction
might be. She wanted the time and the mood to be right before she took the risk of unburdening her heart. No matter
how uncomfortable her inaction was, it was preferable to a
final rejection.

She was halfway into her room when she stopped to re-
consider. She was acting as she always did, finding it safer
and easier to play a passive role than to take a chance on
being rejected. Hadn't the events of the last two weeks made
any difference? Or was she going to live the rest of her life

as the same insecure little orphan girl, willing to fade into the wall if it meant achieving acceptance?

Quickly, acting before she could change her mind, Margret crossed the hall to Jude's room. Raising a trembling hand, she knocked firmly.

The door swung open before she had time to lower her hand. Her eyes widened in surprise as she looked up at Jude's face. Whatever vulnerability might have been conveyed by his tousled hair and bare feet was totally negated by the raw power inherent in his bare, muscular chest and arms and the tense, closed expression on his roughly carved features.

All her cleverly rehearsed speeches totally forgotten, she blurted out the first words that came to mind. "You scared me!"

The forbidding expression on Jude's face eased momentarily. "Damn, Maggie! You're the most contrary woman I've ever met. When I want you to be afraid of me, I get nowhere. And now when I..." He left the sentence unfinished, his tone shifting to one of concern. "I thought I heard someone moving around. I was just coming out to see who it was. Todd is still okay, isn't he?"

Margret nodded, touched by his caring. How could she ever have doubted his feelings where her son was concerned? "He's fine. I just got up to check on him. Then I noticed your light. I...Jude, I need to talk to you."

She looked down, suddenly afraid that all the hope and yearning she'd struggled to hide would be revealed in her eyes. Her gaze skittered over his chest and across his hair-dusted abdomen to the intriguing shadows that lurked below the unfastened waistband of his jeans. One large hand dropped into her line of vision and covered the metal snap, forcing it closed with a dull popping sound.

"I want to talk to you, too," Jude said, throwing the door wide. "Come on in."

As she crossed the threshold, Margret automatically raised her gaze to meet Jude's. His somber expression had been softened by a faint smile. That smile and the knowing look in his eyes brought a hint of color to Margret's pale cheeks. Instinctively she tried to tug the lapels of her robe together as if the material could somehow shield her from the feelings he was arousing.

She felt the heat in her face intensify as Jude's gaze dropped to the front of her robe. Unbidden, her thoughts traveled back to the last time he'd touched her. She could almost feel his fingers tracing the contours of her body, his tongue...

Shocked by her lack of control, Margret dropped her hands to her sides and abruptly turned away from temptation. With difficulty she forced her thoughts back to the purpose of her visit. "I came here to tell you something, Jude. Something that I hope will make a difference in the way you've been thinking of me since the day the will was read."

Needing to see his reaction, she willed herself to meet his gaze. She saw wariness where desire had been seconds before. But he was listening. Resolutely she forged ahead.

"I've decided to give the ranch back to you. You and I can go into Layton City tomorrow and have Sam Perry draw up any necessary papers."

She had expected a word of gratitude, a smug smile of triumph, anything but the same wary, suspicious look he had shown her when she'd first broached the subject. Her heart gave a painful thump, and then seemed to sink directly to the floor. She'd finally felt strong enough within herself to give up the only real security she'd ever known. She was finally offering him everything he'd wanted. Wasn't that going to make any difference to him at all?

"Why?" he asked finally, breaking the uncomfortable silence. "Why would you want to do that?"

Hurt and confused, Margret struggled to find words that would explain her feelings without baring her too-vulnerable heart. "In the beginning, when you pulled me from the creek, I trusted you instinctively. Then, after the will was read, you were a different man—so angry, so hard. You assumed the worst about me and that hurt me very deeply. I began to doubt that you were worthy of the trust I'd placed in you. I began to doubt that you deserved to be Ed's heir."

She looked at his closed, scarred face, silently pleading for understanding. "Then, that day under the oak tree, you were so gentle and so giving. You made me believe in myself, in my worth as a woman. But as soon as it was over, the doubt came back. Were you just playing a role, trying to seduce me into giving up the ranch? I couldn't be sure until a few hours ago. When you came through those flames to save me and my son, I knew you had to care."

Jude hung his head, a flare of emotion eclipsing his stoic expression. "Last night when you and Todd were almost—" He left the sentence unfinished as if he couldn't bear to say the word out loud. "Last night I realized just how much of a fool I'd been. I was angry when Ed left you the ranch, Maggie. Hell, I'd been angry at him for years because he didn't give me his name and my rightful place in the world. I told myself it didn't matter, but the resentment was festering in me all along. The ranch was just the final straw."

He combed one hand through his unruly hair and paced a few steps away. Then he swung to face her again. "I saw signs of your sincerity all along, but I ignored them because I wanted the ranch more than I wanted to believe in you. I didn't want to accept the fact that you might have a legitimate claim to it. But even a blind man could see you cared for Ed. You were there when he needed you. God knows, I never was."

His voice held more weariness than regret. "Ed never told any of us he was dying. But I doubt I'd have gone to see him even if I'd known—unless the old man had asked me with a please in front of it."

Margret heard her own thoughts, her own justifications, being thrown back at her. She found herself protesting, arguing Jude's right of inheritance. "But he promised the ranch to you from the time you were a baby!"

"That was before Ed knew that I would grow up to despise him as much as he despised me. And it was before he met you. He knew you needed a secure income and a home of your own, and he had every right to give that to you and your son."

A corner of Jude's mouth curved in appreciation of the irony of the situation. "It seems we've both come full circle in our thinking, Maggie. If there is a God, he must be laughing now."

But Margret wasn't amused. A feeling of dread began to gather in her chest. She'd thought that once she agreed to sign over the ranch, she and Jude would be free to acknowledge their feelings for each other. She had not even considered the possibility that he would refuse to take advantage of her generosity.

"I don't understand," she said hesitantly. "If you're not taking the ranch back, where do we go from here?"

"You're not going anywhere, Maggie. I am. I'm going to take the twenty-five thousand that Ed left me and use it as a down payment on a few acres of my own."

The cold, numbing shock of his words crept up through Margret's toes and found a home in the pit of her stomach. "But why?" she asked. "Why would you want to give the Double Diamond up when it's yours for the taking?"

"I appreciate the thought, Maggie. But I had a chance to think things over last night, and I decided that I'm too proud to take anything that old bastard didn't want me to have in the first place. I wasted years waiting for him to hand the ranch over to me. Instead I should have spent those years carving out my own place in the world. I can't change the past, but I can sure as hell choose my future."

Margret's mind flitted from thought to thought, as she desperately searched for some argument that would persuade him. "If you leave, who'll run things here?"

Jude walked to the closet, pulled out a suitcase and tossed it onto the bed. "Rob can take over as ranch manager. He's young, but he's worked on this ranch all his life. He can handle the job."

Rubbing her arms to ward off a sudden chill, Margret examined Jude's face for some hint of caring. But his expression was a closed book. She risked her newfound and fragile pride in an effort to breach the wall he'd raised around his feelings.

"I thought we could make a life here together, Jude—a new beginning for both of us."

Jude opened the suitcase and answered without looking at her. "I don't have anything left inside to offer any woman, Maggie."

With a feeling of hopeless frustration, Margret watched him pull clothes from their hangers, fold them and drop them into the suitcase. There had to be some way to reach him, some way to stop him!

"I know why you feel that way," she told him, her voice rising. "Because you can't stop living in the past! When are you going to stop punishing yourself?"

Jude placed the shirt he was holding inside the suitcase. Then he straightened and turned to face her. "Even if I could absolve myself of Anne's death, Maggie, there's one thing I can never forgive or forget. She was seven months pregnant when she died. I caused the death of my own son."

Stunned by his revelation, Margret squeezed her eyes shut against the anguish and guilt of those words. She wanted to argue that it was still illogical for him to blame himself, but she knew this wasn't about logic. If Todd had drowned when her car had plunged into the creek, or burned to death in Pete's cabin, she would have felt exactly the same way.

At a loss, she voiced the first thought that occurred to her. "Are you even sure that the baby was yours?"

Jude's eyes narrowed. "It was mine. Anne was pregnant before we ever got married." He squared his shoulders, physically bracing himself against the pain that always came with reliving the past. "I met her in a bar in San Antonio. I got to talking about the ranch, and she assumed that it belonged to me. I wanted her, so I didn't bother to correct that assumption. Looking back on it now, I'm almost certain she got pregnant on purpose—not that she had to twist my arm real hard to get a proposal out of me. By then I thought I was in love with her."

"But she only wanted you because she thought you had money," Margret said softly, understanding his suspicion of her own motives a little better.

"Let's just say that when she found out that we had to live on a ranch manager's salary, and that it would probably be years before the ranch belonged to me, her 'love' for me died very quickly. I came home one day and found she'd left me. I was afraid I'd lose my child for good if I let her go, so I followed her and asked her to come back with me."

Jude smiled; a small, bitter smile filled with self-derision. "She laughed and told me that even pregnant she'd been able to find a better meal ticket than me. She'd been writing to an old boyfriend, a businessman in San Antonio. He'd finally asked her to come back to him, and nothing could stop her from going. She told me that if she had to wake up one more morning to the sight of my ugly face, she'd kill herself. I told her that if she tried to leave again before the baby was born, I'd do the job for her."

Margret felt his pain as surely as if it were her own. "You didn't really mean that."

"I meant it when I said it. I grabbed her suitcases and forced her to get into that car with me, Maggie. We argued every minute of that ride."

His voice was calm and even, but his face was deathly pale. "It was a pitch-black night. I could hardly see the road. And then it began to rain. On the curve by the creek, I came face-to-face with another car. I swerved to avoid it and skidded down the hill. I was thrown clear. My car went into the creek. I don't know how long I was unconscious, but by the time I came to and managed to get Anne out of the car, she was dead. There was no one out there, no way I could call for help. But I could still feel the baby moving."

He stuffed both hands into his jean pockets, but not before Margret had noticed their tremor. The look in his eyes raised goose bumps on her arms. "I used my pocketknife to take the baby from her, and to keep it warm I put it against my body, inside my shirt. Then I walked home."

The very starkness of his words made Margret's breath catch in her throat. She could only imagine the horror of what he'd had to do on the night of the accident. The agony he must have suffered as, severely injured himself, he'd walked the long miles necessary to get help for his child. Even as she struggled to absorb the enormity of it, he kept on talking.

"At the hospital they told me that the baby was alive in an incubator. But by the time I was well enough to drag myself out to look, I found out that he had only lived for two days. No one had wanted to tell me he was dead because they knew the thought of my son was the only thing keeping me going."

"So you walked out of the hospital," Margret said softly, remembering the story Rob had told her at dinner during her first night on the ranch.

"Crawled out is more like it. I hitched a ride to old Pete's cabin. I knew he was fiercely independent himself and I could count on him to keep my secret and let me die in peace."

Margret wanted to put her arms around him and just hold him. Yet somehow she knew that her sympathy was the last thing he needed. "Only you didn't die," she said, her voice hoarse with repressed emotion. "At least, not physically. And you've never forgiven yourself for that."

Jude turned away from her without responding and resumed his packing as though he'd never been interrupted.

Margret took a deep breath, trying to recover from what he'd told her, praying for words that would help him. "Jude, maybe you were wrong for forcing Anne to go back with you. But she was wrong for deceiving you about her feelings in the first place. And what about the driver of the other car? The accident was at least partially his fault, and he might have saved Anne's life if he'd stopped to help. You can call what happened coincidence, or fate, or plain bad luck. But the only way you can escape it is to drop out of life completely, to hide yourself and your emotions away. That's what you've been trying to do ever since the accident. But now it's past time to come out of hiding."

Jude looked up at her, his eyes telling her it was hopeless. "Maggie, you more than anyone should understand that feeling guilty isn't something you can change just because you want to. You're still hanging on to the idea that you're responsible for your husband's suicide."

Margret stiffened at the mention of the ghost that had haunted her for so long. But to her surprise it was only a shadow of its former self. Paul was a fading memory, it was Jude who was important now. She stepped closer to him and reached out to touch his arm. At the last minute she decided against it, afraid he'd reject her touch as he seemed to be rejecting her words. "So you're just going to go away and leave me, your family, the ranch?"

"The ranch was never really mine to begin with."

He snapped the suitcase closed, and this time Margret did grab his arm. "It *is* yours, and I'm yours, too! I'm not Anne, Jude. I love you. That's the real reason I've stayed on at the ranch—although I wouldn't admit it to myself at first."

Jude looked at her for a long moment, as if weighing her words. Then he shook his head in negation. "It would never last, Maggie. You've just got good sex and gratitude mixed up with some fairy-tale notion of happily-ever-after. The sexual obsession we feel for each other would burn itself out sooner than you think. Then you'd wake up one morning and see me as I really am."

Maggie lifted her hand and gently stroked his scarred cheek. "I know what I feel, and I already see you as you really are."

Jude grimaced and grabbed her arm. He used it to spin her around so that they were both facing the dresser mirror. As she watched apprehensively, one muscular forearm clamped across her throat and drew her closer until she was standing directly in front of him, her back pressed against his chest, his chin brushing the top of her head.

His gaze met hers in the mirror. "Your words are straight out of some romantic fantasy, Maggie. Look at our reflections in the glass. Look, damn you! That's reality."

Margret dutifully examined the image in the mirror, and told him what was in her heart. "I only see the man I love."

Her words started an ache in Jude's chest, a longing that was all the more painful because he knew it to be futile. "Maggie, you only think you love me now because I was the first man to make you feel like a woman. The man who coaxed the real Maggie Brolin out of hiding and set her free. I won't put chains on her now. There's a whole wide world full of good men out there. One of them will be a man who can make you happy for a lifetime.''

A feeling of panic began to rise in Margret. Had she come this far only to lose him now because he was too blind to see how special they were together? How precious a thing they had shared and could continue to share? "You're that man, Jude. You make me happy.''

Jude shook his head, frustrated by her stubbornness, afraid that it would persuade him against his better judgment—afraid that he would let himself be persuaded. ''Maybe I could make you happy in bed, but you've got to get up sometime! In a few weeks or months you'd come to your senses and realize that you'd settled for less than full measure.''

His voice drowned out her words of protest. "Don't you see how it would be with us, Maggie? With a plain woman, I'd just look homely. I'd hardly draw a second glance. But next to your beauty, I'm as ugly as sin. People will turn and stare wherever we go. Beauty and the Beast. That's what they'll call us.''

''No!'' Tears stung Margret's eyes, and she struggled in his grasp, trying to escape, trying to turn toward him.

But he forced her to face the mirror, to face the truth he saw reflected there. "The ranch hands already do.''

A sound came from Margret's throat, a low sound of pain. And of defiance. "I don't care! I don't care what anyone else thinks or says!''

''I do.''

Those two words put an end to Margret's struggles as nothing else could have. She went still in his arms, her face a contorted mask of pain. "I thought you were different from other men. I thought you could see past the way I look! But you can't see the real me at all!''

Jude turned her until she was facing him and drew her into a tight embrace. ''There's nothing wrong with you,

Maggie. Nothing. You're beautiful inside and out. It's just the two of us together that won't work.''

Margret felt a rush of despair so sharp that for a second it took her breath away. Why couldn't he accept the truth of her love? He had so much to offer, they could be so happy together, if only he would give them a chance!

Shaking with the force of her emotions, Margret found the strength to raise her chin defiantly. "There's nothing I can say that will change your mind, is there?''

"No."

"Then make love to me before you go."

Jude's dark eyes cleared, revealing a wealth of hard-won determination. "You think that will hold me here?''

"No," she lied, vowing that it would. She would make love to him so skillfully, so passionately, that he wouldn't be able to leave her. A single tear escaped to trickle down one pale cheek as all her old doubts rose up to weaken her resolve. But she had no time for doubts now. She had to succeed! It would be her last chance to change his mind, her last chance to convince him that her love was strong enough to negate both his past and any differences that stood between them.

Jude's thumb moved up to sweep the tear from her cheekbone as his lips lowered to hers. His mouth was tenderness itself as it claimed hers in a poignant prelude to goodbye.

"Remember," he whispered, as he backed her across the room one slow step at a time. "Remember that you're more than enough woman for any man. And remember the man who made you believe it."

Firmly, but gently, he pushed her out into the hallway and closed his bedroom door.

Maggie stood frozen in place, staring at that door in shocked disbelief. As seconds turned into minutes, her disbelief became despair. Despite his loving words, Jude had held her at arm's length. He hadn't let her get close to him either physically or emotionally. He'd taken her last chance away from her.

Her heart aching dully with the realization, Margret walked the few steps to her own room. The door shut behind her with a hollow click. Leaning back against it, she stared at the too-familiar reflection in the dresser mirror.

Why? Why had she been cursed with a face and form that were destined to bring her only unhappiness? Her looks had been a burden to her all her life, a barrier between herself and others. Now they'd come between her and the man she would always love.

Anger flared within her until it burned with the same heat as passion had burned such a short time before. Because of Jude she had discovered her own sensuality and had laid old doubts to rest. He had seen qualities in her that she'd never suspected she possessed, but he would never recognize the real Margret Brolin; the flawed, imperfect woman who loved him with all her heart. He could only see the beautiful, empty reflection that filled the mirror.

A cold, numb feeling claimed her as she finally accepted the reality of the situation. There was a part of Jude that her words could never reach, a part of him that only he could change. And he didn't want to. There was no way for her to keep him from leaving, none at all.

Tears coursed down her cheeks, blurring the lines in the glass. She staggered forward and slowly sank to her knees in front of the dresser. She sobbed helplessly, hopelessly, shaking with frustration and despair. She cried until she had no more tears. Then, drawing a ragged breath, she dragged herself to her feet.

As she straightened, her gaze fell on a pair of sewing scissors that someone had left on the dresser top. Suddenly it came to her that words weren't the same as deeds. Offering to give up the ranch wasn't the same as giving it up. And saying that her looks didn't matter wasn't the same as doing something to prove that that statement was true.

Slowly she reached out a trembling hand and grasped the cold metal implement. Her gaze fixed once more on her reflection in the mirror. Her intent never wavering, Margret raised the sharp blades of the scissors toward her face.

Chapter Ten

Jude came awake slowly. Straining to focus his eyes in the dim half-light, he checked the time on his bedside clock. It was after noon. He'd meant to sleep for only an hour or two and then get an early start. But he'd been so exhausted, he hadn't even heard the alarm.

Stretching, he turned on his side and saw the golden skein of hair spread over the pillow next to his. His lips curved in a smile of reluctant admiration. "You don't take no for an answer, do you, Maggie?" he whispered.

Despite his resolve to end their relationship, his body swelled with a passion too long denied. He hesitated for half a heartbeat. Then, with a groan of defeat, he reached out his hand and wrapped it in the silken mass. He tugged gently, intending to draw his tormentor into his embrace. But to his shock and horror, he encountered no resistance at all.

Shooting to a sitting position, he reached up and pushed the heavy drapes aside. Light suffused the room. It reflected off the yard of spun-gold hair that lay pooled in his lap like the shimmering pelt of some mythical creature that had existed only in his dreams.

A sharp and painful sense of loss and regret seemed to fill his chest until it was an effort to breathe. He shouted her name aloud, but in his heart he knew that there would be no answer. Maggie was gone.

Dazed, feeling as if his world had suddenly tilted on its axis, Jude moved to get out of bed. His thigh brushed against something cold and metallic, and he looked down to see Maggie's transcription machine sitting on top of his bedcovers.

"What the hell...?" Thinking that she must have left him a taped message, he hit the Play button.

His anticipation turned to anger when he heard Ed's voice instead of Maggie's. It was one of the damned *Legacy* tapes!

Feeling betrayed, he jumped out of bed and started dressing. He was buttoning his shirt before the words Ed had recorded finally began to penetrate his consciousness.

"I knew that only the threat of losing the Double Diamond could bring you back to the world again, Jude. And only a woman like Margret could make you want to stay there. She healed my wounds, and I know she can heal yours—if you'll let her. In return, she needs a home and a strong man who knows how to make her glad she's a woman. She's my legacy to you, son. A legacy more important than money or land.

"My will was intended to throw you two together and keep you together until you realized that the perfect solution to the problem was to share the Double Diamond and each other's lives. And I thought if I willed Margret these tapes to transcribe, she would eventually see to it that you heard what I had to say.

"Even if my plan failed, Jude, I think I will have made you angry enough to get into life again and put

*the past behind you. And you, Margret, even if you're
listening to this alone right now, I can rest easy knowing that you have a home for yourself and Todd. And
I hope that, win or lose, squaring off against that
stubborn son of mine has helped you realize your own
worth.*

*"If all this seems like the act of a desperate man in
the last stages of senility, forgive me. My only motivation was love for both of you. You can't blame an old
gambler for wanting to play just one more hand."*

Only silence followed. Jude leaned over and switched off
the tape. Then he reached for his Stetson and walked toward the door.

Margret checked her watch and looked down the road.
She straightened the scarf that covered what remained of her
hair as her foot took up a fast, rhythmic tapping on the
sidewalk. The bus to El Paso wasn't due for another fifteen
minutes, and she was already a nervous wreck!

Her face creasing in a worried frown, she turned and
glanced at the Layton City Drugstore where Todd was sup-
posedly selecting an activity book for the bus ride. He had
protested long and loud when she was getting him ready to
leave the ranch house. But after she'd explained that Jude
planned to leave if she didn't, he'd settled into a tearful, resigned silence that tugged at her heart.

Her own tears had all been shed last night. The pain of
Jude's rejection was still there, but it was gradually giving
way to a slow, simmering anger. She had offered him everything she possessed, and he had brushed her aside as if
that offer was worthless. How dare he treat her that way!

"Rob said I'd find you here."

Margret whirled around to find the object of her thoughts
within touching distance. The shock waves traveled all the

way to her toes. The pain she'd had under control only moments ago leapt up and danced around her, taunting her, threatening to consume her entire being.

Then slowly her anger came back in full force, eclipsing the pain. She had accepted Jude's rejection. She had convinced herself that there was no way she could have lived with him happily, loving him the way she did and knowing she wasn't loved or trusted in return. And now he had the nerve to come looking for her?

"What do you want?" she demanded in a fine, self-righteous rage.

"I guess you've got a right to be angry—" Jude began. He didn't get to finish his sentence.

Suddenly all Margret's hurt and frustration came rushing out in one breathless flow. "Yes, dammit, I *do* have a right to be angry! I have a right to be angry at the foster parents who either exploited me or ignored me. At the husband who killed himself and left me to deal with the mess he'd made of our lives. And at you for ignoring what I am because you're so concerned with how I look. All I've ever been guilty of is offering those I care about unconditional love and acceptance. But no one is willing to accept me!"

There was a part of Jude that wanted to stand up and cheer because Maggie had finally realized her own worth. And there was a part that was terrified she didn't want him anymore. "I'm willing to accept you, Maggie," he said softly. "If you still want me. I know I want you."

Before Margret had time to react to his words, Jude was acting on them. He pulled her into the shadows by the side of the drugstore and took her into his arms.

The all-too-familiar warmth of his body, the passion of his kiss, swept her away on a tide of feeling so powerful that for a moment she wasn't aware of anything but the exquisite sensation. Then he made the mistake of lifting his mouth from hers. Her vision cleared. Rational thought returned and so did anger.

Margret planted both fists against his rock-hard chest and pushed until there was a decent amount of space between his body and hers. She glared up at him defiantly.

"What do you mean, you want me? Wasn't it you who said good sex wasn't enough to hold a relationship together?"

The icy hostility of her words drained away the elation that had begun to build in Jude when she'd responded to his kiss. He let his arms drop slowly to his sides, releasing her.

"I was wrong, Maggie. It wasn't just sex between us—it was love." He looked down into her eyes, his gaze intense. "I tried to deny it, to run away from it because I'd been burned so badly before. I wanted to play it safe, to stay numb and cold inside—alone with my guilt and regrets. But when I woke up and found you gone, I realized I couldn't go back to the way things had been before. For the first time in years I was thinking of the future instead of the past. A future that looked pretty bleak. I had the ranch and everything I'd always thought I wanted, but it didn't matter. Nothing meant anything without you to share it. Once I realized that, I had to come to you."

Margret wanted to believe him. But Jude had hurt her once. She wasn't going to let him walk back into her life for an instant replay. Margret Brolin was never going to be any man's willing victim again.

"You wouldn't believe me when I told you I loved you last night, Jude. You didn't listen when I begged you to give our relationship a chance. What made you change your mind?"

Jude began to pace the alleyway, trying to frame words that would convince her of his sincerity. "When I told you that all you felt was gratitude and sexual attraction, I honestly believed that was true. I guess my guilt over the accident made me feel so ugly that ugliness was all I could see when I looked in the mirror. That's not what I saw this morning. I saw a man who's paid enough for his mistakes. A man who has the right to some happiness."

He came to a stop directly in front of her, his gaze locking with hers. "I'm finally able to accept the fact that my feelings for you are real, Maggie. So I have to accept the possibility that yours could be real, too."

Seeing her hesitation, Jude reached out to gently clasp her arms. "Look, I know I hurt you, Maggie. I can't undo that. But I can promise you that I'll never hurt you again."

Part of Margret was urging her to throw herself into Jude's arms as if no harsh words had ever been spoken between them. But another, more cautious, part warned her to remain aloof, to avoid being hurt again.

"*If* I were to agree that there was a chance for us," she said, stressing the *if*, "you'd have to promise me that my appearance would never be an issue between us again. My looks are a part of who I am. I'm through apologizing for them."

Jude repressed a sigh of relief. If that was all she wanted, he was home free. He would have accepted any terms in order to win her back. And, in fact, he liked this new assertive Maggie even better than the Maggie he'd first fallen in love with.

But before he could voice his wholehearted agreement, she was jabbing him in the chest with one hard fingernail. "And no one's going to dictate how I dress or how I wear my hair! I've learned that what's important is what I think of myself, not what anyone else thinks of me. Even you."

"Maggie, I think you're wonderful. You almost gave me a heart attack with that stunt you pulled, but you sure got your point across. I swear I didn't even think about your looks once you were gone. What I found myself missing was your sweet smile, your caring, your warmth and your giving."

Slowly, ever so slowly, Jude reached up and grasped the edges of the loosely tied scarf that was covering Maggie' hair. Instinctively her hands moved up to prevent him Then, with a sigh of resignation, she let them drop back to her sides.

Jude pulled the scarf down until it rested on her shoulders. He felt a wave of remorse and an even stronger surge of love as he saw the uneven, hacked-off ruin of what had once been Maggie's crowning glory. He let his fingers thread through the sparse, silken locks and leaned forward to place a soft kiss on her tightly closed lips. "No matter how you look, to me you'll always be the most beautiful woman in the world."

He felt her tremble and drew back to gaze into her face The hopeful, hesitant look he saw there—knowing that he was the man who had put it there—nearly broke his heart Then she reached up and took his face between her hands.

"Are you sure, Jude? Are you very sure?"

He kissed one soft palm as he shook his head. "No love comes with a guarantee. Maybe some time in the future *you* feelings toward *me* will change. But I'm going to spend the rest of my life doing everything I can to make sure they don't. That is, if you'll let me."

Feeling awkward as hell and just as determined, he dropped to one knee on the asphalt. "When I saved you and Todd from the fire, maybe I was being given a second chance. A chance to live my life the way it was meant to be lived." Taking both her hands in his, he looked up into her eyes. "Will you share that life with me, Maggie? Will you marry me?"

Tears in her eyes, Margret gave him a tremulous smile "Just try and stop me!"

Jude got to his feet and almost cried, himself, when she threw herself into his arms. "Maggie, I was so afraid I'd lost you. I was so afraid you were going to say no."

"I've always had a hard time saying that word to you."

"Thank God!"

His lips took hers, coaxing, willing, demanding a response. Margret met his passion with an urgent desire of her own, trying to make up for hours of longing and loneliness in the warmth of his arms.

When they pulled apart, Jude finally noticed the tears in her eyes. "You're not having second thoughts already, are you?" he asked, misinterpreting her mood.

Margret held him even tighter. "Never!"

"You won't mind living out on the ranch? I'm warning you now, you might not be able to find a secretarial job any closer than San Antonio."

"Then maybe I'll just make myself useful by helping you run the Double Diamond."

She raised her head in time to catch his look of apprehension before he masked it. She smiled and leaned her cheek against his chest. Life with Jude was going to be anything but dull!

"And what about Todd?" Jude persisted, finally broaching the subject that had been troubling him most of all. "You're going to have a hard row to hoe if you plan on keeping him away from the horses and the hands."

Margret thought about the implications of that, then gave him the only answer she knew. "I trust you to take care of him."

"I lost one child, Maggie. I don't ever intend to lose another. I'd die before I'd let any harm come to him."

"I know," Margret whispered. "I know that now."

They began to walk back to his truck together, his arm around her shoulders, her arm around his waist.

Jude cleared his throat. "By the way, I . . . uh . . . listened to that tape you left me. At least, I listened to part of it. I was more concerned with finding you, than with what I was hearing."

Margret smiled at his admission.

"Just before I left the ranch house, I played the last *Leg*
acy tape. I knew what was on it wouldn't change your min
about us. But for your sake, I had to try one more time t
get you to listen—to hear Ed say in his own words that h
loved you."

Jude still hadn't had time to absorb it all. "It's hard fo
me to accept. If I didn't know better, I'd swear he made
all up. It's the craziest thing I've ever heard."

Margret shook her head in negation. "After listening ▮
all of his tapes, I can tell you that what he did was typicall
Ed. He loved dramatic gestures—the long shot, the las
chance. And he loved to bet everything on a single roll of th
dice. The crazy thing isn't that he set up that plan in the firs
place. The crazy thing is that it worked."

Jude looked down at her. "Would you mind if I listene
to some of the other tapes?"

Margret stopped walking and hugged him tightly. "No,
wouldn't. Not at all."

Feeling a sudden tug on her sleeve, Margret looked dow
to find Todd standing next to them. His expression was
mixture of apprehension and hope. "Are we going back ▮
the ranch, Mom?"

"Uh—huh."

Her son grinned up at her. "I'm glad."

"Not half as glad as I am, sweetie."

Jude reached out to include Todd in their embrace, an
Margret felt tears come to her eyes again. She was puzzle
by her reaction until she realized the cause of it. She had f
nally found the security she'd been searching for, ever sinc
her parents died.

She gave Jude a smile filled with gratitude and love
"What are we waiting for?" she asked huskily. "Let's g
home."

Epilogue

'**Y**ou may kiss the bride.'

Margret treasured the feel of her husband's lips on hers, sure that at this moment she was the happiest woman in the world.

She turned to hug Rob and accept his kiss. Rob made the most of the opportunity, bending her backward over his arm while she giggled uncontrollably.

Laughing himself, he released her and turned to Jude. His eyes shining with admiration and love, he gave his older brother a rib-cracking hug. "Well, *hermano,* at least now he knows who the *best* man is!"

Every one of the relatives, ranch hands and friends in the crowded living room groaned aloud. All except, Margret noticed, for one pretty young lady who actually laughed. Even as Margret watched, Rob made his way over to the woman and gave her a smile that seemed to light up the room. Blushing, the woman responded with a shy smile of

her own. It seemed that Rob's broken heart was on th
mend at last.

Todd gave Margret a rare kiss and shook hands with hi
new father. "Now we're a real family," he declared so
emnly. Then he grinned up at both of them. "And I get t
be a cowboy!" He had disappeared outside with severa
other children before either of his parents could think ho
to respond.

Margret squeezed Jude's hand, tears threatening. But the
were tears of pure joy.

Nilda came up to them, her face radiant with happiness
"This was well worth postponing my trip for!" She kisse
Jude and took Margret's hand. "My son is starting a ne
life today, happy and whole again—thanks to you, m
dear."

"I finally finished listening to Ed's tapes today, Mama
Maybe that old gambler really did care about you. An
about me."

Nilda touched her son's cheek and smiled. "Haven't I al
ways told you so?"

After the last guest had been shown out, Margret mad
her way to her room and switched on the bedside lamp. Sh
carefully took off her wedding dress and hung it in th
closet. As she slipped into the white silk nightgown she'
chosen for her first night as Jude's wife, she caught
glimpse of herself in the dresser mirror. Her fingers trace
the smooth, classic lines of the long gown, then moved u
to touch the thick blond strands that curled at her nape.

The nightgown might have been considered conservativ
by some, but it was anything but dowdy. She was dressin
in a way that pleased her now, in attractive clothes tha
flattered her figure without emphasizing it. And, after
much-needed styling at the local beauty parlor, she'd eve

discovered that she liked the coolness and convenience of short hair.

Once she'd gotten over the first terrible wave of anger and despair that had prompted her to cut her hair and abandon the legacy Ed had left her, she'd discovered that she was free at last. It was as though, through that one symbolic act, she had cast off Paul and Ed and even Jude's expectations of what she was and what she should be. Somehow, after all she'd been through, she was finally free to be herself.

Content with what she saw, Margret turned away from the mirror, mentally reviewing her list of things she had to do before she left on her honeymoon tomorrow. The plane tickets to Acapulco were in her purse. Nilda had agreed to watch Todd for the week they'd be gone. All the bases were covered. Now if—

Margret shrieked as two arms closed around her from behind. "Jude!" she exclaimed, twisting around to give him a playful punch. "I didn't even hear you come in."

Ignoring Margret's halfhearted protest, he pulled her down on the bed. "I missed you, Mrs. Emory," he whispered as he trailed kisses along one cheekbone.

His lips took hers, and Margret responded eagerly. But when she felt his hand slide up beneath her gown, she reached down to stop its progress.

"I missed you, too," she admitted. "But we have an early flight tomorrow. I've got to finish packing."

"You don't have to worry about bringing any clothes, honey. I don't intend to let you out of that hotel room until it's time for our flight home."

He took possession of her mouth again, entering, exploring, claiming it as his own. His hands moved over her soft, familiar curves. Impatient to touch the warmth of her skin, he pushed aside the cool white silk and let his fingers trace the rough velvet tip of one lush breast.

Margret closed her eyes, her whole body responding to the exquisite sensations he was producing. Burying both hands in his thick, midnight hair, she pulled his mouth down to quench the fire that his fingers had so skillfully aroused.

They fell back on the pillows together, hungrier for each other than they had ever been before. His hands shaking with passion and restraint, Jude removed her nightgown an inch at a time, worshipping each millimeter of exposed flesh with his tongue and his touch.

Margret sighed in his arms, feeling cared for and cherished, even though no words were spoken. Not for a moment did she consider how she looked, only how she felt. Her heart pounded, and her blood seemed to sing as it surged through her veins. She gloried in being in love and feeling more alive than ever before.

Jude was aching to take her but determined to show her how much he cared. "You'll never have cause to doubt my love again," he told her. "And you'll never have to pretend with me—that's a promise."

She gasped as he trailed a path of kisses down across her abdomen, intent on fulfilling that promise. He continued his ministrations until a searing bolt of pleasure pulsed through her, until she had to fight to catch her breath.

Still Margret's body strained against his, demanding a closer union, a more complete satisfaction. She looked up at him pleadingly, all modesty forgotten. "Love me," she implored. "Love me now."

Jude didn't wait for a second invitation. He threw off his clothes in record time. When he came to her again, it was flesh against flesh. The feel of her writhing body beneath his threatened to drive him insane.

Thrusting into the tight, wet warmth of her, he fought the waves of pleasure that nearly consumed his last fragment of control.

She reached up as he slid into her, wrapping her arms and legs around him, trying to pull him deeper, closer. He moved slowly, relentlessly, heedless of her moans and urgings.

Grasping his buttocks, she felt the powerful muscles contract beneath her hands and gasped as each movement increased the terrible yearning inside her. His mouth returned to her breasts as his hand eased downward.

She arched into his touch as the wave of pleasure began deep inside her and spiraled outward to engulf her whole being. His lips muffled her cries of ecstasy as he thrust into her harder and faster, doubling the intensity of every sensation until she was sure she would die of it. Then he arched up and back, groaning her name over and over as he found his own release.

When Margret became aware of her surroundings again, she found herself lying on her side in Jude's arms, their bodies still joined. He kissed her softly, lingeringly. She raised her hand and traced the jagged ridge of scar tissue that was so much a part of his face.

"Does the scar bother you?" he asked, his voice concerned. "I could always see a plastic surgeon—"

Margret pressed her finger over his lips to stop his words. "I wouldn't change a thing about you, even if I could."

It was on the tip of her tongue to ask for yet another confirmation that he felt the same way about her. Instead, she looked away, ashamed of the hint of residual doubt that still haunted her.

Then she felt Jude's fingers beneath her chin, and reluctantly she raised her gaze to his.

"I love you, Maggie," he said softly. "The truth is, I fell in love with you in total darkness. That night I pulled you from the creek, before I even knew what you looked like, I loved you for your courage and your caring. In my heart I knew that you were the woman for me. It was just hard to recognize that truth after the lights came on."

"I know that's how it happened," Margret whispered, "because that's just the way I fell in love with you."

All her doubts banished, Margret switched off the bedside lamp. She snuggled into Jude's embrace and welcomed the darkness with a kiss, secure in the knowledge that their love would burn just as brightly in the light of day.

Minutes before they were due to leave for the airport, Margret and Jude walked up the hill behind the ranch house. They stood together and looked at the graves where Ed Tanner and Ben Emory lay buried side by side.

Jude put his arms around his wife and spoke a vow that hadn't been included in the marriage ceremony. "Today we put the past behind us, Maggie. Today we start to build a future together. We take the inheritance these two men left us and build it into something even better and stronger. Something that we can be proud to pass on to Todd and any other children we might have."

Margret sealed that vow with a kiss. But in her heart she knew they could share no greater inheritance than the one Ed had given them. A legacy that had transcended pain, anger, jealousy, greed and even death, itself. A legacy of love.

*   *   *   *   *

Is your father a Fabulous Father?

Then enter him in Silhouette Romance's

"FATHER OF THE YEAR" Contest
and you can both win some great prizes! Look for contest details
in the FABULOUS FATHER titles available in June, July
and August...

ONE MAN'S VOW by Diana Whitney
Available in June

ACCIDENTAL DAD by Anne Peters
Available in July

INSTANT FATHER by Lucy Gordon
Available in August

Only from

Take 4 bestselling love stories FREE

Plus get a FREE surprise gift!

Special Limited-time Offer

Mail to Harlequin Reader Service®

3010 Walden Avenue
P.O. Box 1867
Buffalo, N.Y. 14269-1867

YES! Please send me 4 free Silhouette Romance® novels and my free surprise gift. Then send me 6 brand-new novels every month, which I will receive months before they appear in bookstores. Bill me at the low price of $1.99* each plus 25¢ delivery and applicable sales tax, if any.* I understand that accepting the books and gift places me under no obligation ever to buy any books. I can always return a shipment and cancel at any time. Even if I never buy another book from Silhouette, the 4 free books and the surprise gift are mine to keep forever.

215 BPA AJCL

Name _____ (PLEASE PRINT)

Address _____ Apt. No. _____

City _____ State _____ Zip _____

MEN MADE IN AMERICA

Fifty red-blooded, white-hot, true-blue hunks from every
State in the Union!

Beginning in May, look for MEN MADE IN AMERICA!
Written by some of our most popular authors, these
stories feature fifty of the strongest, sexiest men, each
from a different state in the union!

Two titles available every other month at your favorite
retail outlet.

In May, look for:

FULL HOUSE by Jackie Weger (Alabama)
BORROWED DREAMS by Debbie Macomber (Alaska)

In July, look for:

CALL IT DESTINY by Jayne Ann Krentz (Arizona)
ANOTHER KIND OF LOVE by Mary Lynn Baxter
(Arkansas)

You won't be able to resist MEN MADE IN AMERICA!

You're Invited

Silhouette Romance celebrates June brides and grooms and *You're Invited!* Be our guest as five special couples find the magic ingredients for happily-*wed*-ever-afters! Look for these wonderful stories by some of your favorite authors...

WED

Silhouette

ROMANCE™